Praise for the novels of Claire Cross

Double Trouble

"For a fast-paced, captivating story of romance, family relationships, and following your heart, *Double Trouble* is not to be missed."
—*Romance Reviews Today*

"A fun, funny, *Sex and the City* kind of tale." —*The Romance Reader*

"This quirky, funny book made me laugh while tugging at deeper emotions." —*All About Romance*

"Cross's cutting-edge romance proves that not all identical twins are alike while giving the reader insight into Web etiquette that is as entertaining as the story." —*Booklist*

Third Time Lucky

"Funny, quirky, touching, and romantic. *Third Time Lucky* is a gem of a novel with facets of pure brilliance." —Suzanne Forster

"It's a cross between a Julia Roberts romp and an episode of *Seinfeld*." —*The Romance Reader*

"A screwball comedic romance that stars several interesting characters. Claire Cross writes a warm, witty, and often wild novel that shows the expanse of her talent." —Harriet Klausner

"I rarely laugh out loud while reading, but this gave my smile muscles a good workout while engaging my brain. The writing is snappy and refreshing . . . This was my first Claire Cross and I plan to pick her up again when I need a good laugh." —*All About Romance*

"Laced with a good deal of humor . . . [An] emotional, riveting tale." —*Romance Reviews Today*

Don't miss black sheep Zach Co~~xw~~~~ell'~~

All or Nothin~~g~~

Coming in April 2007 from Be~~r~~

One More Time

Claire Cross

BERKLEY SENSATION, NEW YORK

THE BERKLEY PUBLISHING GROUP
Published by the Penguin Group
Penguin Group (USA) Inc.
375 Hudson Street, New York, New York 10014, USA
Penguin Group (Canada), 90 Eglinton Avenue East, Suite 700, Toronto, Ontario M4P 2Y3, Canada
(a division of Pearson Penguin Canada Inc.)
Penguin Books Ltd., 80 Strand, London WC2R 0RL, England
Penguin Group Ireland, 25 St. Stephen's Green, Dublin 2, Ireland (a division of Penguin Books Ltd.)
Penguin Group (Australia), 250 Camberwell Road, Camberwell, Victoria 3124, Australia
(a division of Pearson Australia Group Pty. Ltd.)
Penguin Books India Pvt. Ltd., 11 Community Centre, Panchsheel Park, New Delhi—110 017, India
Penguin Group (NZ), Cnr. Airborne and Rosedale Roads, Albany, Auckland 1310, New Zealand
(a division of Pearson New Zealand Ltd.)
Penguin Books (South Africa) (Pty.) Ltd., 24 Sturdee Avenue, Rosebank, Johannesburg 2196,
South Africa

Penguin Books Ltd., Registered Offices: 80 Strand, London WC2R 0RL, England

This book is an original publication of The Berkley Publishing Group.

This is a work of fiction. Names, characters, places, and incidents either are the product of the author's imagination or are used fictitiously, and any resemblance to actual persons, living or dead, business establishments, events, or locales is entirely coincidental. The publisher does not have any control over and does not assume any responsibility for author or third-party websites or their content.

ONE MORE TIME

Copyright © 2006 by Claire Delacroix Inc.
Cover art by Masaki Ryo/CWC International.
Cover design by George Long.

All rights reserved.
No part of this book may be reproduced, scanned, or distributed in any printed or electronic form without permission. Please do not participate in or encourage piracy of copyrighted materials in violation of the author's rights. Purchase only authorized editions.
BERKLEY SENSATION is a registered trademark of Penguin Group (USA) Inc.
The "B" design is a trademark belonging to Penguin Group (USA) Inc.

First edition: November 2006

Berkley Sensation trade paperback ISBN: 0-425-21198-3

An application to register this book for cataloging has been submitted to the Library of Congress.

PRINTED IN THE UNITED STATES OF AMERICA

10 9 8 7 6 5 4 3 2

Chapter One

Ladies and gentlemen, step right this way!" It's Leslie's father, who had never been a barker anywhere other than Leslie's dreams, his voice as familiar as her own name. In life, he'd said little and never been an entertainer, though he'd always drawn attention to his darling daughter.

This is her recurring dream and she fights it, although she knows that she will lose the battle.

"Step right this way," her father continues. "Put your money down and see the Monkey Boy, raised in the jungle by chimpanzees. See the Snake Man: Watch him eat live mice. See the Tattooed Lady with the map of the world on her skin—find your hometown." His voice falls to a hush. "See the amazing Leslie Anne, my own daughter, as she walks the tightrope for the first time."

The crowd gasps in anticipation. There is a flurry of activity, the clink of coins changing hands, then Leslie abruptly is standing on a platform high above the crowd. Her dream, which she could only hear before, suddenly erupts into view; this is always her first vision.

That doesn't make it any better.

She's on the tiny platform, the wire stretched out in front of her. Her father is beside her. She can feel his presence, but she can see only the wire that is her destiny.

It bobs slightly, as if promising to toss her to her death. It is perhaps fifteen feet above the ground, a little more than the height of two men, but it might as well be a mile high. The crowd whispers then falls silent in anticipation of her feat.

Leslie is maybe six years old in this dream, wearing her favorite pink swimsuit and a tutu that her mother had once made her for a recital. She wears pink leather ballet slippers, the ones she had always wanted, the ones she never got outside of this relentless dream, the ones she would never have paid this price to possess.

"Go on," her father says, giving her a little push. "You can do it."

There is no arguing with him. Leslie knows this. She is his child, his possession as surely as his favorite hat. It's not her place to question him.

Much less to defy him.

She doesn't look at the ground or at the crowd. She swallows, watches the wire, then carefully places one foot on it.

"You can do it, Leslie," her father urges when she hesitates. "You're the one who can do it. We're all counting on you."

Trembling, feeling the weight of the audience's stare and her father's expectations, Leslie slides her weight out onto the wire. It wobbles and she sticks out her arms, stiff, panicked. The crowd gasps, but the wire settles. Leslie's heart is thundering, a trickle of sweat eases down the center of her back, but as she steadies, she feels a surge of triumph.

She's done it!

She glances back, sees the look in her father's eyes and knows that this accomplishment is not enough.

No accomplishment is enough.

Even at six, she knows that he will add another challenge before he congratulates her, that he never will express pride in her triumphs, at least not to her. Success always means the ante is upped.

He frowns. "You've got to carry something, to make it look better."

Leslie has only a moment to form an expectation, that maybe he will give her a pink umbrella to carry, before he conjures a box.

It looks like a gift, all wrapped in fancy paper and topped with a fabulous bow. It's big and shiny and when he puts it into her arms, she can barely see past it.

"Perfect!" he says, then adds another. And another and another and another, until there is a pile of boxes in Leslie's arms. "Now, go! Remember, you're our last hope!"

Leslie takes a step, sliding her foot along the thick wire that isn't nearly thick enough. She shifts her weight from one foot to the other, then pauses to catch her breath and her balance. The crowd exhales a long low ooooooo.

Maybe she can do this.

Maybe her father is right.

She swallows the lump in her throat. She eases one foot forward again, feeling the curve of the wire through her slipper, calculating how soon she can shift her weight.

Just when she's sure she's found the perfect moment, just when she begins to slide her weight to the front foot, she feels the top box begin to slip. She glances up in fear, sees the shiny foil-wrapped box sliding quickly to her right. She snatches for it, then loses her own balance.

And falls.

*   *   *

The alarm clock rang insistently. Leslie bolted upright before her eyes were open. Her heart was hammering and a bead of sweat was on her upper lip. She was disoriented and terrified. She looked around herself, half-expecting to find glittering boxes of various sizes scattered on the floor around the bed.

But no. It was just that stupid dream again.

Leslie braced her hands against the mattress, reassuring herself that she wasn't falling, and took three deep breaths.

Stupid dream. A portent of failure was not what she needed.

Thank you, Dad, for the vote of nonconfidence.

She felt both jangled and groggy, snared in a shadow world

halfway between dream land and real life. Her new blue negligee, an expression of optimism if ever there had been one, was knotted around her waist.

The sheets on the other side of the bed were smooth, untouched. Matt hadn't come to bed at all.

Sex was the simplest and most powerful form of marital diplomacy—Leslie was convinced of this—but all the same, she would never beg. She had believed Matt would come to bed last night, because bed had always been the one place they could negotiate détente, no matter what was going wrong.

And there was a lot going wrong right now.

Maybe that was why Matt hadn't shown.

She became cranky at that thought, irritated with him for losing the court case that could have made his career, afraid that they would have to have a fight over it since they hadn't made love to smooth the marital ripples.

In fact, the prospect of not talking had finally become even more frightening than that of a fight.

That was scary stuff. There had been a lot left unsaid over the years, a lot more these past two years, a lot that could prove explosive if the locked Pandora's box of grievances was ever opened.

They weren't the kind of people who fought. Maybe they were too polite. Their relationship had proceeded directly from "I love you" to "pass the salt," with nary a glance back. For years Leslie had been afraid they'd suddenly drown beneath the flotsam and jetsam of unvoiced frustrations and unexplored annoyances.

What if that time had come and it was right now?

She growled and flung herself out of bed. What she needed was a cup of coffee, which meant that she needed Matt.

But then, she'd needed him all night long.

If not all of her adult life.

The newspaper hit the front door, seemingly coaxing her to face the day as if it were business as usual. Leslie forced herself to think of practicalities, as if this were a day like any other. She had a staff meeting this morning, and Annette had a math test. God only knew what Matt would be doing, seeing as he probably didn't have a job anymore.

Better not to think about that, at least until she was caffeinated.

Leslie hurried into the bathroom. She brushed her hair vigorously, making it bounce and shine, then put the brush down slowly to study her reflection.

Why hadn't Matt come to bed?

Her hair was still dark—albeit with a little chemical encouragement—thick, and long. She wore it past her shoulders, at least when she left it loose—which was pretty much only at night. She'd never been bombshell material, but the man had known that eighteen years before. The new lace-trimmed blue nightgown suited her, she thought, accentuating the slenderness that cost her so much to maintain. She pulled on the matching robe and shoved her feet into satin mules. She looked from the mules to the smooth sheets on Matt's side of the bed.

It was clear that they wouldn't easily patch this up, not even with the oldest stress buster known to mankind. There comes a point when you can't just wrap your tongue around the tonsils of a man and make everything better—even when the man in question has been your husband for fifteen years, your partner for three more than that, and is the father of your only child.

Maybe because of that.

Leslie would have been willing to try, all the same. She knotted the belt of her robe firmly, then adjusted the neckline, feeling armed for battle.

She opened the door and noticed immediately that there was no smell of coffee, a smell that had been present every other morning of their entire married life. Leslie knew with sudden terrifying conviction why Matt hadn't come to bed.

He'd left instead.

Funny but flotsam and jetsam had a way of making Leslie no longer feel any need for caffeine.

* * *

Matt Coxwell could pinpoint the moment he had known he couldn't do it anymore.

It hadn't been when he'd finally lost that court case, against his father's explicit wishes. It hadn't been when he had turned in triumph to his wife, certain she would be proud that he had clung to his principles—*their* principles—and found her visibly disappointed instead. Leslie didn't show her emotions readily, so the fact that he could read her response across a crowded courtroom had told him more about the magnitude of her feelings than he'd wanted to know.

But it hadn't been then. He'd still had a shred of optimism then, a hope that they could work things out.

It hadn't been during the silent ride home, the two of them trapped in the Subaru with the air crackling hot between them. It hadn't been during the painfully polite dinner at home that had followed, the tension so palpable that even their teenaged daughter had noticed something beyond herself.

Not then. Even then, he'd imagined that they'd be able to really talk at some point.

It hadn't even been when he had left the table and poured himself a triple shot of scotch without apology.

No, not then, either.

It had been, in fact, several hours later, after he had spent the bulk of the evening alone with the bottle of scotch, when the phone rang.

Matt had known just from the imperious sound of it that his father was on the other end of the line. He had debated answering it. He decided that it would be better to get the inevitable reckoning behind him.

Matt's mistake, which he was certain of by the time the newspaper hit the door the next morning, had been answering the phone.

If he hadn't done so, his father might have reconsidered.

If he hadn't done so, he wouldn't have become convinced that compromise was doomed to failure. He wouldn't have known that there were people who would not accept anything less than their own way; he wouldn't have known that he was the son of one of those people and the husband of another.

If he hadn't answered the phone, he probably wouldn't have found himself stone drunk, knowing he had to walk out of his marriage when his wife came lurching down the stairs.

In hindsight Matt knew he should have just let the phone ring.

* * *

Leslie tripped when the heel of her mule snagged in the carpet on the stairs. She saved herself from a nasty fall by grabbing the bannister, then kicked the shoes off with rare temper. She stumbled over one of them at the bottom of the stairs, winced, but kept on going.

The kitchen was as pristine as she'd left it the night before. Not an encouraging sign. The dining room might have been in a furniture catalog, it was so perfectly organized and clean.

Leslie's heart started to pound. No. He couldn't have just left. Not without saying a single word to her. Things hadn't been fabulous lately, but he wouldn't just walk away without a word after eighteen years.

Would he?

She looked out at the back deck, which was perfectly dusted with undisturbed fresh snow, and told herself she shouldn't have been surprised that Matt wasn't on the deck in January.

The spare room! Why hadn't she thought of that sooner? She pivoted and raced back toward the stairs, seizing the newel post to hurl herself up the steps precisely as she had forbidden Annette to do.

That was when she saw their old reliable navy Samsonite suitcase standing by the front door. Packed. Her gut went cold, because Matt's briefcase—considerably thinner than it had been lately—leaned against it. For some strange reason, she glanced into the living room that they never used. It too was neat, the curtains still pulled against the night, but a cut crystal glass winked in the shadows.

Leslie froze, one foot up and one foot down, fighting to steady her breathing as Matt's silhouette became clear.

He was sitting in the chair they had inherited from some auntie of his, a woman Leslie had never met. It was the only antique they owned, and it had a position of honor in the living room, although no one had ever sat on it before.

Matt lounged on it now, bracing his weight on the back two legs of the chair as he rocked slightly. The Matt she knew would never have done that to an old, potentially fragile, chair. He was still wearing the dark Italian suit he'd worn in court the day before, the one that made him look like a model, though he'd shed the jacket. He'd rolled up his shirtsleeves, loosened his tie, and unfastened the top button of the shirt. He was unshaven, rumpled and he looked sexy enough to eat.

Matt's smile tugged at the corner of his mouth, a roguish and alien smile. He sat wreathed in shadows, looking mysterious and unpredictable, two traits Leslie knew her husband did not possess. Her spouse had been reinterpreted as a swashbuckler; even the stubble on his chin looked newly dangerous.

There was a stranger in their living room, a doppelganger in her husband's suit, a lost secret twin who might toss away the keys to the kingdom just for the heck of it.

And she didn't know what to do or say. Her mouth was so dry that her tongue seemed to have sealed itself to the roof of her mouth.

One thing was for certain: This twin of Matt's could conjure the same old black magic as the husband she knew. He glanced over her, his gaze heating. His smile became a little more wicked, and Leslie felt her knees melt. He could dissolve her reservations with a glance.

He was still drinking, something he never did to excess, or at least never had done in the past. The amber of the scotch gleamed in his glass as he took another sip.

Would the real Matt Coxwell please stand up?

"Looking for someone?" he asked, his voice rough and only slightly slurred.

"You. Of course."

He smiled, though it wasn't a merry smile. "I guess the staff slipped up and didn't make your coffee this morning. Oh well."

"I thought you liked making coffee in the morning." Leslie hated how breathless she sounded. "Or I would have learned to do it."

"Just like you learned to do everything else. Competent, efficient, organized Leslie Coxwell." He saluted her.

"Somehow that doesn't sound like a compliment."

He raised his brows in mock surprise and sipped his scotch. "Independent," he added, with emphasis. "Driven. Ambitious."

Funny but the list of her attributes didn't sound that positive this morning.

He paused, as if waiting, and though she knew it was an old trick, Leslie couldn't help but fill the silence he left between them.

"You haven't been drinking all night, have you?"

He shrugged. "What if I have?"

"I thought you might have come to bed last night."

"Why? So you'd have the chance to toss me out?"

"Do I look as if I would have turned you away?"

He considered her, letting that simmering glance slide over her curves. Leslie felt her flesh heat, felt his gaze as surely as a touch, and was achingly aware of just how long it had been since they'd made the mattress squeak. He met her gaze finally, smiled slightly, then unfolded himself from the chair. He moved with athletic grace, as he always did, a grace that made Leslie want him all the more.

She gripped the newel post so she wouldn't swoon at his feet and tried to remember why wrapping her tongue around his tonsils had seemed like a bad idea. He reached for his jacket, which was draped across the couch. Light glinted on gold and Leslie's heart skipped that he was still wearing his wedding ring.

That had to be a good sign, didn't it?

Or was he just so used to it that he'd forgotten it?

He crossed the floor to her and once she caught a whiff of his cologne, she couldn't take a breath. He stopped right in front of her, his eyes glittering, then leaned closer. "I haven't been drinking all night, not quite," he whispered, and she surveyed him, fearful of what he might say. "By the way, have you seen the paper this morning?"

Leslie frowned at the change of subject. "What does that have to do with anything?"

"Everything." He lifted it from the hall table and put it into her hands.

Matt was cocksure, though Leslie couldn't imagine why. His manner would have been puckish if she hadn't sensed a tremendous anger in him. Was it directed at her? What had she failed to do? She thought again of the triumphant smile that had lit his face when the verdict had been announced the day before. She watched him for a long moment, unable to understand this man she had thought she knew so well.

It had been a landmark case, the Laforini trial that had ended yesterday afternoon, but not because of the case itself. The defendant was charged with a variety of mob-related crimes, which might have been interesting to some people. What had seized the imagination of the press in this case, though, had been that the two lawyers arguing the case, one for the defense and one for the prosecution, were brothers.

Robert Coxwell, now a judge and retired from practice, had compelled all of his children to go to law school. The eldest, James, had been his father's protégé, his pride and joy, until it had been revealed that James was not in fact his father's biological son. The irony was that James had the most in common with Robert in terms of personality. Matt, always the number two son, always passed over for favor, at least in Leslie's view, had never been given his opportunity to shine.

And when James accepted a position at the District Attorney's office and Matt moved into the senior position at Coxwell & Coxwell, Leslie had been convinced that her husband was finally getting the break he deserved.

Matt, however, had lost the Laforini case, poisoning his father against him forever, and worse, Leslie was sure he'd done it on purpose.

"Chicken?" he asked now, eyes bright with challenge, and she flicked the paper open without further delay.

She took a deep breath, knowing there would be a picture of a triumphant James Coxwell crossing the courtroom to graciously shake his opponent and younger brother's hand. The press had gone wild when James had made that move and the flash from their cameras had been almost blinding.

But that picture wasn't on the front page. Instead a file shot appeared of Leslie's father-in-law, Robert Coxwell—the potent patriarch: handsome, confident, successful, and rich—with the headline, "Prominent Former Judge Dead."

She had to read the headline twice, it was so different from her expectation, then she looked to Matt for an explanation.

The glint in his eyes was definitely hostile. "I don't suppose you heard the phone ring last night?"

Leslie shook her head, still confused. "No. You know that I unplugged the extension in the bedroom when that Chinese take-out place was assigned almost exactly the same number as ours—"

"My father phoned last night," Matt said, interrupting her with a savage tone that she'd never heard him use before. "He summoned me to the house in Rosemount. I didn't want to go, but he promised we'd never talk about the Laforini case again if I agreed. It seemed like a good deal at the time." His lips twisted in a parody of a smile. "But he meant exactly what he said. We didn't talk again and we never will."

"I don't understand." Leslie glanced at the paper in her hands. Dead? Matt's father was dead?

"He killed himself, Leslie," Matt said tersely. "He committed suicide because I fucked up that case, the one he wanted so badly to win." He shrugged, his eyes glittering. "In fact, as a special present to me, he killed himself while I was driving to Rosemount. He made sure that I found him while he was still warm."

Leslie shook her head, unable to accept that, even disliking Robert Coxwell as she did. "But how can you know for sure? Maybe somebody else killed him. Maybe someone broke into the house, or he confronted a burglar, or . . ."

"No, Leslie, this was his way of getting even with me for letting him down yesterday."

Leslie looked at her husband, saw the mingled anger and shock and hurt in his eyes, and she knew she couldn't hold back the one question she had to ask. "Then why did you do it?" she whispered. "Why did you lose the case on purpose?"

She was hoping that Matt would deny it, hoping that he hadn't lost deliberately. For some reason, she could have accepted incompetence better than an unwillingness to comply with expectation.

But Matt's eyes brightened to a vivid green, a sign she recognized as a mark of his strong feelings. "Don't you know? I thought you, of all people, would understand. Don't you?"

Leslie could only shake her head, because she didn't understand. His lips tightened to a thin line and the shame she had felt in her dream, the certainty that she had let down expectations, flooded through her again.

Matt drained the last sip of scotch from his glass, then dropped the empty glass into her hand so abruptly that she nearly let it slip through. It was heavier than she remembered, smoother, and she barely caught it. He tilted his head to regard her, almost snarling. "I thought you of all people would get it."

"But I don't." As soon as the words left her lips, Leslie knew she'd failed a test, one she hadn't even known she'd been taking. "Tell me."

"There's no point." Matt's lips drew to a taut line. He stepped past her, his manner dismissive. He straightened his collar and tie as he looked in the mirror. He shoved a hand through his hair, ran a hand over the stubble on his chin with what might have been regret.

Leslie remembered the suitcase then, a bit later than was ideal, and a couple of points got together to make a line. "You're leaving? Just because I don't understand why you did what you did?"

She might not have spoken for all the response she got. Matt checked what looked like a computer printout before tucking it into his jacket pocket and reaching for the suitcase.

"There was a time when we would talk about things," she said with some desperation. "There was a time when we would give each other a chance."

"We were different people then," he said softly, the murmured words breaking her heart.

She stepped after him, put a hand on his arm. "Where are you going?"

"To get Zach out of jail, of course." Matt smiled then, looking more rakish than Leslie knew him to be. "But then, I doubt you'll miss me anyway."

"That's not true . . ."

"No?" He considered her for a heartbeat, then suddenly caught her nape in his hand and kissed her. He tasted of alcohol and of himself. Leslie felt the stubble on his chin and smelled his cologne, which mingled with his own scent. She felt that old black magic stir between them once more. She had a heartbeat to realize that she wasn't the only one savoring this long-overdue kiss.

Then Matt stepped away. "One last kiss," he said, which made Leslie panic. He smiled that crooked smile, the one that melted her knees, which softened his retreat a little.

"Be good, or at least, be careful," he murmured as he ran his thumb along the line of her jaw. Leslie leaned into his caress without meaning to do so, loving the feel of his hand against her skin, yearning.

"Don't go," she whispered.

But he was gone, striding out the door with purpose, as if he had already forgotten her. An airline limo idled at the curb. Matt put the Samsonite in the trunk, then made for the door to the back seat.

This had all been arranged in advance.

"Wait!" Leslie shouted. "Where are you going?" She was standing barefoot on her porch, which had a dusting of snow on it, her sapphire silk peignoir visible to all, and for once in her life, she didn't care what the neighbors thought.

Matt turned back and grinned, as if he had been possessed by the devil himself. He gave her a look of such pure mischief that she dreaded his words. She always loved his affection for the truth, his ability to be candidly honest about everything, although right here right now, she realized she'd never been afraid of the truth before. "New Orleans."

Leslie's heart headed for her toes. "Are you coming back?"

"Why would I?" He waited two beats for her shocked response, then blew her a showy kiss—her husband's cocksure twin—and leaped into the cab.

"You have to come back!" she shouted, but the cab was already at the end of the block and no one was looking back.

*　*　*

New Orleans wasn't a city name that could be easily mistaken for another one. It didn't sound at all like New York or New Haven or even New Hampshire, though none of those places would have been so threatening to Leslie.

She lived in New Orleans.

Leslie eyed the glass in her hand and wished Matt had left her a sip of scotch. She optimistically lifted the glass to her lips and tipped it, hoping to get the last drop out of the bottom, just as a casement window creaked overhead.

She looked up, unsurprised to find the elderly widow who lived next door studiously cleaning snow off the top of her window boxes. Mrs. Beaton did such an elaborate job of pretending to be unaware of Leslie that it was utterly unpersuasive.

She was tending her window boxes, at 6:45 in the morning.

In January.

Leslie was tempted to ask her what was planted in there. Alpine tulips, maybe, or arctic phlox.

Instead, she squared her shoulders and did a passable imitation of her usually composed self. "Good morning, Mrs. Beaton. Looks like it will be a nice day, don't you think?"

"Oh! Good morning, dear. Why, I didn't see you there! You've given me a start." Mrs. Beaton adjusted her glasses, the better to observe any damning details, and beamed. "I was just adjusting the window boxes, Leslie, and didn't hear a thing."

"And really, you can't get them ready early enough in the year," Leslie said, without meaning to do so. She routinely thought such things but never uttered them.

Funny how watching your husband walk out will throw your game.

Mrs. Beaton peered at Leslie, perhaps fearful that she was being teased. "Was that your husband leaving, dear?"

Leslie was tempted to claim that it was her Latin lover, that they had made boisterous love all night long, until he had begged allowance to go home to sleep for just a few hours. It would be interesting to see what kind of a reaction she'd get, but Leslie knew that the gossip grapevine would have a field day with that kind of tasty morsel.

There was no question that Mrs. Beaton would pass it along.

"Well, yes, it was. He's off on a business trip."

"Is that so, dear?" Mrs. Beaton's gaze flicked tellingly to the glass in Leslie's hand. She wasn't going to assume that it had held apple juice, that was for sure. Her lips tightened and Leslie acknowledged one of the reasons she'd always hated this house: The neighbors were too close.

Or maybe more important, they were too nosy.

"I didn't think Matthew traveled that much, dear."

"Still happens once in a while."

Leslie would have gone back into the house, but Mrs. Beaton cleared her throat. "I do so hope you haven't had a fight, dear. Now, I know that it isn't my concern and I would simply die rather than pry into someone else's personal business, but I have become quite attached to you as neighbors."

Leslie blinked, startled to have her own fears so closely echoed by a comparative stranger. "We're not moving, Mrs. Beaton."

"Well, if you got divorced, of course, you'd have to sell the house . . ."

"Mrs. Beaton, we're not getting divorced!"

"If you say so, dear, but you never know what kind of people are going to move in when a house sells. I would miss you, of course, but I would worry terribly about new neighbors . . ."

"*We're not getting a divorce!*" Leslie shouted this, which was precisely the wrong choice. Several neighbors en route to work looked up with interest.

"My goodness, dear, I never knew you were so touchy!"

"It's a business trip, Mrs. Beaton, no more than that." Leslie spoke so firmly, in her most fearsome Crabcake Coxwell voice, that an astute observer might have wondered who she was trying to convince.

Mrs. Beaton surely did. "Hmm," she said, taking another look at the empty glass.

"Have a nice day, Mrs. Beaton." Leslie retreated into the house and shut the door, locking the deadbolt as if that could keep various nasty developments at bay.

Time for an executive summary. It would be ugly, but she could take it.

Leslie closed her eyes and leaned back against the door, summoning the familiar rhythm of Matthew of Paris, medieval chronicler and—for a medievalist like Leslie—an old friend.

- Item the first:

Leslie's husband was heading to New Orleans, where his former fiancée lived, and had as much as said that he wouldn't be back.

- Item the second:

This would be the same former fiancée who had never married, the one who routinely enclosed personal letters with her Christmas cards to Matt every year, letters that he read over and over again.

- Item the third:

This would be the exotic beauty with legs up to her neck, a figure like a Barbie doll and a come-hither manner that made men salivate at forty paces.

- Item the fourth:

This would be the same husband with whom Leslie had not had intimate relations in a good three months.

And four days.

And twelve hours.

Leslie licked her lips and braced herself for the last titbit.

- Item the fifth:

She had no correlating data confirming that Zach was even in New Orleans. Matt's troublemaking brother had been in Venice, Italy, the last she'd heard, and New Orleans wasn't exactly around the corner from there.

And if Zach was in trouble in New Orleans, why hadn't James gone to bail out Zach, as he usually did? It seemed very suspect that Matt would suddenly take on this fraternal responsibility—had that happened before or after he'd learned where Zach was?

Maybe Leslie shouldn't have been so gracious about not reading Sharan's Christmas cards. Maybe she shouldn't have trusted her husband to have a platonic friendship with a biteably sexy and willing woman. Maybe she should have dragged him off to bed and wrapped her tongue around his tonsils, no matter how he had fought her en route. Any which way, he was probably going to be welcomed to the Big Easy with open arms and open thighs, and there wasn't a damn thing she could do about it now.

She set the glass down on the hall table with a decisive thump and halfway wished she had dropped it earlier. It would have shattered nicely, seeing as it was lead crystal, and that might have been satisfying.

It had been a wedding gift, too, so it might have been appropriate to break to a zillion pieces on this day of days.

"Is Daddy gone?"

Leslie jumped and turned to find her daughter peering over the bannister with what was either hostility or suspicion.

Maybe both. Welcome to lucky thirteen.

"Annette." She smiled as if everything was normal though it took some doing. "Good morning."

"Where's Daddy?"

"He just left."

Annette used an expletive that Leslie would have liked to believe her daughter had never heard before, then fled to her room.

"Annette! Stop!"

Annette did not stop. Even taking the stairs three at a time wasn't enough—her daughter had too much of a head start. Leslie heard the bedroom door slam before she reached the summit, and the key turned in the lock before she even started down the hall.

Leslie pounded on the door, just because it seemed the thing to do, and it felt remarkably good. "Annette! Annette, open this door."

"No."

Leslie didn't like threats or recriminations much, and the severe tone of voice that worked so well on her students had never had any discernible effect upon her daughter.

So she took a shaky breath and leaned against the door, rubbing her brow with her fingertips. With an effort, she summoned her usual demeanor but it was tougher than she ever remembered it being. "Annette? Will you please open the door so we can talk?"

"I want to see Daddy."

She forced herself to sound more patient than she felt. "Well, come and talk to me in the meantime."

"No. I want to talk to Daddy, just Daddy."

Leslie gritted her teeth, but still managed to keep her voice level. "Your dad has gone to the airport, Annette."

"I know. He told me he was going away."

That was news. "Did he tell you when he'd be back?"

"No."

At least her daughter didn't have that morsel of information. "I don't think he's sure when he'll be back," Leslie said with an assurance she didn't feel. "You could be waiting for him for a while."

"I don't care."

Leslie leaned back against the wall and pinched the bridge of her nose. When she finally spoke, her tone of voice was amazingly cheerful, though it cost her in spades.

She would keep up appearances, even if it killed her.

"Fine, then you just wait there as long as you'd like. I'm going to brush my teeth and go to the bathroom and have a muffin for breakfast, then I'm going to have a shower and go to work. You can't stay here alone all day, so the sooner you come out, the better your chance of getting a muffin for yourself."

It was a cheap trick, but she was short of options.

"You wouldn't eat them all," Annette whispered, her voice much closer to the door.

Aha. She had found a nerve.

"This morning, I just might." Leslie paused, then twisted the proverbial knife. "They're chocolate chip, you know, your favorite kind."

Then she left her daughter to think about that. She tossed the newspaper in the recycling bin under the sink, determined to tell her daughter about this family tragedy in her own way.

What exactly that way might be wasn't clear to Leslie at the moment, but with luck, Annette would fume for a while.

* * *

Life, Leslie decided in the midst of her second muffin and her third cup of instant coffee, was apparently a lot like childbirth. Just when you think you can't stand any more, the universe will demand a bit more. Against all odds, you will be able to accommodate that additional increment of stress, which starts the whole process again. It doesn't end, at least not soon enough to please the participants.

There's always more pain to be borne.

And somehow you always manage to take it.

There was a cheery notion, and one that wasn't easily accommodated with only instant coffee for consolation. Leslie had labored thirty-seven excruciating hours to bring Annette into the world. Maybe the blessing was that she couldn't quite remember all (let's do the math) 2,220 minutes—give or take—or every single one of those 133,200 seconds in glorious Technicolor detail anymore.

On the other hand, Leslie could recall an awful lot of them. She drained her mug and considered the dubious merits of another cup of instant java. Even cafeteria coffee promised to be an improvement, which said nothing good about her abilities to boil water and mix it with little brown crystals.

Maybe there was nowhere to go from here but up.

Either way, it was definitely a La Perla kind of a day.

Chapter Two

There are days when the business traveler should just give up, hit the bar in the lounge of the airport terminal, and wait for his or her luck to change. Matt Coxwell was having one of those days, and given events of the last twenty-four hours—and the quantity of scotch swimming solo in his belly—he was not in any condition to accept his fate amiably.

His marriage was over. He knew that. He knew that he had compromised all that he could compromise and his father had provided the reminder that it was never going to be enough. Leslie was like his father in that she saw only her own way, saw only what she wanted to see in him.

Instead of seeing the truth. Funny how people could insist that they loved you when they had no idea who you really were.

Matt had a dream of his own now, one that would require a lot of him, and one that would accept no compromises. He had to protect it, and thus, he had had to leave. It was that simple.

It was also remarkably painful. At least he'd had the chance to talk to Annette, though he hadn't been able to tell her all of the truth. Not yet.

He owed her the truth, but he owed it to her gently.

Matt had learned young that marriages only had room for one ambitious partner: It had been his father in his parents' marriage who had been possessed of the drive to make his mark. Proof positive had come when his mother tired of his father's rules and their marriage had collapsed as a result. Only one person could have an agenda, which required one to be support staff. That was the only way that Matt knew marriage worked.

The problem was that his days as an admin were over. He didn't expect Leslie to understand that: He expected, in fact, that she would try to persuade him to do it her way again. And he expected that he would weaken—for the sake of Annette, for the sake of stability, for the sake of the affection and admiration he still felt for his wife.

An abrupt parting was the only possible way to protect his newfound desire.

There had been no room for negotiation in his parents' marriage, no chance of compromising his father's demands. And Leslie had that visionary drive in common with Matt's father. For eighteen years, Matt had followed her agenda, mostly because he didn't have one of his own. He knew that the balance of their partnership couldn't be renegotiated, because that would mean Leslie sacrificing some of her ambition.

Which just wasn't possible.

He wouldn't ask her to do it, because he couldn't bear to compel her to deny him his dream.

It had all made perfect sense, until he hadn't been able to resist one last kiss—and she'd responded in spades. There had been a time when they had always kissed like that, though it hadn't happened lately.

Where had that kiss come from? Why had she kissed him like that? Why now? He could taste her on his lips and the sensation didn't fade. He couldn't remember when they'd last had sex, but he could swear she would have done it in the foyer this morning.

And that was a pretty distracting idea. How could she so easily undermine his conviction in what he knew to be true? Or was it all a game, to keep him doing what she wanted?

Matt didn't know and that troubled him.

It turned out that he had to connect through Chicago to get to New Orleans, on account of booking late. It wasn't that hard to believe that a lot of people wanted to leave Boston for sunnier climes in January, but a four-hour layover at O'Hare (also in January) wasn't something to anticipate with enthusiasm. And at this particular moment, Matt was singularly devoid of enthusiasm.

"Couldn't you just route me through Seattle instead?" he asked the ticketing agent, who hadn't been very amiable, however friendly the skies might prove to be. "Or maybe Osaka?"

She clearly didn't think he was funny. Matt could tell by the way she slapped his boarding pass onto the counter between them.

"Look at the bright side, sir," she said sweetly. "You'll accumulate more frequent-flier miles this way."

"And, if traffic is stacked up in Chicago the way it usually is, four hours might just allow me to make my connection."

"Have a nice flight, sir," she said with narrowed eyes and a tone that implied she wished his plane would bounce through air pockets all the way to Chicago. "Next!"

He had a good two hours until his departure, so Matt could at least hope for a restorative scotch before boarding. The haze induced by his binge was beginning to lift, and the danger in sobering up was that he might start to think.

That could only be bad news—there was one thing that he really didn't want to remember and another he didn't want to think about—so the best course of action was obviously to remain drunk for as long as possible.

Matt, however, had forgotten about the new security protocol. It had been years since he had flown anywhere, after all. His bag had to be X-rayed, his laptop started up to prove that it wasn't full of plastic explosives, ditto his Blackberry and cellphone. His shoes had to be X-rayed, which left him standing on the cold tile floor in his stocking feet along with everyone else intending to get on a flight this morning.

A decade-plus of child care left Matt wondering how many of his fellow passengers had plantar warts or a toenail fungus or some other podalic virus that this security strategy would give them the opportunity to share.

It also made him remember September 11, not just the devastation of that day but his own dawning sense that if he had been among those lost that day, he would have wasted his life. Nine-eleven had made Matt realize that he didn't even know what his dream was. Nine-eleven had made Matt see that he'd been coasting aimlessly so far. The tragedy had started him on a furtive quest, a quest that had brought him to this time and this place, a man with ambition and a goal and a clearer sense of his own direction than he'd ever had in his life.

It had also left him with his guts ripped out and strewn all around him, but on some level, he knew he was heading in the right direction.

At least if his number came up on this day, he'd know that he hadn't wasted his life so far.

And that had to count for something.

*　*　*

Who says no one wears armor anymore? Not Leslie Coxwell. Lingerie—silk and wires and elastic—gave her the stamina to face even an auditorium of bored undergraduates. It was armor, hidden armor, that bolstered her confidence, lifting and separating all the while.

And let's face it: There's nothing like an underwire bra with a frothy lace edging and matching panties to put a bounce in any woman's step. Leslie had always loved lingerie, the further from sensible white cotton the better, and long ago she had made a bargain with herself.

If she could tame the dragon known as Slow Metabolism and keep herself from looking like a zeppelin in jeans, then she would buy herself all the lingerie she desired.

And that had proven to be a lot.

She'd worked all through university to support her habit, probably the only thing she had done that had not led directly to better grades. Her dresser drawers—pun intended—overflowed with bras and panties, garter belts and camisoles, slips and teddies, tap pants, tanks and corsets. She had matched sets in red and pink and orange and yellow and jade and blue, and lots in black.

Matt had always preferred the black.

There were flower prints and stripes, polka dots and swirls, paisleys and jacquards. Leslie had a veritable cornucopia of satin and velvet and lace and silk jammed into every corner of the closet, and it wasn't enough.

It could never be enough.

On better days, she could admit that she had a bona fide addiction.

But it was a pretty harmless one.

French lingerie, American lingerie, Italian and Brazilian—you could tour the world and make a lot of conclusions about a whole lot of people just by doing a label tour of Leslie's collection. Some had eyelet trim, some had beading, some had ribbon roses or just plain ribbons. She had carefully cultivated a cross-selection of every kind of lace known to womankind, in more delicious colors than you'll find in an ice cream shop.

There was always one more that she needed, one more that captured her heart, and no trip to a lingerie store (or a department store, for that matter) left Leslie empty-handed.

If this was a disease, she'd decided long ago that she'd happily die of it.

The best part about it, in Leslie's opinion, was that no one in the big wide world had a clue. She might have a passing resemblance to a lingerie model in her underwear, but once she was dressed, she was Marian the Librarian all the way.

She wore her long dark hair wound up in a demure knot, her twin sets were as modest and sensible as her shoes and plain straight skirts. Leslie's wire-framed glasses made her look as wildly passionate as a loaf of Wonder Bread. Dressed for work, she was ageless and virtually genderless—which was a feat, given the dropdead glamor of her hidden balcony bra.

There had been a time when she had worried about what would ensue if she ever had a car accident, but that terror had passed. Leslie was too good of a driver to worry much about that—if she had an accident, it would be horrific and she would die. A tanker trailer would have to explode in front of her or something similar.

Which meant that explaining her addiction would be somebody else's problem, if indeed, the underwear survived the inferno.

On this morning, faced with challenges above and beyond expectation, it was clear to Leslie that the new La Perla set had come into her life for a reason. She'd been saving it for something special, and this day was going to be it. The fact that she had found it, discounted, in her size, was as clear a mark of divine intervention as any woman could need.

On this day, she was going to need all the support she could get.

La Perla, for those unaware of the splendors of intimate apparel, is the Everest of lingerie. Italian-designed, Italian-made, handfinished, made of exquisite materials, priced as if the goddesses themselves are the company's best clients, it is the best of the best.

Which is saying something.

This particular combination was smoky purple, though it might look silvery in some light. It was made of pure silk, woven in satin—Leslie's favorite—and trimmed with a substantial border of lace that had been dyed to match the silk.

The lace trim was about three inches deep and shaped like overlapping leaves: It followed the curve of Leslie's breasts, the lavish V lushly framing her modest décolletage. That lace would have looked divine peeking out the neck of a low-cut sweater, if Leslie had possessed such a garment or been inclined to wear one. The lace also accentuated the leg line of the panties, which were cut high to make her legs look longer and slimmer.

It was a shame that no one would see her like this, at least not in the foreseeable future. The plunging line of the bra reminded her of the night she had revealed her secret to Matt—that had been a black satin underwire bra, if memory served—and she blushed in mingled recollection and desire.

(Desire for Matt, in case you aren't sure. She still had the bra in the bottom right drawer and it still fit.)

Leslie pulled on a dove gray turtleneck with curt gestures, concealing that Italian silken marvel from those unworthy of seeing it. She checked, but there was nary a lump or a ripple to reveal her hidden glory. The black straight wool skirt, the sensible Hush Puppy loafers, the cardigan that matched the turtleneck, all combined to give her a serious and reliable air. No one would be surprised to learn that she was an academic, not when she was dressed like this. Pearl stud earrings were her only jewelery, along with her watch and wedding rings.

Leslie considered her reflection critically. She was as ready to face the day as she would ever be. To her surprise, she didn't look any different than she did any other day. No one would guess that she'd been emotionally drawn, quartered, and disemboweled before breakfast.

She checked twice to be sure, but her reflection told her what she already knew: Good lingerie is worth its weight in gold.

* * *

By the time Matt got through the line, his flight was already boarding. Just as well: the bar in the departure lounge was still closed. The flight attendant sold him a small bottle of scotch for a large price, but wouldn't sell him another.

He began to sober fast as they flew west, seeing blood and his own failure with relentless clarity, etched in the clouds that stretched across the sky in every direction. He saw Leslie in more than a few clouds, too.

He'd been so sure he was right, that this was the only course forward.

Could he have been that wrong?

*   *   *

It was 1988 and Matt Coxwell stood in an ivy-clad courtyard at his college. He and Sharan Loomis were sleeping together; no, they were virtually inseparable. He had skipped a class on the history of jurisprudence to do this favor for her, although on some level, it irked him that she had asked—if not expected—him to cut his favorite class to do this.

But he would have done anything for Sharan, a woman so different from all the women he'd ever known that he figured he could just stand back in awe for the rest of his life, entranced by her beauty and her passion for life. Matt had understood from his first encounter with Sharan that Art was the serious competition for her affections. Art was the one thing that could oust him from this relationship, the relationship he had thought he needed more than air to breathe. He had known this intuitively and with terrifying certainty.

In the service of Art, he had moved massive canvases for shows, had hung art, and picked up flyers at the printers. He had gone to meetings, too, of new artists' collectives, and attended performance art, and listened to speeches by earnest young artists who had no clear idea what they were protesting except that they had to protest something, and he had tried to persuade himself that he shared Sharan's enthusiasm for such things.

It was late October. The sky was clear blue, the wind had a bite that promised of winter around the corner, and there were golden leaves scuttling around his feet. Matt could feel the wind ruffling his hair, slipping its chilly fingers through his sweater. Any joy he felt at being asked to participate was tempered by the very real sense that he was being used.

The group of artists mounting the show—along with their sup-

*porters and various hangers-on—had decided that they needed in-
credible attendance at this show, that they needed the hall filled to
bursting. They needed public approval of this first modern art
show at the conservative college, in order to set the stage for more
such spectacles in the future.*

*So there was Matt, a law student and thus token and testament
that anyone could like this art, that everyone should like it, that anyone remotely enlightened would come in and see it. He handed out
flyers, he cajoled people to go inside and take a look, he reminded
complete strangers that the show was free. It was unlike him to be so
garrulous, but Matt knew that he didn't have that much choice.*

*The simple fact was that if he wanted Sharan, this was the role
he had to play. He was representative of the ignorant bourgeois
masses, a decoy positioned to coax his conservative (if not ignorant)
fellows inside, so they could sip of the cup of artistic enlightenment.*

Something like that.

*He didn't even see Leslie that first time, beyond the fact that a
student with a ton of books in her arms was crossing the courtyard.
He just shoved the flyer between her nose and the top book and
started his spiel.*

*"'Piercing the Veil,'" he said, thinking for the umpteenth time
that the title of the show made no sense. "It's a student art show in
the common room, the first one in years, and you've got to come
and see it."*

*She looked at the flyer, then at him, adjusted the weight of the
books, then took the flyer in her right hand to study it. There was
a color photograph of one of the paintings in the show, one done
by Sharan in fact. It was red, as red as blood, with a jagged black
line running from top to bottom just slightly to the right of center.
It was called* Pandora's Redemption.

*"Is this the kind of art in the show?" she asked, clearly referring
to the photograph on the flyer.*

*"What do you mean?" Matt bristled at a potential criticism of
Sharan's work.*

"Is it all modern art?"

"Well, it is all abstract, though much of it is postmodern. You should come . . ."

"I don't like abstract art," she said, then handed him back the flyer. "Save this for someone who's interested."

Surprise made Matt look at her. Her hair was a brown so rich that it was almost black, dark and thick and glossy, tied back in a ponytail. Hers wasn't a cheerleader ponytail, caught up high on the back of her head and dancing in the breeze, but a low one, clasped demurely at the back of her neck. She wore no makeup, though she was pretty in a bookish way. She held his gaze for a moment, unapologetic about her view, and he saw that her eyes were as blue as the autumn sky. She then shrugged a little as if aware she might be hurting his feelings and made to step past him.

"But why not?" he asked, not quite ready to let her slip away.

She glanced back, studying him for a moment, hesitant to reply.

"I'd like to know. Really."

"It doesn't mean anything," she said with another of those little shrugs. "At least not to me." She smiled a bit then, and he braced himself for another candid confession. "It doesn't seem to me to be about what people say it's about, like maybe they're just making up stories to make it seem more meaningful than it is. And that's just not interesting to me."

"This show is different," Matt insisted, struck that she'd expressed what had been bothering him in a more vague and general way. "It might change your mind."

She studied him steadily for a moment then nodded at the flyer he still held out to her. "What does that mean, then? Pandora's Redemption? Why is it called that?"

Matt looked at the flyer, hating that he didn't really know. He struggled to remember something Sharan had said about blood, but he knew he couldn't express it coherently.

"It doesn't make sense," she said. "Does the artist even know who Pandora was? Pandora opened the box that released all evil

into the world, then closed it just in time to keep hope inside. What does that have to do with red and a line of black? I don't get it."

Matt smiled, caught. "Neither do I, actually. But that doesn't mean it's worthless, or that there's no point in seeing it."

"Why are you doing this, if you don't like this art, either?"

"I didn't say I didn't like it!"

"No, but I saw the look on your face when you were looking at it. You didn't have to say it." She smiled then, really smiled, and he couldn't help staring at her. She was much prettier than he'd realized. She tilted her head, eyes sparkling. "So, why do this?"

It seemed inappropriate—or ignoble—to admit that he was doing it for sex.

"Hey, Matt!" Sharan called from behind him at exactly the wrong time. "You're doing a great job!" He turned to see her leaping down the steps, all long legs and loose hair, slender and sexy and headed straight for him.

"Oh!" Book Girl said, and Matt didn't miss that she sounded disappointed in him. "I get it." She ducked over her books, letting her bangs cover her eyes shyly, and started to turn.

"No, you really should come and see the show," Matt insisted, not wanting her to walk away.

She glanced over her shoulder, her gaze darting to Sharan. Her smile was gone. "I don't think so," she said then, with the surety that would become so familiar to him. Then she smiled again, polite to a fault, but this smile was a pale imitation of her earlier one. He wanted the first one back.

"But good luck with it." She paused, her gaze flicking to Sharan and back to him. "Good luck with everything."

Then she was gone, leaving Matt Coxwell staring after the one person in his experience who had the nerve to tell the truth. In a short conversation, Book Girl had been unafraid to speak her thoughts honestly.

Sharan fussed over him and kissed him, apparently thinking that he needed sexual encouragement to persevere, but he kept thinking about the other girl's smile. He kept thinking about how she had nailed exactly what had been bothering him, that she had dared to say what he had thought was the unspeakable. She was right: There was so much of the art game that was bullshit, just fancy talk covering a lot of emptiness.

It was more than unworthy of interest: It was dishonest.

Even his own involvement was dishonest in a way, because he wasn't involved for any passion of his own. He just wanted to keep Sharan happy, to keep Art from wiggling in between them in bed. Sex with Sharan was his passion, not the art itself.

That made him wonder whether his passion was enough.

He would never tell Sharan that truth, never be honest with her, because he instinctively knew that such a confession would cost him everything. But that other girl had been honest, honest as if she couldn't imagine being anything else.

What would it be like to be able to be so open with someone else? Matt could barely imagine such a thing, given his own family history, but was tantalized by the possibility. What would it be like to say what you thought, with no prevarication or gilding? Were there people who had relationships with no secrets, no hidden objectives and goals?

* * *

Some twenty years later, Matt Coxwell watched out his window as his plane sliced through cloud cover over Chicago and remembered how desperately—and how suddenly—he had wanted to find out. Leslie had shone a bright light into his life the first time he had met her, compelling him to assess his motives. She'd called him on his principles. He hadn't even known her name, and she had changed everything with a chance two-minute conversation.

Icy rain enveloped the aircraft as they descended, turning the world below to gray as it pounded on the wings. But Matt was lost in the past. He had turned to Leslie when the Laforini verdict was pronounced the day before, turned to her with a smile of triumph. He'd been sure that she would see that the truth had prevailed, that he had ensured justice had been served, that they were still fighting the good fight together. He had been sure that she would be proud of him and that whatever obstacles had erupted between them recently would be swept aside.

But Leslie had caught her breath and averted her gaze, her disappointment in him as cutting as a knife. How could she have forgotten the first lesson she ever taught him? How could she have lost the value of the first gift she had ever shared?

He decided that it was time he found out.

He decided that the least he could do after eighteen years together was to remind her of the valuable gift she'd given him that first day.

* * *

Leslie was late for her staff meeting, which shouldn't have surprised her, and given the circumstances, shouldn't have bothered her as much as it did. Annette had slouched down to the kitchen so impossibly late that Leslie had had to drive her to school, and she had been forced to tell her about her grandfather while doing so.

After all, people at school might well have read the paper and figured out the connection.

She wasn't sure that ultimately she did any better a job than the newspaper might have done. Annette didn't respond, just stared straight out the windshield as if she hadn't heard Leslie at all.

They didn't talk about Matt any more than they already had.

For once, Leslie didn't fight for some sign of life from her daughter. She was tired of trying to find the elusive right answer, of trying to discern whether Annette was having a mood or a nervous breakdown. She told herself that it was because she was too late, but the truth was that she was afraid of what Annette might ask. She'd never lied to her daughter and didn't want to start now.

At work, she took five minutes in her office to call and leave a condolence message for her mother-in-law. She wasn't really surprised to get Beverly's answering machine instead of Beverly live, and left a standard polite message of the "if there's anything I can do" variety. She didn't expect Beverly to be more than shocked by Robert's demise: The couple was estranged, after all, and their divorce had taken a nasty turn at Robert's instigation.

Still there were things you had to do, and leaving messages of condolence was one of them.

Even if they did make you even more late.

Leslie charged into the departmental meeting, aware that she had never been less than prompt before. She was probably out of breath for the first time ever, too. Dr. Dinkelmann granted her a glare, clearly disappointed that one of his stars was slipping, then looked pointedly at his watch. Leslie forced a smile of apology, sat down, and noticed the murmur of her fellows.

She took a deep breath, felt the hand-shaped La Perla underwire press against her ribs and was reassured.

Dinkelmann cleared his throat portentously. "As I was saying . . ."

Leslie had never been able to pinpoint what had made her despise Dr. William Dinkelmann, the new department head, on sight. She had felt an instinctive dislike of him the very first time he offered his sweaty little hand to her—but why?

He was clever, but that's not so special in a group of historical scholars. He was passionate about his opinions, which also wasn't much of a surprise, but he had a slick persuasiveness about him that Leslie distrusted. He was smooth, possessed of the kind of charismatic charm more typical of politicians than academics. He had a way of marketing his plans, of choosing words that made terrible ideas sound better than they were, of tricking people into endorsing things that they fundamentally disagreed with—and without them realizing what they'd done.

In a room full of smart people, that was quite a trick.

And—this was petty—he wore pink shirts. Someone must have told him once that wearing pink made his eyes look more blue, which was true, but Leslie found it very hard to take a man seriously who was wearing a bright pink shirt.

So she was conservative. Don't shoot.

In fact, she had a sneaky feeling that maybe that was the reason Dinkelmann wore them: So that everyone underestimated him. His accomplishments were hard to belittle: He had to be ten years younger than Leslie and he was already department head, brought in from Duke for big money. He was confident and handsome in his way, which made it likely he'd soon be lured off to another deserving institution.

That couldn't happen soon enough for Leslie.

She kept all of this neatly to herself, of course, and sat demurely in the staff meeting as if she were fully supportive of Dr. Dinkelmann and his schemes.

Let him think she was on his side. Favorites were watched less closely than those in his sights.

He beamed at the assembled group and adjusted his gold-rimmed glasses. Leslie wondered whether they really had lenses in them or just plain glass, whether they were just a prop to make him look older and more distinguished.

See? There was something about the man that made lots of nasty little suspicions start whispering in one's mind.

Dinkelmann checked his notes with elaborate care, ensuring that everyone had time to understand that they were waiting on him. "So the reason for this meeting is to discuss with you the impending policy changes in this department and in the institution at large."

As the group stirred in early consternation—there is, after all, no single group more resistant to change than academics—Dinkelmann held up a hand and smiled benignly. "Now, there's no cause for concern, but the university has targeted some areas for improvement in the ongoing pursuit of academic excellence."

"Here it comes," Naomi Tucker muttered, earning a castigating glare from Dinkelmann. Everyone else present developed a sudden fascination with their shoes.

"The university has become aware of an issue with our image in the marketplace," Dinkelmann said with a salesman's polish. "High school students apparently perceive this institution to be a 'tough' school, and this preconception is affecting our rate of applications from prospective students. Compared to other schools of our size offering a similar curriculum, we have experienced a net drop in real applications, adjusted over time, of five percent per year. If this dangerous trend continues, the financial foundation of the university will be at risk."

It was impossible to look around this chunk of prime real estate and ever imagine that the university's financial health could be at risk. Also Leslie knew firsthand how aggressively the alumni society pursued donations and bequests, because they phoned her constantly. She looked down at the pad of paper she had brought and scribbled something, as if taking notes like a good camper.

Defiance, meanwhile, boiled beneath her fabulous bra. Leslie didn't say anything, didn't even look up from her lap. You really can't argue with (or at least can't win against) an historian who has a specialty in Napoleon's battle strategies. Leslie had realized very quickly that she wasn't Dinkelmann's Waterloo, and never would be.

He, as was typical of him, assumed that silence meant assent, so continued with merry confidence. "The university board of governors has decided to address this false perception by improving upon our already excellent grading standards. Beginning with this semester, fifty percent of all students registered in a given class must receive a grade of B-plus or better. In addition, the former policy of eighty percent of all students achieving a passing grade still stands. I'm sure that you can see . . ."

Leslie's mind absorbed half of that and stalled in shock.

"But wait a minute, sir," Naomi said. She was still young enough to go looking for trouble, and Leslie felt a twinge of sympathy for her. "How does giving away good grades for nothing contribute to the pursuit of academic excellence?"

"You must encourage excellence, Dr. Tucker. I'm sure that your fellows can provide some suggestions for you to use in the classroom."

It was ridiculously easy to tell one's place from Dinkelmann's manner of address: He only called the favored few by their first names. Leslie had found it a dubious, if not an unwelcome, distinction to be called by her first name.

Naomi was not in that club, it was clear.

"But sir, rewarding substandard efforts is counterintuitive." Naomi was wading in deep here, too deep to be saved. Everyone began to avidly take notes, which Leslie doubted were any more substantial than her own.

She, for example, had written "Matt" on her notepad and drawn a box around it. She wrote "New Orleans" beneath his name, then crossed it out because she felt obliged to add "Sharan" and would not do that.

Not even on paper. Instead she wrote "Zach," but couldn't keep herself from adding a question mark. Her stomach roiled.

Could a marriage end, just like that? Without her really knowing why? Without her having a chance to make it better? Leslie supposed that this happened all the time.

To other people.

Instead of thinking about that, she focused on her urgent desire to not yack chocolate chip muffin on her shoes.

Naomi frowned as she spoke. "I don't really see the problem with being known as a tough school. Surely that means that graduating students have a more marketable asset in their degrees?"

"The university, in these challenging times, feels compelled to ensure its own marketability first. And we will do that, each and every one of us, by stimulating our students and motivating them to learn! Academic excellence must be cultivated!" Dinkelmann drove his fist into his palm, his favorite gesture of emphasis. "Academic excellence must be courted with enthusiasm! Remember that our students will blossom into the researchers and instructors of the future. It is our obligation to ensure the future!"

"But . . ."

"Your point has been made and noted, Dr. Tucker. This is an expectation from the board of governors and thus it is an expectation of mine. You will ensure that the grades you give this semester cohere to the new plan or you will find yourself seeking other opportunities."

There was a collective inhalation, and a few furtive glances were exchanged between the professors still seeking tenure. Leslie added little circles around her doodle, as if her husband's name had become a Broadway sign.

Or was reflected in another woman's makeup mirror. Leslie began to scribble over everything but his name. Matt had to come back.

Didn't he?

"But the scheme for grading has already been given to the students," Naomi insisted. "And I've already marked their first essays. I can't change the grading scheme without giving them cause for appeal." She smiled, confident she'd scored a hit. "And that would make more work for you, Dr. Dinkelmann."

Dinkelmann's tight smile said otherwise. "Then you must find a way to balance the two, Dr. Tucker. The solution is your problem to resolve, not mine." It was clear to everyone in the room that Naomi had lost this particular battle.

A dull flush tinged her neck. "I suppose I'll have to think about that."

"Don't think about it, Dr. Tucker. Do it."

There was a heartbeat of awkward silence in the room. Leslie would have been quite happy remaining invisible for the duration of this meeting, but Dinkelmann had other ideas.

He gestured to her, and she had a heartbeat to dread what he might say. "Here's another example of finding solutions: Leslie, you have the distinction of the lowest grade averages per class in the entire department."

So much for no one noticing what she did. Clearly she should have done a better job of fading into the woodwork.

Or this was her bonus prize for being late.

She forced a smile. "I take pride in rewarding excellence, sir."

"While that is commendable, I've looked at your grading schemes. You could make a marked difference in your grade averages by awarding full participation marks to all students."

Leslie blinked. "I beg your pardon?"

"Yes." Dinkelmann referred to his notes, which were apparently about Leslie's grading. She felt a childish urge to snatch them off his lap, tear them up and stomp on them.

Of course she didn't move at all.

"You've allowed fifteen percent of each grade in each course for participation. It clearly follows that if you granted each student that fifteen percent automatically, your averages would be then be fifteen percent higher, and at that level, more consistent with the university's expectations."

Leslie glanced around, seeing a few smirks. Some people were enjoying that she was being targeted; others were just glad it was her instead of them. She felt, suddenly, very alone.

But that didn't mean that she was afraid to fight. "With all respect, sir, students are supposed to participate to get that participation mark, hence the name. They're supposed to show up, to do the readings, and to contribute to any discussions, to actively be a part of their own educations. It is my understanding that the intent of that mark is to acknowledge the efforts of students who actively participate but are not outstanding scholars."

Dinkelmann smiled thinly. "Perhaps it was a meaningful measure once, but now it is no more than a curiosity from the past. As historians, we can all appreciate that the social mores of former times seldom make sense later on." He nodded to the group, inviting them to concur with him.

An astonishing number of them did.

He fixed her with a look. The Look. "With respect, Leslie, participation in any real sense is impossible to gauge, given current class sizes. It's an arcane expectation and we need to look to the future of scholarship. We cannot expect more from students than they can reasonably be expected to give." He removed his glasses and smiled benignly, exuding a paternal concern that was so at odds with his own ambition that Leslie felt an uncharacteristic urge to deck him.

So it was unreasonable to expect students to learn? Leslie had a hard time biting that comment back.

She really needed to get herself a decent cup of coffee.

"I do not need to remind any of you that annual tuition at this institution costs in excess of twenty-thousand dollars, not including any living costs or even books, and that the people paying those bills, by and large the parents of the students, expect a commensurate value with that cost."

He fixed Leslie once more with The Look. She looked back, determined not to blink first, unpersuaded as she was. He was surprised, she could see it, because she'd never defied him this much in the past.

But this was important.

The question was how important.

Important enough to lose her job?

At that thought, Leslie dropped her gaze. She knew she didn't imagine Dinkelmann's satisfied chortle.

"Parents want their children to be A students and the university is determined to fulfil that expectation," he lectured to what he believed was a converted audience. "I merely suggest you all reconsider your marking criterion. Update it, perhaps, because even as historians, we dare not live in the past." He chuckled, pleased with his joke, and there were a few smiles in response.

Leslie pretended to make a note to herself. There was no chance she'd forget this travesty of a suggestion, even though she wasn't sure what to do about it. For the moment, she hoped that Dinkel-mann proved himself to be like past chairmen determined to inflict change on the department; she hoped his attention was fleeting and his memory poor. She hoped she could keep her head down and by the time the marks came in, he would have forgotten all about this nonsense.

It was worth a shot. It had worked before, after all.

Was that what Matt had done? Had he been slipping away, or changing quietly, over the years while her attention had been diverted?

Leslie sat up straight. If so, he had every justification for being angry with her. She'd been so busy tap-dancing here, ensuring her tenure, guaranteeing their income, that she hadn't done much else.

Dinkelmann peered around and must have noticed how many sat with heads bent, apparently cowed. He smiled, content with what he had wrought. "Anyone else?" There was a lot of shuffling and mumbling that could have passed for assent, then Dinkelmann dismissed them.

One more meeting survived. Leslie felt as if she should get a commemorative plaque.

Maybe a new bra.

Twenty-four hours of wild sex with Matt. That would be better. They'd be too tired to fight then.

Of course they'd have to be in the same city for that to work. She would not think about him having twenty-four hours of wild sex with Sharan.

She wouldn't. Not for one minute.

Troubled by the turn of her thoughts, Leslie headed quietly back to her office alone.

Or so she thought.

Chapter Three

"So why do I feel like we've just been sent to the arena?" Naomi Tucker asked. Leslie glanced back to find her younger coworker closing fast. "Naked Christians chucked out to feed the lions, while the crowd goes wild watching the show. For Christ's sake . . ."

"Wasn't that the point?" When Naomi looked blank, Leslie explained her attempt at a joke. "It was for Christ's sake that so many of them put themselves in circumstances that would lead to their martyrdom, if I recall correctly."

"Ha ha," Naomi said without humor. "I'm serious, Leslie. It's outrageous that he could demand that we do this."

Naomi was a tall and easygoing kid, relatively new to the department. She had a sparkling fresh doctorate degree on the wall of her office from this very institution and was easy to like. She was also an excellent scholar of Roman history, with several published articles already under her belt.

"It's pretty easy to see Dinkelmann as an emperor demanding to be entertained," Leslie admitted, then immediately wished she could pull the words back. It wasn't like her to be so indiscreet.

But Naomi laughed. "Let's get him a gilded wreath of laurel leaves. I can have the theater department rig up something and leave it anonymously."

"He'd figure it out. You're going to need a sense of self-preservation, Naomi, if you intend to have a career in academia."

"A tolerance for double-talk, maybe," Naomi scoffed. "You're probably going to follow his edict, aren't you? Always the one to make the rest of us look bad." There was no malice in her words, but Leslie was still surprised.

She stopped. "I don't try to make anyone look bad."

"No, you just make everything look easy. It kind of falls out. More grad students to advise? Everyone says it can't be done, but Dr. Coxwell takes on three more, and remember she's already advising more than any of us. Bigger classes? Everyone's ready to fight tooth and nail to have classes split, but you handle it with aplomb." Naomi glanced aside, smiled, lowered her voice. "You know, I've always wanted to use that word. Aplomb. It has a ripe Renaissance kind of feel to it, don't you think?"

"I think it is Renaissance, from the French."

"Oh, so I'm not allowed to use it, is that it?"

Leslie shook her head solemnly. "Anachronism, Naomi. You've got to watch out for it."

The other woman laughed easily. "I don't remember you making jokes before, Leslie. You should do it more—you're funny."

Before Leslie could decide whether there was something significant in that, Naomi charged on. "But back to my point, and I do have one. You accommodate everything Dinkelmann asks, even when the rest of us think it's impossible. Lecturing to five hundred? No problem if you're Dr. Coxwell. Grading their five hundred essays? You'll have it done over the weekend." She sighed. "I could hate you, Leslie, if I didn't like you so much already."

"Thanks for that." Leslie shrugged. "Remind me never to introduce you to my teenage daughter."

Naomi chuckled.

Surely Naomi was exaggerating about people disliking her? Leslie wished she could be sure. She didn't usually give advice, but felt she should make an exception today. "The thing is, Naomi, I don't think Dinkelmann is going to change his mind. There's no point fighting him, especially in front of the whole department. You'll only annoy him."

"You know him that well?"

"It's human nature. And he's ambitious. He won't like anyone who doesn't make him look good."

"You're not even going to quibble over this edict?" Naomi was incredulous. "I might have to get over liking you, Leslie."

Leslie took a deep breath and didn't say anything. She didn't know yet what she was going to do.

Naomi seemed to sense her indecision. "He's going to be watching you, you know, to set the tone. He already singled you out, mighty star Coxwell."

Leslie shifted her load of books, disliking the logic of that. "No, you're wrong. He was just making a point." She didn't quite believe that herself and wasn't able to summon enough oomph for the assertion to sound persuasive.

"Imagine, a full fifteen percent participation mark in a class of Crabcake Coxwell's, just for having a pulse." Naomi nodded with enthusiasm. "There's going to be cheering in the streets. I wish I was a few years younger: I might have aced your course instead of scoring a B."

"A B-plus, as I recall."

"Your memory's better than mine, then." She grinned. "Of course, they don't actually have to prove they have a pulse, do they?"

"It hasn't happened yet," Leslie noted.

"So what are you going to do? Defy him?" There was a gleam of anticipation in Naomi's eye.

Leslie shook her head, knowing she couldn't risk making waves. "Dinkelmann will let it go, you'll see. He can't fire all of us—a lot of us have tenure."

Who was she trying to convince?

"What about grad school referrals? You know they're due next week."

"Thanks for that. I'd forgotten."

"I'm sure this means that we're supposed to give glowing referrals to students who barely showed for class. Gotta keep those bill-
ables up in the graduate school." Naomi made a sound beneath her
breath that could have been an expletive.

Although Leslie agreed, she was cautious about voicing her
thoughts. "Be serious."

"I am." Naomi gave her a wry look. "But what have you got to
worry about? There can't be that many brave enough to ask you
for a referral."

"Sixteen."

"I've got forty."

Leslie smiled despite herself. "They think you're a soft touch.
You'd better nip that in the bud, Naomi, because Dinkelmann will
hear about it if some of them are disappointed. With that many,
odds are that someone will be displeased."

"How about yours? Are they all deserving?"

"Sadly, no." Leslie shrugged. "But they don't expect a glowing
referral from me. If I say any one of them is acceptable or has potential, he or she will be over the moon."

"What about the ones who aren't? No one's going to welcome
the 'keep this kid out of grad school at all costs' letter."

"Oh, there are ways to say things."

"Aha, someone finally admits that there is a secret language of
the referral letters!" Naomi rubbed her hands together in mock
glee. "Do I get a decoder ring so I can play, too?"

"Not until you get tenure. It's like seeking the Holy Grail:
You've got to earn your reward before you get it."

"Now, wait a minute." Naomi propped a hand on her hip, eyes
sparkling. "Don't you think it's fundamentally wrong for a Roman
scholar to be seeking a Holy Grail?"

"You were the one comparing yourself to a Christian martyr."
Leslie smiled as she stopped to unlock her office door.

"Touché."

The stupid lock was jammed again, and Leslie wiggled the key in the push-pull-turn-wriggle combination that had worked the last time. To her amazement, it worked again.

Maybe her luck was changing.

As if. She could almost hear Annette's snort.

Naomi lingered. Leslie hoped with every bit of hope left in her—which wasn't much—that she didn't want a favor. She didn't want to turn Naomi down, but really, she was at hour thirty-six in the labor analogy and she was pretty sure she couldn't take on anything more.

Giving away the 15 percent participation mark to everybody. What was in Dinkelmann's head?

Naomi shoved one hand in her pocket, looking suddenly young and uncertain. "Leslie, I'm concerned about this. You're not really going to back Dinkelmann on this policy, are you?"

Leslie looked up and down the hall before she answered, and even then, she lowered her voice. "Just do yourself a favor: Don't challenge him in meetings and this whole thing will blow over."

"You don't think he's going to go over your grades with a red pencil?"

"He wouldn't. It would be wrong." She shook her head, even as she wondered. Would he? "He'll be on to the next reform tomorrow and by the time the marks come in, he'll have so many changes to manage that he'll forget to police this one."

Unfortunately, that didn't even sound plausible to Leslie.

"I don't think so." Naomi peered at her, suddenly sober. "I've heard about this edict being handed down in other departments, too. The university is serious about it—low grade averages are affecting their ability to draw new students."

"So it's all about revenue." Leslie spoke without thinking. "Like we're selling a consumer product, not an education or a future."

That was just the kind of reality check she needed.

Naomi added another. "Did you hear that Dias got tenure as part of the deal when they hired him?"

She stared at the younger teacher, aghast. "Tenure? That kid?" Naomi nodded. "But he's coming here directly from Austin, he hasn't even defended his thesis yet . . ."

"Dinkelmann thinks he's a star. You should check out his website." Naomi smiled wryly. "Dias thinks he's a star, too, so they're in agreement."

"A website? Why does a scholar need a website?"

"Maybe he's going to do an HBO deal on the side."

"Since when is academic research about entertainment?" This was outrageous. "And besides, *you* don't even have tenure yet!"

"Don't remind me." Naomi glanced at her watch. "Ah, the unwashed heathens await me, in all their splendid ignorance. Though my fate may be unpleasant, I cannot resist their siren call." She bowed, then lifted her right hand high. "*Ave, Caesar, morituri te salutamus!*"

Leslie chuckled. *Hail, Caesar: We who are about to die salute you!* It was the traditional greeting given by gladiators to the emperor before facing battle and almost certain death in the arena.

"You're not going to die, not even metaphorically," Leslie chided. "Not unless you do something stupid."

"Without tenure, I'll starve in a gutter." Naomi shrugged. "It doesn't look like I'll be seeing that deal anytime soon, so I've pretty much got nothing to lose. I'll go down defending the moral high road, if I've got a choice." She gave Leslie a look. "It'd be nice not to be fighting the good fight alone."

Leslie didn't say anything and she noticed Naomi's disappointment.

"Well, then *ciao*, doc."

Leslie watched her go, hating that Naomi's achievements weren't being appreciated by Dinkelmann. The new-hire Dias with tenure . . . and a website.

Could she defy Dinkelmann without him noticing?

On the other hand, how much further could she bend to accommodate his demands? Surely the rest of the department didn't really dislike her for putting up and shutting up? She had to keep her job; didn't they?

But at what cost? She would have given a paycheck just to talk to Matt again, to get his thoughts on what she should do. Maybe he was really just going to New Orleans to fetch Zach and she'd have that chance to talk to him.

As if.

A glance at the clock made Leslie jump. There were unwashed heathens awaiting her, too, clamoring for higher grades for less work, and this despite their splendid ignorance. Duty called, putting Leslie in mind of Naomi's earlier comment.

Because, really, lecturing to a hall of university students *was* a lot like being tossed to the lions.

* * *

Matt marched through the terminal to the first bank of telephones he saw, then punched in the number he knew as well as his own name. The line had already connected before he checked his watch and realized Leslie would probably be giving a lecture.

The phone rang and rang, giving him plenty of time to curse the university and their failure to install voice mail. Or maybe they had it and Leslie the Luddite hadn't read the instructions to install it on her phone.

Either way the phone was clearly going to ring until Tuesday.

He looked at his watch and winced. He did have four hours to kill, and he did need to talk to her just one more time. He could punch redial as well as anybody.

One more call, just one.

* * *

Leslie marched into her lecture hall, to the general disinterest of the students who had bothered to gather there. About half had showed up, which was pretty much an average measure of the burning desire to learn in a postsecondary institution in mid-January. Over the course of the term, their numbers would dwindle to a few hardy survivors, then she would be astonished by how many were present for the exam.

Sometimes the process seemed to have little point.

But then Leslie had a feeling that if Matt was really gone, there was going to be a lot of her life that didn't feel as if it was worth the trouble.

She put her papers down on the podium, glancing through them as if they contained her lecture when in fact they did not, and braced herself for one of the rituals of her job.

Leslie was a scholar of medieval history. The particular focus of her own research was social history in high medieval society, and she had studied, in sequence, table manners, rituals of courtship, and—her current mare's nest of choice—the dances, songs, and pageants of secular and/or seasonal festivals.

Everyone knows about May poles, of course, and Yuletide festivities, but there were lots of other ones. Often the customs were particular to a certain region or town; sometimes variations on the same theme occurred throughout an entire region. If the sources had been complete or even close to it, the topic would be a massive one. But these were primarily pagan celebrations—or the vestiges of them—and since most medieval source materials were recorded by churchmen, there was either no information or very biased information to be found.

Leslie had to look for snippets, dozens of them, hundreds of them, then try to fit all those jumbled bits together in a coherent way. It was like a puzzle, or solving a detective story, and she found it fascinating. She'd spent as much time as possible—which hadn't been nearly enough—reading chronicles in the past three years, sifting through court records and reading the marginalia in vernacular stories. She didn't have a whole lot to show for it as yet, at least not much that was new, except for some hauntingly weird and interesting vignettes.

This was one of those subjects that made her realize just how little we know about the great swath of a millennia of time and a continent of dirt blithely lumped together as "the Middle Ages," never mind how poorly we understand the thinking and motivation of the people who lived then. Ferreting out details, finding the patterns, and making cautious conclusions was the primary reason Leslie had become a scholar.

Teaching a second-year medieval history survey class to two hundred and seventy-five inattentive twenty-some-year-olds—most of whom had other majors and were looking for an easy breadth credit, preferably not below a B—was not.

This was a lecture she had given a thousand times, more or less: the emergence of centralized secular authority under the regimes of Henry II of England and Louis VII of France, compared and contrasted. It was chock-full of statistical figures that made students all scramble to take notes quickly enough, generated at least one essay question on the final exam, and took precisely fifty-three minutes to deliver.

Matt, who had endured numerous versions of it, invariably told Leslie that it was as dry as a popcorn fart. She had to admit that he was right. She had no real interest in political history, but when teaching a survey course, it was inescapable.

And it was part of her job to teach no less than three survey courses each year, as well as three or four seminars on more specialized topics. The seminars could be interesting, but it was hard to consider the survey classes, with their massive registration, to be more than a waste of everyone's time.

She thought of popcorn farts, wondered how dry they really were, and smiled.

Then she thought of Matt—gone for good, never listening to another test run of one of her lectures, making wry comments, and making her laugh—and felt faint.

The gathered masses straightened at her demeanor, newly nervous. Crabcake Coxwell never smiled, unless she envisioned a particularly nasty future for you, and when she frowned right afterward, well, word was you'd better watch out.

That was the party line and they all knew it. Leslie wasn't known for giving good lecture either. "Tough but fair marking, dry lectures" was inevitably what it said about her in the alternative calendar compiled by the student union based on actual student feedback.

Nobody but Matt ever mentioned popcorn farts.

She spared a glance to the large wall clock—a purely theatrical move—cleared her throat—ditto—and commenced the lecture.

At least she would have commenced the lecture if she could have remembered it. Not one word came to Leslie's lips.

Not one.

Leslie cleared her throat and tried again. No luck.

In fact, as she stared into that sea of expectant faces, she couldn't even recall the title of the lecture.

Or what it was about.

This despite the bolstering effect of new La Perla lingerie.

What she thought about was Matt, the look on his face that morning, the angry glitter in his eyes, the taste of his kiss.

What she thought about was coming home to find the house empty.

What she thought about was coming home to find the house empty every day for the rest of her life.

And her mind stalled cold, refusing to process such a distinctly possible and horrific notion.

Such a thing had never happened to Leslie before. She'd never been uncomfortable at the front of a classroom, never been at a loss for words. She'd certainly never drawn a blank. She could never have anticipated that this lecture, of all lectures, would abandon her thoughts completely.

But she was a veritable tabula rasa, as well as left feeling as if someone had ripped out her heart and stomped that sucker flat.

Leslie looked at her students—expectant, impatient, amused—and the words didn't just leave her: They left town. They were crossing the border to Mexico, never to be seen in the contiguous forty-eight states again.

What the hell had happened to her?

Or more important: What was she going to do about it?

Leslie adjusted her glasses and gathered her papers, frowning in apparent concentration. She forced herself to breathe. In and out, in and out. The situation might be dire, but dying would only exacerbate matters.

And then these kids would know about her lingerie.

She had to grip the podium to steady herself at that prospect. Leslie tried a prayer, but still the lecture did not pop into her thoughts.

So much for divine intervention. She must have used up her allotment by finding the bra and panties on sale. Pick your divinity of choice: He, She, or It clearly had better things to do in this moment of moments.

Leslie was on her own.

This called for showmanship of the highest order. Above all Leslie had to get out of the lecture hall before her deodorant failure became apparent.

"There will be no lecture today," she said as if this was no big deal. A ripple passed through the lecture hall, but Leslie lifted her chin. "This is due to circumstances beyond my control. I apologize for any inconvenience to you."

And before they could ask about makeup classes, about getting their money's worth, whether any of the material that should have been in the lecture would be on the exam, Leslie left.

No, that's not quite true.

She fled. As she ran down the corridor, her mind turned over and over the improbable truth, trying to make sense of nonsense. She had forgotten a lecture.

She had failed.

And she had failed spectacularly. No half measures for Dr. Leslie Coxwell. No losing an essay paper or forgetting a well-turned segue. Nope, she'd forgotten an entire lecture in one fell swoop.

She made one stop en route to her office, at the vending machine in the lobby below the offices of the history department. She had enough change to buy two chocolate bars, and even though they were just Hershey's, she inhaled one of them immediately.

Sometimes even a great bra wasn't enough.

*   *   *

Leslie was shaking when she got back to her office: The aftershock was setting in. She was still mortified, but already thinking about the repercussions of her screwup.

She could hear her phone ringing on the other side of the locked door, and haste made her drop her keys. Of course the lock jammed again, fighting her attempt to open it. She finally got the door open and lunged into her office, half-convinced that whoever was calling would hang up as soon as she touched the receiver.

"Hello?" Leslie winced at her tone. Great. She sounded breathless, like a telephone sex provider—or at least how she imagined they would sound. She took a deep breath and tried for a more professional tone. "Dr. Coxwell here."

"Hi."

One word and her knees gave out. The man's power over her was frightening sometimes.

No, it was only frightening when she believed that what she had always been afraid would happen was happening, right this minute.

The fact was that Leslie had been blindsided by Matthew Coxwell one random Wednesday morning years before and been smitten ever since. She hadn't believed then that he—wealthy, handsome, wry, destined apparently for success—had been interested in her—middle-class (if you measured with your thumb on the scale), plain, destined for a dry-as-dust academic career.

She had spent much of their marriage (and all of their so-called dating) pretty much convinced that he was going to figure out at any minute that he'd made a mistake. His mother had figured it out right away, after all. Leslie had expected for eighteen years that the other shoe was going to drop at any moment.

She could hear that shoe hitting the ground somewhere, with Matt's single word of greeting, and suddenly, the bottom fell right out of her universe. She had hoped and yearned and tried for eighteen years, and it hadn't been enough.

She dropped into her chair, knowing she'd sound breathless again. "Hi." She reached over and flicked the door shut with her fingertips, glad for once that her office wasn't big enough to swing a cat. She could reach everything without getting out of her chair, and on this day, that was an advantage.

"I'm in Chicago."

Hope woke up and took a look around. Had he changed his mind? "I thought you were going to New Orleans."

"I have a connection here, and a bit of time."

Hope died, a writhing death on hot pavement with a stiletto through its heart. It was a nasty death, the kind of death nothing could ever deserve.

Leslie didn't say anything more, couldn't say anything because of the lump in her throat. Matt's voice sounded gravelly, rougher than it usually did but maybe it was the connection.

Maybe it was the scotch.

Maybe it was regret.

Maybe she'd never know for sure.

Leslie felt again the burden of things unsaid, secrets that she'd never meant to become secrets—no, there was only one thing she'd never mentioned to Matt, one thing that had grown in silence beyond all expectation. Her tongue was swollen with it now, especially given what she had just done.

But where do you start to talk, to really talk, when you haven't done it for years? How do you begin to tell someone you love about the sacrifice you made to keep him around, especially when he's going going gone? How do you admit that you haven't told him what you were really feeling because you loved him enough to protect him from your nasty little truth?

How do you cough up the nerve to show your vulnerabilities, especially when he's already out the door, maybe forever?

Leslie didn't know.

Finally Matt cleared his throat. "You're so quiet."

"I was always taught that if I couldn't say anything nice, then I shouldn't say anything at all."

"But you're usually quiet."

Leslie kept silent, letting him work that out all by himself.

"You don't get it, do you?" he asked softly. He sounded so close that his voice made the hair on the back of her neck rise. She could imagine him, leaning in a telephone stall, receiver tucked under his chin, hand braced against the wall. Maybe he'd loosened his tie again. She closed her eyes, imagining that he was whispering directly into her ear.

His next words were somewhat less than the romantic murmur that would have been ideal. "Laforini was guilty, Leslie. There was absolutely no doubt about it. I had to lose the case."

"Had to?" She couldn't bite back her sarcasm completely, not this time, not this day. "I thought it was your job as defense attorney to, um, *defend* your client."

"Right. How could I have lived with myself if I had encouraged any mitigation of his sentence?" His tone hardened. "He was a mobster through and through. He'd killed lots of people himself and ordered the killing of many others—the charges were only the tip of the iceberg. The police reports were something else. Do you want someone like that on the streets? He didn't deserve a defense, so I didn't give him much of one."

A new fear seized Leslie. "But wait, if he has mob connections . . ."

"Don't worry about that." Matt was dismissive. "He just thinks I'm incompetent. You know, I was sure he would change lawyers. I don't think he had a lot of choices, though, or as many allies as people thought. You're one of the few who know that it wasn't stupidity on my part."

Leslie wasn't so sure that she was glad to be in on this particular secret.

Matt cleared his throat. "The point, Leslie, is that I couldn't have done anything else. How could you have looked at me if I had kept the truth from getting its day in court?"

Leslie straightened in her chair, a spark of anger lighting within her. "You aren't suggesting that you did this for me?"

"No, I'm saying I did it because of you."

"I don't understand. Why wouldn't you want to win the case that was your golden opportunity to have a successful career?"

"A golden opportunity to become like my father." He snorted. "Thanks, but I'll pass."

"But it was the one you had to win to permanently join the partnership with your father. You won't blame me for your not having a high power career. I wouldn't have stopped you . . ."

"But I didn't want that partnership. I never did."

Leslie fought to push her feelings back into their neatly labeled boxes. She never lost her temper, and she wasn't going to start today. She pulled away the neck of her sweater, reassuring herself with a peek at the silvery Italian bra. "You might have mentioned as much," she said, then balled the chocolate bar wrapper in her fist and flung it toward the garbage can.

She missed.

"Wait a minute. You can't have really expected me to win."

"Why not? You were his defense attorney, and I know you're neither stupid nor incompetent."

His voice rose in anger. "You expected me to win?"

Hers was not an unreasonable expectation. Leslie took a shaking breath. "Matt, you're a lawyer. Winning court cases would be your job . . ."

"I never wanted to be a lawyer."

One more time, Leslie was shaken not only by what Matt said but how firmly he said it. How could she not have known this? Her sense that he had become a stranger returned, redoubled. "But you went to law school," she said more cautiously. "People who go to law school become lawyers. You must have wanted to be a lawyer!"

"I never wanted to go, but I never had a choice."

"But, but, you never told me that!" Leslie was startled to learn that she wasn't the only one who hadn't been sharing secrets.

"Do you really think I'm like my brother James?"

"No, but most lawyers—most men—aren't like your brother James." Leslie rubbed her temple with her fingertips. Her words faltered. "Matt, you graduated at the top of your class. I thought you loved law."

"Well, I don't. I never did. I did what I had to do to get people off my back."

He was so definite, almost accusatory, as if he was disappointed in her for not guessing what he hadn't told her. And that made Leslie mad. "Funny you never mentioned it."

"I thought you must know, on some level, that I wanted to do something else."

"How would I have known that without you telling me?" What else had he wanted to do?

"Why do you think I stayed home with Annette?"

"You had a home office. Lots of people work at home when they have children: you had a choice to do so and I didn't."

"I had a home-based real estate law practice because I never wanted to play the game."

"But if you didn't want to play the game, what were you doing even taking the Laforini case? Then why didn't you just say no to your father in the first place?" Leslie found her voice rising. This was not her fault! "Why didn't you just decline the privilege of being his partner two years ago?"

Why did you have to give me such hope? she wanted to shout at him but bit it back.

"For the same reason I went to law school and took the bar exam. My father never took no for an answer when he wanted that answer to be yes. The only way to persuade him that I wasn't cut out to be his successor and partner was to prove it to him in a courtroom. So that's what I did. He always wanted hard evidence, preferably from a court of law, so that's what he got."

It made a treacherous kind of sense.

Worse, Matt was proud of himself. Leslie spun in her chair, her frustration rising to dangerous levels. She should have hung up, she knew it. She should have just cut the conversation short before she said too much.

But she couldn't do it.

Not today.

Not when she had hoped for so much and it looked as if she'd get nothing at all. Not when she'd spent two years hoping that he'd win the case, get himself a partnership that would pay a decent wage, and leave her with an option when Dinkelmann got demanding.

"So you just decided," she said, unable to hide her unhappiness with this. "You didn't think that maybe we should talk about such a decision before it was too late? Or had you already decided that you were going to walk out of our marriage?"

The words were like poison on her tongue. Leslie was sure that her mouth would swell with hives just for letting them pass.

Matt's voice hardened. "I was sure that we were in agreement. I thought you'd be glad that I hadn't compromised my principles. I thought you'd be glad that I wasn't following the Coxwell legal eagle career path."

"You don't maybe think you might have bent that principle a bit, just to get yourself a paycheck? Even just for a while?"

"What for? I don't need fancy cars and big houses and acres of lawn to feel like a big man. I'm not my father, Leslie. I don't measure my own worth by what other people think of my toys."

"Well, maybe it's time for you to think about what other people want," Leslie said before she could stop herself. "Don't take this wrong, Matt, I want you to be happy. I just wouldn't mind if I got to be happy, too."

"But you are happy. You're the most contented person I know. You love your job . . ."

How could he be so unaware of her feelings?

"Contented? You make me sound like a cow!"

"That's not what I meant . . ."

"I'm as far from contented as anyone can get. *I hate my job!*" Leslie shouted, interrupting him, only realizing how true it was when the forbidden words left her mouth. "I despise it! But I don't have a choice, do I? Principles don't pay for groceries or property taxes or electricity or gas for the car or even the car itself."

Her voice rose with every sentence and she didn't care. She had kept such a tight lid on these thoughts that they were almost revelations to her, as well. "Principles don't cover mortgage payments or provide for university tuitions, much less retirement plans. Principles don't mean anything!"

"You can't possibly believe that . . ."

"It doesn't matter what I believe." Leslie took a deep breath. "If you'll excuse me, I'll get back to work, so I can pay off the credit-card bill for that new suit you're wearing."

Then, because she remembered belatedly that Matt was headed straight to Sharan, because she realized that she had given him a whole lot of reasons to not just hurry there but stay there, and because she knew she was going to cry, Leslie threw the receiver back into the cradle.

Well done, she had time to tell herself before her tears started. She never cried, though it was hard to remind herself of that truth while the tears were streaming down her face.

She dropped her forehead to her desk and wailed like a baby.

The only mercy was that her office door was closed.

Leslie hated her job. It was true, and now that she had uttered the thought, it was inescapable. She hated the lectures and she hated the politics and she hated all the energy she had to expend on people who really didn't care about history. She hated that she couldn't pursue her own research—and she despised Dinkelmann and his agendas.

But she was trapped here, trapped as surely as a rat in a cage. Annette and Matt, the house, the car, the 401(k), everything was dependent upon her and her paycheck.

And if Matt was gone, her responsibilities were doubled. There wouldn't even be a trickle coming in from his practice.

It was depressing to think that Mrs. Beaton was right: Leslie would have to sell the house to give Matt his half, and she and Annette would have to move to an apartment.

She'd have gone full circle, just as her father had always threatened. Maybe they'd end up in a grubby little tenement like the one she'd grown up in.

Only now did she realize how very much she had wanted Matt to want that partnership with his father. How terrific that he could choose to pursue his principles, while she was going to have to give undeserved As, sacrificing *her* principles to keep her job.

It wasn't Leslie's habit to feel sorry for herself, but she figured that she was past due and allowed herself five minutes of self-indulgence. Her face was on her desk, wet with tears, when the phone rang again.

It was the department secretary, she was sure, calling to request a course syllabus for a student to copy.

The phone kept ringing, long after the secretary would have been distracted by another call.

It was the library, then, about the reserved text list for her summer course load. Some volume was unavailable. It happened all the time.

The phone kept ringing, long after any reference librarian would have given up.

By the twelfth ring, Leslie knew damn well who was calling, but she still didn't answer the phone. She called herself a chicken, but she really didn't have the gumption to hear Matt tell her flat out that their marriage was over.

Maybe hope wasn't really dead, after all.

She fingered the lacy edge of her power bra, closed her eyes, and wished for things to miraculously get better. Maybe she could rewind her day and wake up all over again. No, she'd have to rewind the day before as well, go right back to the end of the trial, then seduce Matt in the Subaru.

Even that might not set this straight.

The phone rang twenty-five times before he gave up—she counted—and Leslie stared at it for most of those rings. She was shocked when it finally went dead.

Maybe Matt was gone forever. The possibility made Leslie want to crawl under a rock—preferably one made of bittersweet chocolate—and cry forever. Maybe gnaw on the rock periodically to console herself. She had been prepared to make a thousand sacrifices to stay married to Matt Coxwell, but if he was really gone, none of it seemed to have much point.

On impulse she rustled up the change in her desk drawer and hit the vending machine in the foyer again. There were only Nestlé Crunches left, but she wasn't proud.

She bought all three of them and told herself she didn't care who was looking.

One thing was for sure: If this wasn't the worst day of her life, if days were going to get worse from here, Leslie was in serious trouble. She just didn't have the artillery in her lingerie drawer to hold up for long under such duress.

And if she kept having chocolate for lunch, she'd need bigger panties. There was a depressing thought, but it didn't stop her from finishing the third chocolate bar.

Lunch. That was lunch. Not a particularly balanced meal, but there you go. If this wasn't a day to make exceptions, she didn't know what was.

* * *

The gods had it in for Matt, because his day only got worse.

Which was saying something after that disastrous call to Leslie. Worse, he'd known she was there when he called back and she hadn't picked up. He'd only given up because they'd called his flight, but this wasn't done yet.

Not by a long shot.

She hated her job.

And she'd never given him so much as a clue.

What the hell kind of trust was that?

His outgoing flight from Chicago was delayed two-and-a-half hours for mechanical difficulties, which wouldn't have been so bad except that they had boarded and the aircraft had been pushed back by the time the malfunction had been discovered. Someone had made a bad choice and concluded that the repair would be done quickly—and undoubtedly the gate was needed for another flight—so they sat on the tarmac, feeling the aircraft interior get more stuffy with every passing moment

Ultimately they did depart, but the meal that had been scheduled for their enjoyment had to be trashed because it had been unrefrigerated too long. Matt doubted that he would have enjoyed it anyway. There was no replacement meal apparently available, or it would have delayed them further to have loaded it, but Matt didn't care. He could do without another pizza thing in his life of ingestion, could do without more mystery meat having even a passing acquaintance with his gut.

Besides they offered free drinks as compensation for the inconvenience.

Which meant that by the time Matt's cab was cruising down Canal Street in the rosy late afternoon, he'd had at least twenty shots of scotch and two tiny bags of pretzels since lunch the previous day.

On the upside, he really couldn't tell anymore whether this was the worst day of his life or not.

Leslie had hated her job and he hadn't had a clue. Now he could see that she'd stopped making jokes and stopped talking to him, and that he should have asked why. But instead he'd been so absorbed in pursuing his newfound dream that he hadn't noticed.

And he'd always thought he was a pretty sensitive guy.

So much for that self-delusion.

He watched the city slip past him and was amazed at the extent of the rebuilding from Katrina that had already occurred. It gave him a sense of kinship with this city and its residents and a sure sense that he had made the right choice. After all, he was rebuilding his own life. It wasn't going to be easy but the result would be worth it.

It would have been a lot easier to get started on that if he could get his wife out of his thoughts.

Matt strode into the hotel lobby, which boasted acres of wall-to-wall broadloom in glorious red, the hue of which prompted an unwelcome association. He smelled the faint whisper of mildew that is so pervasive in New Orleans, recalled the smell of blood, dropped his bags abruptly with the bellman and headed for the bar.

He was already too far gone to call Leslie back and have a decent conversation. He'd call her tomorrow, one last time.

Tonight it was simpler to be drunk.

Chapter Four

Dinkelmann heard about Leslie's humiliation in record time.

He rapped on her office door within thirty minutes of her leaving the lecture hall, all solicitous concern, which only confirmed her suspicion that he had antennae tuned to staff failure. She stuffed the last piece of Nestlé Crunch into her desk drawer, swallowed the bite in her mouth and tried to sound composed.

He was in her office before she realized that her eyes were probably swollen. He took a good look at her face and Leslie cussed under her breath.

It was easier to like Dinkelmann when he was an officious jerk. At least it felt honest. When he turned on the charm, this new department head with his love of soundbites and affection for appearances, Leslie just wanted to excuse herself and wash her hands.

Twice.

As it was, she was trapped in her woefully small office with the primary reason that she no longer loved her job. Or at least Dinkelmann was the most recent reason, the coup de grace culminating a long battle with disillusionment.

He apologized prettily for not realizing that the dead Coxwell in the newspaper was a Coxwell related to her, made several insult-

ing assumptions about the ability of women to deal with stress—
which was remarkable for a man of his age—then suggested that
Leslie take a week off.

She might have done it, if he hadn't implied that she couldn't be
expected to do otherwise, what with her being female and all. She
might have done it if she hadn't had swollen eyes and chocolate
crumbs on her skirt.

Leslie declined.

Then she insisted.

Finally, she argued with Dinkelmann, which did precious little
to improve her mood but at least got him out of her office. He
paused in the hall and looked back, pert as a sparrow and as un-
trustworthy as a weasel on the hunt.

Perky in pink.

"I don't suppose you've made much progress on your research
lately?" he said, clearly knowing that Leslie had not. "I was looking back and it's been several years since you had an article published. I recognize that it would be premature for you to have
completed a book on such a complex subject, Leslie, but a few
more recent credentials would be timely additions to your CV."

Leslie smiled, which was a better choice for job security than
throttling the department head with her bare hands. "Thank you
for the reminder, Dr. Dinkelmann."

"You did have a splendid run of articles a few years ago. I was
impressed by the caliber of the faculty I was inheriting in this department." He smiled, showing all his teeth, with all their perfect
caps, in all their bleached splendor.

Leslie didn't miss the threat. "Yes, it's been a hectic few years,
what with the new course load we're all juggling, and I have more
graduate students than I did before."

"We all have our obligations, Leslie."

"I'll see what I can do."

Dinkelmann waggled a scolding finger. "No, Leslie, no prevarication. You will do it. The dean is watching the achievements of the faculty with a close eye these days." His eyes narrowed ever so slightly and then he was smart enough to leave.

Leslie slammed her office door and leaned her back against it, fuming silently. On the upside, she hadn't bitten Dinkelmann—that had to be worth something. The man had left her office with nary a chomp mark upon his flesh—or at least no more bites than he had had when he arrived.

Did anyone think Dinkelmann was biteable? Was there a Mrs. Dr. Dinkelmann, who couldn't wait to get her hands on him, to get his pink shirt of choice off his back?

That was a scary prospect. Leslie definitely needed more sleep.

She also needed to be cloned to keep everybody happy—or maybe just to keep Dinkelmann happy. Of course if she was just going to give every student an A in every course, that would cut down on the time she spent marking papers. Leslie was beginning to feel that academia was a lot more about showmanship than she'd ever imagined.

Or hoped.

But there was no escape. She had appointments with four of her graduate students this afternoon, who did need her help and direction and had contributed nothing to her current (bad) state of mind. She needed to summon up some serenity for them, and could only hope she wouldn't bomb in her other lecture today.

Where had she put the last piece of that Nestlé Crunch?

*   *   *

No messages.

There were no messages for Leslie when she got back to her office at the end of the day, and even though she lingered, her phone didn't ring. She'd survived lecture number two by relying on her notes, which had made for a painfully dry delivery, but those kids would live.

She wished on the drive home that she had a cell phone, something she'd never desired before.

But then wouldn't it be worse if she had a cell and it didn't ring? Maybe ignorance was bliss, in this case. She charged through the front door of the house, hurrying as she never did, and headed straight for the answering machine.

It was better than noticing that the kitchen was gapingly, vacuously, alarmingly empty. It was better than giving any attention to the fact that Matt wasn't home, and wouldn't be home anytime soon. She realized a little bit late how much she savored coming home to him each day—then wondered if he had any idea.

After all she'd never told him so.

The light was flashing madly on the answering machine, which gave hope a surge, but not one that lasted. Leslie listened to message of condolence after message of condolence, all well-intended, all heartfelt. Each one made her expect that the next voice would be the one she most wanted to hear. She'd need to deal with the replies later, so she saved the messages, every last one.

Until there were no more. That was when Leslie's heart plummeted to her toes with awful certainty. She really had done it. She really had driven Matt away for good.

One glance into the pristine kitchen told her all she needed to know about the merit of honesty. It had been easier to think about the truth before she got here and had to witness it.

She supposed she should be consoled that she didn't have to be afraid of Matt leaving her anymore.

Leslie crossed the kitchen and hauled open the freezer door, looking for more tangible consolation. She intended to snag the carton of Chocolate Fudge Swirl ice cream that she knew was there.

It was gone.

And it didn't take a ten years of postsecondary education to figure out where.

Or more accurately, with whom.

The sliding glass door to the patio was slightly open, testament to a passing teenager. Leslie noticed because of the cold draft swirling around her ankles. She braced her hands on the counter beside the sink and peered out the window, muttering, "Aha!" under her breath.

Annette was sitting in one of the plastic lawn chairs in her winter coat, snow around and undoubtedly under her, the carton of ice cream clutched in her arms. She was eating it with a tablespoon, eating right out of the carton in an outright violation of household cleanliness standards. She stared across the limited expanse of the backyard, almost certainly in open defiance of something.

Leslie admitted to herself—silently, because that was the only way she could face this particular truth—that the last thing her daughter needed was a carton of ice cream. Slow metabolism was the legacy Leslie had given to her daughter, maybe the only one she had to share, but while Leslie still fought the good fight, Annette surrendered the battle early.

She watched her daughter for a moment, noting for the umpteenth time how long Annette's legs had suddenly grown. The girl was sprouting, almost before her eyes: She must have grown a foot taller in the past year.

But it wasn't enough. Annette would have to become nine feet tall to outpace her so-called baby fat, and Leslie couldn't see that happening.

Everyone was comparatively short in her family, after all.

Leslie snagged herself a tablespoon, retrieved her coat, and shoved open the sliding glass door. Her daughter gave her the look of loathing she was starting to get used to.

She was never going to like it. That was another reason to not talk about Annette's weight—the last thing they needed was another barrier between them. They had a whole system of trenches and walls topped with barbed wire as it was.

"Hi," Leslie said cheerfully and fetched herself a plastic lawn chair from the stack by the wall. She plunked it down beside Annette and dropped into it with a sigh.

Then precisely because Annette expected something more from her, Leslie ignored her daughter.

Let her ask for a change.

It wasn't bad outside, a bit chilly. Even though the houses were kind of close together in this neck of the woods, patio use was low on this particular night. Funny how that happened in January in Massachusetts. And here Leslie had thought New Englanders were supposed to be tough. She and Annette had the collective expanse of snow-covered lawn to themselves and it was blessedly quiet. Oh, there was the muted tinkle of people in their kitchens, maybe with a window open a crack, the muffled sound of distant laughter and car engines. The sky was that pretty shade of turquoisey-indigo it turns just before sunset.

"Want to share?" Leslie suggested when Annette didn't offer.

"No." Annette averted her gaze as she took another mouthful.

Leslie twirled her tablespoon, fighting the urge to match defiance with anger. That would only make it worse. "Do you know that some mother mammals, like rabbits, eat their own young?" She hadn't expected to say that, but once it left her lips, she decided it was the perfect thing to say.

Her daughter looked only momentarily alarmed. "Only domesticated ones. Not wild ones."

"And do you think I'm domesticated or wild?"

"You're no rabbit."

"That's for sure. There'd have been a lot more kids in this house if I'd been the kind of woman who gets pregnant just thinking about sex." Leslie waggled the spoon in the face of her daughter's astonishment. "But that's beside the point. Wild or domesticated? What's your call?"

Annette looked at her mother, really looked, so clearly ill at ease with this conversation that Leslie was tempted to try out a maniacal laugh. "Grandmother called. Do you know what she said to me?"

Ah, so the foul mood was due to an exchange between Beverly and her granddaughter. At least some fixtures in the universe remained in place: the hostility between these two was legendary. "No, but I can guess." Leslie frowned into the distance. "Eeny meeny jelly beanie, the spirits are about to speak."

"Just listen," Annette supplied.

Leslie pretended to be a fortuneteller, gazing into her crystal ball which was, in fact, an awful lot like the back of a tablespoon. "Yes, yes, it's becoming clearer now, not the exact words, but I'll guess that you had your mouth full when you answered the phone."

"She shouldn't have been able to tell."

"She is frighteningly clever. Especially when she's sober."

"I'm not sure she was sober. She didn't make much sense." Annette rolled her eyes and sucked back another spoonful of ice cream.

Leslie considered that information for a moment, then dismissed it. Beverly was duct taped on to the AA wagon and wouldn't be falling off anytime soon, if ever. After all, she'd have to answer to James if she did, and Leslie wouldn't wish that confrontation on anybody. "She can't have been drunk if she managed to say something to tick you off."

"So I admitted that I was having some ice cream. It's not a crime!"

"And I'll guess that she made a comment that had something to do with it being inappropriate for you to inhale a carton of ice cream before dinner."

Annette blushed. "I was hungry."

"So am I. And it's your lucky day. I'm here to save you from the pending wrath of Beverly Coxwell."

Annette was suspicious. "Why?"

"Because I want some of that ice cream. And I want it right now."

"You don't eat sweets. They're not on your diet." Annette said this last word with a sneer.

"I'm getting over that." Leslie tried out her maniacal laugh and it wasn't bad. Her daughter took a beat longer than usual to hide her surprise. "Hand it over or die, girlie. I'm feeling like a wild domesticated bunny tonight."

Annette giggled then, as if she didn't want to, but she surrendered the ice cream. A good two-thirds of it was gone but Leslie didn't care. She made a couple of heaping tablespoons disappear fast under her daughter's incredulous gaze and her mood improved almost instantly.

"So, what? You're going to skip all meals for the rest of the month now?"

"No, why?"

"Because you always do stuff like that when you eat ice cream or cake." Annette rolled her eyes. "You'd think a hundred calories threatened world peace or something."

"There's a lot more than a hundred calories in this carton. Or at least there were." Leslie shook her head when her daughter didn't reply. "But I'm not going to do anything like that, not this time."

Annette's eyes narrowed. "You're just doing this to make me feel better."

"*Au contraire.* I'm doing it to make myself feel better. You're on your own." Leslie softened that last comment with a wink and offered the carton to Annette again. She dug in, then licked the ice cream off the spoon with an inscrutable look in her eyes.

Leslie figured she didn't have a lot left to lose, so she leaped in where angels would fear to tread.

Smart angels would, anyway. Leslie was tired of being the smart one. She decided to try on "the impulsive one" for size.

She gestured with her spoon at Annette. "You probably don't know that this easy-weight-gain thing was my gift to you. I would have really liked to have not come up with that particular genetic present, but it's not as if anyone called me in to sign off on your DNA string."

"As if." Annette looked pointedly at Leslie's butt, which was a good bit smaller than hers. "I don't think so."

"Denial goes a long way to managing it. I don't know when I last ate more than a teaspoonful of this stuff. It's dangerously good. How did I forget that?" Leslie treated herself to another mountain of 30-plus-percent dairy fat, studying its chocolate swirled and studded perfection briefly before popping it into her mouth. "You know we could save time and just smear this all over our butts right now. It's headed there anyway."

Annette snorted with laughter. "Wouldn't taste as good."

"There is that." Leslie remembered with sudden clarity an evening very early in their marriage during which she and Matt had taken turns licking ice cream off each other. The sheets had been sticky but, oddly, neither of then had cared. Where had those horny people gone?

Well, one of them was still present and accounted for.

"How come you're blushing?"

Leslie didn't bother to hide her thoughts as she usually did. Truth be told, she was getting a bit giddy, which wasn't surprising given how much sugar she'd just dumped into her empty stomach— which had only had chocolate bars today anyhow.

"Thinking about your dad." Leslie smiled at her daughter. "Thinking about some fun we once had with ice cream."

Annette burrowed in the carton with her spoon, letting her hair fall over her face. "I seriously don't want to know about it, if it has anything to do with you two having sex."

For once Leslie couldn't let it go. She decided to tease her daughter a bit. "We did it at least once, Annette. You're the living proof of that."

"I could have been adopted."

"Think so?" Leslie smiled mysteriously, then sucked on her ice cream while Annette thought about that.

"Deposited by aliens, then. Left on your doorstep by envoys from a more intelligent planet."

"You watch too much *Star Trek*."

"It's not a crime."

"True enough. There are worse things you could be doing, but you've always been a pretty good kid."

Annette glared at her. "Don't try to butter me up. Is this going to be some talk about the birds and the bees? Is that what you want to talk about—sex?"

Well, yes, Leslie did, but not with Annette. "No, that's not what this is about. You know that you can ask me anything you want, but you probably know more about sex than I do."

"Is that an accusation?"

"No, it's just an observation on the way of the world."

Annette turned abruptly to face Leslie, her cheeks rosy and her lips glistening from the ice cream. "So what's this all about? You're supposed to be the tough guy parent, the one who never lets me see you sweat. You're the enforcer. What are you doing out here, being all chatty? What's going on?"

Leslie winced at this description of her role, because it was probably a fair call. "Well, that would be the million dollar question. Just for interest's sake, who's your dad in the role-playing lottery?"

"The soft touch. The buddy parent. The one who understands."

"Is that an accusation?"

"No, but he's . . . easier sometimes." Annette sat back, satisfied with her assessment, then cast Leslie a glittering look. "So how come you're out here, trying to be my pal?"

"Maybe I figure it's time we redistributed assignments." Leslie grabbed another spoonful of ice cream. "Maybe I didn't know the limitations of my job description when I took it on."

"Maybe you don't think Dad is coming back."

Bang. Out of the mouths of babes. Annette made this assertion in a tone that revealed that she expected Leslie to refute it. Leslie rolled ice cream around in her mouth before she leapt in to do just that.

Maybe it was time that she and her daughter had a different relationship.

Maybe it was time she stopped protecting Annette from every stray vestige of truth, especially when truth was looking ugly.

The girl was thirteen going on thirty, after all.

Leslie turned and saw the fear that had been conjured by her hesitation. "I don't know what your father's doing, Annette. He said that he was going to New Orleans to help Uncle Zach get out of jail, which would imply that he's coming back."

"He has to come to Grandfather's funeral."

Leslie thought about that over another bite of ice cream. "He doesn't have to do anything, Annette. He might be too angry with your grandfather to come to the funeral."

"You would make him go to it if you could."

Leslie looked away, less certain of her persuasive abilities than her daughter. "I'd be concerned that he might have second thoughts about not coming to the service later. It's not something that you can rewind and do differently, and I expect there will be a lot of people at your grandfather's funeral."

"You mean Dad should come for the sake of appearances." She curled her lip, looking suddenly a great deal like Matt when he had a truth-on. Mr. Tell-it-like-it-is.

Could she really have been proud of him if he'd defended his client successfully? Leslie was shocked to realize that Matt was right. She hadn't thought it through, hadn't thought past her own burden of obligation, but he was right. She would have hated being married to someone like his brother James, who was more concerned with winning than with a pesky detail like truth.

She set down the spoon, seeing her own role in his departure, wondering how she could make this right.

"Well?" Annette prompted.

"Um, I mean that if he makes an unconventional choice, he needs to be absolutely sure that he won't later regret it." Leslie looked at Annette, and in the fading light, saw her wariness. It had probably been fed both by recent events and her choosing to sit with her out here. Leslie chose to push her daughter a little. "Why do you think I would worry about such a thing happening?"

"Because you think of everything?"

Leslie shook my head. "Nope. I never claimed that."

"Well, you didn't have to. You're the most organized person on the planet. You're like one of those androids."

"Except androids don't reproduce biologically, do they?"

Annette studied Leslie for so long that Leslie thought she might not say anything. Finally she did. "Okay, maybe you're worried about it because you once didn't do something that you later regretted."

"Bingo." Leslie saluted Annette with her spoon. "The incisive Coxwell legal mind nails it. It's in your genes, Annette. That alone proves you weren't adopted."

"How come Daddy lost that big case yesterday?"

Leslie frowned and considered the merits of her stainless steel tablespoon. It had, in fact, gathered a few stains in its lifetime of service, as well as a few dings and scratches. Kind of like herself. "He thought it was more honest," she said slowly, appreciating the nobility of his decision. "He thought it was the right thing to do."

"Why?"

"Because he didn't think he could live with himself if the bad guy didn't get what he deserved. Because he didn't want the bad guy to get away with the bad things he'd done."

"And you don't agree with him?"

"I didn't. I just wanted him to win." Leslie admitted then shrugged. "I guess I just wished that I hadn't been as surprised as everybody else." The carton was empty and Leslie was getting cold. Apparently eating ice cream outside in the winter will lower one's body temperature. Who knew?

It sounded like something a mother should know though, didn't it?

Maybe she was a lousy mother, as well as a lousy wife. She stood up, uncomfortable with the part she had played in creating her own marital disaster.

Annette meanwhile was looking as if her mother had suddenly been replaced by an alien, maybe a more interesting alien than she knew her mother to be.

"Come on, let's go inside," Leslie said. "I'm getting cold and there's no more ice cream anyway."

"I'll just stay here."

Leslie paused at the door and looked back. "I going to get take-out tonight, but I don't know what kind. If you want a vote, you'd better come in soon." Annette hunkered down lower in her coat, clearly having no intention of moving. "Of course, if you don't, you'll just prove your grandmother right about ice cream spoiling your dinner. Maybe I'll phone and tell her that. You know how she likes to be right."

No response. Leslie tipped her head back and considered the first stars. "Maybe I'll just order a pizza from Macetti's," she said idly, fully expecting a reaction. "I mean, if you're not hungry, I might as well get what I want."

"Gross!" Predictably, Annette was on her feet in a flash. "You can't order from there." But instead of protesting that she hated their pizza, which was what Leslie expected, Annette had a completely different issue. "Scott Sexton does their deliveries now, so you can't order from there! I'll die! *Scott Sexton!*"

Scott Sexton. Leslie didn't know why she was shocked that her daughter knew the name of a boy who had to be a good three years older than her—given that he had a job that required him to drive around—much less that she knew where he worked.

This was puberty. *Be still, my intrepid heart.*

"So?" Leslie said, pretending to be unaware of the reason for Annette's objection. "Was he mean to you at school or something?"

Annette flushed crimson. "No, he doesn't even know . . . you can't, you just can't," she insisted, unusually furious. "I won't let you. I won't even be here if you do."

The devil in Leslie was tempted to order from Macetti's and insist that Scott did indeed make the delivery—just to see what he looked like, maybe assess her daughter's burgeoning taste in teenage boys—but for tonight, she'd let it go.

The La Perla bra had already done more than double duty. It was owed a nice soak in her gentle washables detergent.

"Well, if you don't vote, you can't count on anything," she said and returned to the kitchen. "That's what my father always said."

"I thought he said that if you didn't vote, you couldn't complain."

"It's pretty much the same, don't you think? And I like pizza."

Annette was right behind Leslie, fuming. "Not Macetti's, then. Get Domino's."

"But we should support a local business over a big chain." Leslie couldn't resist teasing her, as Matt would have done. "That's what your father always says."

"Well, he's not here. And if you order from Macetti's, I'll hate you forever."

"Here I'd thought that I was already in that club," Leslie said. "Maybe there's hope for an enduring maternal bond with the fruit of my womb yet."

Annette braced to go at it again, but for the sake of world peace—or an approximation of it in this particular corner of Eden—Leslie made a compromise suggestion. They could both do with some vegetables, though she wouldn't get them into Annette without a few carbs.

Like noodles.

"So how about Vietnamese instead?"

* * *

"Hey, you're not going to wake up tomorrow if you keep this up." The bartender gave Matt a nudge. "Don't you got somewhere to go?"

"Here is working just fine for me." Matt drained his glass and pushed it toward the bartender.

That man braced his massive elbows on the bar. "Maybe it's time you squared up with me and went off to bed, my friend."

"You think I can't hold my booze?"

"I think you're holding enough for a good four or five men your size."

"I'm not that small."

"No, you're tall, but you're lean, man. You're the kind that takes it on good at the beginning but can't keep it up." He framed his considerable paunch in his hands, jiggled it and grinned. "You need bulk to go the distance, and you ain't got it."

"Give me another." Matt looked around and realized it wasn't nearly as blurry a view as he'd prefer. "Please."

The bartender leaned on the bar again. "You don't need another drink. What you need is a coupla aspirin, a coupla bottles of Perrier, then you won't hate either one of us in the morning."

"But . . ." *But I can still taste my wife's kiss . . .*

"You don't think I seen lots of drinking in this city? You look like a smart man, a man smart enough to know when to quit."

"Just one more." *Just one more call home.*

"Don't you got somewhere to go, my friend?"

And that was the crux of it. Leaving the bar meant having to decide. A hotel room was not the most appealing prospect. The last thing Matt wanted was to be alone, to be left to sober up and face the shadows lurking in his mind. He wanted to be with someone, not just anyone.

He wished suddenly that it could have been Leslie, then told himself not to live in the past.

On the other hand he didn't want to appear unannounced at Sharan's house, ready to embark on phase two of his life, drunk out of his mind. It seemed that might be a bad start.

And he wasn't even sure about going to Sharan anymore. Funny how the choice he'd been so sure was the right choice didn't feel so right anymore.

All because Leslie hated her job and he hadn't known.

All because Leslie had kissed him as if she'd swallow him whole.

All because the Leslie who had once surprised him half a dozen times a day and stolen his heart away had made a sudden and startling reappearance.

The bartender opened the dishwasher, releasing a puff of steam. He started to unload glasses, giving each one a wipe with a towel before sliding it into the overhead rack. "You got a woman? You look like you're thinking 'bout one."

Matt deliberately chose to refer to a woman closer to his current locale. He was drunk. He was seeing things as they couldn't possibly be. He was afraid to leave the past behind. It couldn't be more than that.

"I haven't seen her in years." Matt shook his head. "Maybe I shouldn't call her. I'm still married."

"And not to her?"

"No."

The bartender chuckled. "Hey this town's like Las Vegas. What happens here stays here. Everybody comes here gets a little something going on. Where's this woman live?"

"Algiers."

" 'Cross the river?" He looked at his watch. "You better get it in gear, then. The last ferry goes by midnight."

"That early?"

"People sleep in Algiers; they don't party. Or they party at home maybe." The bartender shrugged massive shoulders. "Don't make no never mind to me. I never seen the appeal of the place myself, but that's just me. I like the city, whatever price she demands of me in hurricane season." He grinned. "I like meeting boys from the north like you, who git away from home and go wild."

Matt chuckled despite himself. He deliberately remembered how Sharan had looked at him once, refused to admit that Leslie had also once looked at him that way, and told himself that his decision was made.

He stood unsteadily and grasped the brass rail on the bar to stay on his feet. "Give me the tally, my friend," he said to the bartender who smiled at Matt's poor imitation of his accent. "Let's square it up."

"You northern boys just can't drawl, can you?" The bartender worked the word "drawl" so that it stretched out past Tuesday. "You just don't got it in you."

Matt looked back at him. "I could never touch that, drunk or sober."

The bartender laughed when he handed Matt back his credit-card receipt. "Go find your woman, my friend."

* * *

Matt hadn't called.

It was incomprehensible. Leslie sat in bed and stared at the clock. She'd been hoping and hoping . . . But it was almost midnight. He should have called, he would have called if he had any intention of doing so. He had tried to call her back earlier today.

She had been stupid to not pick up the phone then. Maybe it had been the last mistake he'd allow her to make.

He must have arrived at the hotel already.

He wasn't going to call. Leslie slid down in the bed, finding it all too easy to imagine what—or who—might be keeping Matt busy. She tried to swallow the lump in her throat, tried to tell herself that she couldn't expect a grown man to check in regularly like she was his mommy, tried to insist to herself that it wasn't that important.

Except that it was.

Because Matt always called in. Promptly. Frequently. It was as if being away from home were so strange to him on those rare occasions that he was away that he felt compelled to call in and make a connection of some kind at regular intervals.

The telephone rang and Leslie nearly jumped out of her skin. She'd plugged the extension in the bedroom back in—optimistically—but had forgotten how loudly it rang. She seized the receiver and forgot to make sure that she didn't sound desperate.

"Hello? Hello?"

"Hello, Dr. Coxwell. This is Chief O'Neill from the Rosemount police." Leslie sagged against the pillows, deflated. "I'm sorry to be calling so late."

"That's fine. How can I help you?"

"I'm sorry, but I don't know how to ask you this delicately, so I'll just ask. I've been trying to contact your husband in New Orleans but he hasn't checked into the hotel where he said he would be staying. Now I've checked with the airline and know that he arrived this afternoon, and I was just wondering whether you had heard from him. It's entirely possible that he changed his mind about which hotel, after all."

Leslie gripped the phone, wide-awake now that the police were interested in the location of her AWOL husband. "I haven't heard from him since he was changing flights in Chicago this morning."

"Really? And is that typical when he travels?"

Leslie forced a light laugh, one that sounded contrived even to her ears. "Well, Matt seldom travels, so I don't have firm expectations of what he will do when he does. It's possible that the hotel was booked up and he just went to another one. I don't believe he had made an advance reservation, since this all happened so suddenly."

"That's what I was thinking," the chief acknowledged. "Though I was hoping you might be able to tell me which one." He cleared his throat. "I surely don't need to tell you how important it is for me to keep track of Matthew Coxwell right now."

He was a diplomatic man, this police chief of the sleepy town of Rosemount, but Leslie understood the thread of steel in his tone. Unfortunately she also understood that her husband could be in a lot of trouble. She kept silent in defense of him. Matt had told her years before that she was a lousy liar and he was right.

After an awkward pause, the chief cleared his throat. "Perhaps you don't understand the root of my concern, Dr. Coxwell. One of the things I need to ensure is that Matthew has access to some counseling as soon as possible. There's a tremendous shock in discovering a body in such state as that of Robert Coxwell, and cases of posttraumatic stress syndrome are not uncommon. He promised to do as much last night, but it's fair to assume that he might not recall what we discussed."

Leslie had to ask. "Because he was drinking?"

"Because he was in shock."

"This sounds as if Matt isn't a suspect."

He made an indecisive sound, as if debating whether to confide in Leslie, and so she was a bit surprised when he did. "The coroner has yet to make a formal judgement, you understand, but I think it's pretty safe for me to work with the assumption that Robert Coxwell committed suicide. I don't know why he would do so, but his choice of method and a lot of forensic details add together quite coherently in support of this theory."

"Couldn't it have been a burglar he interrupted?"

"Few men put on their full military dress uniform to confront intruders. There were no signs of forced entry or of another person's presence, such as one might expect to result from such a confrontation."

"Maybe an accident . . ."

The police chief interrupted her. "Dr. Coxwell, with respect, there are two types of people in this world: people who are careless with firearms and people who are not. Robert Coxwell and I may have frequently disagreed, but we had a common ground in our respect for guns. I assure you that this was not an accident."

When she said nothing, he cleared his throat. "I will confess to you that the primary reason for my concern is that I did know Robert reasonably well, and I'm afraid of Matthew making similar choices, to his own detriment. Robert clearly believed that he could resolve psychological issues himself, without professional assistance . . ."

"Excuse me, but I was not aware that my father-in-law had any psychological issues."

"People who commit suicide are frequently in a state of clinical depression, which interferes with their judgment. I believe that Robert was in such a state. So, I'm concerned that Matthew may have learned to not confess a weakness to anyone else, especially one that could be concealed. I want to be sure that he receives counseling immediately if not sooner."

Leslie gripped the phone. "It was that bad?"

"It was worse."

Leslie couldn't even imagine it. On some level she hated Robert for having done this to Matt; on another, she felt a certain sympathy for someone so depressed that he would feel suicide was the only option.

She decided to trust the chief. "I do think it's a bit odd that Matt hasn't phoned," she admitted. "I was, in fact, just wondering whether he'd looked up an old friend from college who lives in New Orleans. He might have wanted someone to talk to, and if they're doing that, it might be why he hasn't called."

"That's a very promising possibility, Dr. Coxwell, and I would be very encouraged if Matthew had sought out a friend. I don't suppose you might be able to share the address of that individual?"

"Well, Matt's taken his Day-Timer, but I think I know where last year's Christmas cards are. There might be a return address on the envelope."

"That would be extremely helpful. If you don't mind, I'll just wait on the line."

Leslie knew exactly where those cards were and exactly where in the pile she'd find the one she wanted. Mercifully Matt was less organized than Leslie and never chucked the envelopes.

She came back to the phone in record time and read off the address to the chief.

"S. Loomis?"

"Sharan," Leslie admitted, exhaling mightily when she did so, then deciding that she might as well toss out the rest. What else did she have to lose?

"They were engaged once," she said quietly.

"I see," the chief said, as if he really did. "I'm sorry, Dr. Coxwell, that this tragedy seems to have created a lot of ripples in your life." Leslie heard the smile in his voice. "Though I have always heard that you were the most organized person imaginable."

Leslie found her teeth gritting, getting a bit tired of everyone being so sure she could handle anything. "Thank you. I wouldn't want to keep you, Chief O'Neill. It sounds as if you still have work to do before you can quit for the night."

"I do indeed. I'm sure that we will be talking again, Dr. Coxwell. Good night."

Was it a good night? Leslie hardly thought so.

Chapter Five

Never mind Algiers being asleep: New Orleans was asleep.

Matt crossed Canal Street, sobering fast at how deserted the core of the city had become. It was dark, close to midnight, the streets vacant except for velvety and ominous shadows. He could smell the river, hear distant music from the French Quarter, but shivered in the hush here. There were a few shops open, mostly selling garish T-shirts and cigarettes, a bit of booze, ice cream maybe, though the street was dark beyond the yellow gleam the streetlight cast on the sidewalk.

That kinship he had felt earlier left him now, making him feel like a target, or a stranger in a strange land. He was out of his element and didn't doubt that everyone around him knew it.

Matt hunched over, shoved his hands into his pockets, and tried to look both inconspicuous and purposeful. Given the cut of his suit and the fact that he still wore a tie, "inconspicuous" was probably a stretch, but he tried anyway. He found the claim stub for his bags in his pocket, realized he'd forgotten them, and decided against turning back.

He made his way past the casino, the trade center, through the deserted plaza, following the signs to the dock. It was darker here, even more deserted. The loading zone for the ferry had a low roof, or one that felt low because it was dark metal and was walled with metal mesh. The floor was concrete and the light from the river shone at the far end like a beacon.

It was not the most inviting space he'd ever stepped into. There was an ominous sense to it, an industrial grunge and emptiness that made Matt feel vulnerable.

That was about to get worse. Matt was all the way down the abandoned dock before he realized that the end wall, the one facing the river, was also made of metal mesh. It was actually a gate, presumably to keep people off the dock before the ferry was tied up.

But it made the waiting zone into a closed box. Anyone who was assaulted here would be trapped. There was nowhere to run, except all the way back to the street entrance.

Which was a pretty long sprint. Matt was not in his physical prime on that night, not by a long shot.

He fitted his fingers through the mesh, glanced once over his shoulder at the encroaching darkness, then watched anxiously for the arriving ferry. His pulse thudded in his ears.

To his relief, it wasn't that far to the other side of the river, though the current was clearly strong in the murky water. The little boat was just leaving the opposite dock, so he wouldn't have long to wait. It turned and immediately was tugged on an angle by the river. Its course was corrected, its lights cutting like blades across the dock where Matt waited. Its engines churned and it came closer. He swallowed nervously and silently urged the ferry to hurry.

Matt was so fixed on the ferry that he never saw them coming.

He barely heard the stealthy whisper of a boot on concrete before he glanced over his shoulder and took a blow to the face.

He stumbled and came up fighting, but there were at least three of them, it was dark, and he was drunk. He swung, missed, took a hit to the gut and fell against the mesh, stunned by the pain. He felt himself sliding down the metal mesh to his knees and couldn't stop himself from falling. He wondered whether they would kill him, what he could or would do about it.

Then he felt fingers in his pocket. Once they had his wallet, they gave him one more hit, presumably to make sure he couldn't chase them. Matt fell to all fours and vomited. His assailants' footfalls echoed on the concrete, their shadows dissolving like wraiths mingling into the greater darkness.

Matt knew he could never identify them and didn't much care. He'd had fifty bucks and a couple of credit cards that could be replaced. They were welcome to the lot of it.

Because he wasn't quite dead yet. That fact suddenly held more promise than he might have expected.

* * *

Leslie turned over the envelope from the Christmas card that was still in her hand, eying the elegant cursive handwriting. It was so unabashedly feminine, so flamboyant, so unlike her own practical script.

She listened, but the house was silent. She was unlikely to be caught by Annette in any nefarious deed.

It was dark in the bedroom, the only light falling from the lamp on one nightstand. Leslie reminded herself how much she loved the color of this shade, of how it turned the bulb's harsh glow to a warm golden light that seemed to encourage the sharing of secrets, the exchange of intimacies.

She and Matt had made love in this light once. The memory came quickly, as bright as quicksilver, filled her with heat and was gone. Filled with yearning, impatient with herself for wanting what it seemed she could not have, Leslie fingered the card inside the envelope.

What had gone wrong between them?

Was the answer inside this envelope?

There are people who can read other people's mail without a qualm, much less a second thought. There are people who think that their own objectives are so overwhelmingly important that nothing else matters. Leslie had worked with these people. She was related to these people.

She was not one of these people.

She was a medievalist: She had sipped of the cup spilling with the wisdom of the greatest theologians of the Western world. Leslie was quite certain—though the citation eluded her in that precise moment—that Thomas Aquinas had written about the wickedness of reading missives addressed to another person in his *Summa Theologica*. Maybe it was part of his treatise on the Just Price, that there was no just price for nosiness.

Or maybe it had been Gregory the Great in his *Moralia* who had weighed in on the issue.

Either way Leslie knew that her reading this letter, which had never been intended to slide beneath her gaze, was plain wrong. There was no middle ground. The right choice, the only choice, was to replace the letter where she had found it, unread.

Still Leslie wanted to know. And under the circumstances, she could justify her desire to know, perhaps even her need to know.

If not her right to know.

People talk about having a devil on one shoulder and an angel on the other: Leslie's devil had always gotten short shrift. What else could be expected when the angel was a saint, none other than Bernard of Clairvaux, founder of the Cistercian order? Leslie had written her doctoral thesis on Bernard's interpretation of the Song of Solomon, and she knew far too much about how ol' Bernie's mind had worked.

That's what Matt had called him: ol' Bernie. There had been three of them in the marriage for a while, but since one had been dead for a good eight centuries and the other two had been gloriously alive, it hadn't been an issue.

Leslie could feel the thick card inside the envelope. It was slippery, as if it were glossy on the outside. It would be rich with ink and shiny with foil, some splendid confection to celebrate the Yule.

If nothing else, she reasoned, she deserved to know the woman's taste.

The devil in her managed to whisper that she should go for it before Bernard—in his hair shirt, no less—took a swipe at him with a bishop's crosier and sent him scampering. Leslie could almost see the founding force of the Cistercian order smiling at her with beatific satisfaction at his success in saving her from herself.

From her inevitable feminine weakness. Susceptibility to temptation was the price of being the lesser vessel, of being no more than a little woman, at least in terms of medieval theology.

Maybe ol' Bernie had been having a chat with Dinkelmann before he stopped by here.

Come to think of it, Leslie had always thought that ol' Bernie was a bit proud of himself. It's not much of a tribute to your brilliance or even your piety to be successful when you're born with a silver spoon in your mouth, is it? Bernard had been born noble, with every advantage, and it wasn't so amazing in a feudal society that he had turned advantage to advantage.

He'd had charisma in spades, too, which never hurt.

And really, he had stunk at obedience and humility, two of the monastic big three, though he'd apparently been good with chastity. One for three doesn't give a very compelling performance review. He hadn't been much for retiring from the world to contemplate the glory of God, either. Nope, anytime there had been a dust-up over theology or pretty much anything else, ol' Bernie had been right in the thick of it, slinging words around like arrows and having the time of his life.

He'd been nothing if not articulate, as well as a prolific letter writer: It had taken multiple secretaries to keep up with him. Only an unappreciative skeptic would wonder how the great man had reconciled his active engagement in politics with the monastic ideal of retreat from the world of men to better contemplate the divine mysteries.

Which was a long way of saying that maybe ol' Bernie wasn't the best possible source of advice in this situation.

* * *

Leslie pulled Sharan's Christmas card out of the envelope before she
could change her mind. There was a cartoon reindeer on the front,
standing on its hinds, Christmas balls hanging from its antlers and
a martini in its paw. A sprig of mistletoe hung over its head and it
was winking, the other paw on its hip in an expectant pose. It had
long eyelashes, so presumably was supposed to be female.

She flipped the card open and blinked at the caption: *Wanna
share a little festive spirit, buckeroo?*

That wasn't encouraging. Mae West as a reindeer.

On the other hand Leslie needed only to glance at this to recall
Sharan's flirtatious sense of humor, or the fact that she was an artist.

Or the fact that she was sexy and provocative.

What did Leslie's Christmas cards say about her own personality? They were usually embellished with holly or something equally
predictable, red and green and white, always had a culturally sensitive, nondenominational message like *Happy Holidays* or *Sea-
sons Greetings*. They were safe and inoffensive and utterly boring.

She suspected only now that what they said to the recipient was
not much at all. *Here's another card from an unimaginative, dutiful person. Look inside for a deeply personal message: BEST OF
THE SEASON—MATT, ANNETTE, AND LESLIE.*

"Boring" was not the most reassuring adjective to be applying
to herself right now. Impatient, Leslie read the letter written on the
inside of the card.

Matt—

> *Great to hear from you, as always. You must be relieved
> that the trial (ha ha pun intended!) with your father is almost
> done. When you lose the case, that will call for a drink—or six!
> Let me know and I'll have one for you, just to do my share.*
> *Or you could come here and drink with me.*

Hey, have you finished that book yet? I'm still waiting to read it. Sometimes fiction, like art, is the only way to present the truth. I know you'll do a great job with it. Mr. Wordsmith, that's always been you! Remember?
    Best to Leslie and Annette.

Love,
Sharan

Leslie had always loathed people who used a lot of exclamation points, on principle alone. The enthusiasm lacked a certain dignity that she thought written notes should have. That Sharan had made a little heart for the "o" in "love" wasn't exactly adult either.

Those items, however, weren't the most troubling things about this note. In several short sentences, Sharan had revealed that she knew a great deal more about Leslie's husband than Leslie did.

Like, just for example, the fact that Matt had intended to lose the case, something Leslie had learned only after he had done so and she'd seen his smile of satisfaction.

(It had been, come to think of it, a very Bernard-like smile, a smug smile. It had been a smile that Leslie would never have expected to have seen on her husband's face, and one that she would be happy to never see there again.

She might get that wish, actually.)

And there was another example. A book? Sounded like a novel. Leslie didn't know anything about Matt writing a novel.

He'd never said one word about it. She knew he liked to write, and he had worked for years on a compilation of anecdotes about Boston's history, but a *novel*? That was news.

It wasn't welcome news, not by a long shot.

Leslie had always believed that sharing secrets was the most powerful flavor of intimacy in the freezer case. It takes trust to share your most hidden thoughts and desires, more trust even than it takes to share your body.

So it shook her to learn that she hadn't been the recipient of her husband's trust. What else hadn't he told her? What was the book about?

And most important, where was it? Oh, that devil was back, all frisky from finally having one triumph. Leslie considered temptation for about three seconds before she shook her head.

She shoved the card back into the envelope. She had her limits and they had already been surpassed by a long shot. She went downstairs and put the card back precisely where it had been before the chief had called.

Don't ask how she knew its exact location, wedged between Matt's books and invisible to the eye.

Let's leave her some pride.

* * *

Matt lay on the concrete against the mesh gate and closed his eyes against the pain. He could have done without that last kick to his gut. He wondered whether he had broken a rib—or had one broken for him—then jumped in shock as the metal grate abruptly slid back.

"What happened to you?" The ferryman cussed under his breath when Matt looked up. "No, wait, I know. Those kids!" He helped Matt to his feet and gave him a critical look. "Jesus, don't you have the sense to not come down here alone so late?"

Apparently Matt was hale enough to get a lecture.

"You're going to have a helluva shiner, mister. You wanna call the cops?"

"What's the point? I can't identify them."

"Well, there is that. And it's late."

Matt forced himself to take a step and when he didn't fall flat on his face, he walked slowly to the bobbing ferry. "Let's just go to Algiers," he suggested, wincing as he took a seat in the little interior lounge.

The ferryman watched him with a frown, then shook his head. "Looks like you drank all your sense away."

"No, it was gone long before today."

He smiled ruefully, and the ferryman half-laughed. Matt shoved a hand through his hair and wondered if things could get worse. The ferryman bit back something he had been going to say, then shook his head and went to do his job.

The ferry had a pleasant hum, a vibration that slid through Matt and soothed him in an unexpected way. All too soon, they were docked and Matt opened his eyes to find the ferryman beside him.

"I'm giving you a ride home, so's I can be sure you make it," he said gruffly, covering solicitous concern with a tough crust.

"Thanks. I appreciate it."

And so it was only moments until Matt found himself in front of the house that must be Sharan's. The address matched the one he knew. Even now he could see that the clapboard house was painted a bright color, maybe yellow, and that there were plants crowded in the windows and in pots on the veranda. The lights were out, which made him hesitant to knock on the door and awaken her.

That was when he saw the wicker settee in the sheltered corner of the porch. Perfect. He went straight to it, took off his shoes and placed them neatly beneath the settee. He sat down and let exhaustion roll through him.

Matt felt like ten miles of rough road.

Maybe twenty.

Maybe twenty miles of gravel road with potholes big enough to swallow a small truck.

He rubbed his face, knowing he'd trade his soul for a mint candy or even a cough drop, knowing too that there was no chance of anyone making him that offer any time soon. He took a deep breath and let the silence soak into his skin. He could hear crickets and bullfrogs and not much else. The air was lush here, a little damp and cool but filled with the scent of plants.

He rubbed the leaf of whatever was drooping over the railing and smelled its pungency. It was minty almost, which would do. He rubbed it between his fingers and beneath his nose, was reminded of the shampoo Leslie used. He wondered what she was thinking or doing, and easily imagined her sleeping, her long dark hair strewn across the white pillowcase like the pennant of a medieval knight.

That made him smile.

He didn't think anyone would see him here in this shadowed corner, and if they did, well, there wasn't much more anyone could take from him. Matt Coxwell loosened his tie, folded his arms across his chest, hunkered down and went to sleep.

*   *   *

Runt dunt dada dadala dunt da.

The tinkle of circus music fills Leslie's dream, then the barker starts his spiel. "Come on down to the Big Top. Step right this way . . ."

Leslie fights the recurring dream but knows she has already lost. There she is, up on the tightrope. Here's her father, insisting that she needs to carry something to make her feat "look good."

She still expects a pink parasol, even after all the years she's had this dream. She's still shocked at the box he gives her.

This time she sees that it says Good Daughter *on one side. Leslie accepts the burden without complaint, good daughter that she is, but is surprised to find the box as heavy as it is.*

Then the dream takes a new twist, each box turned so that she can read the text on their sides. Previously she only saw the colors of their wrapping paper and bows.

The next one, the red one, is Academic Excellence. *Huh. It's followed by* Winner of University Scholarship.

Well-groomed.

Polite.

Respectful of Elders.

Thoughtful of Others.

The boxes add up quickly into a towering pile.

At the same time Leslie is growing with alarming speed. The wire slips away from view as she grows. Her arms become longer and better able to bear more boxes.

Dutiful Spouse.

Organized Housewife.

Passionate Partner. *Did her father really add that one?*

Attentive Mother.

Patient Griselda.

Conscientious Worker, Team Player, Responsible Homeowner, Family Adjudicator, Bill Payer, Mortgage Negotiator, Quartermaster, Cleaning Lady, Ms. Reliable in a Crisis.

Then come more boxes with just adjectives on them: Nice, Dependable, Discreet, Ladylike. *Leslie loses track of them. Finally the last little box, the one that always threatens to fall, a little glittering gold confection.*

Labeled Success.

"Do it for all of us," her father whispers, reminding her with painful vigor of the stories of his own past, of his lack of opportunities, of her splendid good fortune, of the sacrifices he made to make it possible for her to bring home—to bring to him—the proverbial brass ring.

"Go on," he urges, eyes shining with hope. "You can do it."

Leslie has to do it.

And maybe she can. The pile of boxes is precariously balanced and it obscures her vision. Would her father really stack the odds against her?

The Grateful Child *box suddenly seems much heavier, just for her having that thought.*

She takes three steps, feeling the location of the wire with her toe before settling her weight upon that foot, then sees suddenly that the ground beneath her is no longer a mere fifteen feet away.

It has dropped into an abyss of such overwhelming darkness that Leslie can't see the bottom, though her tightrope spans it.

Worse, someone has smeared the tightrope with Vaseline.

A wind rises from the canyon, a hot wind that leaves Leslie no doubt of this canyon's awesome depth, a hot wind that ruffles her tutu and makes the wire vibrate.

Maybe it's actually Hell down there. Maybe that's what happens to people who don't fulfil expectations. She's not sure she wants to find out.

Leslie looks back and her father waves encouragement from his safe stance at the lip of the chasm. She trembles. She looks down again and this time sees the light of fires far, far below her.

The fires are in rows, she thinks at first, then sees that they are the outlines of letters, burning orange against the blackness.

The letters spell FAILURE.

So that's what happens when you fall. These letters are the truth of Dante's circles of hell, and they are waiting for Leslie, their flames hot and hungry.

She squares her shoulders, then takes a step. The boxes jiggle, their weight shifting, but then they settle in place. Leslie takes another step, cautiously feeling her way along the tightrope, carefully settling her weight.

And that's when she sees the tiny box perched on the top, the precious little gold one, start to slip. She reaches for it and feels the shift in her center of balance. She knows the moment she stretches too far to recover her footing.

Oh no . . .

* * *

Leslie awakened in a cold sweat, breathing hard. She flicked on the light on the nightstand and shuddered to her toes. It was 2:39 A.M. and her nightmare was so vivid that she might still have been trapped in it. She thought she could smell the fires.

She sniffed, but nothing was really burning. Leslie rubbed her eyes and hoped she hadn't cried out, but the house was still silent.

Certainly no one rushed to console her.

Maybe she should have cried out. Leslie wrapped her arms around herself and shook silently, willing her heart to slow as she considered the dream while it was still clear in her thoughts.

There was truth in its metaphor, that's for sure.

She was on the tightrope and had been on it long enough to know that once you get on the tightrope, you run out of choices. Suddenly everyone around you is commenting on how well you walk the line, how easily you carry burdens across that great divide. They express admiration of how organized you are.

Organized. How Leslie hated that word.

Then they hand off their loads to you. You must really like it on the tightrope if you get on there, if you can walk it with ease—that seems to be the logic.

But what if you hate it? What if you just want to chuck all that crap down, lose all those expectations forever? What if you want to tell everyone to learn to do something for themselves?

What if you don't want to be the one obliged to make the money and do the budget and pay the bills? What if you don't want to mark the papers and give the lectures and prepare the reports and sit through the interminable staff meetings and be the living proof that Dinkelmann's new scheme can work?

What if you want to do something else?

What if you don't even know what you want?

Well, if there are no other volunteers, you lose. That had been Leslie's experience. You keep walking that tightrope because you have responsibilities and a sense of obligation to fulfil them—no, a burden of obligation. It's duty that gets you up there every morning, and it's sheer survival instinct that keeps you watching your footing.

On your toes, so to speak.

But if your heart isn't in it, then every day out there, your footing feels a little more tenuous. Every night that you go without sex or intelligent conversation or just anyone noticing what this is costing you, makes the great chasm below look pretty damn appealing.

Leslie wasn't suicidal, but she could admit—in the darkness of her bedroom in the solitude of the night—that there had been days when she had thought about not taking the turn that would take her home, or the one that would deliver her safely into the arms of her alma mater. There had been days that she wanted to just drive, maybe all the way to Nevada to play the slots.

Why not?

But that was impossible. Leslie was the responsible one, the delivery team for parental ambitions, the person who saved the day and could be relied upon. She was Ms. Spock—not Dr. Spock because she'd never known nearly that much about kids, and not Mr. Spock because she'd almost failed science—the dispassionate one, the one who never slipped up on the logic front.

It was the only trick she knew.

But she didn't know if it was a good one anymore, much less one worth knowing. To tell the truth, the reward ratio was looking a bit skewed. Without Matt, without the sense that she was making sacrifices to keep him in her life, it all seemed pretty thin.

She'd thought she'd been letting him live his dream, or find what he wanted to do, or wait for the opportunity he wanted most—she'd thought that was what love was about—but in this dark night Leslie was afraid she'd only been a convenient source of income for her handsome husband.

She was afraid that she had been the only one in love—desperately, achingly in love, to boot.

There was a thought to put some lift in her loafers.

There was a secret that made for cold comfort.

Leslie turned out the light and pulled up the blankets, then stared at the ceiling until her alarm finally rang. She felt a strange, unexpected link with Robert Coxwell, who—if the chief was right—had been afraid to let anyone see his weakness.

And now he was dead.

Could she have saved her marriage by telling Matt the truth sooner?

Could she save it by telling him the truth now?

Would she have a chance to do so, or had his first taste of the truth been too toxic to tempt him back for more?

Leslie didn't know, and there wasn't much to like about that. The fact was that without Matt, without knowing that she'd come home and find him here, there didn't seem to be much point in hauling herself onto the tightrope at all.

* * *

Leslie chose to arm herself for Thursday with a lime green balconet bra trimmed in black ribbon with white polka dots and matching bikini panties. It was a 1940s pin-up girl special that gave her rocket boobs and made her want to lean against a bomber, pretending to be Rosie the Riveter. But she'd need really red lipstick for that, and really red lipstick wasn't part of the academic uniform.

A demure pink would have to do. She didn't even own a really red lipstick. She rummaged through her makeup, just to be sure, but there was just a variety of pale pinks and mauves, lipsticks that were almost invisible when applied.

Hmm.

Leslie wasn't generally a lime green with black ribbon and white polka dots kind of a woman, but this morning—the morning after Night of Troubled Sleep Number Two—called for a little extra oomph.

The bra had oomph, even if she didn't. The only hint of her hidden defenses was an unusual pointiness to her breasts beneath her modest twinset. She decided no one would notice, shoved on a pair of loafers and opened the bedroom door to embark on her day.

Across the hall the fruit of her womb was sleeping, sprawled across the bed, blankets knotted and nightgown spiraled around her waist. Annette's dark hair was coiled around her shoulders and her bare bum was as ripe and smooth as a new peach.

A big peach.

Annette's beloved fuzzy puppy was on the floor, cast off during the night as so much else would be in the next few years. Maybe even Leslie. It's natural to hate your mother when you're a teenager, right? Either way it was a lot easier to love Annette unconditionally when she was asleep.

Leslie stepped quietly into the room, put the puppy back into the nook of Annette's elbow, remembering a thousand puppy-related traumas. She readily remembered Annette as a baby, suckling at Leslie's breast, for she had been cherubic then and was still pretty close to it now. Just bigger.

Almost grown-up.

Scary prospect. Annette was starting to look like Matt more, his genetic bonus of striking good looks shaping the ripe curve of her lips, the arch of her dark brows, the vivid green of her eyes. Matt's sister, Philippa, had said for years that Annette would be a classic beauty, though Leslie hadn't seen it.

Until Annette started growing up.

Leslie tapped her daughter's shoulder with her usual crisp gesture. "Wake up, sleepyhead." When Annette groaned and rolled over, Leslie said, "My work here is done," as she always did, then headed to the kitchen.

Where there was no coffee brewing.

She was determined to not drink instant coffee again.

That was when Leslie realized she didn't even know how to make coffee. She hadn't made any in eighteen years, and couldn't remember if she'd even drunk it in B.M. (Before Matt) days. That was before the effective dawn of time, after all, so Leslie dated the events of her life B.M. and A.M.

How about A.A.M.—After After Matt?

A.M.L.—After Matt Left?

Or maybe A.M.D.H.F.H.O.T.L.—After Matt Ditched Her For His One True Love? That one seemed a bit unwieldy to be useful.

But maybe true, all the same. Leslie could admit that to herself this morning—when her moat was breached, the drawbridge shattered, and the siege engines were sending Greek fire over the walls. She knew, even if he had had the grace to deny it, that Matt had married down the social ladder when he had married her, way down, further down than any Coxwell had previously dared to go.

She believed he had done it because Sharan had broken his heart. Oh, he'd never said as much, just that he and Sharan were through, but why else would he save Sharan's Christmas cards? She was the one who got away, and Leslie guessed that at some recent point, Sharan had crooked a finger to beckon Matt back to her.

And he'd gone.

Leslie wasn't sure it was best to let herself think about this. It certainly made her feel even more crummy about the current situation than she had before. If ever there had been a morning that she needed a major dose of caffeine, this would be it.

She would not think about the Java Joint, that grubby student-run café where she and Matt had talked on their first date, and many many times after that. Like it or not, Matt Coxwell and coffee were forever entwined in Leslie's thoughts.

If she couldn't have one, she would definitely have the other.

Which was easier said than done.

Leslie stared at the coffeepot Matt had insisted on buying several years before, with its sleek European aluminum styling, and didn't know where to start. You'd think, for what this baby had cost, that it would make the coffee for you.

Or come with staff. A little barista in a cute apron who would stand beside the machine, be perky twenty-four hours a day (proximity to all that caffeine had to have some effect), and make coffee on demand.

Instead a red light blinked patiently on the front of the machine, signaling something imperative that Matt would understand. Maybe it was displaying Leslie's dire need for artificial stimulants.

She had two graduate degrees, she reminded herself sternly. She had to be able to figure this out.

First there had to be water. Leslie knew that much. She managed to open the reservoir, fill it with water, and get it closed again, which was a lot harder than it seemed it should have been. The quantity was a raw guess: She'd just filled it to the top.

Was the reservoir more crooked than it had been before? Had it always jutted out a little bit at this top corner? Or had that last impatient swipe been too much for its glamorous fragility?

Maybe she'd broken it. Would Matt ever know?

Better not to go there.

Next there had to be coffee. Leslie rummaged through the cupboards, ashamed on some level that she didn't know precisely where to find the coffee in her own kitchen, then was astonished to discover that the coffee in question was whole beans.

The bean grinder was right beside the beans, which was a gimme. The contraption looked easy enough to use, if she'd known how many beans to use and how long to grind them. There was no sign of a measuring spoon in the vicinity.

While she deliberated over that, she managed to open the holder for the filter and chuck out the two-day-old filter with its residue of coffee grounds.

Filters. She didn't know where Matt kept the filters.

She looked toward the trash. Could coffee filters be reused? Could she just run another load of water through those old grounds?

Starbucks was sounding good, but Leslie couldn't live on take-out food until Matt came back.

Whenever that might be.

If that might be.

And it irked her to think that she couldn't accomplish a simple task like making herself a cup of coffee, especially one she so desperately needed.

As a matter of fact it infuriated her. How could she have become dependent on Matt for something so simple when there were a thousand infinitely more complicated things that she could have depended on him for?

How could he have left?

How dare he leave, not call, and not even leave instructions for the (expletive deleted) coffeemaker?

She opened a drawer, didn't find anything she needed, and slammed it shut. She flung open a cupboard, again without a successful find, and slammed it so hard that it bounced open again.

She began opening drawers and cupboards faster and faster, each one that didn't obviously contain a package of filters making her more angry. Leslie left them open, moving around the kitchen like a furious whirlwind, then when they were all gaping wide, she let out a primal cry of outrage. It was the first bellow she had ever allowed to cross her lips.

It was even an obscenity.

And it felt good. She shouted it again, just for good measure. When she was done, she kicked a chair so that it skittered across the tile floor. That felt so good that she did it once more, but this time, she kicked harder and the chair fell over with a resounding clatter.

"Um, are you all right?"

Leslie froze midkick and glanced over her shoulder to find Annette in the kitchen doorway.

Oops. So the *Perfect Decorum* box was hurtling into the abyss, as was *Keeping Up Appearances for the Child* and *Temper in Control*. One glance over the kitchen revealed that *Fastidious Housekeeper* was also a goner.

If that was such a bad thing, then why did she feel so much better?

Lying to Annette would have been a shabby way to cover her mistake. And the façade was shattered anyway: The girl did have eyes in her head, so she might as well go with the old tried and true of honesty.

"No," Leslie said firmly. "I am not all right. I don't know how to use this coffeemaker and I don't where the filters are and I don't know how much coffee to use and I need a cup of coffee, and no, instant coffee will not suffice."

"Dad always made the coffee?"

"Always!"

"I thought you knew everything."

"Well, you were wrong." Leslie glared at the entire kitchen, focal point of most of her domestic inadequacies. "There's a lot of stuff I don't know."

"I thought you never got angry."

"Everyone gets angry. I've been holding it back, to work on my ulcer. If I get colitis, I might get time off with pay."

Annette smiled tentatively. "You never make jokes."

"That's not true." Leslie took a deep breath. "I haven't made any recently, but I used to make jokes all the time."

To make Matt smile. She sat down heavily and fought the urge to weep again.

"I've watched him," Annette said, then took a tentative step into the kitchen. "I could make coffee for you, if you like."

Leslie looked up, surprised by this offer. "And if you did, I would love you forever."

Annette smiled. "Aren't you supposed to anyway? I mean you are my mom."

Leslie smiled in her turn and exhaled, reassured by just the promise of real coffee. "It's true that moms are required to love their children, but I'm talking about love in excess of Mom-Love. A bonus offer. Limited availability, contingent upon the timely application of coffee, but oh, it's worth the trouble."

Annette's smile widened. "Promise?"

"Cross my heart and hope to die." Leslie crossed her heart and touched her fingertips to her lips.

Annette headed straight to the demon machine, showing an astonishing intimacy with it. "It's not that hard, once you know how." She plucked a package of filters from the back of an empty cupboard where Leslie had never seen them, ground beans, moved with an easy economy that smacked of Matt.

Soon the blissful smell of fresh coffee was filling the kitchen. There was a deity after all, and apparently Leslie wasn't on His/Her/Its hate list after all.

That had to be a good start.

Chapter Six

T hank you," Leslie said when she sipped of the nirvana of the first cup. She even closed her eyes for the second sip and if she saw the olive green walls of the Java Joint, a young Matt earnestly trying to persuade her of something, well, let's call it a weakness. "Anything you want is yours, my child. Name your reward."

Annette poured herself a glass of milk, then looked around. "There aren't any more muffins."

Right. Leslie should have stopped at the grocery on the way home the night before, but she'd been in too much of a hurry to get home and check the phone. She had gotten so used to Matt buying groceries and making dinner that she hadn't thought about it.

"Fire that muffin fairy," she muttered, then winked at her daughter. "She's been living off our mercy for too long."

Annette giggled, watching Leslie over the lip of her glass. "You're not usually funny."

"I warned you that the job descriptions were being reevaluated." She felt much more human now that there was coffee flowing into her belly. "So what's your price, Queen of the Coffeemaker?"

"Okay, if I can't have a muffin, then I want to ask you something."

Oh, here it came. Leslie braced herself for a soul-scorching question. "Shoot."

"Is it okay to not be sad about Grandfather?"

Leslie considered this. She knew the right answer but she liked the new accord between them. She chose to seek more information before she answered. "Why do you ask?"

"Because I didn't really like him very much, you know?" Annette sat down, letting her hair fall across her face. "And I'm not really sad that he's dead. Is that awful?"

"Well, it's not very nice, but you're right: He was a difficult man to like."

"I just remember that time that we were there for his birthday and Auntie Phil had—"

"Philippa. Aunt Philippa."

Defiance flashed in those eyes. "Uncle Nick calls her Phil and she said I could, too. It suits her better. Philippa is a frumpy name, but Phil is cool for a girl. And Aunt Phil is cool."

"Well, if she okayed it, who am I to argue?" Leslie sat down opposite her daughter. "Is Leslie a frumpy name?"

"It's a serious name."

"What about Annette?"

Annette smiled. "It's a pretty name. I like it a lot."

Leslie saluted her with her mug. "At least I did one thing right."

This confused Annette for a beat. "But you do everything right. Always."

Leslie laughed. "Hardly. Go on, tell me about Aunt Phil."

Annette studied her for a moment, considering this morsel, then shrugged. "Anyway, I remember the first time Aunt Phil brought Uncle Nick to Rosemount, it was for Grandfather's birthday, and he was so mean to her. I mean Aunt Phil is so nice. How could anyone be mean to her?"

Leslie remembered that night well. It had started badly and gotten worse, mostly because Robert had been impossible. He had been a man who hadn't been able take it in stride when everything didn't go his way.

Had Matt been right to show him that he was wrong instead of declining his offer?

Had Matt thought that she was like his father?

Was she?

Leslie became aware that Annette was waiting for an answer. "You're right. That was a really difficult evening. It turned out that having no potatoes was the least of it."

"I didn't remember anything about potatoes."

"Your grandmother forgot to cook any, and your grandfather wasn't amused."

"How could she forget?"

"She was drunk." Leslie smiled. "But she has such good manners that you have to know her to see it."

Annette frowned at her milk. "Did you like him? Grandfather, I mean."

"Promise not to tell? Not anyone? Not even your father?"

Annette crossed her heart and touched her fingertips to her mouth.

Leslie held her daughter's gaze. "I thought he was cold and a bit mean, though I'd never say that to your dad. Robert was his dad, after all."

"So you're not sorry, either?"

Leslie shook her head, then crossed her heart and touched her fingers to her lips again. They shared a conspiratorial smile that Leslie would never have believed possible twenty-four hours earlier.

Then she opened the fridge and surveyed the limited array of options. "So what do you say to yogurt and fruit?"

"Blech!"

"Well, it's that or nothing. The grocery fairy is slacking off, too."

"Off with their heads," Annette said in a growly voice. When Leslie looked at her in surprise, she clapped a hand over her mouth and giggled. Annette was so abruptly cute that Leslie caught her breath at the glimpse of the little girl she once had been.

* * *

"Coffee?"

Matt opened one eye and groaned under his breath. He felt as if he'd been kicked in the head as well as the gut. He was rumpled and hot and had a crick in his back from sleeping on a wicker settee.

In his suit.

Sharan was in front of him, offering him a steaming cup of what looked to be a café au lait, milk frothed on top. Her hair was as long and shiny and golden as it had always been, she was tanned and lithe, and really, he had to look twice to see that she was almost twenty years older than the last time he'd seen her. There were a few lines around her eyes and her mouth, maybe some new shadows in those eyes, but he wasn't going there.

She was wearing a floral sleeveless dress that came only halfway down her thighs and followed every curve so closely that it might have been a second skin.

"Good morning," she said, her smile turning wicked. "Or is it?"

"Very funny. Maybe you could feel sorry for the injured and keep your voice down."

She laughed, as he'd known she would. "But your wounds are self-inflicted, from the look of you. It's tough to feel very sorry for you." She bent to kiss him but he turned aside so that her lips just brushed his cheek. "Shy boy," she teased. "I thought you were an illusion when I came out the door."

"No illusion."

She still used the same perfume—he recognized it right away. "Was it at least a good party?"

"The ending was a bit of a downer. I was mugged."

"No!" Her eyes widened with shock, and Matt was surprised to feel so little response in his body. There had been a time when that expression on Sharan's face had awakened even the dead parts of him.

"Yes, it's true." He moved and winced at the pain in his back. "I was stupid and paid for it. I'm sorry. This wasn't how I planned this . . ."

"Don't be ridiculous. It's good to see you, Matt, no matter what shape you're in. It's been too long."

He averted his gaze, feeling uncomfortable with the glow in her eyes. "Thanks for the coffee. You're a lifesaver." He took an appreciative sip of the coffee and was startled by the taste of chicory.

"I remember how you love your coffee." Sharan sat down on the chair opposite. She seemed to be assessing him. "Are you staying long?"

"I don't know. My brother's in jail, and I need to find out what I can do for him." Matt frowned. "And I guess I'll need to cancel my credit cards and go back to the hotel."

"Oh, you can't stay in a hotel! Not when we haven't seen each other in so long!" Sharan eased closer, the move making her skirt hem slip up a few inches. "You have to stay here. I insist."

It wasn't hard to be persuaded to do what he had told himself he wanted, though Matt made a token protest. He suspected that his reasons for accepting weren't fully aligned with her reasons for offering. Not anymore, though that didn't make a lot of sense.

It's tough to think things through with a whopper of a hangover.

"Are you sure?" he asked. "I don't want to be any trouble . . ."

Sharan stood up and waved off his protest. "Old friends aren't trouble. Especially not you." She put her hand on his thigh, slid it a bit higher, and her voice dropped. "It's good to see you, Matt."

"Well, I don't feel that good right now."

She laughed again. "That will improve. In fact I can help."

Matt swallowed as her eyes darkened with intent. Her hand slid closer to his crotch, caressing and stroking all the way. She leaned close, studying him before bending to kiss him.

"Ah, no, don't do that. I've got to brush my teeth . . ."

Sharan laughed and let him pull away. "Is that all? Or has marriage taken all the wind out of your sails?"

"It was a one-two punch that took that."

Sharan glanced at her watch, then stood and brushed down her skirt. "Well, I have to go to work. See you around five or so?"

"Work?" Matt straightened. "Wait a minute. I thought you came down here to paint, but you make it sound like a job."

"I do have a job."

"But you're the original free spirit . . ."

"It's expensive being a free spirit." Sharan laughed curtly. "The art market isn't that good right now. So I do another kind of painting and get paid by the hour. No big deal." She smiled though it didn't reach her eyes. "I work at the place that makes floats for Mardi Gras."

"That doesn't sound like you . . ."

"Oh, it is now. Yesterday I painted sixty-five neon green palm leaves. Today, I think we'll get into the gold ones." She raised her hands. "It's fabulously exciting stuff."

Matt was disappointed by this confession and a bit disoriented. "You were the one who was never going to sell out," he felt obliged to remind her.

She laughed lightly. "Well, I needed a place to live. Banks don't lend money to unemployed artists who can't sell their work. Life sometimes takes you places you never thought you'd be."

"Isn't that the truth," Matt muttered, not thinking about Sharan's painting. He looked down at his suit and winced at its condition. "I must look pretty rough."

"A sight for sore eyes. So will you stay?"

"Yes, that would be great." So why didn't he sound enthused?

"Will you make dinner?"

Matt forced a smile. "I guess I could."

"Good, here's the key to the house." She tossed him a key ring, which Matt in his current state barely managed to catch, then issued instructions. "There's more coffee in the pot, milk in the fridge, sugar in the cupboard over the coffeepot. Use the phone if you need to. Towels are under the sink in the bathroom if you want a shower—"

Matt laughed that she could even consider that optional and she smiled.

"I have an account at the corner store down the way if you need anything. And yes, whatever you make would be wonderful. I'll bring dessert: In fact, I *am* dessert." She winked, then pivoted and bounced off the porch.

I am dessert. It was exactly what she had said to him every night when they had virtually lived together in college. Matt blinked, certain he must be imagining things. There had been a time when it had thrilled him.

Just how hung over was he?

Sharan blew him a kiss, just as she used to, and then her car was backing out of the driveway.

It was like watching an old video. One that starred a guy who looked the way he had looked once, but otherwise had little in common with him today. He knew that for the privilege of sleeping with her, she'd demand no fewer than three orgasms.

But the prospect of delivering them—and any ensuing pleasure of his own—didn't have the same appeal Matt had expected it to have. They'd broken up because he couldn't understand her drive to create, and she couldn't understand that he didn't feel the same urge. Now that he did feel that urge, he'd expected to have common ground with her.

He'd always admired her, cutting her own path, making her own way. She always got up and kept on going, no matter what happened to her. He looked around the porch of her house and couldn't imagine that Katrina had ever struck here. Sharan always made things come out her way.

Or so he'd thought.

But now she had a job, a nine-to-five job, a grunt job. That was something he could never have imagined the Sharan he knew doing. He felt as if he'd crashed into the life of a stranger. Given that, he was a bit disconcerted by how readily Sharan had welcomed him into her life and, by extension, into his bed.

Since when had he become so conservative?

Since he'd gotten married?

Since he'd married Leslie?

Since he'd been mugged and beaten up maybe. Matt snorted and got to his feet, thinking of Leslie's lingerie collection. She might be monogamous but she wasn't conservative, not once you got beneath the schoolmistress uniform.

Matt strode into the house in search of coffee and a shower. He was restless, impatient and irritable, though he couldn't pinpoint why.

This, after all, was what he believed he wanted.

Funny that it felt all wrong.

*   *   *

Beverly Coxwell had had it up to her eyeteeth with death.

Death was, in fact, showing the social graces of that inevitable guest who doesn't have the grace to leave the party when he should. You know the one, the guest who stays through dawn, the last one alone on the dance floor, the one regaling his yawning host and hostess with old jokes when they're yearning for bed.

With events of this week, Beverly had almost forgotten that she had agreed to attend the reading of an old friend's will. She might have skipped that ritual, conveniently "forgotten," if Marissa's lawyer hadn't phoned to remind her first thing Thursday morning.

So she went, albeit in bad humor. She parked her Jag a bit more aggressively than was customary for her and swung out of the car with impatience. She really didn't know why she had to be here.

Having known Marissa seemed a slender credential.

Marissa Fitzgibbons had been a nitpicking pain in the neck in life, and death apparently hadn't changed that. How many people included a list of those who must be present for the reading of their wills? Beverly didn't doubt that the lawyers would be checking off the attendance list at the door. And what would happen if she skipped out, just headed down the street for a latte instead? Would Marissa haunt her?

Beverly decided she didn't want to find out. It would be like Marissa to get tetchy about noncompliance.

The two women had met when they had both served as volunteers on the refreshment committee for the tour of gardens hosted by the horticultural society. Beverly had been incredulous to learn that Marissa had stipulated in the memo to the caterers that the chives in the egg salad sandwiches had to be cut to sixteenth-inch lengths or less—she had discovered this when she came upon Marissa poking through the sandwiches to confirm that her order had been followed to the letter.

Or to the sixteenth.

Beverly glanced back at the car out of habit, suddenly seeing Robert when he'd triumphantly presented it to her. He'd been like a boy again, a kid with a new toy, so anxious to show her all the features and gizmos that she'd never use. She could almost hear him, could see the rhododendrons in bloom around the driveway at Gray Gables, could feel him come to take her hand in his excitement.

Then Beverly blinked and he was gone.

Funny how you could forget something like that. Funny how you could forget a surprisingly spontaneous kiss in your own driveway, one that sent you both stepping backward in astonishment, left you eying each other as if you were strangers. Strangers were almost what they had become by that point in time.

Funny how you could miss someone, even though you hadn't gotten along in years. Beverly knew she missed the knowledge that Robert existed, not his company, which had been irritable and impatient and unpleasant the vast majority of the time. She had failed him and he had made sure that she had known it, virtually every time their paths crossed.

And she knew she would miss him more than she did now, before she could begin to miss him less. She knew she missed the sense that everything was under control, which Robert always exuded—whether it ever had been true or not was anyone's guess.

Funny how she'd been able to drink when Robert was alive, because he had managed everything, but she wanted to drink now, because no one would be managing anything in the foreseeable future, because she would have to manage things herself for the first time in a long time. A little nip of sherry would have set her straight on this morning, but Beverly was trying desperately hard to be sober.

She didn't want to answer to her son James for any weakness.

And she really didn't want to be numb again. The only problem was that the damn stuff tasted so good.

When she stepped into the empty elevator redolent with the scent of food, Beverly fought a smile. She hoped to God that the chives were chopped properly, or Marissa might feel obliged to rise from the dead.

Now that would be interesting.

But what was about to happen, unbeknownst to Beverly, would be just as interesting.

Maybe more so.

*   *   *

A memo had been slipped under Leslie's office door, copied onto vivid pink paper so that there was no chance of missing it. She bent and picked it up, not needing to guess who it was from.

She got it in one. The head of the history department wanted suggestions for new courses for the fall. He wanted his staff to "sex up" the curriculum, which was where Leslie stopped reading.

The illustrious Dinkelmann was apparently determined to

destroy scholarship as it had endured for centuries and to do so by the end of the week.

"Ah Dinkelmann, how do I despise thee? Let me count the ways," Leslie muttered under her breath, tossing the metaphorical box labeled *Team Player* down into the void. Then she balled up the pink sheet and cast it in the direction of the round file.

Maybe she should start calling it the Dinkelmann file.

A snicker and a scamper of footsteps alerted Leslie to the fact that she wasn't alone. She pivoted to find the Harris-tweed-encased buttocks of Charlotte MacPherson, Dinkelmann's biggest toady, disappearing around the corner of the corridor.

Naomi was right, though Leslie wasn't just being watched: She was dead meat.

In a very real sense, she had nothing more to lose and that—also in a very real sense—was a tremendous relief.

*   *   *

Matt did his best thinking in the shower, and in Sharan's shower he was thinking about Leslie. This wasn't how leaving your marriage was supposed to work out, especially if you managed to get yourself into the house and the bathroom of a sexy woman who made no secret of wanting you.

But Matt had never done things the easy way. So now he was thinking about Leslie, the woman who was several thousand miles away and supposedly left behind him. He couldn't figure out where he'd gone wrong, how he'd misread her so completely, so he went back to the beginning again, back to when they had met.

It had taken him six weeks to find Book Girl, as Matt had begun to call her in his thoughts, six weeks to figure out that he should have looked first in the most obvious place.

He'd found her in the library.

Duh, as Annette would say. He still couldn't believe he'd been so stupid.

*   *   *

She was buried in a back corner, as if hoping no one would notice her, her hair tied back and her ankles pressed chastely together.

She was as pretty as he remembered, and he had to stop to take a breath before approaching her. It didn't matter: She was so buried in her studies that she was unaware of him.

So he looked. He took his time.

The way she tucked a stray tendril of her hair behind her ear revealed how finely boned she was. Delicate. Her fingers were long and elegant, and there were a couple of freckles on her nose.

She was wearing glasses, which he thought looked both solemn and adorable. She frowned slightly as she read, moving between the various books in the three stacks she had made, her pen flying as she made notes.

She was left-handed, just like him, which gave him a ridiculous surge of pleasure.

She was so deep in concentration that she didn't even see him watching her, didn't even hear him step closer, didn't feel his presence when he stopped beside her desk. He cleared his throat and her pen never slowed.

"Hi," Matt said, feeling immediately that he could have thought of something more brilliant as an opening line. But Book Girl didn't glance up, apparently assuming that he was talking to someone else.

He bent lower. "Hi. How are you doing?"

She looked up then, startled, her gaze flying over his features. For a moment he was afraid she wouldn't remember who he was, then she flushed, averted her gaze, then looked at him again. "Fine." She removed her glasses. "So how did the art exhibit go?"

"I don't know." He shrugged. "You were right: I wasn't that interested in it, after all."

She watched him for a moment, and he guessed that she was re-

membering Sharan's enthusiastic embrace. "You didn't need to come and tell me about, um, your change of interest."

"I know. I just wanted to see you again."

"Why?" She almost laughed, her gaze sliding away then back to him. "Need help with an essay?"

"No. Why would you think that?"

Her smile turned rueful. "That's usually the reason guys come looking for me. Especially the hunks."

Matt grinned, pleased. "I'm no hunk."

She lifted one brow, then went back to her books. She wasn't reading, though, and she wasn't writing, either.

He had her interest.

Matt leaned his hip on the desk. "I do all right on my own essays, so you don't need to worry about that."

"Shhhhhhhhhhh!" came an indignant hiss from behind the bookshelves behind them.

"You're not supposed to talk in here," she said in a whisper. "You'd better leave."

"Maybe we could leave together. We could have a coffee some place you're allowed to talk."

Her eyes widened slightly, then she shook her head. "I have a test to study for."

"When's the test?"

"This afternoon."

"So maybe I could meet you afterward. Where's your class and when does it end?"

She picked up her glasses, put them on, took them off again, then looked up at him as if she meant to lecture him. "Look, I don't know who put you up to this, but . . ."

Matt leaned his hands on the desk, bending so that he was close to her. "Nobody put me up to this," he whispered, letting her see that he meant it. "I'd like to talk to you, over coffee, after your test today if possible."

"But why?"

Matt grinned. "Because you're cute. Why else?"

She flushed crimson and her hands shook as she put her glasses back on. "Now I know you're joking. Go away already."

Matt opened one of his notebooks and tore out a page. He began to write his name and telephone number on it. "My name's Matt Coxwell. I'm in the law school so you can ask anybody there whether I'm a rapist or serial killer."

"And if they say you are?"

"Then they're lying."

She chuckled at that, and he grinned.

"Shhhhhhhhhhhhhhhh!"

She glanced over her shoulder and dropped her voice lower again. "You've got lousy references, then."

"A guy's gotta do what he's gotta do." He met her gaze again. "Or you could just tell me where your class is."

"I don't think so. What would your girlfriend think of that?"

"If you mean Sharan—"

"The blonde. The affectionate one."

"We're not seeing each other anymore."

She thought about that, though there was still suspicion in her eyes. He debated the merits of telling her that he'd dumped Sharan after meeting her, but seeing as he didn't even know her name yet and she was half-convinced he was a nutcase, that was unlikely to help his case much.

But he had to say something, so he did. "Alternatively, you could just meet me at the Java Joint after your test. Name the time."

"It ends at four," she said, folding the paper he had given her and tucking it into her knapsack. "But you won't be there."

"Yeah? Let's make a bet."

She leaned back, her eyes twinkling. "Oh that's an easy deal to make. If you don't show, you can't pay any stakes you owe for not showing."

"You've got my number. You could tell my mother on me, and believe me, she has no sense of humor about bad manners."

She laughed a bit, though he could still see that she wasn't convinced. "Four o'clock at the Java Joint, then."

"Good luck on your test."

"Thanks." She smiled then, a brilliant and genuine smile that lit her features and left Matt blinking like a deer in the headlights. All too soon she ducked her head, dismissing him by her inattention.

He wasn't quite ready to leave, though.

"You never told me your name," Matt whispered and her answering smile was so mischievous that his heart rolled over and played dead.

"If you show up at the Java Joint, I'll tell you then."

*   *   *

Matt smiled into the stream of hot water, recalling Leslie's certainty that he wouldn't be there, that he was putting her on.

Oh, he had shown. There hadn't been any doubt that he'd do so, even though he'd had to skip one of his toughest classes to do it.

There'd been hell to pay from that old snarly prof—what had been his name? Bentley or something. Mean bastard. Probably a pal of Matt's father . . . Matt neatly sidestepped the direction that thought was going to take him—but it had been worth it to see Leslie's astonishment when she stepped into the Java Joint at five past four and saw him there, waiting just for her.

He'd had his first glimpse that day in the library of an ability of Leslie's that had never failed to amaze him—her ability to remember so much information and to pull it together into a coherent whole. She integrated vast amounts of data so easily, never guessing how difficult it was for other people.

And when she had talked about her test afterward, he had seen her love for learning, her passion for history. Her eyes had shone with an intoxicating enthusiasm, one he wanted to see over and over again. Given his indifference for his own studies, her excitement was both alien and fascinating.

So why did she hate her job now?

How could she hate her job as a tenured professor of medieval history? It was the only thing she had ever wanted to do—she'd told him as much. Anger roiled within him, anger that she hadn't taken him into her confidence.

It was anger that he knew didn't have its root in Leslie's behavior, but just needed a focus. Even recognizing that didn't make him less angry.

Matt rubbed himself dry and knotted the towel around his waist. There was only one way to get to the bottom of this and Sharan had said that he was welcome to use the phone.

One more call.

He snagged some aspirin out of the medicine cabinet and got himself another cup of coffee before he called north, in the hope that he would sound more human than he felt.

There was an outside chance that he could pull it off.

As he was dialing, he decided not to tell Leslie about the mugging. If he was disconnecting their lives, then he couldn't expect her to console him or worry about him. It was time to start living apart in every sense.

Lying about his reason for needing his credit-card numbers was the only decent thing to do.

* * *

By the time Leslie strode into her lecture hall, her tolerance was running at a dangerous low. This was a third-year class on the society and culture of the high middle ages. There were only about seventy-five bodies in this section: In each successive year, as courses became more specialized, the numbers dropped in a kind of natural selection. By fourth year, there would only be twenty or so in each seminar, and they would pretty much be the ones aiming for grad school.

Leslie put the folder filled with their first essays down on the podium with a thunk. They kept talking to each other, which always infuriated her. She looked pointedly at the clock, which was at the hour, to no avail.

So she looked at them. No, she glared.

Here was the future of scholarship and it was a depressing sight. It was even more depressing that academic excellence, curiosity, and learning were being sacrificed to the greater good of the university as a financial entity. Leslie hadn't signed up for bureaucracy and bullshit, but that's what Dinkelmann seemed determined to bring to the table.

And thinking about that made her impulsively decide to chuck one of her burdens into the abyss. She might regret it, but you only live once.

Sayonara to the big heavy box called *Dutiful Professor*. It could keep *Team Player* company, down there in the bottom of the abyss. Oh, look, there went *Compassionate Teacher*.

Look at them tumble down, down, down.

Dinkelmann had pushed Crabcake Coxwell too far.

*   *   *

Poodles?

Beverly couldn't believe it. She must have heard the bequest incorrectly. Marissa's lawyer and his assistant beamed at her, so certain she would be thrilled by her windfall that she felt it would be rude to express displeasure.

Or astonishment.

"Did you say *poodles*?"

The lawyer's smile broadened. "Yes! Two of them. Wonderful dogs. They were Marissa's pride and joy. You're very fortunate that she trusted you with their welfare."

"They would be dogs, then," Beverly said. "Actual live dogs."

The lawyer chuckled and nodded, apparently thinking she was overwhelmed by her good fortune. "Of course."

Dogs. Beverly didn't have dogs. She didn't particularly like dogs and she was developing a sudden vehement dislike of Marissa Fitzgibbons.

Dogs. Plural, as in more than one dog.

"Is there any sherry, by chance?" she asked. It would take two glasses to set her straight at this point, but she couldn't believe anyone would begrudge her that small indulgence.

The lawyer shook his head. "Marissa was a teetotaler."

"I could make you a cup of ginseng tea," the younger man offered.

"Thank you, no." Beverly decided she'd stop at the liquor store on the way home, James and AA be damned. If she doled it out in nice little glasses, no one would ever know that she'd fallen off the wagon. She rose, filled with purpose, and made to leave.

"But don't you want to meet the girls?" the lawyer asked, apparently surprised.

"We assumed you'd take them home with you today," the younger man said, so earnest that Beverly wanted to shake him.

"What girls?"

"The poodles!"

"Today?" She was supposed to take dogs home with no warning? "I'm supposed to take them with me now?"

"There's no one to take care of them, and they can't stay in Marissa's empty apartment alone." The lawyer shook a playful finger at Beverly, and she glared at him for such inappropriate familiarity. "Marissa was so sure you'd love her girls."

"They are not girls from what you have said: They are dogs."

"Not dogs," the lawyer said with a shake of his head. "Poodles!"

"You'll see once you meet them. They're the most amazing dogs," the younger man said with an enthusiasm that was equally inappropriate.

Beverly passed a hand over her brow with resignation. She had clearly stepped into a universe in which everyone was insane and the only way to escape was to humor them.

"Well, why wouldn't I want to meet them?" she said, though it was difficult to think of making the acquaintance of dogs as one met people in a receiving line. She forced a smile. "I assumed they weren't here."

"Oh, they're here, just being as good as can be!" The assistant opened the kitchen door and two massive dogs trotted into the living room right on cue.

Beverly nearly had heart failure at the sight of them. Poodles were little, weren't they?

Poodles were lap dogs, tiny fragile things that yelped and yapped. Beverly was quite sure of that. Poodles had curly hair and stupid haircuts.

But these dogs were massive.

Though they did have curly hair and moderately stupid haircuts.

There was little time to think about it. The dogs bounced directly toward her, as if they had known the terms of Marissa's will in advance, and Beverly was the one who yelped.

She had time to notice that one was jet black and the other was whiter than white, that the white one led the way. Although their fur was long with an enviable curl, their faces and paws were shaved. There was a pompom on the end of each one's wagging tail and something glittered on their pink patent leather collars.

The fashion faux pas of rhinestones on pink patent alone could have given her palpitations.

"These aren't poodles!" Beverly protested. "Poodles are small!" She lifted her hands up and away as the dogs circled her. She was afraid they would jump on her, but the dogs immediately sat down before her, their manner expectant. They sat with front paws tightly together, chests thrust out, brown eyes fixed upon her. They were as tall as her hip, the largest frilly dogs she'd ever seen in her life.

"They're standard poodles," the assistant said. "Originally, the breed was this size."

Beverly glanced at him. "Really?" seemed the sum of safe comments she could make.

"Meet Caviar and Champagne," the lawyer said. "The two richest dogs in Massachusetts, and now, your wards."

The dogs' tails thumped against the carpet, probably in recognition of their names, and Beverly Coxwell felt faint.

And she'd thought she needed a drink before.

Chapter Seven

Leslie cleared her throat and thought that the clearing of the professorial throat is always a portent of doom.

Funny how Gregory of Tours had never noted that.

Maybe that was why her students didn't seem to know what it meant.

"Perhaps some of you think that the assigned reading is not actually reading that you should do," she said, projecting her voice so that her students stilled. The bright ones were already wary, though the few in the back who sprawled in their seats and chewed their pens were still muttering cracks to each other.

She paced the front of the hall, not adverse to a little showmanship. She'd been playing this game long enough to know that a lot of it was performance art. "Perhaps you think that my time is well-spent preparing lectures that none of you will heed. Perhaps you think that I enjoy reading your feeble if not incoherent attempts to write an essay, in English, comparing two elements of medieval society. Perhaps you think that doing any work for this course would cut into your social life." She pivoted and faced the pranksters in the back of the hall. "Perhaps you think that obtaining a university degree without actually learning anything is funny."

Leslie waited a beat, then smiled thinly. "Unfortunately I do not agree."

One of the anxious ones who always sat in the front row put up her hand, then unable to wait, blurted out her protest of innocence. "But Dr. Coxwell, I did the readings!"

Leslie chose not to test her comprehension in front of the entire class, but spared her a curt nod. "Those of you, like Ms. Smith, who troubled to do your preparatory readings, as well as those who managed to read three lines on your syllabus, will be aware that today's lecture was to concern the emergence of the individual, as Georges Duby has labeled it, in the high middle ages."

She paused, letting them worry for a moment. Dinkelmann wanted something done with the participation mark: Well, he'd get something, if not what he wanted.

"There has been a slight change to the schedule."

A rustle passed through the group of students at this ominous comment, and they looked a little less smug than they had. Leslie was surprised to find herself enjoying this. She was pretty sure that unpredictability hadn't been part of her reputation.

Maybe it would become part of it.

"We will, instead, see the emergence of a number of individuals in this class."

They began to take notes.

Leslie paced. "I admit that my notion of education is somewhat anachronistic and owes more to the medieval model than the contemporary one, in which a degree from an institution of higher learning is no more than a commodity to be bought and sold, or even a product in which consumer satisfaction must be assured." She faced them, rocket boobs pointing to the back left and back right corners of the room. "In short, I expect you to actually learn something, not to simply memorize, regurgitate, and forget the material from this course, then complain to the dean if you do not receive an A."

Leslie picked up a sheet of paper from the pile she had brought in, pretending that she was referring to it. "If you turn to the second page of your syllabus"—there was a rustle of activity, and the predictable murmurs from those who had not in fact kept the syllabus that Leslie had provided to them at the beginning of the semester—"you will note that fifteen percent of your mark is allocated to participation. The more keenly observant among you will have noticed that I do not take attendance in this lecture, so your presence alone cannot possibly be the full requirement to obtain this grade.

"In past years the mark has been derived from a general sense on my part of which students were familiar to me—because I had seen them in lecture all semester and/or they had come to me to discuss their essays—and observation of the answers on the final exam. Although it is generally clear when marking the final exam who has attended my lectures and who has not—from which one can extrapolate attendance and consciousness, if not participation—that is not a direct justification for granting all or part of this participation mark. It has been brought to my attention that this is not an entirely fair assessment."

They didn't need to know what Dinkelmann had really said.

The students who sat in the front row were leaning forward, intent upon not missing a single word, and even the jokesters in the back were quiet.

"As a result this year, I have changed the requirements for the participation mark. The bulk of this mark will be assigned in our lecture next Tuesday, based upon your individual participation in a discussion. In that two-hour lecture period, we will discuss the evolution of the concept of the individual in the medieval context."

A ripple of panic rolled through the ranks, but Leslie kept talking. "This is a broad and meaty topic and one that has been subjected to increasing scrutiny among medieval social historians, of which I am one. If you have access to notes from this course in a previous year, I must remind you that my own lecture has a particularly narrow focus and reference to it alone will not suffice. I would suggest that you refer to the list of secondary reference materials supplied in the syllabus"—the rustle of papers was louder now—"and spend some time in the library familiarizing yourself with current scholarship on this subject in preparation for this discussion.

"Those of you who have other obligations scheduled during Tuesday's lecture or who simply do not appear will receive a zero for the participation grade. I remind you that that's fifteen percent of your grade. Next week a roll call will be taken, though I cannot guarantee whether it will be done at the beginning or the end of the class. You may find it prudent to attend the entire discussion. Those of you who have misplaced your syllabus can pick up another copy from the secretary in the history department—I will ensure that she has an original from which you can make copies, at your own expense, by five o'clock today."

This was fun.

"Now about your essays." All of Leslie's students were listening now, even if they would have preferred not to do so. "It has been brought to my attention that grades in my courses have been found to be lower than the department average. In plain language, I fail more students than other professors and I give fewer excellent marks. Certainly there are those who would argue that I am being unfair, but generally those are the people who would prefer not to do any work."

It could have been a funeral, they were so serious.

"This is a third-year course," Leslie said sternly. "In order to register in this course, you must have completed two prerequisites, one being the medieval history survey course offered in second year and the other being any other history course of your choice. This means that you must have a grounding in the basic concerns facing any student of medieval history, and also that you know how to perform certain tasks, such as writing a history essay. Because of this, the grading standards—or perhaps more accurately, my expectations—are higher than they would be for a first-year course. A superficial consideration of the variables will not get you far. Using only general sources will not get you far. Failing to develop any argument or forming any conclusion will not get you far."

She held up a finger as they began to fidget. "Yet in all fairness, I understand that some sources will not be available to those of you who do not plan to continue with medieval studies. I recognize that students no longer learn Latin and that, as a result, vast quantities of source materials remain indecipherable to such students. In fact, in what is an appalling failure of the educational system or our expectations of it, very few students at this university, regardless of their discipline, will master a second language, let alone the four that used to be considered a minimum for scholarship in the medieval era. This is not your fault, and I do not hold it against you, although those of you who do read other languages and do consult source materials in those languages can expect to be compensated accordingly."

Leslie turned, paused, then patted the stack of essays. At this point, she didn't think she needed to bother to gild the lily. "You have the collective distinction of creating the worst suite of first essays I have ever marked." Consternation passed openly through the assembly. "Mercifully for those of you who care about your marks, this essay is only thirty percent of your grade. Even with a zero on this paper, you can still achieve a decent mark in this class."

"Are you going to grade on a curve?" demanded one student who was familiar for consistently asking such questions.

"There is always the opportunity to improve your own grade and to receive an excellent mark on any assignment, Mr. Carmichael, but I will not be adjusting these grades. I do not believe in bell curves, as each class is unique. I do not mark to a quota: I give each paper the mark it deserves in my opinion, and if that meant that every student got an A, I assure you that I would be delighted. Sadly it usually means that the vast majority of students receive a C or an F." She gave them a heartbeat to worry about that.

"But . . ."

"I am interested in the pursuit of academic excellence," Leslie said, interrupting Mr. Carmichael crisply. "And the future of scholarship. It would be irresponsible on my part to mark overgenerously. If none of you prepare an excellent essay or write an outstanding exam, it is my duty to give you a commensurate grade."

"But . . ."

"I have tenure, Mr. Carmichael. They can only fire me for a few things, and telling the truth isn't one of them."

And Leslie could see, from one glance over the lecture hall, that she finally had their attention.

She hoped, a bit belatedly, that she was right about the tenure bit.

"Any questions? No? Fine, then I will leave your essays here for you to claim—surnames A through M in this pile, surnames N onward in this pile—and I look forward to our discussion on Tuesday. I remind you that the last date to drop any half course this semester without any mark of its presence remaining on your student record is tomorrow."

Leslie left the lecture hall just as pandemonium erupted.

Wait until Dinkelmann heard about this.

The best part was that Leslie didn't care. She had embarked on Naomi's course of taking the high road and the only question she had was why she hadn't done it sooner.

With those boxes gone, their burdens cast into the abyss to burn, she felt lighter on her feet. She felt like dancing, with a rose clenched in her teeth.

Maybe she should take tango lessons.

Except she'd want to take them with Matt and only with Matt, and that wasn't likely to happen anytime soon. There was a thought to bring her back to earth.

Thankfully, there was one last Hershey's in the vending machine below the history department offices.

* * *

The phone was ringing in Leslie's office and she was pretty sure it was Dinkelmann, calling to chew her out for failing to play by the new rules of the game. The man had a sixth sense for knowing when things in his kingdom were diverging from his edict of the day. She bit off another piece of chocolate once she got the door unlocked, crossed the office in one step and picked up the phone.

"I don't care what you think, Dr. Dinkelmann," she said with defiance. "It was the right thing to do and I'm glad I did it. Go ahead. Do your worst."

There was a beat of silence, then a different male voice echoed in her ear. "What did you do that Dinkelmann won't like?" Matt asked, his tone wary.

Ooops.

Leslie sat down at her desk, reminding herself to breathe. The chocolate bar was less interesting than it had been.

For the moment at least.

"I didn't expect you to call," she said, instead of answering him. "Since you didn't call last night."

"I was too drunk to punch in the number," he said, with a rueful laugh. Leslie silently gave herself ten bonus points for not asking if he had been too drunk to do the horizontal boogie with Sharan.

There was an awkward pause, one that Leslie was reluctant to fill with chatter about Zach or Sharan. She waited instead, not wanting to hang up the phone, either.

What did she want? She wanted a sign from Matt—a portent, like the ones Gregory of Tours recorded so diligently—that he still cared, at least a little.

An eclipse or a shooting star would do. She checked out the window, only to find thin winter sunlight on dirty snow.

"You never answered my question," Matt said irritably. "Why do you hate your job? You never said anything before."

"You never said you were going to lose the court case."

"I thought you knew."

"Maybe I thought you knew about my job, or would guess."

"I had no idea," he confessed. "So we have that in common. Is this new?"

Leslie straightened, not feeling inclined to bare her thoughts when she was so uncertain of his intentions. "I don't think it really matters . . ."

"Well, I do," Matt interrupted her, that new tinge of impatience in his tone. "The thing is that I expected everything to be right between us again once that case was over, and it isn't and I want to know why."

Leslie liked the sound of his determination, but she wasn't going to cave in too easily. "I thought you were leaving instead."

"Well, maybe I am."

"No maybe about it. You did."

"All right, I did." Matt exhaled and lowered his voice. "But you surprised me, Leslie. I was sure that you loved your job. Look if I'd known otherwise, maybe I would have done something different in court."

Leslie toyed with a paper clip, well aware that she was hearing what she most wanted to hear yet afraid to trust it. "It didn't sound like compromising your principles was an option."

"Is that it, then? Do you feel you've compromised yours?"

"Does it matter? We need my paycheck—or I guess now I should say that I need it."

Matt ignored that opportunity to pledge his return. "Yet you did something today that you knew Dinkelmann wouldn't approve of. It's not like you to be inconsistent. What aren't you telling me?"

What wasn't she telling him?

Leslie thought of the Christmas letter from Sharan, that Sharan knew about his intent to lose the case and about his novel, neither of which Leslie had known. She recalled that he was at Sharan's home, maybe sitting at her kitchen table, using her phone, which maybe had a smear of her lipstick on it (maybe there was a smear on him to match), and yet none of that seemed to be worthy of conversation.

What wasn't *she* telling *him*?

She probably should have guessed that she'd lose it. "What aren't I telling you? Hello, aren't you my husband who is several thousand miles away, staying at the home of his former girlfriend, and noncommittal about returning to the family domicile here? I think you've got a few confessions of your own to make, Mr. Coxwell."

He wasn't daunted at all. In fact he came back hard and fast, as if he was still in court facing his brother. "Fair enough. We haven't talked enough lately. How does your not telling me that you hated your job fit into fixing that? How does refusing to discuss it now change anything?"

Leslie paused and swallowed, hearing the truth in his words. Every journey began with a small step, just one.

Maybe it was time she took that step.

Maybe she should take it first.

"Okay," she agreed, twining the telephone coil around her fingers. "You're right. I should have talked to you about it. But I haven't felt as if I even knew you lately, Matt, and this whole situation isn't helping." She wished she could see his eyes, wished she had evidence beyond the tone of his voice to measure his sincerity.

New Orleans might as well have been the moon.

"Fair enough," he said tightly. She heard a chair being dragged across the floor. "So talk to me now, Leslie. Tell me what's wrong with your job."

"Why should I bother?"

"What have you got to lose? And I'm asking."

She thought about that for three seconds, then straightened and pushed her door with her fingertips. The door didn't quite close, so she lowered her voice, sure that no one was around anyway. "It's Dinkelmann."

"The department head?"

Leslie found herself nodding. "Yesterday he insisted that we have to give higher grades."

"You're whispering."

"This isn't the best place to express doubts about the emperor's choice of wardrobe."

Matt chuckled and Leslie was inordinately pleased that she had made him laugh, even a little. "I've missed your humor," he said, his voice warm. "Why did you stop making jokes?"

Leslie felt herself blushing. "I don't know."

"When you became disenchanted with your job, I'll bet," he mused. "I've really got to become more observant."

"I didn't even notice," Leslie admitted and there was a warm moment of understanding between them.

Matt cleared his throat. "So presumably these higher grades are for the same work or lack thereof." His disgust made Leslie feel better, as if she wasn't fighting this battle alone.

She turned the paper clip over and over. "He wants me to just add the fifteen percent participation grade to every student's marks . . ."

"Fifteen percent for free?" Matt was so incredulous that Leslie smiled. "Not even for showing up? The participation marks are already gimmes!"

"I know. And more students have to get As under the new policy. They're going to calculate percentages."

"I thought they did that already."

"It was a request last time, not a formal policy."

"So why the change?"

"Apparently the university is unable to compete for new students because of its reputation as a tough school. And people paying tuition want something great to show for it."

"Straight As, regardless of what the kid has done. Welcome to the consumer society."

"Exactly."

"So it's all about money."

"Yes! Money and marketing and bureaucracy and . . ."

"Bullshit."

"Yes!"

"You know, there was a time when the antidote for low grades was more work on the part of the student."

"Oh, but that's not all. There's more . . ."

"I get the Ginsu knife, too?"

Leslie chuckled. On some level she was astonished by how easy this was. Beginning to talk was difficult, but once they were rolling, their old rhythms kicked right in. "This morning, I got a memo that Dinkelmann wants course offerings sexed up . . ."

"Sexed up? He actually used that phrase?"

"Um hmm. Listen, here's his example." Leslie retrieved the pink sheet from the trash and read to Matt. "'A sample of a new course might well be Submissive Whores, Lusty Heiresses, and Dominant Queens: The Unexpected Women of the Middle Ages.'" Leslie snorted, knowing she could express herself honestly to Matt. "What's 'unexpected' is his suggested course title."

"That's incredible. Could such a course even be taught?"

"Well, at some level. Maybe like a cable television script, not like a history course." Leslie forced herself to consider the root of Dinkelmann's suggestion. "Maybe he just wants to get away from political history, which I can understand. I would be the first person who would welcome a women's studies course focused on the middle ages and the role of women in medieval society. It's intriguing stuff and the origin of a lot of our notions of gender roles and courtship."

"But . . ." Matt prompted, drawing her out.

"The problem is, as always, source material." Leslie warmed to her theme. "How many churchmen wrote extensively about whores—or even about heiresses or queens? How many women were even taught to write, so they could write about themselves? How much raw stuff is available?"

"Not much," Matt guessed. "Some, but not much."

"Exactly. Is it reasonable to extrapolate from some bits and ends to half of the population of Europe?"

"Dangerous stuff, statistically speaking."

"Exactly. Here's a comparative for you. Could you take a case history of a hooker working in Manhattan and make conclusions about the role of women in general in twenty-first century Western society?"

"No way."

"Even the United States? Even Manhattan? It would be risky to even extrapolate to hookers working in Manhattan: One point does not make a line."

"How much material is there on medieval woman?"

"We have three well-documented examples and not much else. Three, for roughly a thousand years of history that encompasses all of Europe. It's a pretty meager sample, but they are remarkable women. There's Blanche of Castile, Eleanor of Aquitaine, and Hildegard von Bingen: that gives us a queen regent who ruled with an iron fist, an assertive heiress who became queen twice by virtue of her inherited lands and sheer force of will, and an abbess who had remarkable dreams on theological themes."

"But the million dollar question is how typical are they of medieval women?"

"Right. Probably not any more typical than Ivana Trump or Princess Diana are of your mother or me." Leslie heaved a sigh. "Maybe even less so. And none of them wrote without a scribe, none of them wrote themselves, so there's always the chance that their words have been edited or revised."

"Not very reliable stuff."

"No. My own suspicion is that chroniclers who wrote about these women did so because they acted often in the ways men were expected to act, ways in which women were not supposed to act. They were considered abominations by clergy, and were newsworthy, so to speak."

"Wasn't Eleanor of Aquitaine the one someone called Queen of England 'by the wrath of God'?"

"Yes! Giraldus Cambrensis said that she had brought the wrath of God upon England, and ultimately she used the phrase to describe herself." Leslie was thrilled that he remembered some of this stuff. Her stuff. She balled up the pink sheet and tossed it back into the trash. "So that's why I hate my job. I can't even pursue my own research, what with the number of classes and number of graduate students to advise . . ."

"But you like teaching, don't you?"

"Not this way. Not when they're going to dictate the resulting grades, independent of the work that gets done. And I don't like having all these burdens piled on my back that keep me from doing my own research, then being told that I'm not publishing enough articles. There are only so many hours in a day!"

"And if you can't keep up, Leslie, no one can. You've got to be the most organized person on the planet . . ."

"Could you stop saying that, please?" Her words were lightly spoken and she heard Matt chuckle. "I'd like to be given another adjective, even if it's only for a while." Leslie swung in her chair, surprised to find herself smiling. She felt better for venting, better for having Matt agree with her, better for tasting their old camaraderie again.

Reality, of course, was quick to intervene.

"But you see, they're asking exactly the same thing of you that my father asked of me," Matt said, with a levity that the assertion certainly didn't deserve. "You're being asked to compromise your principles, your ideas of what makes good scholarship or even good teaching."

Leslie froze, startled by the truth in this.

"It sounds as if you know exactly what I was facing, as if you understand now what you didn't get the other day. You always were the moral lodestone, Leslie, so I know you'll do the right thing." He thought it was resolved, as easily as that. "Back to the topic at hand."

Which was his leaving her. Leslie was in shock.

Matt apparently took her silence for assent. He cleared his throat, making her think he was uncomfortable with whatever he meant to say. Leslie had a heartbeat to marvel at that before he shocked her again.

"Look, this is kind of embarrassing to admit, but I lost my wallet last night." His voice was strained, and Leslie intuitively knew that he was lying. "So I'll need to get the credit-card numbers from you so I can cancel the cards."

What had happened to his wallet? Or maybe it was just one item in that wallet, one credit card maybe, for which he needed the number. Matt never lost anything, so Leslie knew his story was exactly that.

A story.

A *lie*.

Which made her angry all over again. How dare he challenge her for not telling him everything? How dare he spout about the value of honesty? She had just shared her concerns with him, only to have him lie to her in return.

Her silence clearly concerned him. "So when do you think you could get me the numbers? A couple of those cards have a lot of open credit and I'm a bit worried."

Leslie grit her teeth and deliberately didn't answer his question. "I don't have the numbers here. Remarkably."

"I wouldn't expect even you to be that organized." Matt laughed. When she didn't laugh with him, he cleared his throat again. He was nervous. Because he was lying? Because he guessed that she knew it? Because the truth was something that would really infuriate her? "Well?"

"I think you have to report the loss within twenty-four hours," Leslie said crisply, "so tonight will probably be fine. If you call the house around dinner, I should have all of the statements collected by then."

"Thanks."

"Glad to be of assistance." The words came out terse and hard.

"Leslie, don't take this wrong. You know that there's no one else I could ask about this . . ."

Being convenient was not a credential Leslie wanted to hear she possessed, not in this moment. Nor did she want to be told that she was organized or useful or held any number of other safe wifely traits.

For once Leslie wasn't going to make nice and swallow her frustration. Matt wanted honesty? Well, he was going to get some. "Well, it's terrific to find myself useful, especially when you're lying through your teeth."

"What do you mean?" He was hesitant, as if he knew that she was going to call him on something—and be right.

"You've never even lost a hair off your head, Matt. You never lose anything and no matter how drunk you might have been, you would never ever lose your wallet. You could at least tell me the truth, after I've shared my truth, Mr. Honesty-Is-Everything."

He whistled low, but didn't deny her accusation. "Cutting right to the chase, just like old times." In fact there was admiration in his voice. "I remember this Leslie. Where have you been?"

"Working, because somebody has to," she said bitterly.

"Look, Leslie . . ."

Leslie could hear that he was preparing to negotiate something, but she wasn't inclined to give him another chance right now, not considering where he was and how little he was telling her about what he had done.

She was too angry.

"Ooops, gotta go. Give my love to Sharan." Leslie blew a kiss into the receiver then chucked it into the cradle. She shoved a piece of chocolate into her mouth. There's only so much truth a person can face after being sheltered from it for so long.

Leslie gathered her stuff and left her office, telling herself that she didn't care that the phone didn't ring before she got to the end of the hall. She was leaving early and she didn't care who knew it. Thank God she had underwires to hold her up straight.

In fact, she left the building with a certain aplomb.

*   *   *

Matt met his brother in the usual colorless, featureless room reserved for meetings between lawyers and their incarcerated clients. He was in a sour mood after that morning call to Leslie, not particularly inclined to kiss his younger brother's boo-boos better. He was tapping his toe with impatience when Zach was ushered into his company.

"It's about time you got here," Zach complained and Matt's back went up.

The two guards exchanged a glance and Matt saw that they were already used to his brother's attitude. And they were bemused by it. They gave the usual instructions about where they would be and how to summon them and Matt nodded, letting Zach fume.

"Good to see you, too," Matt said with forced politeness, as if they were strangers instead of brothers. "Maybe you'd like to sit down."

"Nice shiner! How does the other guy look?"

"Shut up and sit down."

"Jeez, no sense of humor today." Zach sat. "What's wrong with you?"

"There's nothing wrong with me."

"Yeah? Then why do you seem so officious? More like James than yourself." Zach grinned and lounged in his chair.

Matt considered his brother, the man so accustomed to having everyone else clean up his mistakes. He had a sudden conviction that he might not be so helpful this time. "Imagine that someone could be less than thrilled to be summoned the length of the country to serve your whim, with no hope of compensation."

That made Zach pause, but then he braced his elbows on the table. He was too handsome for his own good, this kid, and too smooth to have ever gotten what he deserved. Even after a couple of days in the can, he had a certain rakish charm. "You've got to get me out of here, Matt. These guys are apes. It's got to be a violation of my constitutional rights to be detained for so long on trumped-up charges."

"I can only assume that you have told them as much."

"Well, yeah! I'm an innocent citizen . . ."

Matt glanced at the charges. "With five pounds of pot in your backpack."

"Look, it wasn't even my stuff . . ."

"Be serious, Zach. You had it in your backpack, which was apparently zipped closed."

"I am serious! It was a plant, no pun intended. Somebody set me up. What do you think I am—stupid? I never carry that much at once, even when I'm selling, because you're dead meat if you get caught."

Matt couldn't resist the impulse to pointedly look around. "Clearly."

Zach scowled. "This is no time for joking! Look, I'm in a jam and I need your help."

Matt tapped his finger on the table between them. "Correction, Zach: You're in deep shit. Three counts of resisting arrest, one count of assaulting a police officer—"

"He deserved it! He was twisting my arm behind my back, so I decked him."

"Good plan. It always makes things go better for you when you're innocent, if indeed you are, if you can manage to deck a cop who's doing his job."

"Wow, you're cranky today. No sex in Belmont these days?"

Matt lowered his voice to a growl. "Shut the fuck up and do it now."

Zach swallowed. "It was just a joke . . ."

"Too bad it wasn't funny, then." Matt flipped through the dossier he'd assembled upstairs. "Let's see: driving under the influence, possession of marijuana, intent to traffic marijuana, soliciting . . . You were having yourself a good time for a Tuesday night, weren't you?"

"I was at a party, that's all." Zach sat back, displeased with something. Whether it was the litany of charges or Matt's attitude, Matt couldn't say.

And he didn't much care.

Especially when Zach criticized him again. "So where were you? I've been here two and a half days. I called James Tuesday night."

"Wednesday morning, actually."

"So? Did you walk from Boston? It's Thursday."

Matt forced a thin smile, determined as he was not to lose his temper. "You heard, perhaps, that Father is dead."

Zach sat back, folding his arms across his chest. "It's not like anyone would care. Don't tell me you were too busy crying to get your ass on a plane and come to help me out."

That was it. Matt leaned abruptly across the table and seized Zach by the shirt collar. He had always been strong and fury made him stronger. He lifted his little brother so that his butt came off the chair and gave him a shake. "You stupid bastard," he snarled, then once he started, he couldn't stop. "Let me tell you about Father's death. Let me tell you what it's like to be summoned to a man's study, a man who eats his gun while you're en route."

"Jesus, I didn't know . . ."

"Let me tell you about the library at Gray Gables, all those books behind his desk dripping with blood and little bits of his brains."

Zach swallowed and averted his gaze. "Jesus, Matt, give it a rest."

"Let me tell you how he looked with his head exploded. Let me tell you about the smell . . ."

Zach looked at Matt with fear in his eyes.

"So the timing is a little inconvenient for you maybe, but I'll be

seeing—and smelling—that scene for the rest of my life." He released his brother abruptly, tossed him back into his chair, then
straightened his own tie. "Sorry to hear that his suicide didn't suit
your schedule."

"You never lose your temper like that," Zach said with care, as
if Matt had become unpredictable.

"Maybe that was my mistake." He sat down and riffled
through the paperwork. "So I can't defend you here, because I'm
not admitted in Louisiana, but as your brother, I can offer you
some advice."

"Don't you know anybody here? James always knew somebody . . ."

"Then it's too bad that he's not inclined to help you out anymore. Guess you went to that well too many times, huh?"

"What is this, Honesty Day?"

Matt ignored that. "What you want to do is admit to the possession and pay the fine—or do the time, however it shakes out
here—and I'll guess that they'll blink on the intent to traffic since
they don't have much more than an assumption that one person
couldn't use that much . . ."

"But didn't you hear me? I'm innocent!"

Matt laughed a low humorless laugh. "Yeah, right. I'm not sure
you can get around the assault charges, seeing as they were police
officers in uniform and you've obviously been busy making friends
during your time here."

"What's that supposed to mean?"

"You may be the favored prince in Mom's kingdom, but being
demanding in this place isn't going to get you far. You should have
used some of that charm to have them think you a nice guy, instead
of working to persuade them that you're a selfish prick."

"Hey, don't mince words on my behalf."

"I won't."

The pair glared at each other, then Zach shook his head and

grinned. "You know, I was expecting you to come in here with this all fixed up, that I would, you know, walk out of here with you today, but I got a feeling that that's not going to happen."

Matt closed the folder and dropped it into his briefcase. "Your day in court is Tuesday. I'd suggest you do yourself a favor and play nice with the locals over the weekend. A little sympathy for your cause could go a long way to mitigating the fines and . . ."

"Tuesday? *Tuesday!* What kind of shit is that?" Zach was on his feet, outraged as a toddler denied a chocolate in the check-out line. "I'm not staying here for the weekend. I've got things to do. I have a date. And besides, I'm innocent! Didn't you hear me? I'm innocent!"

Matt didn't have to call the guards: They were already at the door courtesy of Zach's shouting.

"Zach, this would be a lot easier if you just admitted the truth."

"Okay, okay, resisting arrest: absolutely." Zach raised his hands. "Because I should never have been arrested. Otherwise I'm as innocent as the day I was born."

Matt had long been of the opinion that Zach had been born looking for trouble, but it seemed a bad time to mention as much. "Well, you can tell the judge that on Tuesday. Maybe he'll even believe you. Have a good weekend."

"You're leaving? You're leaving, just like that? Leaving me here?" Zach sputtered and the guards grinned. "What kind of help is that?"

"You know enough about the law to know that there's process."

"I know enough about the law to know that a citizen shouldn't have to do time for something he never did." Zach straightened and gave Matt a disparaging glance, but Matt marched to the door.

"Maybe you're just not a good enough lawyer to get the job done," Zach called after him. "I heard you lost to James this week. What was the matter—couldn't you make it in court?"

Matt felt something come to a boil within him, but he turned a cool stare on his youngest brother. He walked slowly across the room, noting how Zach flinched. He clenched his fist and raised it slowly to Zach's chin, pushing it to a slight angle. "Lucky for you, you're in jail, little brother," he whispered, then waited until Zach's gaze flickered.

He paced crisply to the barred door, then paused to deliver his parting shot. "Well, then, you should be glad that you don't have to put up with me anymore. You're on your own, Zach. Maybe you can wring some value out of those two years of law school that Father paid for."

And he turned and left.

"You're not abandoning me!"

"No, I'm leaving you to your own formidable resources. I understand they're quite impressive."

One guard liked that one; Matt could tell by his snicker.

"I'll call James!"

Matt kept walking. "He didn't come the last time you called and he won't come the next time, either. Maybe you don't know that he promised Jimmy he wouldn't be bending the rules for you anymore: You know that anything James promises to his kids is inviolable."

Zach swore because he did know that.

Matt was almost at the end of the corridor when the inevitable shout of protest came from behind him.

"You bastard! I'll get you for this!"

Matt shook his head as the last guard opened the last gate. "It's just like when we were kids," he said, with a smile.

" 'Cept you grew up," she said with an answering smile and an appreciative glance.

The fact was that Matt had thought Zach should be left to his own resources for a long time. In a way he was glad to be the one to have done it. It hadn't been easy and he shouldn't have lost his temper, but maybe that had been necessary for Zach to take it seriously.

Matt took a deep breath and deliberately pushed his brother's plight out of his thoughts. He heard a bird sing and decided to walk, as it was such a beautiful afternoon.

Maybe he'd cook fish for dinner. There had to be a good seafood market here and he could go for some ceviche.

Chapter Eight

Mrs. Beaton was peering through her lacy drapes when Leslie started up her own front walk. Instead of playing the neighborhood game of pretending to not notice what other people are doing—or even their presence—Leslie gave the nosy widow a cavalier wave.

Mrs. Beaton disappeared in record speed, only a slight sway to the drapes revealing that she had ever been at the window. Leslie imagined her hyperventilating beneath her window and speculated that it would be a while before Mrs. Beaton watched so closely again.

She might have found that more amusing if the front door of her own house hadn't been standing open. This was strange and unusual on a Thursday afternoon, in case you aren't sure. Leslie might have blamed Annette, but there were boxes in the foyer.

And a moving truck parked at the curb.

Leslie's first thought was that they were being robbed.

Her second was that it must be true that thieves weren't often clever. She and Matt didn't have much worth stealing in terms of its resale value—few electronic toys, no new ones, no jewelery, cash, or booze.

Still, it was all theirs.

Leslie ran into the house, forgetting everything she'd ever read about not surprising villains in one's own home. She dodged boxes and shouted for Annette, which wasn't, in hindsight, the most circumspect way of finding out what was going on.

To her dismay, Annette didn't answer.

To her relief, the Coxwell furniture was right where it belonged: There were just boxes and other pieces of furniture in between. Come to think of it, some of it looked familiar, as if it had come from another Coxwell residence. Leslie heard the sound of an argument in the kitchen and was reassured: Thieves surely wouldn't pause to argue.

She made her way toward the kitchen, trying not to think that it would fit her luck to end up confronting the only two stupid violent thieves in the greater Boston area.

"I'm telling you, lady, we don't have a lot of time." Leslie reached the kitchen door in time to see a burly stranger tap his watch. "I gotta know where you want all this stuff, so me and my boys can get this job done and get back to punch out. Everybody's ready to finish this day, that's for sure." He glared at his opponent.

Who proved to be Leslie's mother-in-law, Beverly Coxwell.

Beverly glared back. "Well, you're mistaken if you think that I have any desire to prolong this interaction. Your hourly rates are appallingly high, outrageous really . . ."

"And we can argue about them while you're racking up more of them, or you can tell me where you want all this stuff, I can get done, and we can stop the clock. You're lucky we were able to accommodate you on such short notice."

Beverly shook a finger at the mover, who had to be a foot taller than her and three times her weight. "You are impertinent . . ."

"And you're drunk. Nobody's perfect. Where do you want this junk?"

"It is not junk. That table in particular is a very nice example of a Biedermeier . . ."

Leslie chose that moment to clear her throat and declare her presence. "Hi. Maybe someone could tell me what's going on."

"Leslie!" Beverly swept across the kitchen, giving Leslie an air kiss on each cheek. They might have been meeting at a swish garden party, all flowing chiffon, broad brimmed hats, and little tiny sandwiches. It was odd to be greeted this way in her own currently crowded kitchen, which made Leslie suspect the show of affection was for the mover's benefit.

Something was different about Beverly, but Leslie couldn't put her finger on it right away.

"I'm so glad to see you," Beverly declared, for possibly the first time in their entire relationship. Leslie blinked because her words even sounded sincere. "I just know that you'll have this arranged in no time at all. You are the most organized person alive, after all."

It was on the tip of Leslie's tongue to observe that she was only welcome because she was useful, but that would have been bitchy. She chose to be less confrontational.

For the moment.

"What exactly am I arranging?" Leslie glanced around at the boxes.

"Didn't James phone you?"

"No. Why would James phone me?"

"To tell you, of course, that I was very rudely evicted today from my condo rental and to explain that the only possible solution to the dilemma under the circumstances was for me to stay here." Beverly waved a hand, as if this was painfully evident.

Ipso facto. Leslie could imagine her brother-in-law making the same cavalier gesture, although she found it hard to believe that he would have made the same conclusion. James was usually quite gracious about respecting boundaries.

He hadn't gotten that from his mother, who seemed to think that everyone around her was staff.

Maybe she only thought Leslie was staff, seeing as Leslie never had been and never would be of the same social circle as the Coxwells. And Leslie'd probably never learn enough of those little cavalier gestures to fool anyone into thinking she belonged in those circles.

Beverly gestured to the large man behind her, who watched this exchange with a measure of amusement. "Hence the movers who, I don't need to tell you, charge an outrageous hourly fee. It would be best, Leslie, if you could promptly tell them where you want everything so they could get finished as quickly as possible."

Her expectations clear, Beverly turned as if she meant to leave.

The mover covered his smile with one meaty paw as he watched Leslie struggle to find the words.

Or at least some polite ones. "I don't mean to be slow, Beverly, but maybe you could confirm to me just what 'everything' is?"

She blinked. "Well, *everything*."

"Are we talking about the entire contents of your condo? That's what they're moving into my house?"

"Well, where else would I put it?"

Leslie bit her tongue, because she was about to ask her mother-in-law if she could spell "storage locker."

That *would* be bitchy.

The mover tapped his toe and looked at his watch.

"I suppose some of it could be put in storage," Leslie suggested.

Beverly arched a brow. "Not all of it. The antiques need to be in a temperature and humidity controlled environment, and it's much simpler to store them here. I'll need my clothes and personal effects, after all. Anything else, of course, could be put into storage, if you could just sort them out. I haven't had the time today, with being so rushed."

"You were evicted suddenly?"

"No notice. It was very rude."

"You were lucky to get a moving team," the mover said.

Beverly took a steadying breath as she looked him up and

down, then seemed to decide against expressing any gratitude about the availability of these movers. Instead she smiled at Leslie. "Honestly, it's not as if I have a great many personal possessions."

It seemed to Leslie that her house was full of a great many personal possessions, but then Beverly lived on a different scale. Leslie supposed that could happen to a person who grew up with Gray Gables, the fabulous Coxwell house in Rosemount, as a summer cottage. There was a house that Leslie loved but which would always be beyond her aspirations and income bracket.

And of course, in a house like that, this array of stuff would practically disappear. She supposed she shouldn't be too hard on Beverly for having different expectations.

Beverly waved a hand. "Most everything is at the house and will be tied up with the investigation and settling of the estate, anyway."

That comment made Leslie realize just how much strain her mother-in-law had faced this week.

In fact at the word "estate," Beverly sat down so abruptly at the kitchen table that her legs might have given out beneath her. She immediately began rummaging in a carry-on bag that was dropped beside the kitchen table. She came up with a slender thermos, poured herself a capful of its contents—which did not steam—then tossed it back like a shot of vodka.

Leslie suddenly remembered what the mover had said.

Beverly then exhaled, straightened her shoulders, and smiled pertly at Leslie. There was a light in her eyes that practically dared either of them to ask what she'd been drinking, and her hand shook ever so slightly.

Leslie had a pretty good idea what was in the thermos, and it wasn't herbal tea. Beverly wasn't having as easy a time with Robert's death as Leslie might have assumed.

But then Beverly had married the man once, so must have seen some redeeming features in him. Maybe he had changed. Either way Leslie decided to cut her mother-in-law as much slack as she needed.

"Don't worry, Beverly, I'll take care of it."

"I know that everything will be fine," Beverly said to Leslie, her voice a little bit higher than it was usually. "Now that you're here, taking charge. I trust you, Leslie, to resolve everything in a competent and reasonable fashion. Efficiency is your best trait, after all. It's so nice to have someone to rely upon in a crisis."

"You make it sound as if you're leaving."

"I am! The girls and I have an appointment, so there's no choice. Fortunately you arrived home in the very nick of time."

She stood then and straightened the chic little suit that probably cost more than Leslie earned in a month. She pulled out a compact, touched up her lipstick, tucked a hair into place, then snapped it closed and put it back in her purse.

"I shall see you later then. Don't trouble to wait dinner for me."

Dinner? Leslie glanced around the kitchen, realizing what was missing. No one had made dinner, because Matt wasn't here and the dinner fairy was clearly slacking off in his absence.

The kitchen seemed to yawn with emptiness, and Leslie knew it wasn't just because there were no luscious smells rising to tempt her to the table. She felt flat, as if nothing in her life had any point, as if she were just trudging through an endless desert.

Matt was gone. It seemed a bit late to be doing the math, and Leslie figured she'd be doing it over and over again for quite a while. The house was infused with Matt and she'd be finding his specter at every turn.

Maybe forever.

Meanwhile Beverly smiled, lifted her carry-on bag, scooped up her purse, and sashayed across the kitchen. En route to the front door, she paused to peck Leslie's cheek and murmured a low warning as she did so. "Don't let them take advantage of you."

"I won't."

"I knew I could count on you."

"I know what's different!" Leslie said with a snap of her fingers. "You've changed your hair." Beverly's hair had been a rich shade of brown for all the years Leslie had known her, then her mother-in-law had let it go silver these past couple of years. Leslie smiled, thinking a compliment might be just what Beverly needed. "I like it better this color. It makes you look younger."

Instead Beverly's eyes welled with tears and she turned abruptly away. Beverly said nothing, admitted nothing, simply turned and marched through the foyer.

What had Leslie said?

Wait—Beverly had said "the girls"? What girls?

Leslie might have pursued Beverly, but that woman stepped nimbly aside as something large loomed in the front doorway. Then she darted out of the house while Leslie was confronted with the large something.

It was an antique French armoire, the one that Leslie had last seen in the living room of Beverly's condo. It was a massive and impressive piece of furniture, one that Leslie had always admired. Beverly had told her once that it was seventeenth century, inherited from her family, though what Leslie liked better than the age of the piece was the rich honeyed hue those years had given to the wood's patina.

It was a piece of furniture she always wanted to caress.

And now it was here, in her house, looking more enormous and formidable than she'd ever imagined it to be.

"Where do you want it, lady?"

The mover in the kitchen didn't say anything, just waited with his arms braced across his chest. Leslie looked around her comparatively small house, seeing immediately that the huge armoire wouldn't make it up the stairs or through the doorway to the kitchen. It would fill the foyer to impassable if left there, though.

There was only one place it could go.

"Well, we never use the living room anyway," she said decisively. "Maybe we can move all of my things aside and fit Beverly's in there, too."

That way, Beverly's belongings could go out the door as easily as they'd come in.

There was an optimistic thought.

The man who appeared to be in charge followed Leslie into the living room and began to move her furniture aside with surprising care. "It'll be jam-packed in here," he warned her. "For someone with few possessions, that lady has a lot of stuff."

Leslie shrugged. "I don't have another solution. By the time I sort out the antiques and her clothes to stay, there won't be enough left to bother storing. It would be great if you could leave her clothing closer to the door, so she can reach anything she needs."

"Otherwise I'm betting you'll have to fish it out."

Leslie smiled. "I think you'd win that one."

"She's one crusty bit of work. Old Mass money, I'll bet."

Leslie nodded.

"They're like that. Ready to squeeze every dime until it begs for mercy. Your mother?"

Leslie almost laughed. "My mother-in-law."

He rolled his eyes. "That's some kind of news to come home to, huh?"

Leslie gave him a look, feeling driven to defend Beverly. She might be an elitist snob, but she came by it honestly, and her heart was good. "Actually she's had quite a shock. You might have read in the paper about her husband's sudden death two days ago. Judge Coxwell?"

"That was your father-in-law?"

Leslie nodded again as the mover whistled under his breath. He looked assessingly after Beverly. "Now there was a judge you could count on. He was ex-military, you know. Marines. My cousin knew him in the service, said he was a stickler for procedure but a man you could always count on to do the right thing."

Leslie blinked at this unexpected endorsement of Robert's

character. "Well, if you could leave her personal effects closer to the door here, that would make this situation easier for everyone."

"No problem. Judge Coxwell. Huh."

The two men carrying the armoire made a sound of protest, drawing his attention once again. He waved them into the room, gesturing Leslie out of the way. The armoire moved steadily toward her, like an ocean freighter under full steam. She was a bit stunned at how much of the room that armoire consumed even when it was against the wall.

It looked ridiculous. Good thing she had no chance of ever owning such a thing.

"It's a question of scale," the mover said sagely. "The proportions between the piece and the room are not in sync. You'd need a bigger place to make it look good, higher ceilings and such." He smiled encouragingly. "Maybe your next place."

"As if!" Leslie said, with a laugh. Once she might have agreed easily with him, filled with optimism about the future—now she knew she'd be glad to just manage to keep this house. "It's a lot more likely that we'll just move that monster out of here one of these days."

"Easy for you to say," one of the movers joked as he straightened and rubbed his back. "That's one heavy bas—"

"Hey! There's a lady present!" The lead mover snapped his fingers and set them all to work *toute de suite*.

Leslie supposed that somewhere there was a cold beer waiting somewhere with his name on it.

*   *   *

It wasn't long until the contents of the truck had been disgorged, primarily into the living room, and the paperwork had been signed. The house looked like a train had hit it—or maybe a tornado—and Leslie's nerves were jangled by the complete dishevelment of her home.

She headed for the kitchen in search of Annette and solace, not necessarily in that order.

She could only hope that she wasn't supposed to pay for the movers, too. She was definitely not in the mood to call her brother-in-law James (court victor, champion, etc.) to find out. It would have been an understatement to say that contact between the two factions of the Coxwell clan had been strained these past two years. Leslie wasn't ready to be the one to expend the energy to mend fences. Not right now anyway, though the job would probably fall into her lap eventually.

Family Diplomat. Oh yes, she'd almost forgotten that virtual burden.

Maybe she'd just rip up the bill when it came.

If it came.

Leslie optimistically checked the freezer, but it was empty except for some ice cubes that had wasted away to one fifth of their original size. They looked particularly lonely and pathetic. She couldn't blame them. The fact that no ice cream had spontaneously manifested itself in the freezer left her feeling lonely and pathetic, too.

She prowled the perimeter of the kitchen, finding nothing to eat that was horribly bad for her body and thus potentially satisfying for her soul.

This did not improve her mood. Matt, to his credit, was a bit fanatical about whole foods, a concept that was much easier to endorse when he was home to shop and cook those whole foods into yummy meals. There was something particularly uninspiring about a jar of uncooked lentils, however wholesome they might be, after a long day of battling the encroaching tide of commercialism.

And the buzz from this morning's coffee was long gone. The sliding glass door to the patio was slightly open, and Leslie moved impatiently to close it, assuming it had been the movers who had left it open. Maybe they'd snuck out back for a cigarette before she'd gotten home.

But no. Annette was hunched in a lawn chair on the patio, glowering into the distance like a fat, cranky, elderly cat. Leslie leaned against the door jamb, thinking her daughter's pose and expression echoed her own mood perfectly.

"Hi," she said when Annette made no acknowledgement of her presence. "Guess we've got to fire the ice cream fairy, too."

Annette exhaled in what could have been a disguised laugh. Encouraged, Leslie dropped into the lawn chair she had occupied the night before. It was cloudy, damp, and not as nice for sitting outside. "How's it going?"

"Is *she* gone?"

Leslie nodded. Beverly had no name in many of these discussions, but there was no doubt who Annette meant.

"Then it's going better, thanks very much. Is *she* coming back?"

"I think *she's* moving in."

Annette made a sound of disgust. "She was here when I got home from school, with a moving truck out front, tapping her toe and asking for the keys. No, she demanded the keys, like I was some . . . some minion!"

"That's a new word."

"It was in a book I read. I looked it up."

Some fantasy novel, undoubtedly. Annette had been reading Dungeons & Dragons–flavored fiction for years, ever since Matt had read her *The Hobbit* at bedtime and started an addiction. Leslie could hardly argue against fiction that owed so much to medieval stories. "It was nice of you to let her in."

"I was thinking about not doing it."

"I believe it. Glad to see you two are still getting along famously. Just like oil and water."

Annette almost laughed again, casting Leslie a sparkling glance. "You're full of it. You're not glad at all."

"Actually, I am. It's reassuring to see that some things haven't changed, especially when so much has." Leslie realized a bit too

late that she had said too much, but to her relief, it slipped right
past Annette.

"She thinks I'm too fat. And you know, I don't care what she
thinks, it's just that she keeps on about it. It's rude."

"It is rude."

"You agree with me?" Annette turned in surprise.

"Sure. But being rude in return doesn't solve much, does it?"

"So what am I supposed to do? Agree with her?"

"Do you?" Annette slanted one of those lethal glances at Leslie,
and Leslie smiled. "Not going there, huh?" Annette looked away
again. Leslie straightened and folded her fingers together. "So
maybe it would be easier if you understood a bit more about your
grandmother."

"Like what? That she's mean to kids for the fun of it?"

Leslie smiled. "You're not a child, not anymore." She knew she
had Annette's attention, so she spoke with care. "I don't really
know much about how your grandmother thinks, so this is just
conjecture, but I'm wondering if she sees herself in you."

"Maybe two of her," Annette joked with surprising self-
deprecation, flashing a smile when Leslie laughed in surprise. "Seriously, I'm not like her at all."

"You don't think so? You look like her a little, you know, especially around the eyes."

"No way!"

"Yes way. That's why people said from when you were a baby that
you'd be a beauty, because you always looked a bit like Beverly."

"She is kind of pretty." This admission was made grudgingly
and immediately amended. "For an old person."

Leslie fought a smile. "And maybe there's a less obvious resemblance, too. You like food, maybe you like it a little too much.
Maybe food takes the place of something else for you."

"Like what?"

"Reassurance. Comfort. Security. Pleasure." Leslie shrugged.

"Only you know the key that makes you eat. Maybe it's how you deal with fear or stress—that's my big trigger."

Annette rolled her eyes. "You have no trigger for overeating. Look at you! You can't weigh a hundred and twenty pounds!"

"Well, that's not likely to last." Leslie ticked off her fingers. "In the last thirty-six hours, I've eaten twelve chocolate bars, way too many Vietnamese noodles, two muffins, a serving of yogurt and fruit—"

"Yogurt and fruit does not count as food."

"Then what is it?"

"Fiber." This word came with a sneer.

"This is an inventory. Everything gets included." Leslie considered her count. "I would have eaten a carton of ice cream last night, too, if you hadn't beaten me to it. And I haven't even had dinner yet tonight. I've got to be looking at more than three thousand calories a day. If that's not overeating for someone who gets as little exercise as I do, I don't know what is."

"So what's wrong? What are you afraid of?"

Leslie blinked. Annette had connected those dots more quickly than she had anticipated. "That's no one's business but mine. What you need to decide is what makes you eat, then you can figure out what to do instead."

"What do you mean?"

"If, just for example, I was eating because I was afraid, then I could name that fear. Once I knew what was spooking me, I could reason out a way to make it less scary. Theoretically then I'd have less desire to hoover ice cream and chocolate."

"Sounds too easy."

"No, it works."

"You're going to tell me that you're the living proof of that?"

"Until yesterday, yeah, pretty much." Until yesterday, when she'd faced the unexpected prospect of life without Matt. That was so scary that it was hard to even think it, let alone say it, let alone work out a response to it.

Leslie felt an itch for chocolate.

Annette stared across the yard, considering this slice of wisdom. "So what does this give me in common with Grandmother?"

"Same mechanism, different stressbuster. You know that your grandmother goes to Alcoholics Anonymous."

Annette nodded, eyes widening.

"She's been a compulsive drinker as long as I've known her, probably longer than that."

"Duh."

"So she's getting help to stop that. You have to admire that, at least."

"Maybe."

"My point is simply that maybe she perceives that you two share a weakness, that you also think that putting something in your mouth will solve whatever's bothering you. And she knows that doesn't work from her own experience, but unfortunately she doesn't know how to share that information with you. So she criticizes, hoping to make an impression that way."

"It makes an impression all right," Annette said sourly. "I hate her guts."

"No, you don't. If anything, you hate her mouth."

Annette laughed, a chortle that showed she had been surprised. "I like you better when you're funny."

"Well, thanks for that."

Annette was thinking about Leslie's words, though, the proverbial wood burning so ferociously that Leslie was half-afraid of what her daughter would ask next.

Fortunately the telephone rang.

Leslie snapped her fingers. "That's probably your father. Why don't you talk to him?" Annette's face lit up. "Go! Go, before the machine takes the call."

Annette ran, which had to be good for her. The happy burble of her voice a moment later revealed that Leslie had named the caller right.

Which meant that the Queen of Efficiency had another job to
do before she could sleep or eat. *Household Administrator* was the
duty of choice. *File Master*—or *File Mistress*, as the case might be.
Leslie headed for the filing drawer in the desk in the spare room,
which had been Matt's home office. Within hours, it would have to
be Beverly's pied-à-terre. She was fishing the credit-card invoices
out of the files before she had the brilliant idea of having Annette
give the information to her father.

That way she wouldn't have to talk to Matt herself.

Perfect, if cowardly. Leslie decided that she could live with that.
She had to think about what she would say to Matt, how she could
explain that she couldn't just blow off her own job after he'd
blown off his best chance of having one.

Money didn't grow on trees, after all.

Besides she needed to go to the grocery store if they were going
to eat anything resembling real food for dinner.

And it was past six already.

*   *   *

Beverly hated being late, but late she was. She couldn't find the address the lawyer had given her, not right away, and was compelled
to make a U-turn on a busy street to try it again. The address she
sought was on a street she didn't know well, where there were lots
of little office parks and strip malls, the kind of neighborhood with
fast-food restaurants she would never patronize. And it was rush
hour, so it was difficult to slow down enough to read addresses
without getting rear-ended.

And to be fair, she was irked. Not only had she had two dogs
dumped on her without warning, but they had an appointment
that had to be kept, courtesy of the same lawyer who had pressed
their leashes into her hands. The icing on the cake, of course, had
been her landlord meeting her in the lobby with the eviction notice
for her condo.

It was true that no dogs were allowed in the building, but the paperwork had been done before Beverly even knew she'd have dogs. No, the prime mover was one Robert Coxwell, to whom she had assigned power of attorney many drunken moons ago, who had never been a man to overlook a tool he could use.

Before he killed himself, knowing full well that all of his assets—and thus Beverly's—would be knotted up for months, he had served notice to the condo that there would be no further rental payments made. It had been one last act of vengeance, one that made Beverly hope they did meet in Hell, just so she could give him a piece of her mind.

And really, a trick like that wouldn't look good on his application for Heaven.

Beverly finally pulled into the parking lot of the vet's office, a good thirty minutes late and harried. After one sniff, Champagne whimpered and Caviar laid down on the back seat, hiding her snout under one paw.

It was almost as if they knew where they were. Beverly wondered whether these dogs really were as smart as their PR maintained.

"Well, don't get too worried about it," she counseled. She had already taken to the habit of talking to the girls as if they were people. It seemed as if they understood, but then that impression could have had as much to do with the fact that she was slightly sizzled as with their reputed intelligence. "We're late and they're supposed to be closed by now. You might be home free, for tonight at least."

The girls leapt out of the car with admirable grace and stood patiently while Beverly gathered their leashes and locked the door. She liked their manners. They might not be anxious to go to the vet, but they weren't going to make a scene. Beverly had to admire any creature with social graces. She also liked the way they walked demurely beside her, not pulling or sniffing disgusting things on the ground.

Marissa had trained the girls well.

Beverly hurried to the door, as if that would make a difference to her expectations. There were other businesses in this particular plaza and a few other cars in the lot, though she had no way of knowing which cars were at which establishments. Her heart sank when the door proved to be locked. Sure enough, the hours posted on the door declared that the office had closed twenty minutes before.

Beverly swore slightly under her breath. The girls watched her with some trepidation, poised to go back to the car if she gave the slightest sign.

"I guess we'll have to come back tomorrow," she told them and they pivoted as one, their tails high again.

Beverly was halfway to the car when a door scraped behind her. "Are you Beverly Coxwell?"

She spun in shock at hearing her own name. A man in his forties was holding open the door to the vet's office, his white lab coat giving one good clue as to who he might be.

"How did you guess?"

He smiled. "Caviar and Champagne, of course. Marissa told me about you and when I heard the news . . ." He shrugged. "You could say that I was expecting you."

It was his smile, however fleeting, that unnerved Beverly. It wasn't that he was such a fabulously handsome man, or that she was unaccustomed to people being friendly. Even from halfway across the parking lot, she could see something in his smile, something appreciative and flirtatious, something that made her want to leap into her car and drive far, far away.

"Well, you're closed. We're late." Beverly spoke with uncharacteristic haste. "We'll come back another day."

"Oh, you don't need to do that. I'm in no rush to get stuck in traffic. Come on in." He stepped back, still holding the door.

Beverly looked to the girls for guidance. They seemed to have mixed feelings about this vet. Their tails wagged, but not wildly, and they held their ground.

So he was a nice man, but a vet all the same.

Maybe it would be better to get this over with.

"Come on then," she said crisply to the girls. "Anything is worse if you put it off." She met the warmth in the vet's gaze—which only grew warmer as she got closer—and wondered who the heck she was trying to convince.

"I'm Dr. Matheson. Ross Matheson," the vet said, offering Beverly his hand. She shook it, not knowing what else to do.

"Well, you already know who I am," she said, feeling flustered, and he smiled.

"And it's good to see the girls again." He was a tall man, built lithe and lean, who had to bend down to greet the girls. His hair was thinning but clearly had been blond. His eyes were brown with a bit of green and his smile was easy. Beverly watched him pat the girls and saw gentle strength in his hands.

A biscuit each and they remembered that he was more or less trustworthy.

"Come on in. We'll just do a checkup. It won't take long. No shots this time, either; they have them all done later in the spring along with their heartworm tests."

"Of course," Beverly said, as if she knew what he was talking about. Shots? Heartworm? No wonder they were suspicious of him. She wasn't much for shots herself and though she didn't know what heartworm was, she felt some trepidation in the company of someone who could easily say such a word.

Maybe that was what had her flustered.

"I suggested this appointment so that you could ask any questions about the girls that you might have."

"I don't know what to ask."

"Have you had dogs before?"

"Never."

"Ah, well, they're both spayed, and are almost three years old. The breeder is one I work with a lot, a very careful breeder. I have some of the genetic records for their parents here, if you're curious."

"Not really. So long as they're healthy. Are they sisters then?" Beverly was surprised that she hadn't thought of that.

But then it wasn't as if they had a long intimate acquaintance.

"Yes. Same litter. They have three brothers and two more sisters, though I only see the eldest male in my practice. The others were taken by families farther away." Dr. Matheson glanced up briefly. "He's a chocolate. Beautiful dog. They're showing him and he's doing quite well." He patted Champagne before checking her teeth. "Though you two have the easier life, that's for sure."

Beverly could tell that Champagne didn't like having her lip pulled back, though she didn't bite or growl. It was more the look in her eyes, as if she felt rebellious but knew it would be vulgar to do anything about it.

Beverly could relate to that look.

Caviar watched, then laid down on the examining room floor with her paws curled beneath her. She trembled a little, so she wasn't big on having her teeth checked, either.

Beverly found herself squatting down to pat Caviar, who then leaned against her leg and trembled a bit less. The dog licked Beverly's fingertips, as if to thank her, and remarkably, Beverly didn't mind a little dog spit on her hand.

"I don't know why Marissa left me her dogs." Beverly felt a strange need to say something. The room seemed so small and so quiet. "I never even knew she had them until today."

"Because she knew the three of you would look good together, of course," the vet said, with easy charm.

"Be serious."

"All right. She thought you needed some company."

"I don't think so . . ."

"No? Well, that's what she told me. And she was convinced that there was no better company for a woman alone than the girls. She spent her time with them, after all." He gave her a piercing look. "How's that for a serious answer?"

So Dr. Matheson knew that Beverly lived alone. That was a bit disconcerting. "Sound like something Marissa would say. She always thought she knew what was best for everybody."

"So you'd prefer to be alone?"

"I didn't say that."

"I didn't think so. How'd you like to go for dinner sometime, Beverly Coxwell? I can provide a couple of good references." He gestured to the girls, both pleased with him now that he was leaving their teeth alone and offering them each a biscuit.

"I'm married," Beverly said curtly.

"That's a different kind of being alone, isn't it?" he mused, as if he didn't really expect an answer.

Beverly was intrigued by his comment but said nothing. She liked that he didn't press her for information or confidences, didn't push her about dinner.

What did he know about lonely marriages?

He checked Champagne's ears and Beverly watched him. "See this hair here?" he asked, and Beverly had to move directly beside him to see what he meant. "You need to pull it out, once a week or so."

She looked at him with horror. "You're joking."

"No, I'm not." He grabbed the fine hair in the curve of Champagne's ear and pulled it out. The dog looked bored, so at least it wasn't a painful exercise. "It doesn't hurt them, though it can if you leave it to grow. Poodles have the distinction of having hair grow in their ear canals: If you leave it, it fosters infection."

"I'm too busy to do that."

"Oh? What do you do?"

"If I did nothing all the bloody day long, I'd be too busy to do that."

He laughed. "Did you get the ear drops from Marissa?"

"I have no idea."

"I'll give you another bottle. You just pour in a drop or two once a week. It helps to manage the wax. Do it on a different day than you pull out the hair."

"I told you . . ."

"Well, you can bring them here, then, and I'll pull it out. It'll give me more time to persuade you to go for dinner."

Beverly eyed him, not bothering to hide her suspicion. "Sounds as if I'll need a schedule."

He laughed, a rich sound that put Beverly more at ease. "I doubt it. Marissa used to say that they would remind her, by putting their heads in her lap when their ears needed attention. I guess they get uncomfortable and they're smart enough to know that people can fix the problem for them."

Beverly blinked. "Caviar was trying to do that this afternoon. I wondered what she was doing."

"Well, then we'd better have a look at those ears, hadn't we, Caviar?"

Caviar proved to have wax gathering in one ear, which the vet easily removed. It didn't look much different from human ear wax. Beverly watched, still skeptical that she'd be able to do this task in the future.

When he was done, there was no doubt that the dog was relieved: Shy Caviar licked his ear and wagged her tail in gratitude. "None of that now," he teased her. "You'll be making Mrs. Coxwell jealous."

Beverly laughed despite herself. "There's wishful thinking."

He turned a sparkling gaze on her. "Maybe there is a bit of that. Your husband's a lucky man, Mrs. Coxwell. Maybe you should remind him of it."

Beverly turned away, grief catching her by surprise. She gripped the stainless steel table behind her. "He's dead," she said, not meaning to do so and probably just as surprised as the vet when the words leaped out. "Maybe you read about Judge Coxwell in the paper."

"Oh, I'm so sorry. That was thoughtless of me . . ."

"You could never have known and there are too many Coxwells around here for you to have guessed." Beverly straightened and looked him in the eye. "He committed suicide, and I never anticipated it. I still can't really believe it."

"I can imagine as much. I'm very sorry."

Because he was sincere—a nice man despite being a vet, as the girls might have said—and because it had been a long time since Robert Coxwell had had much claim on her heart, Beverly confessed a little more. "We've been estranged for a while, which was probably what Marissa meant. In fact, we were in the middle of a divorce."

"Been there, done that," he said with a smile. "But my ex-wife just ran away to Seattle with her new girlfriend."

"No."

"Yes." He smiled. "I was the proverbial last person to know. Not quite so dramatic as your story."

"Oh, I don't know. It's a story that would still have people talking."

"But it wouldn't make the papers."

Beverly had to concede that, so she didn't know what to say.

Dr. Matheson patted the dogs, as if he was also at a loss for words, then gave them each another biscuit.

"They're going to get fat, having so many snacks at once."

He was unchastened. "It would be good to do their heartworm tests around the beginning of May, though you're welcome to come back sooner if you have any questions."

He seemed more somber than he had and Beverly felt responsible for the change in his mood. She had the urge to prompt his smile again. "Or if the girls need their ears cleaned."

"Or that. Of course." He nodded, still serious.

"Or presumably if I have a burning desire to go for dinner."

He smiled then, a smile of surprise, and their gazes met. "No, you can just phone for that. No appointment necessary."

Beverly cleared her throat. "You must know that I'm a lot older than you."

He shrugged. "You can't mean to argue that women aren't attractive once they pass thirty, because if you do, you'll get a good fight from me."

"I'm serious."

"So am I."

Their gazes locked and held for a long moment, one that left Beverly's mouth dry.

She really shouldn't have drank that sherry this afternoon. It was clearly affecting her thinking and her judgement.

She made hasty excuses to leave, and the girls were right there with her. Dr. Matheson accompanied her to the door, locking it behind her when the girls made a beeline for the car. When Beverly glanced back, he was still standing there. He smiled and waved, and before he turned away, Beverly smiled back.

"A nice man, for a vet," she told the girls, but they just leaped into the back seat of the car and looked anywhere but back toward the office.

Chapter Nine

The front door was unlocked and no one answered her knock, so Beverly walked directly into Matt and Leslie's house. She shouted a greeting to no reply, though there was music coming from the kitchen.

Loud music.

Beverly grimaced, guessing that Leslie was out and she'd have to face That Child herself. She stepped into the kitchen to find her worst nightmare: Annette making herself a sandwich, probably a predinner snack, one that could have been a reasonable meal for three.

Despite the music, Annette must have heard her. She glanced over her shoulder, giving Beverly a dark glare.

Beverly crossed the kitchen and turned off the radio. She could have sworn that Annette hissed: She certainly hunkered down and glowered.

Beverly refused to consider the origin of the child's manners. She wasn't precisely a snob, but neither had she been pleased by Matt's choice of a wife.

The product of their marriage was no better mannered than a feral cat, Beverly thought.

Witch, thought Annette.

Then they smiled simultaneously, false bright social smiles that faded as quickly as they had appeared. Beverly leaned against the counter, wondering whether the child had learned something from her, after all.

Beverly glanced over the makings of Annette's sandwich, then let her lips tighten. "I hate to be the one to disillusion you, Annette, but mayonnaise is not a beverage."

Annette left the ample dollop of mayonnaise on her sandwich and the knife in the jar, undoubtedly on purpose. She closed the sandwich with care and took a large deliberate bite. Beverly didn't doubt that this bit of theatrics was for her benefit.

Annette then looked her grandmother up and down while she chewed with some exaggeration. "I hate to be the one to disillusion you, Grandmother, but no one really thinks you're toting tea in that thermos."

So the cat had teeth. Little sharp ones. Beverly straightened, because this exchange had just gotten interesting.

At least the child was bright.

* * *

Annette saw immediately that she had drawn her grandmother's fire. "You are an audacious child . . ." the witch began to lecture, though there was an appreciative gleam in her eyes that Annette couldn't explain.

"I'm just trying to get into the spirit of this relationship," Annette said with an audacity she hadn't known she possessed. "You hand lots of truth to me, so I thought I'd hand some back to you. How'm I doing?"

Call 1-800-SMACK-ME, Annette thought as she watched emotion flit across the witch's usually impassive features. That was what she called her grandmother in her own thoughts—the witch—since Beverly was unnaturally young, thin, beautiful, and had an evil heart.

Maybe she ate children instead of just being nasty to them.

Oh, what the hell. "Can't you get wrinkles from looking like that?"

Beverly laughed unexpectedly. "No, you're supposed to tell me that the wind will blow and my face will stick in that expression for the rest of my life. That's what my mother used to threaten."

"My other grandma used to say that."

"Grandma? You've never called me grandma."

"Big surprise."

Beverly braced a hand on the counter, the other on her hip. "You shouldn't take that tone with me."

"You shouldn't be mean to me," Annette retorted. "You're supposed to be my grandmother. You're supposed to spoil me and buy me things and be nice to me."

Beverly considered Annette so shrewdly that Annette was acutely aware of every flaw in her appearance. The hems of her jeans were frayed, her T-shirt didn't quite pull over her skin to meet the waistband of the jeans. To her astonishment, though Beverly clearly noted these items of inappropriate deportment, she didn't comment on them. "Is that what your other grandma used to do?"

Annette nodded, her sandwich not looking that tasty anymore. "Yeah, she did. She bought me stuff that Mom wouldn't. She always made me promise that it would be our secret, so that Mom wouldn't say I was getting spoiled and give her heck for it."

"What kind of stuff?"

Annette shrugged. "Videos, then DVDs."

"Of what?"

"An entire season of *Babylon Five*, or vintage stuff like *Battlestar Galactica* or *Space 2000*." Her grandmother looked predictably blank. "Or whatever other science fiction and fantasy stuff I wanted. We used to play Dungeons & Dragons together when I was little." Annette doubted that the witch even knew what that was, though she was surprised that she admitted it.

"Is that a game?"

"Yeah. A role-playing game."

"I don't ever remember playing a game with you."

Annette snorted. "Because it never happened. It's not like you forgot."

Beverly considered her perfect nails for a long moment—what would Annette give to have nails like that? Lots. Was that what the witch would offer to her in exchange for her heart?—then looked up so suddenly that Annette jumped. "I haven't been very good at this grandmother stuff, have I?"

It seemed silly to lie. They were dealing truth, after all. "No." Annette took a big bite of her sandwich and chewed it with vigor. It did seem to have a little too much mayonnaise, though she'd never admit that now.

"No need to mince words. That's fair enough," her grandmother said, with a certain decisiveness. "I'll bet you miss your other grandma." This time there was a slight emphasis on the last word.

"So what if I do? That isn't going to change anything, is it?"

"Not that she's passed away, no." This grandmother spoke to Annette as if she were an adult, which was appealing in a way. "Be warned that I'll never play games with you or anyone else, that's for certain. It's not my style. Life is full of games and I've already had my fill." She looked tired all of a sudden, but Annette wasn't about to be sympathetic.

It was probably just a trick.

"That doesn't sound very promising, in a grandmotherly kind of way."

Beverly laughed a little. "No, it doesn't, does it? Well I think we've pretty much agreed that I've been lousy at being a grandmother, so there's nowhere to go from here but up."

Annette didn't know what to say to that, but fortunately, her mother came home before things got really awkward.

In fact, her mother marched into the kitchen as Annette was taking another bite out of her sandwich. "Annette! I'm just going to make dinner! Why are you having a snack?"

Annette pushed the mouthful of food into her cheek, feeling an urge to provoke her mother since the witch wasn't biting. "I didn't know how long you'd be at the grocery store."

Her mother's eyes flashed, predictably. "You know better than to talk with food in your mouth. What will Beverly think of your manners?"

"I was hungry."

"I've already seen her manners," Beverly said wearily. "You should give her to me for a month. I'd straighten her out."

Annette swallowed and straightened in alarm. "Mom?"

But her mom wasn't paying attention. "Well, it took longer than I'd hoped at the grocery. I couldn't find what I wanted for the longest time." Her mom put a bag of groceries on the counter and shook her head. "Of course, I don't know when I was last at that grocery store. Annette, would you help me with the bags, please? There are more in the car."

"Can I move the car into the garage if I do?"

Her mom gave her a look, but instead of declining immediately, she seemed to think about it. "Does your father usually let you do that?"

Annette shrugged, finding it harder to lie to her mother than it had been just a week before.

"I've got an idea," Beverly said. Had she deliberately saved Annette from further interrogation? It sure seemed like it, as odd as that was. Probably she was going to offer a more fearsome alternative. *Let's toss Annette into the snake pit instead.* "Why don't you move my car into the driveway?"

Annette looked up in astonishment, just in time to catch the keys that were flying across the kitchen. "Your car?"

"Yes, my car."

Maybe there was some dark diabolical reason for the witch being nice all of a sudden.

Maybe Annette's virgin heart looked particularly tasty.

"Beverly! Are you sure? I mean, the Jaguar is an expensive car."

"True." Beverly nodded to a shocked Annette. "So don't wreck it, all right?"

Annette's mom cleared her throat. "Beverly, I don't think Annette knows how to drive a car with a manual clutch . . ."

"Well, then I'll show her," Beverly said, as if she did this kind of thing all the time. "Come on, Annette. And don't mind the girls. You can help me bring in their accessories when we come back. My goodness, but they have a lot of stuff."

It was hard to believe that anyone had more stuff than her grandmother, whoever the girls might be.

Curious despite herself, suspecting that she was being tempted into participation in some fiendish scheme, Annette wiped mayonnaise from her lip. She cautiously followed her grandmother to the foyer, clutching the keys as if they might suddenly turn to vapor and prove that this wasn't going to happen after all.

"What about the groceries?" Annette's mom shouted after them.

* * *

They brought in the groceries, and under her mother's tutelage, Annette parked the Subaru in the garage. Knowing that her chance to drive the Jag was contingent upon doing this well, she focused.

And she prayed a little. She even put on her seat belt first and adjusted the seat and mirrors, as if she was used to doing this all the time. As if Dad had taught her, when in fact, she was just a good mimic. She parked the car carefully, very slowly. She was sure her mother would hear her heartbeat, it was pounding so loud, but instead she just murmured directions.

"A little more to the right." Her mom reached over and pushed the wheel slightly so they pulled into the garage straighter. "And a little farther in. Maybe a foot more. Now, stop. *Stop!*" After the car stopped—because Annette nearly put the brake pedal through the floor—her mom pointed to the front of garage and car. "You see how that shelf lines up with the front of the car?"

"I can't see the hose anymore."

"Right. That's how you know you're in far enough. Just don't hit the shelf or your father will hit the roof. It was the first thing he built in this house and he's very proud of it."

"How do you know?"

"Because I hit it the week after he finished it." Her mom shrugged. "I told him it was too deep of a shelf, but he measured it to be an exact fit."

Then her mom shut up and went a bit pale, as if she'd suddenly thought of something.

Right. Dad wasn't coming home.

Maybe.

Better not to think about that.

Annette was shaking as she put the car into park and turned off the ignition. Then she turned to her mom, certain of her triumph.

"You've never done that before, have you?" her mom asked, destroying any illusion that it was a habit.

"No, but I've wanted to for a long time." Annette was sure that this would be the end of it, that her mother would take away the bonus round that the witch had offered.

"You should have said something sooner." Her mom took a deep breath, obviously bracing herself for letting Annette down.

Figures, Annette thought. *No one ever lets me have what I want now that Grandma's gone.* And she wanted to tear into the bag of chocolate chip cookies that she'd glimpsed in the grocery bags.

"Now, please, be really careful with your grandmother's car." Annette glanced over in time to see her mom shake her head. "I can't imagine that we can afford to get it fixed if you even ding it. And we might have a hard enough time getting along while she's staying here without a wounded luxury car in the driveway."

Annette felt her eyes widen. Her mother had clearly been abducted by aliens and a sophisticated robot, who looked a lot like her mother but didn't know all the rules and limitations, had been left in her place.

And this robot was sometimes funny.

"Okay," she said, and got out of the car before the alien robot could change its mind.

Her grandmother's sleek silver Jaguar convertible was parked at the curb, the witch standing beside it expectantly. Annette's mouth went dry and her fingers sweat on the keys she held. What would Scott Sexton think if he saw her driving this car? Annette would have bet her last buck that he would talk to her then, if only to get a ride.

The witch opened the door with what seemed to be unnecessary care, then two big dogs leapt out of the backseat. "Champagne!" Beverly shouted. "Caviar!" The dogs made a beeline for Annette, their leashes trailing behind them across the snow.

"Poodles!" Annette cried, with joy.

"God's blood!" her mother said, with something less than joy.

The white one barked happily, the black one sniffed Annette's hands, and they both wagged their tails so hard that Annette thought they might fall off. They circled her, one after the other, moving so fast that they were hard to watch.

The witch had dogs! Annette had always wanted a dog, but a stuffed puppy had been the sole result of her attempt to persuade her mother that she was right.

She laughed with delight as the two bounced around her, then the white poodle leaned against her leg. When Annette rubbed behind its ear, it let out a sigh of satisfaction and seemed to grin at her. The black one, which appeared to be more cautious, then leaned against Annette's other side and looked up expectantly.

She patted them both. They had such pretty eyes. And their fur was so soft and curly. And they weighed a lot—she could tell by the way they leaned against her leg—though she didn't care.

Dogs! The witch had dogs!

Not just dogs: poodles! Annette knew a great deal about dogs, given her lifelong fascination with them, her ardent desire to have one, and her mother's persistent refusal to have one in the house. She had done projects on dogs at school; she had read book after book on dogs and dog care; she was a veritable encyclopedia of dog lore. She had scored a stuffed puppy toy for these endeavors, despite dropping hints every Christmas and birthday since she could talk.

But poodles, big poodles, had always been her favorites.

"Beverly, are those your dogs?" Annette's mom asked, her words a bit strained.

Annette ignored her mom, who had never liked dogs, who had refused to let Annette ever have a dog, who just didn't do the pet thing. Annette was busy, anyway, completely enchanted with these two affectionate poodles. The white one licked her ear.

"Actually, I'm more their person." Beverly came over and picked up the ends of their leashes, brushing the snow from the black leather. "The girls seem to think that they're the ones in charge."

"They're poodles," Annette informed her, forgetting that the witch must know what kind of dogs she had. "They're the smartest dogs."

"So they say," the witch—who was seeming a lot less wicked—acknowledged with a smile. "They seem to have me figured out already."

"Do you walk them?" Annette asked, with awe. Maybe she'd rather have Scott see her walking these two dogs.

"Probably not as far as they'd like to go or as often as they'd like to go." Beverly sighed. "But we have had one walk today. They leave no doubt of their desires."

"But I don't understand," Annette's mom said, as she slowly drew closer. She kept a wary watch on the dogs, which were no more dangerous than ladybugs. At least she watched the dogs when she wasn't watching Annette. "How long have you had dogs, Beverly?"

"Since this morning. An old friend of mine passed away and left her girls to my care."

"That's a bit unexpected, isn't it? I mean, did you know about this responsibility ahead of time?"

"No, it was a complete surprise." The witch paused for a beat. "As was the trust fund that the dogs inherited. Technically I'm their guardian and they're my wards."

"They're rich dogs?" Annette's mom asked.

The witch laughed. "Very rich." She shook her head a little. "Very very *very* rich."

So that was why the witch had taken them on. Annette patted the dogs even as she formed a scheme to save them from the witch who only wanted them for their money.

"And you intend to stay here with them?" Annette's mom asked, her tone revealing what she thought of that.

Not much, but Annette could have predicted that. She had fought the battle over a dog in the house a thousand times—never mind two dogs—and lost, but she couldn't leave this be.

"Mom, you have to let them stay. Poodles are nice dogs, and they're friendly, and they don't even shed. They won't bother my allergies at all. Kids at school with allergies get poodles as pets all the time." She sounded like a little kid and didn't even care. The dogs watched her with complete trust. "Please, Mom, please."

"I'm not sure this is a good idea, Annette. We're out a lot and dogs need company, as well as exercise."

"I'll walk them," Annette volunteered impulsively. "Twice a day, as far as they should be walked. And I'll feed them, and I'll give them water and I'll brush their hair . . ."

"Fur," her mom corrected.

"No, it's hair." Annette insisted. "Poodles have hair; that's why they don't shed."

"I'm not sure about this . . ."

To Annette's surprise, the witch intervened. "I don't see the harm in giving it a try, Leslie. The girls are well trained, at least from what I've seen so far. And I'll be home more than you." She smiled at Annette, who dropped to her knees to rub the dogs. The white one licked her cheek again, then the black one followed suit. "And Annette has always wanted a dog. This would be a good chance for her to see what such a responsibility involves."

It figured that adults could only see the merit of the dogs staying because she might learn something from them. Annette knew better than that, but she played along. "You'll see, Mom. It will be perfect!"

"I think I've been outnumbered," Annette's mom remarked, keeping her arms folded across her chest so the dogs couldn't sniff or touch her hands.

That didn't last. The witch handed off the leashes so imperiously that Annette's mom had no choice but to take them. "We've got to move the car," she said, then winked at Annette.

Annette stood with reluctance, telling the dogs to sit until she came back. They did exactly as she told them, which thrilled her no end. And they stayed, sitting with front paws together, chests out, ears perked up, and eyes locked upon Annette.

"They look like statues," Annette whispered. Her mother was holding the leashes as if they were made of toxic waste. The dogs ignored her, maybe sensing that she wouldn't be converted to the cult of poodle worship anytime soon, and kept their gazes fixed on Beverly and Annette.

"They do," her grandmother acknowledged. "So, am I doing better as a grandmother? I mean, you always wanted a puppy, but this is close, isn't it?"

"Yeah, it is. And Mom can't really say no this way, since they're still yours."

"Sounds like a perfect solution to me."

"Me, too." Especially as Annette was going to figure out a way to keep those dogs for herself forever. She didn't say that, though, just let the witch believe that they were a team.

As if.

Beverly pointed at the floor of the car, her fingernail catching the light. "All right. That left pedal is the clutch . . ."

* * *

Sharan's house in Algiers was a glorified corridor, a shotgun house, called such because you could fire a gun at the front door and the bullet would come out the back door.

Provided you could shoot straight.

One room followed another. From the front porch—which was wooden, shaded, and painted a giddy yellow—a visitor went through the front parlor or living room, a spare bedroom, the dining room, the kitchen, and Sharan's bedroom. The bathroom was notched out of one corner of the kitchen. Only the relatively new bathroom was a closed-off space.

Mercifully.

What was particularly striking about the house was the flamboyant use of color. The exterior, for example, was a brilliant cerulean blue, the exact color of the Mediterranean on a sunny summer afternoon. The porch was yellow, the front door lime green. There was a bougainvillaea climbing the side of the house, covering a good part of it in fuschia flower bracts.

Matt had had a general sense of the house being vividly hued when he had arrived the night before, but when he'd returned this afternoon to find it in full sun, his eyeballs had nearly melted.

Inside was much the same. The living room walls had actually been gilded, as far as he could tell, for they gleamed the gold of the actual metal. The drapes were crimson velvet, trimmed with gold fringe, and so elaborate that they made him think of old movie theaters.

Maybe that was where they had come from. There were a lot of candlesticks in that room and not much furniture, some cushions on the worn pine floor in luxurious fabrics. There were also a couple of creepy wooden sculptures, shoulder-high figures with chipped paint and gilt that must have been saints from churches. One offered her eyeballs on a tray, like hors d'oeuvres.

Maybe she'd been shocked at the color of the house, too.

Either way, Matt wasn't a fan of the living room.

The dining room was full of canvases, many large ones stacked against the walls. They were turned to face the walls and embellished with a good layer of dust. Matt didn't want to pry by looking at them, but they made him realize that none of Sharan's work was hanging on the walls.

In fact it didn't look as if she'd been painting lately. A jar on the sill filled with brushes had clearly been there for a while: the turpentine had evaporated, leaving a ring on the jar and a bunch of dried misshapen brushes within it.

Once Sharan had been fastidious about her tools. Matt guessed that there was a story behind her decision to get a job, and maybe a story he didn't want to know. He was concerned about these signs, because one of the reasons he'd sought her out was that he'd been sure she'd understand.

He'd thought she could show him how to live a comparatively normal life while following a crazy creative dream. He'd thought they would be kindred spirits now that he had the drive to create himself, but that dried-out jar of turpentine made him wonder.

The spare room was spartan, a cast-iron daybed on one side, a kitchen chair on the other. Clouds had been painted on the ceiling but the room was otherwise unadorned. There were four hooks in the wall beside the chair. Matt left his suitcase there, the one he had retrieved from the airport, along with his briefcase.

He wasn't going to make assumptions about where he would be sleeping. Strange but now that he was so far from home, he found himself thinking about Leslie, not Sharan. Funny how he didn't seem to know what the heck he wanted anymore, when once it had been so clear.

Or maybe it wasn't funny at all.

One thing was as clear as crystal. He thought of his novel, secured in the basement ceiling in Massachusetts, and felt the rush of pleasure that thought always brought him.

His luck, the house would burn down while he was gone.

Matt grimaced. He was tired, that was for sure, and unsettled from that interview with Zach. And he was getting too sober for comfort.

That must be why he was tempted to call Leslie again. He'd missed the sound of her voice earlier, though it had been good to talk to Annette. He could call back.

One more time.

Because only a loser would lead his wife to believe that more was possible than was really the case.

This was where he belonged.

So why didn't he feel as if he fit here?

Matt retreated to the kitchen, which was easy to identify and even easier to like. It had a terra-cotta tile floor that was cool under his feet, and the appliances were small and vintage. The cupboards were old and piecemeal, bits and ends snagged from different places and all painted a creamy yellow to give a coherence they wouldn't otherwise have possessed. The tile backsplash was red and yellow, the tiles making up larger patterns by the way they came together. There was an old fireplace still in one exterior wall, fascinating because it was so high and narrow. Sharan didn't seem to use it: Dried palmetto fronds were arranged in front of it.

He liked the unexpectedly generous expanse of counter, which seemed bigger because there was no clutter. He liked the deep enamel sink, and the old wooden kitchen table with its mismatched chairs. It was funky and artistic. Sharan seemed to have bought most of her kitchen equipment from restaurant supply companies, which suited Matt just fine. Her knives were impossibly dull, but she had a stone and he hadn't really expected much different from her.

He hung up his suit on a hook in the spare bedroom, put on some shorts and a T-shirt, and went barefoot into the kitchen to get to work. It was reassuring to sharpen the knives, more reassuring to grant himself a shot of tequila.

Matt was chopping cilantro when the screen door opened and slammed. The ceviche was chilling, and he was moving on to the main course. He jumped at the slam of the door, having lost himself in the reverie of food preparation and almost forgotten that he soon wouldn't be alone.

"Hi!" Sharan waved, her face alight with pleasure at the sight of him.

"Hi." Matt smiled in return, but it was a dutiful smile and he knew it.

"I had the worst day," Sharan said, and he heard her kick off her shoes. "I couldn't believe how many palm branches they need for this crewe's float. I mean, really, you'd think it was Jesus riding into Jerusalem that they were staging or something. Every time I'd get a batch done, they'd come down with another armload to paint. Boring!" She drew this last word out to a paragraph.

Matt heard something hit the floor. He glanced over to see the floral dress in a pile on the terra-cotta tile. Sharan, meanwhile, was wriggling out of her panties.

They were plain white cotton, perfectly decent panties, and they were dispatched to the floor as well. She was nude and tanned and slender, smiling in invitation. She wore no bra, a fact that Matt found ridiculously disappointing. Her breasts were round and firm, the nipples high and pert. There was absolutely nothing about them that wasn't perfect—even their tan was flawless.

But they hung bare and loose, which made him think of the photographs in *National Geographic* magazines. And that didn't turn him on.

"You're not wearing a bra," he said, without meaning to do so. He'd gotten spoiled with Leslie, with the daily revealing of what he called "Leslie's secret." He frowned and chopped cilantro with more vigor.

Unnecessary vigor.

Sharan laughed. "Never do. It's a mark of the patriarchy to insist that women bind their breasts. I don't play that game. I thought you'd remember that."

Matt didn't know what to say to that.

Sharan watched him for a moment, then smiled. "Oh I get it. You've been in the conservative world so long that you've gotten to like all that tarty stuff."

"No, it's not that . . ."

"Or did she put out so seldom that you had to get it off with lingerie catalogues?"

"Look, Sharan, I don't want to talk about the past . . ."

"Neither do I. Here I am, present and accounted for." Sharan's hands slipped around Matt's waist, and he felt her press against his back. "So aren't you glad to see me?" Her hands slid into his shorts.

"Hey, wait, I've got a knife here!"

"So put it down."

Matt glanced over his shoulder. "Don't you want dinner first?"

Sharan grinned up at him. "Life is uncertain: Have dessert first."

Matt returned to his work, irritable for some reason he couldn't name. "Well, I'm hungry even if you're not."

"Oh, I'm hungry, too," she said, then bit him playfully on the shoulder.

Matt put down his knife and turned around. "Look," he managed to say before Sharan kissed him. Her arms were around his neck, her fingers twined in his hair, her tongue between his teeth. Her breasts were pressed against his chest, and he would have had to have been dead to not have responded to her caress.

She lifted her lips from his and smiled. "Phew! Some magic never fades." She licked her fingertip and made a sizzling sound as she touched it to his shoulder. "You are one hot piece of work, Mr. Coxwell."

Matt put his hands on her waist and managed to put an increment of space between them. "Look, Sharan, I've got to finish getting dinner ready . . ."

She took a step back, watching him with narrowed eyes. "I'm definitely picking up a cool vibe from you. What's going on?"

"Well, dinner!"

She laughed. "That never used to stop us. That's why they put those really low settings on stove dials. See?"

"Sharan, I'm serious."

She gave him a shrewd glance. "Maybe it's time for a review. Why exactly did you come here, if not for fabulous wild sex?"

"I wanted to see you, of course, and talk to you."

"Well, that's a good start. What's wrong with touching me, then? It's not as if you don't know how; we both remember that."

"Well, I'm married, for starters . . ."

Sharan laughed. "Is that all?" She leaned a bare hip against the counter and stole a piece of red pepper from his array of chopped vegetables. "That's not fatal. In fact it can be fixed . . . if either of us really cares."

Matt glanced up in surprise. "What's that supposed to mean?"

"Oh, come on, Matt, you must have cheated before."

He shook his head, stoic. "No. Never."

"You never cheated on Leslie?" That she was so incredulous made Matt unexpectedly angry.

"There are things you don't know about her . . ."

"I guess so. But in the end, it doesn't matter, does it? You're here and she's not—I figure that what I don't know about her won't hurt me." She was laughing at him and he knew it but he couldn't help bristling.

"There's a lot more to Leslie than you think . . ."

"Like what?"

"Well, she's driven and passionate about her work . . ."

"You wouldn't be here if you thought she was passionate about you."

There was a truth in that, one that silenced Matt. He looked back down at his cilantro and tried to remember why coming here had seemed the best, if not the only, possibility.

Sharan watched him with knowing eyes, then rapped him in the chest with an imperious finger. "Well, here's the thing: We're not inventing extramarital sex. You'll have to trust me on this, but people do it all the time."

"I'm serious. I made a vow . . ." He tried to figure out, on some level, why he was fighting this so hard, and failed.

"And vows can be broken. It's not exactly a rare occurrence. Besides you left, so that vow is already moot. If you figure you're going to live here until you get divorced, then wait until we get married before we do it, then be warned: I'm going to need dessert before that."

"That's not what I mean . . ." he began to argue, though he wasn't sure exactly what he did mean. "I'm just not ready for this."

"Ready for what?"

"Ready for sex, when we haven't seen each other in eighteen years and haven't talked yet."

"I thought it was women who needed foreplay."

"Looks like it's the other way around here today."

Sharan braced her hands on the counter and stared at him. "So was it marriage, fatherhood, or life in gloriously suburban Belmont that made you bourgeois? Because you didn't used to be, you know."

"It's not bourgeois to keep your word," he said, with unnecessary force. "It's honest."

"Honest?" Sharan laughed again. "Is that what this is about? Well, don't feel any need to lie on my account. You want to confess? You want to tell Leslie?" She crossed the kitchen and picked up the phone. "Let's just give her a call so she's in the loop. What's the number again?"

Matt seized the receiver and slammed it back into the cradle. "You can't mean that."

"Well, actually I do."

"You're just trying to tick me off . . ."

"No, I'm trying to get some honesty out of you," Sharan retorted. "I don't care who knows what I do. I don't answer to anybody, especially your dear wife. And if she's so fucking important to you, then what are you doing here?" She flung out a hand. "Why were you sleeping on my porch? Why are you cooking in my kitchen?" She stepped closer, eyes flashing. "And even if it's honest, it wouldn't be smart to tell me that I'm just a convenient solution to your marital problems."

Matt shoved his hands through his hair, abandoning the cilantro for the tequila, probably for good. "I wanted to see you."

Sharan spread her hands, displaying her nudity to him. "And here I am. There's no more than this to see. Now what are you going to do about it?"

He swallowed tequila, watching her, then shook his head. "I want to talk to you."

"And I want to sleep with you. Honest enough for you?"

Matt shook his head. "I'm not ready for that yet, Sharan. It's not you, it's me." He drained the glass again, under her watchful gaze.

She folded her arms across her chest and sighed. "You're lucky I'm crazy about you," she muttered, then shook her head. She took his next shot of tequila, knocked it back and winced. "So what did you want to talk to me about?"

Matt glanced toward the dining room and the inventory of dusty canvases. They stopped the words in his throat, so eloquently did they speak of her surrendering the fight he was embarking upon. "I wanted to ask you how much a person should give up for their art. I wanted to ask you how you keep going, how you find the strength to create when there are so many other things we're supposed to do." He shook his head slightly. "But I'm not sure anymore that I should ask."

"You saw the canvases."

"They're hard to miss. You gave me the house keys."

Tears welled in her eyes before she turned away and dropped the glass onto the counter. "You want honesty, Matt? Well, here it comes. I don't know the answer to that, except that it's more than I wanted to give."

"You shouldn't have stopped."

"Is that right? Thank you for the advice, Matt Coxwell. What was I going to eat while I kept painting canvases that no one wanted to buy? Where was I supposed to live after my first solo show bombed and my agent ditched me and my gallery reneged on everything they'd promised me?"

"I'm sorry, Sharan, I didn't know."

"You didn't know because I didn't tell you, and I didn't tell you because I was ashamed. So there you go. There's all the truth I have on tap today. Sex now or sex later?"

"Sharan, I didn't mean to start a fight. I just thought you'd be the one person who'd understand."

"Understand what? That creating makes you feel like a god, then leaves you to starve in a gutter? That not creating is worse? I don't need the executive review: I've been living this nightmare for a decade and if I ever figure out what the hell to do about turning it around, I'll let you know."

"You should paint again."

She grimaced. "I don't think so. Here's the compromise position, pun intended: I've had eighteen years of foreplay, eighteen years to think about you since you dumped me, and a whole day today to think about getting it on with you. I like sex. I want sex with you. I thought you wanted sex with me. I came home, expecting to have sex with you. Are you with me so far?"

"Yes."

"So sex or not?"

"Let's eat something first."

"No, let's fuck first and eat later." She was challenging him, deliberately choosing a vulgar word to get a rise out of him. Matt knew it just as well as he knew that he wasn't going to be with her tonight.

"I need to talk to you first."

"I don't want to talk, and I especially don't want to talk about giving things up for art—or even about giving art up for everything else. Reviewing my inadequacies is not going to turn me on, that's for sure." She met his gaze, daring him to take advantage of her offer.

Matt turned off the stove. "This was a bad idea. I'm sorry, I made a mistake. I should go."

She plucked her dress off the floor and put it on, not bothering with her underwear. He stepped past her, sickened that he had brought her pain to the surface in his own quest for understanding.

He couldn't be so casual about sex. He couldn't just leap into bed, not with a woman who had become a stranger. There had been a time when he hadn't understood Sharan's passion for her work, a time when he couldn't fathom how she could paint for hours, all through the night even, and remain on a jubilant high until she was done. He had been certain that they'd make the connection that had proved so elusive years before.

But she was a different person than he remembered, a much angrier person than he ever could have expected from her cheerful letters. If Sharan's house had been full of paintings, if it had been a crummy apartment or a loft filled with her art, if she had been filled with the joy of creation that he remembered so well, maybe his response to her offer would have been different.

If she hadn't been bitter, it would have been different.

And he could see in her eyes that she knew it. He got to the spare room before she called after him.

"Matt. Don't leave." She sounded tired, resigned.

He glanced over his shoulder, tequila making his head swim. "I think it's better if I do."

"And I think it would be better if you stayed. We were friends first, and I'd like the chance to be friends again." She put out her hand, offering to shake, and Matt hesitated only a moment before taking her hand in his.

"But I'm going out." She heaved a sigh, swallowed, and looked around the kitchen, as if seeking an answer amidst the clutter he had made on the counters. "I have to go out, but I'd like it if you were here in the morning."

"Why?"

"Because we're not done with each other yet. Because I've loved you for a long time, and you came here because you needed me." She smiled ruefully. "Just because you don't need me in the same way that I need you right now doesn't mean that I should let you walk away. I'll talk to you, but not tonight."

"Are you sure?"

"No, but if I hate you in the morning, I'll let you know." She grinned then, but her eyes were suspiciously bright. "Deal?"

"Deal."

They stared at each other for a moment, before she turned her back on him, swearing under her breath. He poured himself another shot of tequila, then the screen door slammed again.

*   *   *

It was late when Leslie got to bed. She was dead on her feet after her day, but still anxious. In fact, the yearning that filled her had a certain familiarity.

Leslie sighed that she'd have to solve it herself and reached into the top drawer of her night stand. When her fingers didn't immediately fall on her vibrator, she leaned over to search for it. It must have slipped under something else, she was sure of it, but as she rummaged through the drawer, it became obvious that the vibrator wasn't there.

Someone had filched it.

And Leslie would have bet good money that neither Beverly nor "the girls" were the responsible party.

Was Annette sprawled across her bed, murmuring Scott Sexton's name in this very moment? Had she washed the vibrator first? How did the stuffed puppy figure into all of this?

Did Leslie even want to know?

Hello, puberty.

There was a scary prospect. Leslie stared at the ceiling, eyes wide open, for longer than she could have anticipated just five minutes before.

Chapter Ten

Matt awakened to the sweet perfume of a New Orleans morning, a heady mix of oleander, jasmine, and coffee with chicory. The sun poked its fingers through the parted curtains to jab him in the eye. He got up to close the drapes and saw the sun just on the horizon, hanging low and red.

As red as blood.

With little pink clouds scattered across the sky.

He pivoted and headed for the kitchen, moving quietly past Sharan's closed bedroom door, still shaking his head over her early-morning return and assertion that Mike was here for a good time, not a long time. The guy had been pretty surprised to find Matt here and Matt could understand Mike's confusion. He poured himself an orange juice and gave it a dollop of dark rum to take the edge off his morning.

Then he rubbed his forehead, wincing at the pain there, and tossed back the pair of aspirin that were becoming part of his morning regimen. Tequila, he decided, was not a substance with which a man could have an enduring relationship. Banished to the veranda the night before when Sharan came home with her date, he'd taken the bottle of tequila for company and now regretted it.

Maybe he should have just left.

Maybe he would have done so if he hadn't sensed Sharan's loneliness or her fear.

Sharan's bedroom was adjacent to the kitchen and the house was small, so when her mattress began to squeak, Matt felt too close for comfort. He grabbed a shirt and a pair of shorts and retreated to the veranda again.

There was a nice breeze coming off the river, and the vine beside the porch hid him from view, which suited him pretty well. He sat and drank his O.J. and tried not to look at the crimson eye of the sun.

Tried not to think about little bits on the bookcase behind what had remained of his father. Had they been his father's brains? It seemed reasonable that they might have been.

He gulped orange juice and desperately tried to think of something else that was the same red as the sun, something with a more soothing connotation.

The inside of Annette's mouth, when she had wailed as a baby, often all night long. He'd learned more about the look of her tonsils that first year than he'd ever cared to know.

No. He needed to think of something that wasn't human tissue.

Red had been the color of the sweatshirt Leslie had stolen from him on their third date, the one that she had worn for the next five years, until it had fallen to shreds. Matt smiled into his juice, hearing her consistent protest that she hadn't technically stolen it because he hadn't ever asked for it back.

Which had been true. She'd worn that sweatshirt every time she'd studied, for luck she'd said, and he still liked the idea that he could be her lucky charm.

Even if he wasn't anymore. Matt frowned and drained his glass, setting it aside, letting his thoughts slide into the past.

* * *

It had been April, chilly, almost their anniversary and nearly time for Leslie to defend her master's thesis.

She studied every afternoon and every night. He was working in real-estate law under a genial little lawyer who professed himself glad to have another pair of feet. Matt spent days researching titles, and if truth be told, getting distracted by all the strange details that hung on deeds for old property like cobwebs on an antique lamp.

"No goats." Admonitions against keeping livestock, chickens, or pigeons were common, almost as common as liens against the property that had to be paid back first in the event of a sale.

"Buyer shall not sell said home and property for less than $2,000." Price protection was common, too, though it was laughable to think of the smallest possible piece of dirt in Boston going for less than two thousand dollars.

"Buyer shall never sell said property to the Goodman family of Davis Lane, or otherwise facilitate the passage of said property into the possession of said family." These kinds of edicts always left Matt wondering what had happened between the two families, whether the Goodman clan were even interested in said property or whether it was a fiction in the seller's mind.

You could put anything in a property title, he'd learned that pretty quickly, but still he had been fascinated by the kinds of things that people did put in titles. He had sensed that you could learn a lot about human nature by reading these seemingly innocuous documents.

Which was what he supposed Leslie was doing, with all of her tax rolls and hearth censuses and lists of fines payable to the courts of the lord of such-and-such. He'd understood then the fascination she felt for the way people unwittingly revealed their natures, desires and secrets in documents they believed to be routine.

Red was the color of the sweatshirt she'd been wearing the night he'd come home to find her lost in her books.

Red was also the color of the element on the stove, the element beneath the empty pot.

The apartment was full of steam, the pot on the stove boiled dry, the package of pasta open on the counter.

"Hey! Don't burn the place down!" Matt darted to move the pot and turn off the burner before things got serious.

"Ohmigod, I forgot!" The horrified look on Leslie's face revealed that she'd been somewhere else completely—maybe the thirteenth century. "I was going to make dinner, so it would be ready when you came home."

Red was the color of his wife's cheeks.

Crisis resolved, the pot sizzling in the sink and the burner turned off, Matt kissed her. It was a good kiss, sweet and hot, the way kisses were every night when he came home.

"You don't come back to the twentieth century until I get here, do you?" he teased finally and she blushed.

"It's hardly worth it, if you're not here." Her eyes were clear when she said this, sparkling a little with that honesty he so loved, and he caught his breath.

"You can't mean that."

"I do." She smiled and shrugged, shaking her head as she looked over her books. "I was clearing the table for dinner, putting my books away, and I noticed this footnote that I missed earlier." She pounced on a book, beginning to read the footnote to him.

Matt laughed. "Can you tell me after we eat? I'm starving."

"Sorry. I just forget."

"I know." They smiled at each other, smitten newlyweds still. Matt hadn't yet gotten used to the fact that marriage could be this way, filled with laughter instead of the silence that had always yawned between his parents.

He wasn't exactly sure how his parents had managed to conceive a second son—himself—let alone two more children after that, but he supposed it had been a quiet matter.

Duty bound, maybe, which was a horrible thought.

He shed his jacket then, because it was warm in the apartment no matter what the season, and rolled up his sleeves. "So how about I cook?"

Leslie glanced up, tucking her hair behind her ear. "Can you cook?"

"A bit. I'll learn more."

She laughed, a rich sound that always made him smile, too. "You mean it can't be worse than what I make."

"I don't mean that at all. You're just so focused. I respect that."

"I have to be if I'm going to defend this thesis well." She shook her head. "Why did I take the thesis option instead of the course-based master's?"

"Because it would be harder, and because you knew you could do it." He bent and kissed her just below her ear, liking how she shivered. "And because you knew that it was the right step to take toward getting into the school you want."

"You make me sound very deliberate."

"That's not a bad thing. You're driven. You're passionate about what you do. I admire that."

"Aren't you?"

"No." Matt laughed. "I've never had a burning desire to do anything, not the way you are with your medieval studies. You're going to be a great teacher, because you're going to bring all that passion to your work." He shrugged and glanced around the apartment as if seeking an answer in its corners. "I just get pushed this way and that, and kind of drift along because I don't have a better answer than the one being offered."

"You're too hard on yourself. Not everyone gets into law school, you know, and not everyone passes the bar exam."

Matt saw that he'd never be able to explain to her how they were different from each other, much less the reason why he admired her so much. And it was okay. It was enough that he did. "So one thing I know how to cook is a fettucine alla carbonara."

She looked up in shock. "You know how to cook something that doesn't even have a name in English?"

"It's pasta, with a little cheese sauce and some bacon, some peas. It's not complicated. Really."

Leslie bowed and stepped out of the miniscule kitchen, waving him into it with a flourish. "Then by all means, be my guest. Do you want me to make salad?"

"No, I'll do it. Don't let ol' Bernie get lonely."

Leslie laughed, then gazed at Matt with undisguised admiration, such a sparkle in her eyes that he hoped like hell he could remember the recipe.

And that they had all of the ingredients.

* * *

So Matt had embarked on the culinary adventure that had lasted all of his life so far. Filled with anticipation and ideas, he had climbed that long narrow staircase every night with a bag of groceries, rain or shine, and set to work.

Sometimes it worked out well. Sometimes he bombed. Leslie ate it all and gave her compliments to the chef every time.

And she never made the tacky suggestion that she was dessert.

Ultimately he saw that there had never been a question of one of them learning to cook: The delicious smells rising from the Portuguese restaurant below their apartment had left Matt salivating every hour that he was home. The choices were cook or spend every spare dime they had—there weren't many of those—on take-out food. For the sake of sheer quantities involved, home cooking was the way to go.

In the here and now of New Orleans, Matt yearned for one of those "good to see you again" kisses, kisses that had disappeared when they had started to take each other for granted. Maybe he yearned for the past. Maybe he yearned for appreciation.

Maybe he yearned for what he should have known better than to want.

Leslie had always known what she wanted, where she was going to go, and exactly how she was going to get there. The path ahead was straight and clear for her. That vision had always awed

Matt and in a way he envied it. It was completely alien to his own sense of floating through life, waiting for something to seize his attention and hold fast.

But nothing ever had. Not until Leslie, though that was different. A man couldn't just spend his whole life being in love—well, he could, but Matt needed to do something else, too. For lack of a more commanding option, it had been easy for Matt to choose to be a stay-at-home dad, the better to facilitate Leslie's return to the work she loved after Annette's arrival. He had had a home office until two years ago, practiced real-estate law on his own schedule, picked Annette up from this and that class, made dinner every night.

But something had changed in the last two years. Something good had come out of this experience with his father: Something had awakened that had been dormant all of Matt's life.

He had started to write.

He had done so furtively at first, in stolen moments, on filched sheets of paper. The characters and the story had seized hold of his imagination in a way he had never experienced before. He recognized the passion: He had witnessed it in Leslie.

In fact, he might have run from it, if he hadn't seen how she worked with her passion, corraled it and channeled it and guided it to where she wanted to go. She had a strong hand on the reins: Matt was far from having that, but just seeing it done allowed him to believe it was possible.

Finally something had grabbed him tightly and refused to let go. He was afraid of the writing, afraid of its power over his imagination, afraid of the potent truths it revealed, afraid that the two competitive brothers in his fictional story were just thinly veiled versions of himself and James.

Mostly he was afraid that he had put everything he had into this book's creation and that the result might not be any good. What would that say about him?

In contrast Leslie didn't have doubts. Leslie was resolute and strong, and she was pragmatic. On some level, Matt admitted to his juice glass, he was afraid that she wouldn't respect the one thing he'd chosen to do, the one thing that had commandeered his passion.

He was changing the rules, needing space and time and encouragement for himself. He knew better than to ask her for what he needed. Leslie saw her own way to the exclusion of all else.

It was what he loved about her. It was also what made him believe it was impossible for them to remain together.

But he'd missed his kitchen last night, his familiar tools in their familiar places, the butcher he could count on to trim the fat just right—that was how he'd ended up with fish—the greengrocer who held a little of the best produce in the back of the store for Matt.

But mostly he'd missed that moment, the moment he waited for every day and hadn't even realized until right this minute that he waited for every day. It was the moment when Leslie walked through the front door and, unbeknownst to herself, her expression changed completely. She often arrived home harried or late, her brow furrowed and loads of books in her arms, some explanation or apology falling from her lips. But when she crossed the threshold and caught the scent of dinner, her whole face softened in a way that broke Matt's heart.

Was it relief? Was it love? Was it just pleasure? He'd never asked her to name her response. He liked that she didn't even realize that she did it, that she let her guard down because she was home. There was that moment when the look in her eyes made him believe that she still was as surprised as ever to find him there.

And glad he was.

The glimpse was enough, because she always smiled right afterward and said, "Something smells good." It might be a fleeting smile, it might soon be eased away by the cares of her day or the demands of their daughter, the words might be rote, but for one precious moment every day, Leslie always looked at Matt with eyes alight.

Just the way she had, once upon a time, in a tiny apartment

over Inman Square when he had first offered to cook fettucine alla carbonara.

The sun broke clear of the horizon then, fiercely red. Matt knew with utter conviction that there was only one person he wanted to talk to right now.

Just one more time.

* * *

The phone rang at 7:45 Friday morning, just as Leslie was entering that never-never land between dream and wake. Except she hadn't dreamed the night before.

Was that an omen? There was no time to think about it with the insistent shrill of the phone right beside her.

She reached for the receiver, fearing the worst. "Hello?"

"Good morning," Matt murmured into her ear. "Sleep well?"

It was what he had murmured into her ear a thousand times at this point in the morning. Leslie closed her eyes, easily remembering how that question was followed by a smooth caress, how it usually led to early morning lovemaking.

At least once upon a time it had. Her eyes popped open again, and she reminded herself not to be so easily seduced.

Matt might have guessed that the mood was less than he'd hoped for, because he kept talking, instead of waiting for her to reply. "I was thinking about that first apartment we had. Remember the one off Inman Square?"

"What a dump. The rent was outrageous for what we got."

"How can you say that?" She could hear the undercurrent of laughter in his voice. "The place had character . . ."

Leslie snorted. "That's real estate lingo for 'dump.'"

"I still have bumps on my head from that angled ceiling in the bathroom."

"And I can still smell the *caldo verde* soup from the restaurant downstairs. Kale and potato, day and night, day after day after day."

"Never mind the cockroaches that came visiting from its kitchen."

Leslie shuddered even as she smiled. "Don't remind me!"

"It was our place, though, our refuge from the world." Matt's voice dropped low, low enough to give her goose pimples. "Remember?"

Dear God, but she remembered. She remembered silent love-making, their eyes filled with stars, and showers together and stifling their laughter so that no one would hear them through the paper-thin walls. She remembered the smell of that restaurant permeating everything; she remembered Matt being the focus of her universe. She remembered how they were lost in each other, and the lump that rose in her throat made it impossible to catch her breath. The telephone line seemed to resonate with emotion.

Was she the only one ripped apart by his decision to leave?

Then she recalled something else, a clear mental image of a younger Matt, embellished with paint, lit with pride. "You painted the walls there," she said, her words thick. Someone had to say something. "It was kind of a mocha color. Very cozy."

"I think I got more paint on myself than on the walls." His tone was rueful, intimate, redolent of a thousand mornings whispering abed so that they didn't awaken Annette.

Leslie could have curled up in his voice and slept for a month. Instead, she slid deeper under the covers and tried to pretend that recent conversations hadn't occurred.

"I don't think I missed my calling as an interior painter for hire."

"But it looked better than it had been before." She twined the phone cord around her fingers, savoring the most important part of that incident. "And you surprised me."

"I knew you hated that orange."

"I never said anything!"

"You didn't have to. It was hideous. And you had to study there at night. You needed the right environment to work on your thesis. It was important, the key to the future. We couldn't do much about the kitchen table doubling as a desk or about the smell of the *caldo verde*, but painting seemed the least thing I could do to help out."

Leslie sighed. They had been so close then, so much in love, and the future had seemed full of promise and possibility. "Maybe it wasn't such a bad place, after all."

"It was our place," Matt insisted. "And we were happy there."

She rolled to her side, not wanting to spoil the mood. "Remember when your parents came to dinner the first time?"

"Don't remind me!" Matt chuckled. "I'd rather remember how the morning light came through those drapes you found at Goodwill."

Leslie swallowed. "Thank God for the pill," she joked. "Or we would have had a dozen kids before Annette came along."

"True enough." He cleared his throat slightly. "I wanted to help you finish your thesis, Leslie. You had a passion for your studies, a genuine calling that I never had. You need to find that again."

It seemed somehow important that he hadn't said that he wanted to help her find it. Leslie stared at the ceiling, the warm glow dismissed. "You're whispering."

"Well, I don't want to wake anyone up."

Leslie sat up, knowing exactly who "anyone" was. Was he lying in bed beside Sharan, whispering into the phone to her? What exactly was going on there? How could she ask? Why didn't he tell her?

Or was his continued presence in Sharan's house (bedroom?) all that Leslie really needed to know?

She folded her arms around herself, suddenly cold. She realized that she was sitting much as Annette had on the patio the night before.

"So I've been thinking, if you're not happy in your job, why don't you quit?" Matt's tone was challenging, as if he was daring her to leap off the tightrope, and knew exactly what he was doing.

"Quit?" Leslie squeaked. "Quit a tenured professorship?"

"Why not? It's not even giving you the chance to do the research you want to do. I'd say that walking away from it is a gimme."

Leslie felt her mouth opening and closing, though it took a while for her to force out a sound. "But quit? As in, walk away forever?"

"Yeah, just like."

"But . . . but I couldn't! I can't! It's impossible . . ."

"Nothing's impossible, Leslie," Matt said roughly. If he was trying to shake up her preconceptions, he was doing a pretty good job. "Think about it, it makes perfect sense. You don't like the job. Most people would then find another job, quit the crummy job either after or before."

"Most people don't have tenure."

"Sounds more like a liability than an asset."

Leslie still was having problems forming a coherent objection. "But Matt, if I quit, they'll stop covering my paycheck."

"Well nothing comes without a price."

"You can't be so cavalier about our sole source of income!"

"You can't be so cavalier about your own happiness and job satisfaction. Quit. It'll work out."

That he could believe such a thing left Leslie gaping again. "How, exactly, will it work out?" she asked, her voice higher than usual. "How exactly will we eat and pay the mortgage and send Annette to college . . ."

"You're thinking about it too much. When you make good choices, good things happen. Staying in your job is obviously a bad choice, so take a chance."

"I am not going to take a chance on our losing everything we've worked to gain!" She wondered even as she protested why she was still thinking of them as an economic unit.

"Why not?" Matt asked. "Money doesn't matter that much and it certainly isn't everything . . ."

"But money makes everything easier! Matt, money doesn't matter to you because you've always had it coming out of your wazoo!"

"Objection, your honor. I can categorically state that I have never had money coming out of my wazoo." His words were slurring slightly, she noticed now, evidence that he'd been drinking.

Again.

Still.

"I may not be the most observant man on the planet, but I would have noticed that."

Leslie wanted to push him to seek counseling but guessed how well that would go over. Instead she aimed for a closer target. "Matt, this isn't a joke. You don't respect money. You don't know what it's like to not have any. You're not seeing how important this is."

"No, I see exactly how important it is," he argued, his voice turning harsh. "I'm just saying that your goals and general happiness are more important. And besides you're not being consistent: Why else did you want me to win that case, if not to secure that job and give you the option of quitting?"

Leslie stopped. She rubbed her temple with one hand. "You're right. I hadn't gotten that far in my reasoning. I just knew that if you had won, if we had another paycheck coming in, then I wouldn't feel so pressured."

"Under siege," Matt concurred softly. A change of tone and he undermined her resistance as surely as a tunnel dug under a medieval fortress. Leslie felt the walls she had erected against him crumbling. "Because you're doing something you hate."

Leslie blinked back tears. "Yes. 'Under siege' describes it perfectly." She heaved a ragged sigh. "And Dinkelmann just keeps lobbing more Greek fire over the walls. He's not the first and he won't be the last."

There was a silence again, but it was a thinking silence. It gave Leslie the sense (the illusion? the delusion?) that they were trying to resolve something together again.

Which was probably what they should have done sooner.

Was it too late? She feared it was.

Leslie closed her eyes and imagined Matt shoving a hand through his hair. He would have a shadowy bit of beard as he always did in the morning, his shirt collar would be loose, and he'd have an elbow braced on the wall. He would be frowning, in concentration not in anger, the way he did when he helped Annette with her math homework. A lump rose in her throat at the image and she held the phone closer.

It was somewhat colder than he would have been.

"You make it look so easy, you know," he said slowly. "I never even guessed that you were under so much pressure."

"Well, it's tedious to come home and whine."

"We used to talk about things at other times, in other places."

"In bed," Leslie affirmed.

"Is Annette there?"

"No."

His voice deepened, roughened, dropped to a murmur that undoubtedly couldn't be heard by anyone but her. "Then tell me what bra you're going to wear today."

Leslie's skin immediately heated. "It's one you haven't seen. It's black lace . . ."

"Black is my favorite."

She knew that. The memory of that first trip to his apartment almost shorted her circuits. "It's like a tank top but made of lace and cut to support. I mean it wouldn't work if I was more buxom . . ." Leslie shut up abruptly. She sounded less provocative than she'd hoped. More desperate. She closed her eyes, fearing she'd only made things worse.

Matt said nothing, nothing at all.

"Your mother is here, you know," she said brightly. It was a change of subject typical of Annette's evasive tactics.

Matt's surprise was clear. "No, I didn't know. How did that happen?"

"She got evicted for nonpayment of rent. She thinks Robert did it before he died . . ."

"Well, that makes some sense. He was paying all of her bills while the divorce settlement was being worked out."

"But I thought your mother was the one who came from money. Doesn't she have money of her own?"

"She gave full power-of-attorney to my father years ago—I don't know why—and he was using it."

There was an odd silence then and Leslie wondered what Matt was thinking, whether she had inadvertently awakened another, less pleasant, memory than the apartment on Inman Square. "Are you all right?"

Matt laughed but the sound wasn't merry. "So long as I stay smashed. Why?"

"The Chief of Police from Rosemount wanted you to get into counseling for shock. Did he call you?"

"So you were the one who gave him the number here. I wondered about that."

Leslie tightened her grip on her belly, sensing that this conversation was going to go from bad to worse PDQ. "So I'm not supposed to help the police in locating you when you're not where you tell them you'll be?"

Matt's voice was bright with suspicion. "Where'd you get the number?"

"I didn't." Leslie bristled that she should be the one being interrogated, as if she were the guilty party. "I guessed where you were and I gave him the address."

"And where'd you find that? I have my Day-Timer here."

Leslie gritted her teeth. Her husband was sleeping with an old girlfriend and they were arguing about the location of his Day-Timer. "It was the return address on Sharan's last Christmas card. Does it matter?"

He didn't speak for a moment, which eloquently answered her question. Then he asked the question she most feared to hear in a tone of voice that sent chills down her spine. "Did you read the card?"

Leslie stared across the room, unable to decide whether to lie or have it out.

She went for the middle ground and tried for a mild tone of voice. "Why? Was there something in it that I might have found inappropriate?"

"You did read it," Matt said, with disgust. Leslie had time to think that the problem with knowing someone well for twenty years or so is that you can't possibly lie to them before Matt tossed another firecracker onto the table between them. "I can't believe it."

"You can't believe it?" That was it. Leslie gripped the phone and spoke her mind. To hell with *Demure Spouse*. "I have never opened your personal correspondence because I trusted you. So, yes, I found that Christmas card for the Chief of Police to help him find you, as any law-abiding citizen should do, and then, yes, I did succumb to temptation and read it. And what did I find out? That my trust in you was misplaced. So don't go telling me that I'm the guilty party here, Matthew Coxwell: If you didn't have anything to hide, my reading that card wouldn't have mattered."

He was bristling. "I don't have anything to hide."

"Please! How stupid do you think I am? You're staying in her house and don't want to wake her up . . ."

"Because she's in bed with another guy and the walls are paper-thin in this place, maybe thinner than in that apartment."

Leslie closed her mouth at that. A menage à trois was not something she would ever have imagined would work for Matt.

But then there were proving to be a lot of things she didn't know about her husband.

Maybe he was in an experimental mood.

Maybe she couldn't tell anymore when he was lying.

There was a scary prospect.

He exhaled with impatience. "Look, Leslie, I'm not going to get counseling. That's for other people. I'm working through this on my own, and so far, there seem to be two ingredients to success: a minimum blood alcohol level and evidence that I'm not alone."

His voice was slightly unsteady and Leslie's heart went out to him. "Was it bad?"

"Let's just say that I don't ever need to see something like that again."

"So don't you think that maybe the chief has a point?" Leslie suggested with care. He seemed volatile, which wasn't like Matt, and she didn't know what to expect from him. "That maybe, given the circumstances, counseling might be the way to go?"

Even though she thought she was ready for anything, Leslie was shocked that he shouted at her. "I am not going to get counseling! There's nothing wrong with me. I'm not cracking up, and I'm not losing my grip, and I'm not having problems dealing with this. Understand?"

Leslie understood that this outburst proved not only that the chief had been dead on the money but that she'd only make things worse by insisting on it. "Everyone awake now?"

"Shit. Thanks a lot."

Leslie opened her mouth to protest that his outburst wasn't her fault, but decided against it.

"Let's talk about something else," Matt said dismissively, his tone businesslike and indifferent.

As if she were a check-out clerk who'd slipped up on his change.

And that tone, as much as anything, made Leslie determined to not let the really good questions slip away unanswered. "I don't think we're done talking about that Christmas card," she said, forcing the words out. It wasn't like her to be confrontational, but she wanted to know the worst of it. "There was a time, maybe in that small apartment on Inman Square, when you would have told me your secrets."

"Well, the roaches weren't going to listen."

Leslie refused to be deflected by humor, not now. "You might have told me, instead of Sharan, that you intended to lose that court case."

"But I was sure you knew."

"I didn't know. I never guessed."

"I'm sorry then. I thought I just had to lose to set everything right between us again." He half-laughed. "But I had it backward, didn't I? You wanted me to win and sell myself into slavery in my father's business."

"You make it sound as if I don't want you to be happy . . ."

"Well, it sure doesn't sound like you do."

Leslie acknowledged the silence and the hardness of his tone, but she couldn't let this go. "Or you could have told me about your novel."

He let out a long breath. "Oh, right. I forgot that she mentioned that, too." An awkward silence followed, one that Leslie didn't fill.

Finally Matt spoke, his words spilling over each other in a very un-Matt-like way. Was he embarrassed? That he had written a novel or that he had been caught? "It's just a work in progress. I don't even know if it's going to come together. I just had an idea and started working on it, and I guess I knew that as an artist, Sharan would understand the challenge of it. And the joy of it."

This little speech did exactly nothing to reassure Leslie.

In fact she thought she might be sick.

When she didn't say anything, Matt continued. "We've made some atypical choices, Leslie, but we've done it on purpose, to get further together than we ever could alone. And I didn't mind, because I didn't know what else I wanted. Now I know what I want and you're not going to tell me that I can't pursue it, just because it doesn't leave you with complete freedom to do whatever you want."

"That's not what I'm asking of you!"

"Aren't you? It sounds like it from here. Well, news flash, Leslie." He was angry again, his voice rising. "Something has finally caught hold of me and won't let go. I need to do this. I'm going to do this. And that's why I left. I have to protect this. I have to give it my best shot and that means being with people who understand the impetus behind it. I don't trust you to not sweep me into your agenda and whatever my assigned role is there." He half-laughed. "And I don't trust myself to say no to you when you have that light in your eyes. It's that simple and that complicated."

The news that Matt believed she couldn't be relied upon to supply any encouragement for his dreams, after he had done so much to support her own, was shocking, but Leslie had no opportunity to argue her side.

Because this time, Matt hung up on her.

She stared at the receiver, dumbfounded. Why wouldn't he have at least tried to talk to her first? Had she really been such a crummy partner? Leslie couldn't believe it. Her glance fell on the call display, S. Loomis and the New Orleans telephone number gleaming in red, and her stomach roiled.

She waited, watching the phone, but Matt didn't call back and she knew he wouldn't. He had left because he didn't believe she would help him reach for his dream.

It was the most depressing thing anyone had said to her or about her in a long time, and with Dinkelmann in the accounting, that was bad news.

Aubade, today, Leslie decided as she got out of bed. Definitely Aubade. She'd wear that black lace undershirt that she'd told him about, as a gesture of optimism if nothing else. It had no wires, nothing but an excellent cut to shape and support.

Thank God it was Friday.

* * *

Well, that had gone well.

Matt congratulated himself on his smooth delivery as he snagged another glass of orange juice. This one got a double dollop of rum, just to take the edge off.

"A bit early for drinking, isn't it?" Sharan asked.

Matt pivoted to find her leaning in her bedroom door, a silky kimono tossed over her shoulders. She was naked beneath it and her long hair was tangled.

Her expression was guarded though, all the words of the previous night still between them.

"It's not early to start if you never stop." Matt saluted her with his glass and drank.

The stud du jour slipped past Sharan, gave Matt a nod, then ducked out the back door. He started to whistle when he was a dozen steps away, but Matt and Sharan didn't look away from each other.

Sharan swallowed, looked at the floor, then met Matt's gaze again. "There was a time," she said softly, "when I loved you more than anything or anybody. And you know, even though you left, there was something to be said for just having ever felt that way about someone." She tilted her head to study him. "Why did you come here? Why did you have to steal that from me?"

Matt shook his head. "I didn't mean to. I thought . . ." He gestured as words failed him. "I thought that we could pick up where we left off."

Sharan shook her head. "But we're not the same people anymore. You know that as well as I do. There's something in there that's still the same, but a lot of other stuff has shaped us since."

He looked into his glass, knowing she was right.

She moved to stand in front of him, perfume and her own scent engulfing him. Her voice was unsteady. "I could still love you," she said, then shook her head. "But we'd have to start again." She raised her gaze to his and something in him twisted at the shimmer of tears in her eyes. "The question is, could you still love me?"

She stood there, trembling and vulnerable, the woman he'd once believed to be tough and resilient and certain to succeed. He lifted one hand and touched her jaw, and she looked away, her tear splashing on the back of his hand.

"Why did you stop painting?"

She shook her head, lost for words.

"Tell me."

"I'm no good." Her tears started to flow. "No, I'm not good enough. That's the truth." She stared at him and he saw the depth of her wound, then the words began to fall from her lips in a torrent. "I'm not daring enough or talented enough or visionary enough and when push came to shove and I had my chance, I just couldn't offer anything good enough. I failed."

"You make it sound so final."

"It is final. It's over! I'm going to be painting fucking palm leaves for the rest of my life because I don't know how to do anything else!" She glared at him, moving away from his hand. "And I can't even manage to get into bed with a man who comes thousands of miles to be with me. Failure, Matt. I'm a failure!"

She spun away, but he caught her elbow to halt her. On impulse he pulled her into his arms. He was shocked by how she melted beneath his caress. She was crying, he could taste her tears, and he caught her closer, finding familiarity in her embrace if not passion.

"You need to paint," he told her, with low urgency. "You need to try again."

"No, no, I don't think so." She tried to pull away from him as well as his suggestion. "I don't know what to paint . . ."

Matt caught her chin in his hand and compelled her to look at him. "Yes, you do. In your heart you know what to paint. You can only fail if you quit."

She blinked and he knew he had her. She swallowed and looked toward the dining room and all those stacked canvases. "I'm not sure."

"I am. You have talent. We both know that. Now all you need is luck and hard work."

She smiled then. "That's all?"

"That's all." He smiled at her. "I'm looking for the same thing, if it's any consolation."

She studied him for a long moment and he wondered what she saw that made her sober. Then her gaze slipped to the clock. "Hey, I've got to go to work." She darted toward the bedroom, pausing to glance back, yearning in her eyes. "Will you be here tonight when I get home?"

"Do you want me to be?"

She smiled crookedly, as if she'd heard a joke. "Yes," she said, her smile turning impish. "I'd like to talk."

Matt looked around the kitchen. He thought of his phone call with Leslie and deliberately tried to shut the door on his past. Nobody had ever promised him that he could get the good stuff for free. Sharan wasn't who she had been, but neither was he. That didn't mean that they couldn't find at least friendship together.

"No guarantees," he said.

"Where were you getting those all these years?"

They smiled at each other, then Matt cleared his throat. "Any requests for dinner?"

"No. Whatever you want to make."

Long after Sharan had left, Matt realized she hadn't said anything about dessert.

And that was okay with him.

Chapter Eleven

Leslie thought she strode into the department with some verve, though her confidence faltered when Charlotte MacPherson gasped at the sight of her. When Charlotte scampered away in the direction of Dinkelmann's office with nary a greeting, Leslie figured she was due for a visit from the great man.

Might as well get the scolding over with. She unlocked her office door without spilling her coffee, dumped her books, and booted up her computer.

She had, predictably, a zillion e-mails to download.

Give or take.

No surprise there, since she'd pretty much forgotten to check it for the past week. She wasn't exactly a Luddite, but could never remember that e-mail was one more place to check for correspondence.

It often seemed like one more place to find work.

Leslie adjusted her glasses and sifted quickly through the notes from students—she thought of them collectively as pleas for clemency of one kind or another—stuffed the two messages from Dinkelmann into a separate folder for later viewing, did the same with the condolence messages from friends and associates, and was left with two messages.

One was from her brother-in-law, the devil himself. She could tell, not just by the j.coxwell of his address but by the fact that the server was the district attorney's office. She clicked to open it, bracing herself for a bomb of some kind.

The message was typical of James.

"Call me at your earliest convenience, please."

That polite terse imperative was followed by a telephone number, presumably his cell phone. His message was only half an hour old and she disliked the sense that she was being commanded to do anything. Rebellion roiled within Leslie, but she wasn't prepared to drop the box *Social Niceties*.

It matched *Keeping Up Appearances* so well, after all.

She might as well get this over with, too.

James answered immediately, as if he had known exactly when she would call. After cursory greetings, he got right to the point. "Have you talked to Matt lately?"

Leslie found herself bristling. "Yes, why?"

"How did you find his attitude?"

Leslie preferred to not answer that. "Why do you ask?"

James sighed. "Because I've had a call from the Chief of Police in Rosemount—"

"Me, too. I thought he reached Matt."

"I spoke to him afterward. He didn't think Matt was taking his suggestion of counseling very seriously."

Leslie bit her lip, not wanting to reveal what Matt had told her about his inclinations.

"And I had a call from Zach last night. He thinks Matt is cracking up."

"Why?"

"Well, for one thing, Matt has refused to defend Zach. He told him to solve his problem himself."

"That's past due, I'd think," Leslie couldn't help noting.

"Maybe so." She heard the smile in James's voice. "But Zach said that Matt was angry . . ."

Leslie felt the need to interrupt and defend Matt. "But you know, Zach does have a tendency to be irritating. And maybe he's just annoyed that Matt isn't doing what he wants him to do."

"And so Zach is calling names in order to prompt me to do something instead," James mused. "That would be consistent with the past. Zach has a hard time accepting that his way isn't the only way."

"Funny how the youngest of you would end up thinking himself the crown prince." The words were out before Leslie could stop them, although she didn't usually say such things aloud. She clapped a hand over her mouth, wondering what had gotten into her lately.

Oh right. She'd dropped that *Family Diplomat* box.

To her surprise, James laughed. "You're right. Although the youngest is sometimes the most indulged." He sobered then. "How are you doing with my mother, by the way?"

"I think we have a cease-fire," Leslie found herself saying. "Certainly she and Annette have come to some kind of agreement, which makes life easier."

"Don't tell me that either of them compromised?" James feigned shock and Leslie found herself smiling. It was easier to talk to the shark than she'd expected. "They've got more in common than just their looks."

"Here I thought it was just the poodles."

A beat of silence told Leslie that James didn't know what she was talking about. "What poodles?" he asked carefully.

"The girls, of course. Your mother's new wards." Then, just because she seldom had a chance to leave James with anything to think about, Leslie did. "Oh, gotta go. Give my best to Maralys and the kids. Have a good weekend."

James sputtered incoherently as he never did, and Leslie indulged herself a good chuckle after she hung up the phone.

Maybe she should bite her tongue less often.

It might, at the very least, make life more interesting.

* * *

"Score one for the good guys!" Naomi said, appearing so suddenly in Leslie's office doorway that Leslie jumped. "Ha! I knew you wouldn't be able to just step aside and let him have his way."

Leslie spun in her chair, a little bit spooked by Naomi's jubilant manner. "Am I supposed to know what you're talking about?"

"Be serious. The whole department is talking about the lecture you gave your third-year students yesterday." Naomi punched her fist skyward. "Yes! Crabcake Coxwell says 'no' to higher grades for less work. Crabcake Coxwell says 'no' to full participation marks for just registering for her class." Naomi perched on the credenza, nearly launching an avalanche of books and papers when she did so, her eyes sparkling. "Damn! I wish I could have been there. You were kicking some lion ass!"

Leslie felt a little bit sick. Why hadn't she remembered to check her contract for those possible reasons for termination? It wasn't as if she'd had anything else on her plate this week. "Surely not everyone is talking about it."

"*Everybody*. Even upstairs in classics, they're all over it. You're major hero material." Naomi snapped her fingers. "Hey you want a triumph, I can fix it right up. No problem."

"I'm not sure I really need a triumphant procession into the department right now."

"Department? No, I'm talking about an entry into the university, out in the streets, cheering fans, the whole bit."

The idea made Leslie laugh. "Even you can't fix that."

"But I'd try. Seriously, Leslie, I admire you. Standing up to Dinkelmann is something."

It was, in fact, something that made Leslie feel as if her breakfast was going to make a curtain call.

"I mean, for me to buck him is nothing comparatively, but you've got so much to lose." Naomi stuck out her hand. "Welcome to Team Good Fight. I knew I'd always looked up to you for a reason."

Dinkelmann himself arrived right when Leslie and Naomi were shaking hands. Sadly, Naomi had left the door open, so he saw the whole thing. His gaze flicked between the two women with open disapproval and his lips thinned.

"Excuse me for interrupting, Dr. Coxwell, but there's a matter I would like to discuss with you."

His form of address told Leslie all that she needed to know about his opinion of her behavior the day before.

"Of course," she said, with a gracious smile that belied her inner turmoil.

"If you could come to my office in ten or fifteen minutes, I think we can deal with this before your next lecture." There was a slight emphasis on the last word, which Leslie knew was an accusation. She agreed and he nodded, sparing only the barest glance to Naomi before he left.

"Trust him to change the field," Naomi muttered.

"What do you mean?"

"Oh, it's always better to fight on familiar turf. And there's the whole strategic advantage of having you come to him, on his terms. You watch, he'll be sitting behind his desk, all his artillery mustered around him, and let you sit in one of the armless chairs opposite." Naomi scoffed. "There's a reason I always hated military history."

For her part, Leslie was wishing she'd hated it a little less, or maybe studied it a little more. She might have moats and siege engines and Greek fire and, maybe, if she stretched to the end of her era, even the longbow.

But Dinkelmann had gunpowder. Cannons. Infantry and a paid standing army. Hell, he even had better maps, ones that didn't say "here be dragons" all around the perimeter.

Leslie left her office, knowing she was sailing off the edge of the world, into terra incognita. It was only reasonable, given that she'd never defied expectation in this job, that she was feeling like dragon chow.

* * *

Matt's past showed no inclination to remain placidly where it belonged. He told himself that it was only reasonable that he kept thinking of the woman with whom he had spent the last eighteen years of his life, but it was unnerving to realize what a hold Leslie still had over his imagination.

He caught himself drifting into memory for the umpteenth time that afternoon and surrendered.

* * *

The Java Joint was a dump.

No real estate agent could have put spin on that place's character and Matt had always been mildly amazed that no health inspector had ever shut it down. It had the layer of grunge typical of undergraduate housing but mercifully uncommon in a retail establishment serving food. The kids working there were indistinguishable from the patrons and the music was so loud that you had to shout to place your order.

The tables were quieter and the din was lower yet in the back corner where Matt and Leslie invariably met. He'd still had to lean over the table to hear her, at least until he'd summoned the nerve to sit right beside her.

Come to think of it, that light of pleasant surprise at the sight of him had been a hallmark of her arrival from the very beginning. In those days, though, she'd smiled and blushed a little before she came to the table. They talked about everything and nothing, about politics and history and families and dreams—and gradually he'd found pieces to the jigsaw puzzle of her life. She lived with a maiden auntie who had a house near the T if not near the university. She lived under rules more strict than he'd ever had to deal with, within a virtual cocoon designed to protect her innocence for marriage. She was supposed to be either at school, at her part-time job at JCPenney, or at her auntie's. There were no other options.

He'd understood early that there was no chance of their having a conventional date.

But they had the Java Joint. Weekly, then daily, then several times a day, they met and talked, and when he first kissed her, it had been at that table in the corner of the Java Joint.

Such sweetness. He could remember her surprise, her softness, her uncertainty. He had been sure then—and still was—that she had never been kissed before. He had felt protective of her because of that kiss, had been cautious about pushing her too far too fast as a result of it.

He brought her things. Silly things. A postcard from the pier. A seashell he'd found in Rosemount. The smallest gift gave her the greatest pleasure, and that told him more than he could have guessed about her background and her expectations. He'd brought her ridiculous, playful tokens, things calculated to make her smile: olives from Little Italy and stories of going to the theater. He remembered how she'd fingered those ticket stubs, souvenirs as they were of a world far beyond the boundaries of her own. And that had given Matt ideas, perhaps ideas that would have frightened Leslie's father as much as the ideas that man had feared young men would have about his precious daughter.

Over time Matt had encouraged Leslie to take some adventures during the day: A furtive trip to Gardner Museum had been the first. Then there was another to the Museum of Fine Arts, lobster at Johnny's—at lunch—veal piccata in the North End, a Red Sox game on a spring afternoon. He was an ambassador for the city of Boston, all the while falling more deeply in love with a woman so sheltered yet so willing to embrace the world.

To embrace him. He figured out how to make her laugh, how to persuade her to show him more of her own quirky humor. He earned her confidence in easy steps and found so much more than he had expected. Leslie had a thousand layers of armor, a remarkable self-control that protected the best of herself from casual view. She shared that jewel with those closest to her.

When had he lost access to the treasury?

Was that why he had been so convinced that he had to leave? Matt didn't know, but the reappearance of Leslie's humor in their conversations made him realize how much she had slipped away without him noticing.

Could he be part of the reason for the distance between them?

They had been dating—if that's what it was—for a year before she came to his apartment at lunch one day. It was autumn again, later, closer to Thanksgiving. Matt could remember how the dead leaves swirled around their feet as they walked in silence across the campus. It had been cold, the wind whipping at his cheeks, but he hadn't been able to feel beyond the soft heat of Leslie's hand in his.

And he was nervous. He felt as if he was walking a schoolgirl across the park. He was certain that Leslie couldn't feel the same lust that he did. He was going to explode if they didn't make some progress on the intimacy front, but he was halfway convinced that she would run away from him if he tried anything.

He was not entirely sure of his strategy.

He and a buddy rented an apartment close to campus, more of a dump than the apartment on Inman Square proved to be, but infinitely more private than the Java Joint. His buddy had been banished, the apartment was clean—or cleaner than it ever had been or would be again during their tenancy. This was as good as it was going to get.

"Well, here it is." He unlocked the door with a flourish, feeling brilliantly inarticulate. He needed a smoother move than any of the ones he had; that was his last thought as Leslie crossed the threshold. He followed her, wondering what to do, and was assaulted as soon as he closed the door.

"Really kiss me this time," she whispered, her eyes dancing with anticipation.

Leslie still kissed with sweet ferocious heat, that would never change—it was the frequency of kisses that had changed over the years. Nor, in fact, would his surprise at her hidden passion ever change.

He should have learned that truth that day when they were entwined on the couch. He unfastened her sweater to find her wearing the most sexy black satin bra he'd ever seen in his life.

He was struck speechless. The lingerie was so incongruous with her outward appearance, so mischievous, sexy, and playful. He looked at her and shook his head. She blushed but laughed.

"I like lingerie," she admitted. "A lot. That's why I work at JCPenney, so I can buy what I want."

"I thought you needed money for school."

"No, I could earn that during the summer. This is for me." She said this last with such defiance that Matt had a sudden insight into what it cost to live her father's dreams, to always fulfil his expectations. He saw that she would fight for her lingerie, and maybe for more of her own choices in time.

He shook his head and smiled. "I'm surprised."

"You'll never catch me in a white cotton sport bra."

"Will I catch you in this?"

Her smile turned wicked. She lifted his hand to her breast, then feigned surprise. "Caught!" she said, and triumphant, he kissed her laughter away.

* * *

It was a telling recollection. Leslie fooled the world with her demure exterior, sometimes even fooled him into forgetting how deeply she cared. Matt Coxwell stopped cold in a quiet street in Algiers and wondered whether he had been fooled again.

He certainly hadn't been checking on his wife's lingerie collection lately.

Was it possible that she *wouldn't* have condemned his choice if he'd confided in her?

No, he reasoned, starting the trek back to Sharan's house. No, he was giving credit where it wasn't due, he was sure of it, though a voice in the back of his thoughts nagged him about the possibility. Leslie had said herself that she had wanted him to take a job with his father, which any idiot could see would be a bad choice for Matt, just so that she could pursue her own ambition, whatever it was. Leslie saw what Leslie wanted and nothing else. Matt should know that well enough by now.

Funny how he couldn't stop thinking about that black satin bra, or even his own surprise at its discovery.

* * *

It was no consolation that Naomi was right.

Dinkelmann was behind his desk—a vast expanse of actual oak in contrast to the chipboard with wood-grain-paper-veneer special in Leslie's office—hands braced on its surface, the wall behind him chockablock with books. No, they were tomes with leather binding and gilded script. The window in his office looked over the tranquil quadrangle and the snow there cast a bright white light into the room.

They exchanged greetings, then Leslie claimed one of the straight chairs positioned for guests. It was a cheap chair with a plastic seat and wobbled disconcertingly. She thought of Naomi and wondered whether the choice was deliberate. Meanwhile Dr. Dinkelmann spun slowly in his five-legged, leather-upholstered, ergonomically designed chair and regarded her solemnly.

He did that for a long time, but Leslie resisted the urge to fidget like a toddler caught with one hand in the cookie jar. She sat, perfectly straight, didn't wobble the chair, and stared back.

He abruptly leaned forward and templed his fingers together, the image of paternal concern. Seeing as Leslie had at least a decade of experience on him, it irritated her. "Leslie, Leslie, Leslie. I've heard the most troubling stories about your lecture yesterday."

"Really?"

"Really. I can only conclude that I was right to encourage you to take a leave of absence and that your enthusiasm for teaching has led you to overestimate your capabilities under duress."

Leslie was pretty sure that she wasn't the one overestimating her capabilities. "Thank you for your concern, Dr. Dinkelmann, but I don't happen to share your concerns."

"Even after yesterday's lecture?"

"Even after yesterday's lecture. I've been thinking about the encouragement of excellence and am convinced that the way to do so is to demand more of students, not less."

"That's clearly contrary to our discussion earlier this week."

"But consistent with my experience, all the same. Even my own daughter will take advantage of any opportunity to do less, though encouragement will invariably prompt her to do more."

"You would base your management of a university class with your experience in raising your daughter?"

"And with teaching other university classes." Leslie smiled. "I think it's a better plan than basing my teaching patterns on marketing decisions."

Dinkelmann's eyes widened. "I must confess that I'm surprised to find you possessed of such a defiant attitude, Dr. Coxwell. You've always worked well with me in the past."

Leslie took a deep breath, knowing that she was leaping into the abyss without a parachute. "There are principles worth fighting for, Dr. Dinkelmann. I do not believe that excellence is encouraged with lassitude and I do not believe that any academic purpose is served by lowering expectations and standards."

"This is in direct defiance . . ."

Leslie had had enough, which made her more bold than she had ever been before. "Give me this term. Give me this term and the kids who are already registered in my classes and I guarantee you that they'll have better marks than they would have had otherwise."

Dinkelmann leaned back in his chair and smiled. "Leslie, Leslie, this is foolish."

"I'll do it. We'll tally up their GPAs in history classes thus far and if more than half of them improve upon that, then you have to cede that my strategy has some merit."

"And if they don't?"

Leslie took a deep breath. "I'll quit, because if I can't succeed at this, then I don't know anything about teaching at all."

"Leslie, this is quixotic . . ."

"I refuse to teach to the lowest common denominator or give grades beyond what has been earned."

"You're living in the past, Leslie."

She smiled. "I'm a medievalist and a social historian to boot. The past is the point for me."

Dinkelmann stared at the top of his desk for a long moment, his pen tapping as regularly as a metronome all the while. "You should know," he finally said, with care, "that Anthony Dias will be joining us next week. He's poised for great things, Leslie, and has already begun to make his mark among medievalists for some daring revisionist thinking."

He raised his gaze. "The fact remains that I respect both you and your work, so I'm giving you an option. You can recant everything you've just said right here and right now, and I'll forget we ever had this discussion. I'll attribute it to stress." He wagged a finger at her. "But if you walk out that door without recanting, I'll hold you to the letter of what you've just said. I don't need to have two medievalists in my department, and I won't endorse any challenge of a mandate directly from the board of governors by anyone on my staff. Even with tenure, your appointment here can be made very uncomfortable. Are we understood?"

"We are." Leslie got to her feet, hoping he couldn't see how her knees were trembling. She held out her hand. "So do we have a deal on this term?"

Dinkelmann studied her for so long that Leslie thought he'd decline. Then he stood abruptly and took her hand. He shook it once hard, giving her such a steady look that she was half-convinced that he wanted her to succeed.

Then she was flying down the hall, late for her third-year lecture. She decided impulsively against the prepared format, swung into the room, dropped her books and seized the lectern.

It was all or nothing, a fight to the finish.

Leslie Coxwell was ready.

"I want to talk to you today about my own studies," she said, watching as the students exchanged glances. "I want you to understand the point of all of this, to see what a social historian does once he or she has survived the political history courses and the rigors of grad school. I want you to understand the point of studying the past."

Leslie took a deep breath, terrified because she had nothing prepared but exhilarated all the same. "I want to talk to you about charivari. Have any of you ever heard this term before?"

They shook their heads and several leaned forward.

"Charivari was one of a number of performances or rituals that enforced socially acceptable behavior in medieval society. These kinds of rituals became increasingly common through the middle ages, reaching their peak of popularity in the fourteenth century. It's possible that someone someday will link them more conclusively to the emergence of theater, but today we'll just talk about what charivari was and how it worked."

The kids were listening, Leslie saw with pleasure.

"Charivari was also called rough music, or *katzenmusik* in Germany, *concerrada* in Spain, *scampanate* in Italy. You'll find it listed as *chalivali, calvali, chanavari,* or *coribari* as well. It had many names because it was a phenomenon that occurred all over Europe.

"So what was it? Charivari was a noisy demonstration that was held at night, and it was a means of policing social transgressions—as opposed to legal ones, which would be policed by the sheriff and court. When a social transgression was perceived to have been made, people of the village came to the door of the offender in the middle of the night, or even to his window. They wore disguises, they often dressed as animals or wild men, and they played pots and pans as if they were instruments. They sang rude songs and made coarse jokes. They would rouse the transgressors from bed and humiliate them publicly, maybe by making them ride a donkey backward, maybe by burning them in effigy, maybe by leaving them naked in some public place."

Leslie paused to face the class. "It must have been terrifying, even though people were not physically hurt. Further, the following morning, those who had enacted the 'punishment' would act as if nothing had happened, which must also have contributed to the anxiety of those who were chosen as victims."

The students were riveted.

"So what prompted these attacks? Well, we have pretty limited records of charivari, as the churchmen responsible for most of our medieval records didn't approve of these kinds of spontaneous, perhaps pagan, rituals. But it's clear that one of the main triggers for charivari was the transgression of marital expectations. A man who beat his wife might be humiliated in this way, because the law might not be against him or inclined to take action against him. Similarly a marriage in which the wife was perceived to be in control would often be the target of charivari. Any guesses as to why?"

Four students raised their hands, and Leslie picked one. "Because having the woman rule was perceived to be unnatural?"

"That's right. It would be seen as a violation of God's law, and thus an action that could endanger the souls of everyone in the village. They perceived the question of their salvation to be not only determined by their individual behavior, but by the behavior of the community as a whole. This belief empowered them to chide their fellows.

"Similarly those who were believed to engage in unorthodox sexual practices might be the victims of charivari. Women who beat their husbands were a favorite target, and that seems to have been much more prevalent than we might have expected."

Another student raised her hand. "But I thought women had minor roles in medieval society?"

Leslie spread her hands. "The sources would seem to indicate as much, so what do we do with all of these husband beaters? There are many of them. What does the prevalence of these women mean? Is there something we don't understand about gender roles and their restrictions in that society? Or do we have false assumptions about the agency—that is the power of individuals to act or to make things happen in their own lives—of medieval women? Maybe gender roles in medieval society—or in some places and at some times—were more fluid or more complicated than we've seen in other sources."

They thought about that, a couple of them looking genuinely perplexed, and Leslie felt a conviction that she'd awakened something potent. "Widows and widowers remarrying also were often the targets of charivari, especially if there was a large age disparity between the pair. Any ideas why?"

They were leaning forward now, anxious to speculate. Leslie indicated one student who was waving her hand. "Because it's unnatural for a young person to marry an elderly one? They might not be able to have children."

"There's that." Leslie pointed to another student.

"And other young people might not like one of their fellows being 'taken.'"

"Exactly," Leslie said. "Remember that Europe had a kind of population explosion from the twelfth century until the plague's arrival in the mid-fourteenth century. There was greater competition for assets, including property, tillage, and marriage partners."

"Could there have been people who thought that the younger person consented to the marriage just to get the older person's money?"

"Absolutely. Charivari was primarily a rural phenomenon, something that happened in villages and not in cities. You may know yourself that there are few secrets in a small town." They laughed then and Leslie was excited to have them so engaged in the material. "Any other ideas? Does anyone know how remarriages were enacted, or how the ceremonies were different from first marriages?"

"Weren't they held privately?"

"Yes, exactly. Remarriages were often quiet affairs. The couple might pledge themselves at night, at home, in the company of only a few witnesses. Remember that marriage is the one sacrament that requires only the participants and God as a witness: It did not even require the presence of a priest until the state became concerned with ensuring the legitimacy of offspring. So why would that bother people?"

"No party?" guessed one student, to laughter from his fellows.

"Exactly! There would be no food, drink, and entertainment provided at the expense of the couple and/or their families. In lean years—and there were a lot of them in the early fourteenth century, what with famine and crop failure—that might easily be resented." Leslie leaned on the podium and decided to push them a bit. "So you may not realize this, but a lot of medieval traditions endure in our society in one form or another. Any ideas what happened to charivari? Is it gone, or is it still lurking in the corners of our expectations and behavior?"

"Some religious groups shun people for perceived transgressions."

"Like the Amish and the Shakers. Exactly. That's a formal response, decided in committee by representatives of the group, almost like a court decision. Do we do that informally, though?"

They nodded, and more than a few of them smiled.

Another student put up his hand. "Isn't that why people don't tell anyone where they're staying on the night after their wedding?"

"Yes, people will beat pots and pans, and sing loud songs outside wherever the couple has gone to consummate their marriage, if they find out where it is. The idea is that the honeymoon location is supposed to be a secret. Sounds a lot like charivari, doesn't it?"

"People still say things about couples who get married who are really different in age," suggested one student.

"Things like?" Leslie prompted.

"Like one's marrying the other for money or for sex or for a trophy."

"Exactly. We still hold similar ideas about which partners are suitable. What other kinds of marriages do you think were targeted for charivari? Guess."

"People of different religions getting married?"

"Yes. There's not an enormous amount of that in medieval Europe, but even the idea of someone eligible marrying a foreigner, someone from outside the local region, could make the couple targets."

"What about Carnival? You know, it happens in the winter in Rio de Janeiro and New Orleans?" asked one girl.

Leslie nodded. "That's another kind of costumed revelry, one specifically linked to the beginning of Lent, and it used to happen everywhere in Europe in the middle ages. You all know, of course, that Lent in the Christian tradition is the period of spiritual preparation for the celebration of Easter, and in medieval Europe, Christianity was the religion of the majority. What do you do during Lent?"

"Fast!"

"Give something up!"

Leslie smiled, enjoying herself as she seldom did in lecture. "So what do you think Carnival is?"

"One last party!"

"More than that. What's the origin of the word? Where are my Latin students?" The students blinked and looked between each other. "What if I say, '*carne vale*'?"

"Farewell, meat," called a student from the back row to general laughter.

"That's exactly it," Leslie said. "One last chance to eat meat—as well as to drink alcohol—before the fasting of Lent began. And as you might imagine, things got a little wild."

The students were murmuring to each other, interested as they never had been and Leslie had to raise her voice to continue. "I'm going to change the midterm essay assignment, because I want to make it more interesting for you. I'd like you to identify some element of medieval social history—it can be weddings or funerals or charivari or Carnival or courtship or table manners, any aspect of social history—I'd like you to research what it is, how it worked, and explore any variations in its practice.

"If you choose something more universal, like weddings, or something for which there are a lot of source materials, then you may have to limit your discussion, either by geography or by date. For some subjects, because of a paucity of sources, you'll have to work with whatever is available and try to make some sense of it.

"Finally, I'd like you to look for traces of that medieval practice in our own times and culture. My own suspicion is that the root of much of Western social custom derives from the middle ages, so I'd like you to decide for yourself whether I'm right or not."

They were chattering and Leslie had to raise her voice again. "You have my office hours. Please come by in the next week or two to discuss your chosen topic and I can help you either broaden it or narrow it, as well as point you in the direction of some sources. Questions? Fine, I'll see you next week."

They left the lecture hall, chattering and excited, and Leslie couldn't help but smile.

It wasn't the black cami hiding under her blouse that had her walking so tall when she headed back to her office, or even its fabulous cut. It was the prospect of receiving a pile of essays that she actually wanted to read.

If this wasn't the way to end the week, Leslie didn't know what was. For the first time in years, she had enjoyed teaching, and had seen the proverbial little lights go on all across the hall.

She was right about this and she knew it. Dinkelmann would have to cede, because these kids were going to do a lot better. Best of all, she was following her own instincts instead of swallowing them and doing what was expected of her.

The only dark cloud in her sunny sky was that she had no one to tell about her triumph. Matt would have been proud of her. Matt would have said exactly the right thing. Matt would have suggested a celebration involving the horizontal fandango, Leslie was convinced of it.

Or she would have been convinced of it once upon a time.

But right now Matt almost certainly had someone else's tongue wrapped around his tonsils.

If that wasn't something to take the bounce out of Leslie's step, she didn't know what was.

Chapter Twelve

Leslie shouldered her way through the front door, feeling as if she'd dragged her butt all the way home. Two dogs barked and bounced toward her, giving her a momentary sense that she'd entered the wrong house.

"Champagne and Caviar," Annette scolded. "Sit down and let Mom come in." The dogs sat, though their tails still thumped on the floor.

"This is definitely the wrong house," Leslie muttered. "There are no cheerful teenagers at my place."

Annette playfully stuck out her tongue.

"Are you sure they don't need to go outside?" Leslie asked, eying the dogs uncertainly.

"I just walked them to the school and back. They're fine."

Leslie blinked, trying to connect the notion of exercise and her daughter together and failing completely. "You're pretty happy tonight," she said, as she put down her purse. She dropped her voice. "Isn't she here?"

Annette waved this off. "Dad called!" she said, with a glee that revealed how much she'd been worried about what was happening. "And I talked to him for ages. It was great."

Leslie didn't share her daughter's exhilaration. There was no doubt that the person she most wanted to talk to had called when she wasn't home. No excuses: She was right on time.

It would take a much more stupid person than Leslie to not see that Matt's had been a deliberate choice.

"That's nice," she said, without slowing her steps toward the stairs. If they were going to eat something homemade tonight, she needed to change and get to it. She wasn't going to so much as glance at that empty kitchen for the moment.

Champagne stretched up and sniffed Leslie's purse, probably checking for snacks. Caviar stayed put and watched.

Annette trailed behind Leslie as she climbed the stairs, doing that annoying observant-teenager thing that was mercifully rare. "So, aren't you glad?"

"Sure. I'm glad you had a chance to talk to him." Leslie reached her bedroom and peeled off her cardigan, kicked off her shoes.

"You seem to lack enthusiasm," Annette said, echoing a comment that had been made on one of her report cards years before and that had haunted her ever since. She and Matt had made a joke of it, though her tone wasn't humorous today.

"I'm thinking about what to make for dinner."

"He didn't say when he was coming home." Annette slouched in the doorway, her gaze fixed on Leslie.

"Maybe he's not sure yet of his plans."

The silence stretched between them, pulled like an elastic to nine times its natural length. Leslie expected something to snap and she hoped it wouldn't be her. She rummaged around, found a sweatshirt and jeans, and changed clothes, trying to act as if she hadn't had one heck of a fight with Matt this very morning. Annette lingered, as she never did, and Leslie felt her daughter's gaze like a ton of bricks on her back.

"You don't know whether he's coming back, do you?"

There would be no lies here. Leslie pivoted to face her daughter and took a deep breath. "No. I don't."

"Do you know why he left?"

"I have an idea, but only he knows for sure."

Annette shook her head. "No, I think you do know and I think you're not trying hard enough."

"Excuse me?"

The dogs climbed the stairs and stood beside Annette, their ears folded back and their eyes wide. Leslie would have sworn that they understood what was being said.

They certainly understood that Annette was upset. Caviar sat, leaning against Annette's leg and Champagne nuzzled her hand as if to reassure her. Annette probably didn't realize that her hand had fallen onto the top of the dog's head, or that her fingers had knotted in its fur—hair!—because her voice rose. "You always fix everything—why aren't you fixing this? Don't you love Dad anymore?"

"Of course I do!"

"Then why doesn't he love you?"

That would be the prizewinning question. Leslie was momentarily at a loss for words. "You don't know that . . ."

"Why else would he leave?" Annette lifted her chin in challenge. "I think you need to make him love you again, like you did the first time." She folded her arms across her chest and tears shone in her eyes. "I think you need to show him that you care."

"But I do care . . ."

"How would he know? How would *I* know?"

"Annette!"

She bolted before Leslie could reach her, retreating to her room with the dogs fast behind her and slamming the door. Her stereo was abruptly turned up, making it impossible to talk to her through the door.

Leslie heaved a sigh and decided not to even try.

"Or maybe," Beverly said, at sudden proximity, "you need to stop doing whatever you've been doing that made him forget that he loves you." She closed the door of the spare room behind her

with care, making Leslie aware that her mother-in-law must have
overheard the entire exchange.

"What's that supposed to mean?"

"That once any of my children decide that someone is for them,
it's not an easy feat to change their minds." Beverly shrugged. "In
fact, it's not easy to change their minds about much of anything.
They're all as stubborn as mules." She sighed. "They must have
gotten that from Robert."

Leslie decided it would be tactless to comment on that.

Beverly passed Leslie, trailing her fingertips across the younger
woman's shoulders. "Fight for what you want," she murmured.
"Win him all over again."

But that was the kicker, Leslie realized. "But I never fought for
him in the first place," she said, thinking aloud. She turned to meet
Beverly's gaze. "I never chased him. I never changed anything or
tried to tempt him. He courted me, with that persistence you're
talking about. I just was who I am."

Beverly smiled sadly. "But who are you, Leslie Coxwell? Are
you the same person as you were, or did you lose yourself somewhere along the way?"

That would be the million-dollar question.

Too bad Leslie didn't have the answer just yet.

*   *   *

Matt called Belmont when he knew Annette would be home from
school but Leslie would still be coming home from work. He
sensed Annette's uncertainty and had a long talk with her about
minor matters. They'd done that when she got home from school
for years now, usually in front of the television and some old
science-fiction show. It was different to do it on the telephone and
he was aware of the miles between them, as well as the fact that he
couldn't read her thoughts in her changing expression.

When they were done, he hung up the phone thoughtfully.

The cooked shrimp appetizer was chilling as was the wine; the catfish had been rubbed with spice and were ready to grill. There was nothing else Matt could do in the kitchen, so he strolled into the dining room and turned around the first of Sharan's canvases.

It was painted white, overpainted as she used to do when she was going to reuse a canvas after some idea hadn't worked out as she'd anticipated.

Intrigued he turned the next one over, only to find it the same.

In minutes he'd turned every canvas—and roused an army of dust molecules—only to discover that she didn't have a single painting left.

The largest canvas looked as if it might have once been *Pandora's Redemption*, the painting that had hung in that show all those years ago. He was standing, sipping his drink, considering the import of all of this, when Sharan lunged through the front door.

"Hey, what's for d—" She stopped cold and dropped her bag, the screen door slamming behind her. A flush rose from her throat and stained her cheeks. "You had no right!" she said, moving to turn the closest canvas around again.

Matt stayed her with a fingertip. "I wanted to see your work."

"There is none."

"There must have been some. It's been almost twenty years."

Sharan shook her head. "There was none that was any good." She lifted her chin and left the dining room, her shoulders stiff. "What are you making tonight? Oh, catfish. I love catfish . . ."

"Sharan, why did you paint over your canvases?"

"I told you. Because they were no good."

"So why didn't you just try to do better? Once upon a time, you wouldn't have given up so easily on something you loved."

She spun to face him and flung out her hands. "Who died and made you the Grand Inquisitor? I don't owe you any answers, not anymore, and if you think you're going to stay here and pester me about stuff that isn't any of your business, you've got another think coming . . ."

"It is my business, because you're my friend." Matt put down his drink and caught her shoulders in his hands, forcing her to look at him. "And you're unhappy. I'd like to help fix that."

Sharan regarded him ruefully. "And let me guess: It won't be with wild sex on the kitchen counter?"

Matt smiled and shook his head.

She sighed and looked away, then she leaned her forehead on his shoulder. She seemed to draw strength from that fleeting touch, because she straightened. "Okay, here's the deal. I'll talk to you about my painting if and when I feel like it, and you can talk to me about your book. You can cook, because I don't much, but you won't try to change me and you won't judge me."

"Deal."

"No, there's more. I do, however, reserve the right to try to change you and/or your mind. I'm not someone who's shy about what she wants. You should know that by now."

"I do. That's why the canvases surprise me . . ." Matt turned to gesture to the dining room but Sharan caught his arm.

"I want more than dinner and talk from you. Understood?"

Matt was sure that he understood more than Sharan thought he did. He saw that she was lonely, that she wanted him, that her desire was as much due to romantic notions of the past and proximity as anything else. He saw that she had learned to use sex to get what she wanted, to use it more effectively than she had when she was younger, and that she meant to try to use it now. She knew him well enough to know that if they had sex, he'd feel an obligation to her and their potential future.

And he saw that she wasn't his future; she was his past. But maybe the past they shared could help him to get her painting again, to start her own healing.

"I'm still sorting out who I am and what I want," he reminded her gently. "I wouldn't stay if I didn't think I could help you."

"Are you sorry you came here?"

"No," he said. "It's good to see you again."

Although that was true, Matt couldn't summon as much enthusiasm as he knew she wanted to hear. A cloud touched her gaze and she turned away. "Well then, let's eat. The fish look good."

Matt knew she was stung, just as he knew there was nothing he could do to reassure her because that might give her false expectations.

So he cooked the fish.

And after dinner he went for a long walk alone.

The house was empty when he came home, and he wasn't surprised. Nor was he surprised by the rhythmic sounds he overheard in the wee hours of the night.

He got himself a drink, returned to bed. He rolled to his back and considered the ceiling, and without intending to do so, found himself wondering what Leslie was doing.

*   *   *

It was late when Leslie closed her bedroom door and leaned her back against it. She was deliberately late, because she had tried to ensure her own exhaustion. The kitchen was cleaner than it had ever been but she was so wide awake that she might never sleep.

She stared at the ceiling, doing the Matthew of Paris inventory of her day so far. She'd once done this to amuse her own Matt, and that thought only made her more painfully aware of his absence.

Item the first: She'd cooked dinner tonight for the first time in decades. It hadn't been fabulous—just roasted chicken breasts and rice and steamed vegetables—but it hadn't been instant food, either.

Item the second: No one had died.

Item the third: No one had insisted upon ordering pizza instead of eating what was put in front of them.

That had to be a triumph of some kind.

Too bad she didn't feel very victorious.

She got into bed, knowing that if she did sleep, she'd probably have her stupid dream.

It showed up, right on cue.

* * *

Runt dunt dada dadala dunt da.

Leslie fights against the dream, knowing this battle is lost. She's in the big top, standing before the tightrope, dressed in her tutu and pink shoes. Her father is behind her, urging her on.

It's the same as it always is.

She feels the cable under her shoes, feels her shock and dismay as her father gives her a box. (She's a bit annoyed to find herself still expecting a pink parasol.) He gives her another and another, an astonishing and now familiar litany of titles emblazoned on their sides.

She takes a step, the one that is manageable, and he encourages her.

She takes another step, her heart in her throat, and her foot slips. She tries to regain her balance but overcorrects and the first box starts to fall. Leslie snatches for it, that little gold foil-wrapped box. She grabs it out of the air, feels a moment of triumph, before she tumbles from the wire.

The crowd gasps as one and Leslie swallows a scream. Her fall happens in slow motion. The other boxes tumble from her arms, falling into the abyss far far below, drifting down like snowflakes. She feels herself tumble into the air, feels nothing beneath her, nothing stopping her fall. Nothing saving her. She hears her father mutter in disappointment and fears that she will be consumed by the fires, too.

If the fall doesn't kill her first.

But suddenly she drifts aloft. She clutches the little gold box, the only one she still has. Her terror recedes as she moves horizontally over the crowd.

Instead of falling down.

It's impossible, but it's happening.

The abyss fades from view and is replaced by the floor of the big top, the stands filled with the audience, the clowns standing on the perimeter, the children waving their pink candy floss in excitement.

Leslie doesn't fall. She can't make sense of this. There's no safety harness attached to her back, but she's flying like Peter Pan. The crowd looks up at her in wonder, their eyes round and their mouths open. Leslie sails over them. She swoops, she dips, she does a loop-de-loop just by thinking about it.

She's flying!

She laughs as she soars and the crowd begins to cheer. She flies over their heads time and again, faster and slower, then finally lands as delicately as a butterfly in the middle of the tent. The roar of applause is almost deafening and she looks down at the box she still holds fast. She's pretty sure it's the box that's labeled Success *but as she turns it, the writing melts, the letters changing to form a different word.*

Honesty *is what is written on the side of the box.*

And Leslie knows with sudden clarity that this is the only box she really needs.

*   *   *

Leslie awakened with tears on her cheeks, knowing what she had to do.

*   *   *

It was late Saturday morning and Beverly was looking for her sweaters. She was freezing cold and had been since arriving here. Part of the problem, she knew, was that arranging a funeral was depressing stuff and another part of the problem was that she wasn't sleeping well. Either way, she didn't want to get sick and she didn't want to impose any further on Leslie.

Even borrowing a sweater might tip the scales too far. Beverly never could tell what Leslie was thinking or what she really thought, and she wasn't prepared to be tossed out a door again.

She was imposing and she knew it, but she needed a few days to catch her breath. Just a few days.

Beverly's own sweaters had to be in one of these boxes near the door of the living room, but she couldn't say that she had packed with any measure of organization. The quest was complicated by the fact that she was constantly being distracted by some unexpected item, because the movers had just tossed everything all together when they'd stepped in to help.

It was a mess. Fragile things needed to be righted and rewrapped. Delicate fibers needed to be flattened and folded. As a bonus, it kept Beverly's hands busy and her thoughts occupied. After some initial curiosity, the girls had crashed in the foyer. Champagne was snoring and one of them was farting—Beverly chose not to speculate further.

In the next box she opened, she found a bottle of Chanel Allure, dumped on its side and threatening to spill its contents. She treated herself to a spritz, then set it upright on one of her own end tables (which was not currently at the end of anything).

She found her favorite Cole Haan slingbacks chucked into the top of a large carton, not safely nestled in their individual felt bags within their designated box. Fortunately they had no new dings or creases. She set them aside and looked for that shoe box, without a lot of initial success.

She found the plastic cup from her bathroom swathed in six layers of tissue paper—while the perfume bottle had been unwrapped—and damned all movers to Hell.

Or at least Purgatory.

For a long time.

She muttered under her breath about the merits of a good straw sherry, the disadvantages of a perceptive eldest son taking responsibility for her recovery from addiction, and the woeful appropriation of a very nice stainless steel insulated thermos by said concerned son. She ripped open another crate and stopped cold.

"Oh." The sound left her lips, barely more than an exhalation. The girls heard it though and looked up with interest, poodle dreams forgotten for the moment.

The small familiar boxes were dumped into the larger carton, at sixes and sevens. To Beverly's relief, each smooth orange box was still closed, its contents safe from disarray. There were forty-nine of them. Beverly knew this without counting the individual gift boxes, just as she knew that not a one of them had ever had its contents disturbed.

She caressed the top one, appreciating the idea of it.

They were Hermès boxes, the kind used to package their trade-mark scarves. Flat square boxes that exuded luxury. They were or-ange with gold detailing, so beautiful that they were almost a gift in themselves.

Each year, Beverly knew, Hermès issued a silk scarf, a commem-orative design for that year. They made them now in many colors, but the traditional color of the house was a vibrant orange and the signature scarf was always available in that orange.

It was a color that Beverly could not wear. Yet Robert, con-vinced that he had found the perfect gift, apparently not noticing that Beverly had never cracked a single scarf out of its gift box, had given her one every single year to mark their anniversary.

Forty-nine pristine orange scarves, in their forty-nine pristine orange boxes. Forty-nine gifts evicted from their hiding place in the back of her bottom drawer and forced into her field of vision again, with astonishingly bad timing.

Forty-nine years of memories: good, bad, and indifferent.

Beverly blinked back her tears and flicked open the top box. She pulled out the scarf with some impatience and unfurled it, shaking out the shimmering silk of it. It was large, probably a yard on each side, as gleaming and bright as the robes of a Buddhist monk.

It was gloriously vibrant, the hue of life and optimism. The hue of saffron and citrus. The hue of joy.

What had happened to her joy?

A card lay in the bottom of the box, illustrating a number of ways to tie your scarf. This was clearly for foreigners, as Beverly was convinced that French women were born knowing sixty-three chic ways to tie a square silk scarf.

Or maybe they were initiated into the arcane secrets of the scarf at puberty.

At any rate, she had an idea and one that didn't require instructions. She doubted that there were instructions provided for decking out your dog in a Hermès scarf, but one never knew with the French. The girls were poodles, after all.

She folded that top scarf diagonally, rolled it and twisted it a bit, then wound it onto Champagne's collar.

"You can wear this color," she informed the dog. "And poodles are French, so I think you need a bit more style than this collar offers. It's better than that rhinestone thing Marissa had decked you out with, but the plain black leather is a bit severe."

Champagne sniffled the silk, as if confirming that it had been arranged to her satisfaction. She then shook herself and it did fall a bit better.

It was a French female thing obviously.

The orange looked fantastic on Caviar with her dark fur, like fire against the night. She bit the one corner and tugged, giving the scarf more of a cavalier air.

Beverly sat back on her heels, pleased with the results. The door clicked then and Annette came into the foyer, skepticism marring the prettiness of her features. She was wearing a black T-shirt, emblazoned with the name of something unfamiliar to Beverly, and the color did nothing for her. She dropped her backpack on the floor and surveyed her grandmother skeptically. "Aren't those Hermès scarves?"

"What do you know about Hermès scarves?"

Annette shrugged, a gesture that Beverly despised because it looked common. "Only that some of the girls at school think they're the thing to have."

She wanted to grab her granddaughter by the shoulders and compel her to stand straight, to be proud of her natural beauty, to wear colors that drew eyes to her beauty.

Which gave her an idea.

"Do you want one, then?"

Annette's eyes narrowed with a suspicion that ran so deep it wasn't easily disguised. "Because the dogs don't need any more?"

"Because it will suit your coloring. I've never been able to wear them because of that orange."

"You could wear orange."

Beverly shook her head. "No. I look like I have jaundice if I do. Here, you try. I think the undertone of your skin is different from mine." And the orange would flatter her more than the black, Beverly was certain.

Annette reached out a hand, then hesitated. "You're going to just give me one? Just like that? What are you going to want for it?"

Beverly dug out a gift box and presented it to her granddaughter. "A chance."

As soon as she said it, she knew it was true. She smiled, watching the uncertainty fade from her granddaughter's expression. "That's all I want from you; one more chance to be a grandmother."

Annette's eyes widened and her fingers brushed the box, the slowness of the gesture revealing how badly she wanted that scarf.

"Or maybe even a grandma," Beverly added boldly.

"As if," Annette said, under her breath, clearly thinking she wouldn't be heard.

Beverly arched a brow. "You're not giving me much of a chance."

Annette flushed. "Sorry. Can I still have the scarf?"

"Can I still have a chance?"

Their gazes met. Beverly smiled tentatively and was relieved when Annette smiled in return. "Okay." Annette opened the box and fingered the scarf. "But how do you tie it so it looks cool?"

Beverly's smile widened. "I see that it's time to initiate you into the arcane secrets of the sisterhood of scarf wearers."

Annette's eyes lit in anticipation. "No way."

"Way," Beverly retorted. "Let me show you a few things I learned in Paris."

* * *

Leslie circled the kitchen, one eye on the phone sitting silently on the counter. The house was empty, her privacy was complete. The day had been long and quiet, one spent marking papers like most Saturdays. On this Saturday, though, she'd been planning what to say and how to say it. She'd been revising a script in her head all day long, and it was as good as it was going to get.

She was nervous, her palms sweaty. Asking for what you want was worse than being thrown to the lions.

It was Saturday night in a little town close to the big city and she was barefoot in her kitchen, a flurry of snow tinkling against the windows. Annette was walking the poodles; Beverly had gone somewhere, maybe an AA meeting.

It was time to eat some crow.

If only she could work up her nerve.

If only Matt had been anywhere other than where he was.

But there was nothing for it. She pounced on the phone suddenly, before she could change her mind, got Sharan's number from directory assistance, and quickly punched in the number. A lump rose in her throat and her heartbeat began to pound in her ears.

Great, she had the smooth assurance of sixteen again. That would make things easier.

"Hello?" A woman. Well, that shouldn't have been a surprise.

"Hi, is this Sharan?" Leslie tried to sound as if she called this number all the time.

"Yes, it is."

"Hi, Sharan, it's Leslie Coxwell. Would Matt happen to be there?"

"And it's very nice to talk to you, too, Leslie."

"I'm sorry. It's been quite the week."

"Hasn't it, though?" Leslie didn't have much time to decide what to make of that. "Hang on, he's here."

Sharan put the phone down with a clatter that made Leslie wince. There was music playing, rollicking jazz that put Leslie in mind of speakeasies and people jitterbugging, laughing loudly and cutting loose.

Is that what he was doing? She could only imagine.

"What's the matter?" Matt demanded, his voice rough, and she jumped.

"Nothing's the matter. I just wanted to talk to you." Leslie heard him breathe a sigh of relief. "Well, something is the matter, but not in the way you think. I owe you an apology, maybe more than one. I haven't been listening very well. I haven't been asking very many questions and I haven't been sharing my own thoughts and worries with you. I haven't done a very good job lately of being a good partner."

It wasn't a particularly flattering confession and Matt's silence only made it harder. Leslie charged onward. "And so you were right in thinking that I wouldn't understand you and even in thinking that I might not be very accommodating of you changing the rules. I saw what I wanted, what I thought I needed, and didn't see much further."

Leslie took a ragged breath. "But you were wrong about me, too. I might have forgotten about my principles in order to guarantee my paycheck, in order to make sure that you weren't disappointed, but you've reminded me of that again. I've been making some changes. I've been trying to be the person I want to be."

She smiled and shook her head, knowing that she sounded like she was begging and not really caring.

Maybe she was begging.

Maybe it was about time.

"Annette says that I should just make you love me again, but the thing is that I never did that. You always were the one to make things happen. You always were the one to smooth the way and manage the details, and I just carried on with my own plans. It's been an unbalanced relationship, Matt, though I only see that now. And I'd like a chance to strike a new balance. I'd like a chance to find a way for both of us to have our principles, and to have them together."

She swallowed, achingly aware of his silence. But if you're going to eat crow, you've got to clean your plate. "I love you, Matt, though I don't think I appreciated how much until you were gone. I don't want to split up without giving us one more try."

Those last words might have been a penny tossed down a well. The silence was like waiting for the splash far below.

There was no splash and no response. Leslie figured it would be her luck to have given the genie at the bottom of the well a concussion with her coin.

The line crackled slightly. Having said what she'd called to say, Leslie was fresh out of words. All the same, she didn't want to hang up.

Matt cleared his throat, as if feeling awkward, something he seldom did.

At least as far as Leslie knew.

What else didn't she know?

"So how'd it go at work yesterday?" he asked, as if they were either strangers or so familiar to each other as to be disinteresting. Leslie was disoriented by this change of subject, until she remembered that he wasn't alone.

But what did this mean? Did he even care about what she'd just said? He must have heard her.

Or maybe he was looking for evidence of change.

"Oh, well, I challenged Dinkelmann to let me teach my way and we'd tally it up at the end of the term. If the kids' averages drop, then I'll quit: If they improve, he has to let me teach my way."

She could hear Matt's surprise. "And he went for that?"

"I think he's expecting me to blow it. It will be easier to be rid of me if I quit than for him to try to fire a tenured professor."

"And then what happens?"

"Well, I'm not planning on blowing it," Leslie said, trying to sound humorous and confident. She was pretty sure she failed on both counts. "But I have it on good authority that if you follow your heart, things should work out."

It was a clear reference to Matt's comment the previous day, but he didn't pick up on it. In fact he didn't say anything. There was another unwelcome portent.

Eating crow didn't seem to be bringing in the results.

Leslie's mouth went dry. At the very least, she had to find out when he was coming back, if he was coming back. "Your mother has pretty much completed the funeral arrangements for your dad," she said. "The service will be Wednesday in Rosemount."

"I see."

There was an informative response.

"Did you talk to Zach?" she asked, pretending she hadn't talked to James earlier.

"What?"

"Zach. Did you see him?"

"Oh yeah. Sorry, my thoughts were elsewhere."

Sharan laughed in the background and Leslie scowled at the counter, knowing damn well where his thoughts had been. Here she was yearning for her husband who was probably fondling his girlfriend while he talked to her.

It was disgusting.

Though she wasn't sure whether she was more disgusted with herself or with him.

Matt cleared his throat. "Well, right, I did find Zach. You'll love this: He swears that he's innocent of the charges."

"What are the charges?"

"Oh, there are a ton of them. Possession of marijuana is the one that will stick. He had enough dope on him that they're working on trafficking, as well."

"And he says he's innocent?"

"I know. It's crazy, isn't it? He's so sure that we should all jump to fix things for him."

"Are you going to?"

"No. He was hostile with me from the outset, insisting that I didn't know what I was doing, that I'd taken too long to show up and a lot of other stuff, as if there was nothing else going on in the world beyond the inconvenience of his detention. The truth is, they probably would have released him on his own recognizance if he hadn't handed around so much attitude."

"But that's not like Zach. He's usually very laid-back."

"Well, I'm guessing that they confiscated his stash and that affected his joie de vivre."

Sharan laughed in the background, though Leslie frowned.

"Bottom line, he ticked me off, and he wouldn't let it go. So I did the only sensible thing. I told him that if he was innocent, he didn't need my services and that I had to go."

"But what will happen to him?"

"That's his problem. He's done a couple of years of law school. Let him solve his problems himself for once."

"He must have said some nasty things."

"Maybe." Matt's tone as much as told Leslie that she wasn't in his confidence any longer. "I was out of there anyway. It was a nice day. Why would I want to hang around in a jail?"

"Won't the estate be tied up until the police finish their investigation?"

"And then some. Maybe Zach will work his way free by then." Matt sobered. "It could prove to be a financial problem for Mom, though. I'll have to talk to James about that." He murmured something, covering the receiver with his hand. "I should go."

Leslie's heart sank with the certainty that this would be the last time she talked to him. She would have done pretty much anything to keep him on the line. "Did I tell you about your mother's dogs?"

Matt paused. "Dogs? Like 'woof woof' dogs?"

"Yes, 'woof woof' dogs. Two of them."

"Live ones?"

"Yes." Leslie smiled, savoring his astonishment.

"You're telling me that my mother and dogs have something to do with each other?"

"She has two big poodles now."

"Since when?"

"Since Wednesday. She inherited them from a friend."

"She inherited dogs. Are you putting me on?"

Leslie laughed. "No, wait, I have it wrong. She has been appointed ward of the two dogs, because the dogs inherited the estate of Marissa Fitzgibbons."

"I remember Marissa. I didn't realize she had died."

"Well, I guess she did, because the dogs were hers and that was how she provided for them."

"My mother hates dogs."

"She seems to be getting over that. They're wearing her Hermès scarves today."

Matt made a choking sound, then Leslie heard him snap his fingers. "You know, Marissa Fitzgibbons was really loaded. Those must be the richest dogs in Massachusetts."

"Then maybe I should charge them rent."

"Wait a minute. The dogs are there, in the house?"

Leslie tried not to think too much about the fact that he hadn't said "our" house. The result was, inevitably, that she chattered. "Well, yes. Your mother is staying here, so the dogs came with her. Caviar and Champagne are their names. One's black and one's white: You can guess which is which all by yourself. She calls them 'the girls.'"

"The girls. It boggles the mind."

"Annette really likes them. You know how she always wanted a real puppy and these dogs are well trained already. She's out walking them tonight."

"Annette is outside in winter, walking, and by her own choice?"

"Yes." Leslie smiled at his astonishment.

"And you, you who do not like dogs, allowed not one but two dogs to live in the house?"

"Would you have wanted me to chuck your mother out in the street?"

"Jesus!"

There was a pause, and Leslie thought she heard Matt muttering under his breath. "What are you doing?"

"Trying to figure out how much I've drunk tonight. I'm having aural hallucinations."

Leslie enjoyed his discomfiture enough to serve him up some more. Maybe it would tempt him to come home. "Well, I should warn you we've fired the ice cream fairy and the muffin fairy. They just weren't working out without you here to keep them in line."

"Do you know what I had to pay headhunters to find those two?"

Leslie laughed.

"That's better," Matt said, with approval. "I've missed hearing you laugh."

"Then maybe you need to make better jokes."

That surprised him into a laugh of his own. Leslie might have felt a moment of triumph, if Sharan hadn't suddenly breathed into the phone. "Listen, Leslie, it's wonderful that you and Matt are talking, but this is my phone and my time. Dessert is served, Matt, so say night-night to your wifey."

And the connection, not surprisingly, was broken.

Leslie listened to the dial tone and wished she knew who had hung up the phone.

On the other hand, did it really matter?

*   *   *

"You shouldn't have done that," Matt said to Sharan. She stood right beside him, her thumb on the phone from breaking the connection. He was still holding the receiver, though that seemed kind of pointless now.

And he was still trying to wrap his mind around Leslie's words.

"Why not? Years ago you dumped me and broke my heart. Now you're here, in my house. I get to gloat." Sharan said stubbornly.

"You don't have to be mean."

"You came here, remember? You were looking for something and I don't think it was a telephone."

"You're right." Matt hung up the receiver. "I did come looking for something, but what I found was different from what I expected."

And what he had left had been different than what he expected. In fact what he'd been looking for had been his already.

It was a startling realization and one that left him blinking.

"This is not just about my painting . . ." Sharan began furiously.

"Yes, it is," Matt insisted, realizing that he had another purpose here with Sharan. It was a different one than he'd expected but was every bit as vital. "It's exactly about your painting. You need to paint, Sharan. It's a part of you, it's a gift that you were given so that you would use it. So long as you're not painting, I'm not sure of who you are."

"Art isn't all of me!"

"Would you have said that twenty years ago?"

"I didn't know anything twenty years ago." She folded her arms across her chest and spoke through gritted teeth. "Art isn't all of me."

Matt held her angry gaze. "Isn't it? Then who are you without it? You're more than a palm leaf painter, Sharan, and we both know it. You've got talent and it's your obligation to use it."

"You've got a lot of nerve," she snapped. She pivoted in the doorway to the spare room and glared back at him. "You think you can just come here and shake everything up, toss around what you think is the truth, and everyone will dance to your tune. Well, I've got news for you, Matt. I'm not going to play your game. I like sex and I like you, and if you're not going to ante up some physical affection, then you can leave."

Matt turned off the stove and moved the pot from the burner. He moved with surety, not wanting to anger her, but knowing he would do so anyway. "Fair enough," he said softly.

Sharan was shaken by his agreement, he could see that. "Most people think sex is easy, Matt." She tossed the words at him like grenades. "Most people would be glad to put out a bit to get what they want."

"Lots of people think sex is an important part of something bigger."

Sharan grabbed her purse, shoved her feet into her sandals, and headed for the door. "I'm going out. If you're not going to change your mind, don't be here when I wake up in the morning."

They eyed each other for a long moment, and he knew that she was expecting him to bend to her will. He knew what he had to do, though, and clearly saw his course forward.

Sharan must have seen something in his eyes. "Haven't you heard, Matt?" she asked, her words ragged. "Home is where the heart is, so get your ass out of my house."

He dropped his gaze, realizing that she'd uttered more truth than she knew.

Sharan swore, then spun out the front door. It slammed behind her and her little car started with a vengeance. The tires squealed and she was gone, only the hum of insects and the sound of a distant television carrying to Matt's ears.

He could have told her that she couldn't run away from what was frightening her. He knew that now, knew what he hadn't known just days before.

Sharan wouldn't have listened, though. She had to find the truth in her own way and in her own time, or not at all.

Maybe he could give her a nudge. Maybe he already had. Maybe that was what he owed her for old time's sake.

Matt considered the bottle of tequila and decided against it. He didn't want to be drunk tonight. He didn't want to dull his senses or cloud his thinking. He was filled with purpose and an optimism that he'd been sure he'd never feel again. Leslie wanted to try. Leslie was willing to make changes. Leslie still loved him.

And, albeit a little bit late, Matt realized that that was all he'd wanted. He'd been afraid to ask her for the one thing he desired of her, afraid she'd deny him. The fact that she had offered it of her own accord was a more precious gift than he'd ever imagined he'd find.

There were still, however, a few things he had to do.

Chapter Thirteen

Runt dunt dada dadala dunt da.

Leslie fights against the dream, knowing this battle is lost. She's in the big top, standing before the tightrope.

But something's wrong.

Her father's not here.

She looks around, but there's no sign of him. The music is insistent, persistent; the barker makes her introduction with a flourish.

But where is her father?

Leslie lifts one foot to step onto the tightrope, but the cable wobbles in front of her and she loses her nerve. She pulls back her foot, to the dismay of the crowd, then pivots and runs as they boo and hiss behind her.

She wants to fly the way she did the last night, but she has to find her father first. She runs through the working areas of the big top, pink leather slippers scattering sawdust. She ducks under the elephant's trunk and races around the clowns. She bursts out of the back of the tent to find a midwestern landscape stretching flat and golden in every direction.

The wheat is ripe, that's what she thinks, though she knows less than nothing about farming. It's warm, a sunny afternoon in the *late summer. She looks down and sees that she's an adult now, an adult in a child's tutu, her heels bursting out of those treasured ballet slippers.*

Her father stands just ahead of her, his foot braced on a guyline. He's smoking his pipe, staring across the flat expanse of land. The music of the calliope is muted behind them, but loud enough that she thinks he won't hear her approach.

She lifts a hand to put it on his shoulder, and he moves away, sensing her pending touch.

"It wasn't what you were supposed to do, was it?" he growls, and she pulls her hand away.

"I thought you wanted me to succeed."

"Not at that. Not like that."

"I liked flying."

"I don't care! It's not what you were supposed to do. You were supposed to walk the tightrope."

"But, but . . ."

"Get away with you now," he says gruffly. "You had to go and do what you wanted, didn't you? You couldn't think of others."

"But . . ." Leslie can't understand why her father doesn't want her to be happy, not until his words take a familiar turn.

"You had to marry him, didn't you? You had to stretch too far. I told you that it would end in tears. I told you that it would come to grief, but did you listen to me? Did you give any credit to what I said to you?" He turns and looks at her, accusation bright in his eyes. "Do you see yet that I was right?"

Leslie shakes her head. "It wasn't all bad . . ."

"No? And now you have a child and houseful of obligations and no man at your side. I told you this would happen. I told you that a man like him could not sustain any interest in a woman like you. I told you that you were just an amusement for him, but did you listen to me?"

"You told me to pursue my dreams. You told me to become a scholar . . ."

"You were supposed to find a man to take care of you, not find a man who amused himself for a while in having you take care of him. This was not what I wanted for you!"

"What about love?"

"Love has left you where you are, and where is that?" He looks her up and down. *"You don't want my advice. You don't listen to me, and you have no respect. Go ahead and destroy everything I've tried to give you."*

"I love him."

"You're too smart to make choices on that basis alone." He spares her a glance. *"At least my daughter was too smart for that sort of stupidity."* There was challenge in his eyes, challenge and condemnation. *"Get away with you then. Go ahead and do whatever you want. That's what you'll do anyway, ungrateful child. I don't need to watch you destroy yourself."*

And he turns his back upon her.

Exactly the way he had turned his back upon her fifteen years before.

* * *

Leslie awakened with a gasp and a catch in her throat. She hadn't forgotten a single word of that last exchange with her father. It was every bit as painful to hear his dismissal in a dream as it had been in real life.

And just as she had all those years ago, she started to cry. Who could have guessed that his approval had really been hinged on her marrying an approved choice?

It still hurt, still stung that who she was and what she had done was less important to her beloved father than who she might marry. Leslie rolled over and pulled the covers over her head. She supposed that if she was going to cry, this was a good time to do it. No one would see her, no one would hear her, and her eyes wouldn't be puffy by the time she got to work on Monday.

Because the thing was that she still believed she'd been right.

Love did count. Even if she had known that Matt would ultimately leave her and their marriage, she wouldn't have chosen differently. They had laughed together and loved together and been happy together, at least until recently. There had been the Java Joint and that first horrible apartment and a thousand other sweet memories, so treacherously precious that they would make her cry again.

And there was Annette. It was impossible to imagine her life without Annette, impossible to imagine Annette not existing.

Her father had managed that trick, though. Leslie cried that he had never seen his own grandchild, that her mother had been so afraid of his disapproval that she hadn't seen Annette until he had died.

Annette, mercifully, had been too small to understand, much less to remember. Beverly Coxwell might have been a snob about her son marrying down, but she hadn't forbidden him to do so. She hadn't stayed away. She hadn't made absolute decisions.

Who'd ever heard of someone being a snob about his child marrying up?

It was so unfair. He'd only met Matt briefly once, had made his decision on the basis of Matt's surname and the cut of his suit. He hadn't cared what Leslie believed, what she thought or felt. It had been a final, nonnegotiable decision.

The mattress bobbed before Leslie could wallow too much in this hard truth. She thought at first that it was her imagination, but then it happened again.

A distinct thump. Or a nudge.

She glanced over her shoulder and Champagne wagged her tail. The dog had her chin resting on the mattress and as Leslie made to roll over again, the dog thunked it on the mattress once again. The whole bed vibrated in response to this bid for attention.

"I suppose you want something."

Caviar appeared then, alongside her companion, tail wagging as well. They had nudged the door open just enough to slip through the gap. Champagne stretched to sniffle Leslie, but Leslie recoiled.

"Don't lick me. I don't like dog spit first thing in the morning. Or ever, actually."

Undeterred, Champagne disappeared for a moment, ducking her head toward the floor. Leslie watched, intrigued until the dog deposited a black leather leash on the bed.

"Ooof," the dog said, a low bark of emphasis, almost an exhalation.

Caviar wagged as if in endorsement of this splendid idea.

"It's five thirty." It was nuts to talk to a dog as if it were a person, but the gleam of intelligence in the dog's eyes made Leslie believe she might be understood. "It's too early."

The dogs exchanged a glance, then Champagne nudged the leash closer with her snout.

"Ooof," she insisted.

The dogs sat down and fixed Leslie with unblinking stares.

"You have staff," she informed the dog. "Check across the hall. The door on the right. You'll find your minion there." Leslie pushed the leash off the bed and buried herself in her covers.

All to no avail. The dogs came around to the other side of the bed. Champagne put the leash on the bed, exhaled, "Oof," and the pair sat back expectantly.

"You have a fan club," Leslie said this time. "Across the hall, the door on the left." Again she dumped the leash off her bed so that it hit the floor with a clatter.

"Ooof." One peek revealed that the leash was back on the bed, along with a second leash. Champagne sniffled the leash in front of her, then pushed it closer to Leslie again.

To Leslie's amazement, Caviar was looking toward the window, almost with yearning. She followed the dog's gaze and saw that it was snowing.

The dog was watching the snowflakes fall. It was early and the snowflakes swirled white out of the slate blue cloud-filled sky. The fact that it was snowing at all meant that it couldn't be too cold outside. There was no wind, the snowflakes appearing to dance as they came to earth.

"Ooof." Again the leash was nuzzled and pushed closer.

It didn't look as if the dogs were going to leave Leslie alone.

Maybe they really had to go outside to do things that people did in the bathroom. She hadn't paid attention to when they had gone out the night before. And if they made a mess in the house, Leslie knew who would be cleaning it up.

That made the decision for her.

She rolled out of bed, pulled on a pair of jeans and a sweatshirt. A short walk might even be good for her, might work off those extra chocolate bars.

It was, however, hard to get her socks on with two excited poodles circling her in their enthusiasm.

"Well, bring your leashes," she said to them when she left the room, and to her surprise they did so. Both girls ran back into the bedroom, picked up a leash, and galloped after Leslie. Champagne bodychecked her into the railing on the stairs when she passed on the right, then Caviar did the same from the left.

"Hey!"

They both leaped the last four or five steps, landing in the foyer with a thump, then trotted to the kitchen, tails wagging like banners. Leslie had a hard time keeping up.

By the time she had her boots and jacket on, both dogs were practically tap-dancing at the back door. Maybe this was a matter of some urgency. She opened the door, not accustomed to dogs and assuming that they would wait for her to put on their leashes.

Instead they bounded out into the snow so quickly that she panicked. Caviar skidded across the low deck, slipped off the low edge, and landed in snow that went up to her belly. Champagne leaped off the deck, looking for all the world like a dressage horse. Leslie shouted and they stopped, looking back at her with snow on their snouts, apparently surprised by her call.

Champagne trotted back to her and nuzzled Leslie's mitten, as if to reassure her, then bounded after Caviar and pounced on a snowflake. The two dogs ran circles around each other in the snow, playing like children. Suddenly they pivoted and looked at her expectantly, the snow gathering on their backs, tails wagging.

They wanted to play. Leslie understood as much from the mischievous gleam in their eyes, by the way they tried to catch snowflakes, by the joy in their every move.

"You got me out of bed so you could play in the snow," she accused, with mock indignation.

Champagne's merry bark seemed to be an agreement. Both tails wagged so quickly that they seemed to blur. Caviar bowed down—chest on the ground, rump in the air—and gave a low playful growl.

That gave Leslie an idea. The snow was perfect for packing and dogs like to chase balls, as far as she knew. She bent to gather snow for a snowball and Champagne barked with anticipation. The dog bounced closer as if unable to contain her excitement.

Leslie threw the snowball and Champagne jumped to snatch it out of the air. It was impressive how high she could jump. The dog shook the snowball playfully, then took a bite out of it. She held it down with one paw, eyes dancing, tail wagging, as she ate it.

Then she barked for another.

Caviar barked, as if to say, "Me, too!"

Leslie found herself laughing, just moments after she had been crying. She threw snowball after snowball, and the dogs never seemed to get tired of the game. They jumped and barked and chased snowballs, ate a lot of snow, and generally had the time of their lives.

Leslie was surprised to realize that she was having a good time, too. She couldn't make other people happy—she'd tried that and failed. Other people had to make themselves happy, and if that meant that they withheld their affection or moved out of her life, there wasn't a whole hell of a lot she could do about it.

That hurt, but the truth tended to be like that.

What she could do was make herself happy, take responsibility for her actions and choices, and communicate effectively to those around her about her desires and needs. She'd messed up her marriage by not talking more to Matt. Maybe she'd get another chance, maybe not.

It looked like not, but at least she'd told him what she thought first. That might make a difference. She could only try.

Maybe she'd be better off making herself happy first.

Leslie was so taken by their game that she didn't notice the sky begin to lighten, didn't realize the passing time until the back door opened behind her.

"Mom? Don't you want any coffee this morning?" Annette asked, her astonishment so evident that Leslie laughed and threw a snowball at her.

*   *   *

Annette couldn't believe that it was her mother outside, playing with the dogs in the snow. But when the person outside turned around, there was no doubt that it was Annette's mom.

Even if she did chuck a snowball at Annette.

"Hey!" Annette jumped out of the way and the snowball hit the door with a splat. Her mother—or the alien who looked remarkably similar to her mother—laughed again.

"Did you make coffee already"

Annette nodded, smiling when the dogs trotted over to greet her. She patted them, then looked at her hands. "They're covered in snow!"

"Well, someone will have to dry them off. There are some old towels in the downstairs bathroom." Her mom trudged back to the house and seemed somehow different. Happier. Brighter. More determined. Annette couldn't name it quite but she noticed it. "And your reward, my beloved child, for making me coffee is a good breakfast."

"Chocolate-chip muffins?"

"Alas, we fired the muffin fairy." Her mother shook her head with mock regret, then held up a finger. "But fortunately we have something better."

"Chocolate-chip cookies?"

"Your father would shoot me if I let you eat cookies for breakfast. Come to think of it, I might shoot me, too." Her mom shed her boots and crossed the kitchen, producing a box from the cupboard with a flourish. "We're having Raisin Bran, with fresh fruit on top."

Annette made a face. "Healthy food isn't a reward."

"Sure, it is. Look, it even has riboflavin."

Was that a joke? Annette folded her arms across her chest. "You can be as cheerful as you want. You're not selling that stuff to me."

"You'll go hungry instead?"

"I'll get a chocolate donut at the corner instead."

"I suppose that's what you do during the week."

"No, I buy them at school, in the cafeteria."

Her mom rolled her eyes and got two bowls out of the cupboard. "My tax dollars at work, teaching poor nutritional choices through simple availability in the public school system."

"Donuts aren't that bad for you."

"Be serious." Leslie perched on the stool by the counter, her eyes too bright for her to be entirely trustworthy. Annette braced herself for A Lesson. "Let me tell you a story. Once upon a time, there was a teenage girl a lot like you, and she was sad that boys never looked at her."

"Because she was fat." Annette threw herself into a chair, knowing who the teenage girl in question was supposed to be.

Her.

Duh.

"And so she decided that she would do something about it."

"As if."

Her mom continued on as if Annette weren't saying anything. "She decided to eat less and to be thin, but she knew she'd need a reward. So she decided to buy herself a fancy bra when she'd lost five pounds. And she did."

Annette regarded her mother with suspicion. There was no fancy bra in her life, though there were a bunch of them in her mom's dresser.

"It was red with white polka dots. Then she bought the matching panties when she'd lost another five."

"Who are you talking about?" The dogs laid down on the towels, stretching out by the floor duct that was gushing warm air into the kitchen.

Her mom kept talking. "And then she cut a deal with herself, that so long as she stayed thin, she'd buy herself lingerie. The trick was that she had to stay thin to be sure that all the lingerie continued to fit. And so she's been pretty much the same size and weight for about twenty years, except when she was pregnant, of course."

"Wait a minute. I saw all of your lingerie . . ."

"Did you now?" Her mom sipped coffee, unsurprised. "Was that before or after you took my vibrator?"

Annette opened her mouth and closed it again, not knowing how to defend herself against that. She hadn't expected to get caught, and she'd expected even less that she would be challenged. Her old mom—the one who had been replaced by an alien—had never paid that much attention to domestic detail.

Her mom considered her coffee for a moment before she spoke. "So, did you use it?"

Annette sputtered, then the truth fell out of her mouth. "I'm not sure how."

"Well, that's a relief in a way."

If Annette had expected censure, this wasn't it. As a result, she wasn't sure what to say.

Her mom watched her for a moment, then continued. "So

here's my suggestion. If you want to lose weight, to maybe have someone like Scott Sexton—"

"Hey! I told you that in confidence!"

"—stop to talk to you, then you could give yourself a reward, like I did."

"I tried your bras. They didn't fit."

"So I'll make you a deal. Ten pounds off and I'll buy you a bra and panties."

"My choice?"

"Your choice." Her mom crossed her heart and touched her fingertips to her lips. "It's just between you and me."

"What about the vibrator?"

Her mom laughed. "I'm not going to show you how to use it. You'll have to work that out for yourself."

"Can I have it?"

"No. If you haven't used it, I'd like it back. I'll buy you another one."

"After another ten pounds, I'll bet."

"No, right now. This weekend. I have to go to the mall anyway."

Annette's ears perked up. "Why?"

"I feel a sudden need for a very, very red lipstick."

"You don't wear red lipstick."

"Then maybe it's time I did. You can help me pick one out."

"You'll need something to wear with it."

"Yes, that's right. Something very, very red."

"And a vibrator for me," Annette reminded her, still skeptical that her mother would buy her such a thing.

Her mother looked similarly surprised, then she passed a hand over her brow. "I can't believe I'm saying this, because it sounds more like something your Aunt Maralys would say . . ."

That was interesting.

". . . but knowing how to satisfy yourself might keep you from making mistakes over men." Her mom smiled. "Scott Sexton, for example, might not be as great of a guy as you think he is. I'm already inclined to think less of him for not having noticed what a terrific girl you are."

Annette shared a smile with her newly cool mother, then sobered. "But how am I going to figure it out? I can't ask anyone at school."

Her mother sighed. "Did you look through all of my drawers?"

"No. Just the top one."

"Well, it's a good thing you didn't check the bottom one. Left side at the back. There used to be a book in there called *The Joy of Sex*." Her mom frowned and looked at the ceiling. "You know, it's been so long since I've glanced at it that I've almost forgotten about it." Then she looked at Annette and winked. "Maybe it's not even there anymore."

"Maybe not." Or maybe it wouldn't be there soon. Annette found herself smiling. The alien robot mother replacement wasn't all bad. She thought about the bra, knew it was a lure, but reached for a cereal bowl anyway. "Did you ever make a mistake about a guy, Mom?"

Her mom smiled back at her. "Not once."

"Not even if Dad's not coming back?"

"Not even." Her mom didn't even flinch, though Annette's stomach felt like it dropped to her toes. "The thing is, Annette, that I don't know what your father is going to do. And you know, it's not really up to me. So I've decided to try to not worry about it too much. You can't make people happy, though we often try. People need to make themselves happy, so I'm going to focus on getting myself happy."

"What? So, you don't care about him?"

Her mom exhaled and looked away, and when she looked at Annette again, her eyes were glistening with tears. "I care a lot, maybe too much. I said I was going to try, but it's not a given that I'll succeed."

"So, sometimes acting like an adult bites."

Her mom shook her head at that. "Yeah, that pretty much sums it up."

They eyed each other, almost smiling, almost crying, and Annette suspected they were going to end up having a hug. That was too much. It was, in fact, getting altogether too cozy in the kitchen.

There was a sound upstairs and Annette suddenly saw the upside of the witch finding her eating a healthy breakfast.

She picked up the box of cereal and checked the fine print on the side. "So, what is riboflavin anyway?"

* * *

Leslie's buoyant mood survived the shopping expedition, which was a first. She and Annette got along reasonably well on their adventure, though Annette had insisted that magenta was a better color for Leslie than vivid red. Leslie was new the proud owner of a fuschia lipstick, as well as a matching twinset.

The color made her look younger. She'd be Marian the Librarian with 'tude when she wore it, a prospect that made her smile.

Annette headed upstairs to study, the girls fast on her heels, and Leslie went to the kitchen. The first thing she saw was the package of chocolate-chip cookies on the counter. Her initial reaction was to want one, but then she wondered what it would solve. All the chocolate in the world wouldn't bring Matt back, and gorging on fattening foods wouldn't solve anything.

It sure wouldn't make her happy.

And what if her bras stopped fitting? Her heart nearly stopped at the prospect.

Leslie dropped the package of cookies into the trash just as the front door opened. "Hello?" Beverly called. "Anyone home?" The girls barked and came galloping down the stairs. Leslie glanced down the hall to find her mother-in-law being greeted with enthusiasm.

And laughing.

"Well, what a welcome! I don't know that anyone ever cared this much about me coming home before." Beverly patted Champagne, and Caviar barked for a bit of attention, too. "Go on, into the kitchen, and I'll show you what I've bought."

The girls trotted down the hall, apparently having understood, and Beverly followed. "What a fuss," she said, though she was clearly enjoying it.

"It looks like they missed you," Leslie said.

"It's a nice idea, whether it's true or not." Beverly put down her acquisitions and the girls immediately nosed into the plastic bags, sniffing the contents. "Out of the way, you curious creatures," Beverly chided, and the pair sat back. Their ears were still perked up, and they continued to watch Beverly with avid interest.

"Did you buy pork chops or steaks?" Leslie teased.

"Neither. Although I can't believe that I did buy these." Beverly pulled out a pair of stuffed squeaky toys made of brightly colored fake fur. Champagne barked while Beverly cut off the tags, then Caviar nudged the other impatiently with her nose. "There you go." The two dogs pranced off with their prizes, then flopped on the carpet by the duct—which they seemed to have appropriated as their own space—and investigated the toys.

"What are they?"

"I think one is supposed to be a drill and the other a power saw." Leslie gave Beverly a skeptical look. "Made of fake fur?"

"Yes." Beverly laughed then shook a finger. "Don't forget the squeaker inside."

Champagne found the squeaker in that moment and bounced to her feet at the noise the toy made. She excitedly pushed the toy with her nose until it squeaked again, then barked and pounced on the toy with both feet.

It clearly needed to be taught a lesson, because she settled in to lick it to oblivion. Caviar meanwhile was nudging her toy with greater insistence, seeking its squeaker.

"Well, you've made somebody happy today," Leslie said, with a smile. She opened the cupboards and found the box of sugar-coated cereal as well as a bag of potato chips, adding them to her accumulation of junk food trash.

"What are you doing?"

"Getting rid of pacifiers."

Beverly blinked. "Excuse me?"

"All the substitutes for emotional satisfaction. They're all going away. They're unwelcome here. We're going to be stable and strong and go after what we want without any high calorie crutches."

"Is this for you or for Annette?"

"It's for all of us." Leslie snapped her fingers, remembering the new carton of triple chocolate fudge swirl ice cream. She pulled it from the freezer and dumped it into the trash bag.

"I don't eat any of that stuff, so don't imagine you're doing it for me." Beverly developed a sudden interest in gathering the bags of her purchases. "I'll just take all of this upstairs."

Leslie stepped into her path, having a very good idea what was in one of those bags. "What did you buy today? Besides dog toys?"

Beverly bristled. "Oh, just a few odds and ends."

"That looks like a bottle."

"Shampoo," Beverly said quickly.

"We have lots of shampoo upstairs, which you're welcome to use."

"Oh no, this is for color-treated hair." Beverly rummaged in the bag, produced the bottle of shampoo, then shoved it back into the bag. She wasn't so quick, though, that Leslie didn't see the other bottle in the bag.

"What's this, then? Conditioner?" Leslie reached into the bag quickly and snagged the bottle of sherry before Beverly could step away.

At Leslie's enquiring glance, Beverly exhaled. "Anyone would acknowledge that I've had a difficult week."

"True. But they'd probably also tell you that it's a good test of your determination."

Beverly sighed. "That's exactly what they did say."

"You know and I know that this isn't going to solve anything, not any more than eating that carton of ice cream will fix my marriage."

"And besides you'll tell James on me."

"No. No, I won't." Leslie leaned against the counter. "But I'm trying to go with some new house rules and everyone needs to play along if this is going to work."

Beverly gave her a steely look. "It will not be my fault if Annette doesn't lose weight."

Leslie shrugged and glanced to the bottle.

Beverly grit her teeth and took the bottle. To Leslie's surprise, her mother-in-law marched to the sink, opened the bottle and poured its contents down the drain. She cast one accusing glance over her shoulder as the bottle emptied. "This is reputed to be a very good straw sherry."

Leslie shrugged. "The chocolate-chip cookies were the best of the best. They still wouldn't have fixed anything."

Beverly watched the gold liquid go down the drain and when she finally spoke, her tone was pensive. "I hope that you're not making a similar mistake to the one that I made."

"What would that be?"

"I think that sometimes we women get a bit mixed up as to the role of the men in our lives. I think sometimes that we think of our husbands as the powerful ones in our marriage, almost as if we've married our own fathers. I think sometimes that we transfer our feelings and expectations regarding our fathers to our husbands, and I know that is neither fair nor expected."

Leslie sat down heavily on a stool. Was she expecting Matt to make the same demands for her own success as her father did? Had she hidden her doubts and weakness from him for the same reason that she had hidden so much from her father: because she didn't want to disappoint him?

It sure seemed like it.

Beverly meanwhile was putting the top back on the empty sherry bottle and setting it aside for recycling. "You see, my own father had been raised in affluence. He wasn't the one who had made the family fortune: He'd just had the good luck to be born into it. I don't know that he ever worked a day in his life. He was charming and carefree and had the most exquisite manners. He could dance all night and make anyone laugh, but he wasn't a very practical man. If he had ever managed to spend all of that money— and believe me, he tried—he would have been in a predicament. He had no discipline, no drive, no desire to accomplish anything. He liked to have fun and that was the purpose of his life."

Beverly pulled out another stool and sat down beside Leslie. "My mother and he were two of a kind. They were more like kids than we were, and any discipline in our household came from our governess. That woman found herself outnumbered and outranked so many times that I think she eventually became overwhelmed with it all. I was allowed to do almost anything I wanted." Beverly looked up. "Except, of course, I wasn't supposed to get pregnant before I got married."

"You didn't." Leslie made a token protest, but she knew that Beverly had been pregnant before her marriage to Robert. She knew that James, Matt's elder brother, hadn't been Robert's son because that was why Robert had cast James out of the partnership and insisted upon taking Matt into the firm instead. She'd never heard the details though.

"I did," Beverly said. "Imagine, if you will, that a child has been completely indulged and allowed to do whatever she wanted, whenever she wanted, except for one thing, one thing that isn't even named."

"That's what she's going to try to do."

"Absolutely. I didn't plan it deliberately, but it must have been somewhere in the back of my mind. I was young and I was in love—or so I thought—and I believed that anything could be forgiven. I really believed that there wasn't much I could do wrong that would have lasting consequences. So I did what I wanted, and when he wanted to do that, I was game to try."

Beverly met Leslie's gaze and smiled, her eyes filled with wisdom and humor. "I didn't get pregnant the first time, which didn't teach me anything. I had no appreciation of how lucky I had been."

"You just thought it was something else you could get away with."

"Exactly! It took me about six months to get pregnant, which is pretty amazing given that I was young and healthy and so was he. But then it happened and I didn't know what to do."

"What about your boyfriend?"

"Oh, he left at the first sign of trouble." Beverly shook her head. "He had a great deal in common with my father. We had a lot of fun together, but he has probably never yet had a job of any kind."

"I thought you loved him."

"So did I, until I realized I'd have to pursue him and live in much less luxurious circumstances. The governess explained it all to me in very stern terms. Maybe she was making up for all those years in which no one listened to her: I had no choice but to listen and heed her advice and she knew it."

"What about your mother?"

"She fainted every time I tried to talk to her about it. I don't think that one of her daughters being pregnant out of wedlock was fun, so she refused to have anything to do with it."

Leslie eased her stool closer. "It must have been very frightening for you."

"Well, it could have been worse than it was. You see, there was an ambitious young man who had started to call on me. I hadn't thought that he was very amusing, because he was serious and so driven, but in this crisis, he began to be more appealing to me. He was solid and reliable. He was stern and disciplined. He wasn't much fun, but it seemed to me then that maybe we had had too much fun growing up and weren't very aware of our responsibilities as a result. He was very aware of his responsibilities."

"Robert Coxwell."

"The very same. But here was my mistake: I didn't want to tell him the truth, in case he took it badly or held it against me. He struck me as the kind of person who would have firm ideas of what a woman should be like and what she should do, and although I admired that, I didn't want to fall short of the measure. So I never told him and we married quickly—impulsively, he thought, but I wanted to get down the aisle before I started to show—and we had one of the largest premature babies ever born in Massachusetts."

Leslie laughed. "You had to subtract a couple of months from your pregnancy to make it sound legitimate."

"And James did not play along. How many babies arrive two months early but weigh seven and a half pounds?" Beverly laughed and Leslie joined her. "Mercifully, Robert had no sisters and his mother had already passed away. His only source of information about matters feminine was me, and I lied." She shook her head and met Leslie's gaze. "We never met as equals. Part of it was the times and the expectations people had of marriage . . ."

"And gender roles," Leslie contributed.

"But a lot of it was that lie. That combined with my own sense that Robert was stern and tough, the way a father should be, to put our relationship on an uneven footing. I always felt like the naughty little girl, waiting for him to find out just how I'd disappointed him. I looked for the father I never had in my husband, and that, plus my lie, doomed our marriage to be less than it could have been."

"You can't take all the blame yourself. Robert's nature was not exactly nurturing."

"More so than you might imagine." Beverly smiled sadly and traced an imaginary line on the counter around the shampoo bottle. "I knew him before his defenses were so formidable. I had seen some of his vulnerabilities, so he was more likely to show his weakness to me than to anyone else. That doesn't mean that he did so often, but he did do it once in a while, usually when he had no choice." Beverly looked up. "Those moments kept me there, and those moments are the ones that are assaulting me now." Her tears welled and she averted her gaze.

Leslie studied the shampoo bottle, for lack of a better place to look. "You need this shampoo because you're coloring your hair brown again."

"Yes," Beverly said curtly.

It seemed a good time for a compliment. "You look so much younger than with it gray. I never did understand why you let it go silver the last couple of years."

Beverly gave her a wry glance. "Well, if I tell you that Robert preferred it brown, that might give you an idea."

"You stopped coloring it when you left him?"

Beverly nodded. "Yes. I didn't want my appearance to be shaped by his expectations, and I was tired of looking like the young trophy wife I surely had been." She shook her head and pushed the bottle across the counter. "But, you know, he was right. It does look better this color. I didn't like looking like the grand-mother I know that I am."

"So you colored it back."

"And I was dreading the first time he saw it, because I knew he would gloat that I had agreed with him. I knew he would say I had come to my senses or something equally infuriating." She glanced up sharply. "But now he'll never know. He never did see it. He never did have a chance to remind me that he was right."

Leslie didn't know what to say to that. Whatever she said would sound insensitive, because even though she appreciated that Beverly had fond memories of Robert, it was impossible for her to think kindly of the man who had so cruelly arranged his death for Matt to discover. She turned the shampoo bottle on the counter and said nothing.

Beverly cleared her throat and spoke lightly. "Unless, of course, we both end up in the same camp of the afterlife. Although I doubt that will happen."

"Why?"

"Well, Robert always aimed to achieve the best and so he's prob-ably hoping to make the cut for Heaven." Beverly looked up with a smile. "I'm personally planning on Hell, as it sounds like more fun. That's where the sherry will be, after all. So he'll never know."

"You're forgetting your doctrine," Leslie felt obliged to point out. "Suicide is a mortal sin. In the middle ages, suicides couldn't even be buried in the hallowed ground of the churchyard. They were buried at crossroads, because people believed that would keep the corpses in their graves."

"I didn't need to know that."

"Sorry. Occupational hazard." Leslie touched Beverly's hand. "I think you need to shoot for Heaven, and I think you can get there from here."

"No sherry for all eternity isn't much incentive," Beverly said, with mock solemnity. "But who knows? Maybe it doesn't even taste good to souls who have left their bodies behind." She tapped her chin, then stood up. "That reminds me. I'd better check with the church about the arrangements. Wouldn't it be embarrassing if Robert couldn't be buried in the family plot?"

"I don't think they do that anymore, if indeed it was done consistently in the first place."

"I think I want to check," Beverly said firmly, so firmly that Leslie suspected her mother-in-law wanted something concrete to do.

She could relate to that. Unfortunately, there was no lack of papers to mark, the rest of the house could use a cleaning, and there was dinner to be made. She wondered how Annette was doing with her homework and hoped desperately that she wasn't having troubles with algebra again.

Leslie put the trash outside, then strode toward Annette's room with purpose. Maybe she was destined to get better at math now, too.

Chapter Fourteen

Matt was sleeping like a corpse. The shrill ring of the telephone made him leap, made his dreams change into something horrifying.

It was his father on the phone.

It was his father summoning him.

It was his father, loading his gun.

Matt snatched at the phone. "I won't come!" he shouted.

"Oh, I'm sorry," a polite voice said. "I've connected to the wrong room. Excuse me, sir."

Matt sat there, clutching the receiver, still dreaming, sweat running down his back as the line went dead.

* * *

He was in his father's study at Rosemount. He could see his father at his desk, putting the receiver back in the cradle, straightening his dress uniform. Robert Coxwell opened the drawer of his desk and removed his service revolver. He checked that it was loaded, he brushed a speck from the metal, he glanced around the room one last time.

He put the gun in his mouth, looked straight at Matt and pulled the trigger.

* * *

"No!" Matt screamed, leaping from his bed. The telephone cord wasn't long enough and the phone fell from the nightstand with a jingle and a clatter. The blankets were knotted around Matt's ankles and the hotel room was empty.

He blinked and looked around himself in a panic.

There were no books, no desk, no gun, and certainly there was no sign of his father. His heart was racing, he was breathing hard, and his hands were shaking. Beyond the window, the lights of New Orleans twinkled in the darkness, looking so unfamiliar and alien that for a moment he wasn't sure where he was.

Then it all came back to him.

He peered in all the corners of the room, of the closet, of the bathroom, seeking some clue that things had happened as he had witnessed them.

But there was nothing. He was alone.

Alone with his memories.

Matt licked his lips and shoved a hand through his hair. He was going crazy. There was no doubt about it.

And there was only one person with whom he could share such an intimate and terrifying truth. He took a deep breath, sat on the side of the bed, and dialed home.

* * *

The phone rang in the wee hours of Sunday night, startling Leslie out of a fitful sleep. "Hello?"

"Leslie!" It was Matt. He exhaled her name like a benediction, something that would have been more encouraging if he hadn't been where he was.

She sat up and turned on the light. "Matt, what's the matter? Where are you?"

"Just talk to me."

"But what's going on? But . . ."

"Leslie! Talk to me!" His voice faltered, as if he was at a loss for words, which was not typical of Matt. "Just, um, tell me what you did today."

"Are you all right?"

"More or less." He half-laughed. "Come on, talk to me. Please."

"It's two-thirty in the morning. You must know that."

"Oh? Oh, yeah, it is. Well, there's no time like the present, is there?"

Leslie nibbled on the bottom lip, uncertain how to continue this bizarre conversation. "Are you drunk?" she asked quietly.

"No." Matt took a ragged breath. "Maybe that's the problem."

The fact that he tried to make a joke reassured Leslie. "So what *is* the problem?" she asked in her best Crabcake Coxwell voice. "Why are you calling in the middle of the night to chat?"

"Because, um, I was thinking of you . . ."

"Liar." Leslie whispered the single word and it stopped Matt cold for a heartbeat.

"No, that's not a lie," he said angrily, as if he was prepared to fight about it. "I was thinking of you and that is why I called you. It's that simple."

Leslie thought about where he was and what he might have been doing at this hour of the night and had a funny feeling that he'd thought of her because he'd just done the horizontal boogie with Sharan and felt guilty. It wasn't the most inspiring thought she could have had, but once she'd had it, it was tough to shake.

She folded her arms across her chest and reminded herself that she wasn't going to flinch from the truth anymore. "Why?"

"What do you mean?" His voice sounded steady again.

"Why were you thinking of me? What could possibly have made you think of me in the middle of the night?"

There was a pause, as if he wasn't sure what to tell her, though Leslie thought that the truth should have been easier for Mr. Honesty to cough up.

Maybe it was a question of being overheard. Or of worrying

about waking someone up. Sharan, surely, was snoozing contentedly beside him, exhausted from multiple spectacular orgasms.

Leslie gritted her teeth.

"Okay, here's what happened." Matt's voice lowered. "I don't know how to say this, but that doesn't make it any less true. I think I'm cracking up. I think I'm going crazy."

"Why?"

"The phone rang tonight, it was a wrong number, but it woke me up." He was sounding agitated again and Leslie didn't want to interrupt his story to ask why Sharan hadn't answered the phone. "Or at least it woke me up enough that it started a dream. Or a nightmare. I thought it was that night again, I thought my father was calling." He swallowed audibly. "I saw my father with the phone in his study, putting the receiver back into the cradle, reaching for his service revolver . . ."

"Matt, you need to get help," Leslie interrupted him crisply, knowing that this was not a path of recollection he should go down tonight. He was too shaken for this to be anything other than the truth, and she wanted to help him help himself. "The Chief of Police was right. You can't resolve this alone."

"I know." He took another one of those uneven breaths and her heart wrenched a little. "That's why I called you. I understand now that I need to go for counseling. I need to talk to a professional about this, but I don't know who to call."

"So you're asking me."

"Well, yes."

Leslie bristled. "And I'm such a good secretary. Is that why you called me? So I can do your paperwork and manage your appointments?"

"No, I trust you . . ." Matt protested, but Leslie wasn't interested in any excuses that he might make.

"You trust me to always facilitate everything. Well, it's very sweet to find myself useful after all our years together. Nice to know that being organized is such an asset. Let me get this straight:

You're living with your girlfriend, having sex with your girlfriend, but you're calling your estranged wife to manage your appointments." She lowered her voice and growled. "Don't even think about sending your laundry home."

"I'm going to come home myself," he said, with a resolve that surprised Leslie for a heartbeat.

Then she realized the subtext of what he was saying, and knew that she had to make her own expectations clear. "You may be coming back to Massachusetts," she said sternly. "And it may be that we'll see each other again. But the location of your home is a matter of dispute."

"But . . ."

"You left, Matt. You left and you hurt me and you hurt Annette and you cast everything into doubt. You can't hurt me like that again," she concluded, knowing as the words passed her lips that they were not true. He could hurt her just as badly, but only if she allowed him to do so. "I won't let you do it."

There was silence on the line, silence that Leslie knew was born of shock. He hadn't expected her to say no to him.

"Fair enough," he finally said, his words soft. "I'll call the chief for a reference myself."

It was that single final click, the click that maybe signified that he was slipping away from her forever, that broke Leslie. She closed her eyes and bowed her head and let her tears roll. She listened to the dial tone, felt her stomach roil, and reminded herself that she had done the right thing.

Why did the right thing always have to be so hard to do?

Why did love have to hurt so much?

Love was based on respect, and one couldn't exist without the other. Leslie knew that, although it hurt like hell to so clearly state the stakes. That must be why she had started to cry.

It certainly was why she couldn't stop. She hung up the phone and nestled lower in her bed, trying to muffle the sound of her tears

so she wouldn't have to explain herself to either of the other
women in the house.

Although she knew she could have used a hug.

Her door was nudged open and two shadows slipped into the
room. With a single bound, Champagne was on the bed, cuddling
up beside Leslie, breaking several household rules but so warm and
reassuring that Leslie couldn't evict her. Champagne licked Leslie's
fingers, perhaps liking the salt from the tears, then nestled closer.
She was warm and soft and very reassuring.

When she buried her fingers in the dog's warm fur, Caviar leaped
up on the other side. The two dogs settled in to sleep, pressed
against her like sentinels.

Or warm teddy bears.

It was difficult to remember exactly what she'd had against
them being in the house in the first place.

*   *   *

On Monday morning, Leslie went for a Victoria's Secret bra in soft
blue, an underwire special that promised extra lift. She needed a lift
like nobody's business.

There was no way that she was up for that fuschia sweater and
lipstick on this particular Monday, though Annette expressed disappointment over that on the way to school.

She got to her office without incident and checked her e-mail.
There was a message from someone outside the university, someone named Graham Mulvaney.

Leslie considered the message for a moment. The only Graham
Mulvaney she knew was the student who had failed her medieval
history survey class.

Twice.

It seemed unlikely that this message would contain a ray of sun-
shine. She opened it with some trepidation and had to read it twice
in her shock.

Dear Dr. Coxwell,

You probably don't remember me, but I failed your excellent medieval history survey course twice, once in 1993 and subsequently in 1994. I certainly have never forgotten you!

Since graduation, I have worked as a headhunter, with a specialty in recruiting postsecondary educators for positions at established universities and colleges. I'm contacting you now because a very interesting position has become available at a high profile university close to Boston. They are seeking to establish a medieval studies department that will integrate specialties from across the university. Many professors will be cross-appointed, and their main interest is in finding a candidate to pull everything together. The successful candidate will not only demand excellence from students, but would be capable of guiding such a department—with a considerable administrative staff—and actively pursue his or her own research in order to raise the university's profile in this area. There would undoubtedly be some travel to conferences involved.

Naturally, given their desire for excellence, I thought of you. I am wondering whether you are completely satisfied in your current employment situation. If so, I wish you every success. If not, I would be delighted to hear from you, perhaps to discuss this opportunity further, perhaps to pursue other alternatives.

Sincerely,
Graham Mulvaney

Graham, it seemed, had done rather well for himself since failing Leslie's course.

She read the e-mail again, noting the telephone number in the signature file. She glanced over her shoulder, considered what to do. Did they track e-mail in the department? She wouldn't put it past Dinkelmann to spy on his staff.

But she hadn't done anything. There was no law—or even a guideline from the dean—prohibiting the receipt of e-mail.

She read the message again, marked it *unread*, and shut down her browser. Didn't they say that something that sounded too good to be true usually was?

Still, she was tempted.

*　*　*

Sharan came home Monday night to find a box on her porch.

She eyed it warily, because she hadn't been expecting any deliveries. She finally decided that it must belong to someone else. She was exhausted, having spent the day sticking raffia to tennis balls to make them look like coconuts. She felt like there was raffia stuck to most of her and really wanted a shower.

The box was in the way.

It was, in fact, addressed to her, so she scooped it up and dumped it into the foyer before heading to the bathroom.

She'd had that shower and a drink, taken a call from a girl-friend who wanted to try a new bar tonight, and was thinking about what to wear when she remembered the box. She got it from the foyer and brought it to the kitchen table.

It was, she noticed, from an art supply store downtown. She had bought stuff there once, in such enormous quantities that they had known her by name. She was pretty sure that the entire staff had turned over a couple of times since she'd last shopped there.

But that old curiosity about art supplies was hard to ignore. Sharan opened the box, not certain what to expect. What she found was two dozen tubes of oil paint and a fistful of sable hair brushes in all different sizes. She inhaled deeply, because the box had been in the sun and the paint was emitting the odor that had been part of her life for so long. She rummaged through the colors, feeling a ripple of that old excitement at the familiar names. Prussian Blue. Burnt Sienna. Red Vermilion. Chrome Yellow.

Rummaging revealed that there, at the bottom of the box, was an envelope. It was probably the bill. Sharan pulled it out, opened it, removed the single sheet inside and blinked in shock.

Sharan,

This can't begin to thank you or to apologize the way I should. But I'm wondering whether the problem was that you painted what you thought should be the truth, instead of what you knew the truth to be.

There's only one way for you to find out. I've become convinced that the only way you can fail creatively is to quit, so don't quit and neither will I.

With luck, I'll be home for Christmas and will write to you again then.

Your friend,
Matt

She needed another drink to make her tears stop, another hour to mourn what she'd thought Matt was bringing her, that same hour to consider the gift he had left. She emptied the box then, lining up the tubes of paint on the kitchen table, sorting the brushes by size. It didn't take her long to measure out a sheet of wax paper, to feel that familiar thrill of squeezing raw color out of the tube.

She had to touch it then, had to pick a nice fat clean sable brush and embellish it with color. She held the brush aloft, cerulean blue gleaming wetly on it, and turned to consider the canvases in the dining room. It suddenly seemed very clear that she had nothing to lose and a great deal to gain.

She lifted out the canvas that had once been *Pandora's Redemption*, thought about Pandora and love and loss and hope, then touched that loaded brush to the canvas with new confidence in what she had to express.

* * *

The phone rang Monday evening while Leslie was finishing the dishes. She assumed it was for Annette and scooped it up without thinking or putting down the dish towel. "Hello?"

"I have a collect call for Leslie from Matt in New Orleans," the operator said. "Will you accept the charges?"

Leslie nearly dropped the phone. She'd been so certain that she wouldn't hear from Matt again. "Of course."

"Go ahead, please."

There was only silence on the phone. Well, a kind of silence. It sounded as if someone had dropped the receiver into the street. She could hear traffic and horns but no voice.

"Hello?" Leslie said, uncertain of what was happening.

"Hi," Matt said, with startling vigor. He sounded as if he was right beside her and desperately in need of . . . something. "I need to ask you a question."

"Where are you?"

Matt ignored her query. "Would you do me a favor?"

"Depends what it is."

"Would you go down to the basement right now?"

"Okay," Leslie agreed hesitantly.

Matt spoke with urgency, as if this were a limited-time offer. "Go down to the basement and go behind the furnace, toward that little window that faces the backyard. Push back the acoustic tile that's right over that window. Go do that and come back to tell me what you've found."

Leslie didn't dare to speculate. She took the basement stairs, ran behind the furnace, pushed back the tile and saw nothing at all. She reached up and felt around, disappointment welling within her until her fingers landed on something square.

She grabbed it and lowered it out of the ceiling, staring at the stack of paper in wonder and awe.

It was a book manuscript.

And she could make a pretty good guess as to whose book manuscript it was.

She clutched it to her chest and raced back up the stairs two at a time, her heart thundering as if she'd run a marathon. "It's your book," she guessed.

"Yeah. Yeah, it is." She heard his hesitation now and wondered what to make of it. "Okay, here's the real favor. Would you read it and tell me what you think? Tell me *really* what you think?"

Leslie sank into a chair. "Are you sure?"

"No. I mean, yes." Matt cleared his throat and half-laughed. "No one's read it, Leslie. I want you to be the first." He paused. "Because I trust you to tell me the truth instead of what you think I might want to hear."

Leslie put the book on the counter and pushed it away, not wanting to damage it with the tears that threatened to fall. She kept her hand on top of it, as if it might squirm and run away. She couldn't say anything.

Matt spoke, his voice rough with emotion. "We started with honesty, Leslie. We started with you telling me the truth and somehow we got lost. But I want to go there again. I want that truth between us again and I want it to start with you telling me the truth about my book."

"I'm honored."

"Well, it might stink, so don't be too honored just yet."

She smiled a little.

"I want an honest opinion, no matter how tough it is." She heard him summon laughter into his voice. "So, no saying nice things just to have your way with me, you hear?"

She laughed and rubbed her tears away with one hand. "Rats. So much for that plan."

Matt laughed a little. "Go at it just like you were marking my term paper in Medieval History 101."

"Okay, I promise." Leslie could have sworn that there was a golden glow coming out of the phone. Or maybe it was coming out of her. Maybe she was radiating. She was happy enough to do so.

His novel. He trusted her to be the first to read his creation.

She caressed the stack of pages with wonder. He had written a whole book.

"Thank you," she whispered.

"I'll thank you after I know for sure that you've kept your promise," he teased.

"I will," she whispered, and thought for a moment that he was gone.

"Yes," he said quietly. "I know. I trust you."

Before she could respond, before she could decide what to respond, he truly was gone. At the sound of silence, Leslie slowly put the receiver back in the cradle.

But she had a precious part of Matt on the counter right in front of her. This was a gift and she didn't underestimate its importance to either of them.

She hoped like hell that she liked what he had written, that she could understand his accomplishment. She hoped she didn't disappoint him. She hoped it was all she believed it could be.

There was only one way to find out.

Leslie pulled up a stool to the counter, removed the elastic bands from the bundle of paper, and began to read. By the third page, tears were rolling down her cheeks because she knew there'd be no temptation to gloss the truth.

Because the truth was that Matt's book was very, very good.

* * *

One.

One. The smallest whole number. A number of exclusivity: one-way streets, one-sided arguments, and one-track minds. One soul-mate. One destined lover.

One night stands.

United we stand and divided we fall. Arriving—or leaving—one by one. Single file. One after the other, until there isn't a single seat in the house. One for the money. One for the road.

One is a number of achievement as well, of top place or highest honors. We're number one. To be an ace is to be the best of the best, the numero uno, the one who takes the premier prize.

Acey deucy one-eyed Jack.

Except there are two of those in the deck. Maybe being the star is harder than anyone would like you to believe.

Prime importance and prime examples, prime authorities—like Leslie on the matter of charivari—the prime of youth or a woman in her prime. Prime numbers and primates—or prime mates, depending how you look at it. But why is Prime the second of the canonical hours used to keep time in the Middle Ages?

Maybe the number one is more complicated than we'd like to believe.

Monochrome, monotheism, monopoly: lots of ways of saying that there can be only one. But does monogamy necessarily lead to monotony?

Monophysite—there's one for Leslie—a theologian who argues that Christ had one nature: part human and part divine. Two halves making a whole, as opposed to believing He had to be exclusively divine or not. Wasn't He both alpha and omega?

To achieve anything single-handedly is a great thing, but everything is easier when you don't walk alone. And the fact is inescapable: One morphs to two with surprising ease.

One is the beginning, alpha . . . and maybe it's omega, too. One is a lonely number, or so they say, though every virgin has been taught that one thing leads to another. First there was Adam, then Eve was wrought of his rib, then they begat enough mortal descendants to populate the world.

One and two have a mystical relationship; they always have. One whole that is wrought of two halves is more than it has any business being. Its total is greater than the sum of its parts, though no one thinker can tell you why.

This mystery is right in our DNA, it's wired right into the process of our creation. One egg, one sperm unite into one fertilized egg, which then divides into two, just to keep things interesting. Two come together to make one, which divides into two a zillion times—give or take—and ultimately results in one bouncing baby.

One child. One mortal who grows up, falls in love, cleaves partnership to another, and two halves again make a whole.

Until one sperm and one ovum do their dance again.

If that's not magic, I don't know what is.

It certainly is the foundation of much religious thought. Two cosmic principles—yin and yang: feminine and masculine, dark and light, negative and positive—unite into one force that governs the fate of mortals and the shape of destiny. The Kabbalah identifies Shekinah as the indwelling one, the female soul of God, the source of wisdom, creativity, and enlightenment, the one force without whom no man (or God) could be complete. Shekinah comes from Shakti, the Tantric name for the mother goddess also called Anima, Sophia, Psyche, Kali Ma, whose primary purpose was to make her counterpart complete.

Many religions, one universal notion: Two must become one for either to be complete.

They must unite.

In the unique dance to which only they two know the steps. We can call it fate, destiny, kismet, the pursuit of one true love, but we know it's the magical mystical union that makes any one of us more than we would be alone.

More than we could be alone.

One is the spark of the divine.

Let's give it one last chance.

Once more, with feeling.

One more time.

* * *

The time hung heavy on Matt's hands. He walked the length and breadth of the French Quarter over and over again. He hit every tourist spot, unseeing, and followed a number of tours without hearing what was said. He ate without tasting the food on his fork, though it was probably spectacular, and went through the markets without savoring the scents.

Someone was reading his book.

And not just anyone: Leslie was reading his book.

Matt was terrified—that it was worthless; that it was incomprehensible; that she wouldn't understand it; that she wouldn't like it.

That there would be no common ground from which they could go forward.

That the book would prove that they were too far apart to stay together.

That the book would make his worst nightmare come true.

Because, in hindsight, Matt saw that the one thing he had wanted most in all the world was the one thing for which he had been afraid to ask. Now Leslie was reading his work and his entire future hung in the balance.

He didn't sleep.

He didn't really live.

He just marked time until he could get on his booked flight to Boston on Tuesday, get home, and find out the truth.

*　*　*

Leslie, meanwhile, was up reading most of the night. Beverly came and went, Annette came and went, both spoke to her but Leslie wasn't entirely sure what they said.

The girls slept in the kitchen for a long time, but eventually even they gave up on Leslie and abandoned her for better sleeping facilities upstairs. They'd slip into Annette's room, Leslie knew, because their dog beds were there. She didn't doubt that if she peeked into the room in a couple of hours, they'd both be sprawled on Annette's bed with her.

Tonight she didn't care. She was lost in a fictional world of Matt's making, a tale of two brothers as different as chalk and cheese. It was fiction, and yet it was infused with the truth as only Matt could tell it. His own experience made the brothers real, made them living characters who were both noble and flawed. His ability with words brought the crises to fever pitch, made Leslie laugh, made her cry.

The brothers seemed to be opposites, two very different men in pursuit of similar objectives, two men raised to compete with each other. Yet in the course of their journey, they found a new understanding and compassion for each other, though it was not achieved easily. They wrung each other out, turned things back on themselves, made each other work for a balance and camaraderie that Leslie knew would sustain them for the rest of their lives.

At four in the morning, Leslie turned the last page, exhausted by the emotional journey she had endured along with the two brothers in the story. She looked around her kitchen, saw the darkness gathered outside the windows, saw that all other windows facing the backyards were shadowed.

The house was silent, only the sound of breathing and the quiet hum of the furnace filling its walls. The streets were quiet outside, all of the town lost in slumber.

How much of this story was owed to Matt's competition with James over the past two years? How much nuance and detail of that was owed to their upbringing, as the two Coxwell brothers closest in age? How much was owed to Robert Coxwell and his ambition, either in fiction or in truth? Leslie couldn't tell. She couldn't unfurl what she knew to be truth from what she believed to be fiction.

And that was the power of Matt's book. It could have been all true. It could have been all fiction. But it was powerful in a way that only a work that blended both fiction and truth could be.

It was honest. That realization made her stop and stroke the manuscript, because such honesty could only have come from the

Matt she knew and loved. This book was infused with his percep-
tiveness and his insights and his view of the world.

That was what made it so potent.

And she wasn't afraid to tell him that particular truth.

*   *   *

Tuesday was the kind of day that called for the best armor Leslie
had. She had a fuschia La Perla underwire bra that she had bought
on an adventurous day and only had worn once. This was its day.
It was understated for La Perla, relying upon exquisite cut instead
of ornamentation for its star power. There was no lace, but the
edges were finished with two narrow lines of silk satin piping, one
cream and one a sapphire blue that made the fuschia zing. There
were three scrumptious little freshwater pearls, one at the center
front and one each where the strap met the top of the cup.

It was, Leslie recalled once she had it on, the best fitting and
most flattering bra she'd ever owned.

The pink twinset was a given, on this day of challenges, though
Leslie's hand faltered slightly when she stepped up to the mirror to
put on the pink lipstick.

She looked like a different person, maybe a more interesting
person than she was. No, she finally looked like the interesting person she was, instead of a pale substitute.

Annette was right, though: She needed new shoes.

Leslie descended to the kitchen, drawn by the smell of fresh coffee. The girls came trotting to greet her, although there was no sign
of Beverly. "No snowballs this morning," she told them. "I have to
go to work." Champagne sighed at that and headed back to the
dog bed that now occupied the corner of the kitchen floor. Caviar
strolled over to sit at Annette's feet.

Leslie blinked to find her daughter eating Raisin Bran with
sliced bananas on top. Annette noticed her glance and waved her
spoon in greeting. "You get used to eating sawdust," she said, with
a philosophical shrug. "I like the pink a lot."

Annette couldn't be in that bad of a mood: She had broken out her favorite black *Battlestar Galactica* T-shirt. Maybe something was going on at school.

Maybe it had something to do with Scott Sexton.

Leslie knew better than to ask.

"Have the girls been out?"

"I took them for a walk after I started the coffee," Annette said. "Mission accomplished."

"And your grandmother?"

"No sign of her yet."

Leslie took a sip of her coffee and sighed contentment. "You're spoiling me, you know," she told Annette.

"I could get used to you spoiled. It brings out your inner alien."

"And that's a good thing?"

Annette grinned.

"So do you need a ride to school this morning?"

"No, thanks, I'm going to walk."

Leslie blinked, then blinked again at her daughter's mischievous grin.

Annette leaned over her cereal bowl to confide something of such obvious import that Leslie leaned closer instinctively. "I have found the most awesome bra," her daughter said, "and it costs a fortune and you're going to have to buy it for me soon." She nodded sagely. "Really soon." Then she eyed Leslie, as if expecting the offer to be rescinded.

"Good. I'm ready anytime."

Annette grinned and bounced a bit.

"You know, it's funny, but I seem to have lost a book I once had," Leslie mused. "And it's not like me to lose track of a book, but I just can't figure out what happened to this one."

Annette flushed and Leslie smiled.

"Guess it's gone for good," she said, with a wink.

"I'd think so," Annette agreed and they shared a smile.

Chapter Fifteen

This was it.

That was Leslie's thought as she strode down the hall, out-wardly confident and inwardly terrified, toward her Tuesday after-noon lecture. Everything was riding on this, she felt, all the chips were on the table and she'd called "double or nothing." It was frightening to have risked so much by challenging Dinkelmann.

She hadn't even thought to wear the Rosie the Riveter bra.

On the other hand, she hadn't felt so much anticipation for a class in years. Maybe anticipation mingled with terror was a better description.

Maybe they had all dropped the course.

Maybe none of them had prepared.

Maybe they would have absolutely nothing to say, and all two hundred and seventy-five souls would stare at her in silence for two hours.

Scary prospect. Maybe she should have brought a lion and a Christian or two.

The fact was that there was no way to tell for sure in advance how it would all work out. Which was similar to a lot of other things, which was not the most reassuring thought Leslie could have had.

All possible mortal preparations had been made and the result was left in the hands of the gods. Not being a particularly religious individual—and experience had shown her miserable success rate with divine intervention—Leslie wasn't optimistic.

She gripped the door handle to the lecture hall, took a deep breath, and hauled it open.

The chatter within was abruptly silenced by her appearance. To her astonishment, at least two-thirds of the class as she knew it had shown. She continued to the lectern as if she'd expected nothing else.

"Good afternoon," she said, letting her voice carry over the room. "Is everyone prepared?"

There were some murmurs of assent and a lot of shuffling of papers. Several of Leslie's grad students had offered to help by taking attendance for her and she greeted them quietly, giving them some instruction on how to have the students sign in without disrupting any potential discussion.

The class waited restlessly, either anxious about each having their chance or terrified of being singled out.

"I'd like you all to move down, closer to the front," Leslie said once the grad student cum emissaries were dispatched to their missions. "That way, we'll be able to hear each other better. I'd also like you to meet several of my grad students—Fatima and Stephen and Ilona and Chi-Van—who have graciously offered to take attendance during our discussion. Please have your student identification on your desk and be prepared to sign in with your student number. They will also take note of anyone who arrives late or leaves early."

At that, the back door opened. Everyone glanced over their shoulders to see who was late, and Leslie caught her breath when Dinkelmann stepped into the back of the hall. He seemed discomfited to find all eyes upon him.

Leslie was discomfited that he and she were wearing the same color of pink.

At least, she told herself, that that was what was making her heart leap. He glanced about and quickly claimed a seat, clearly hoping to disappear.

Leslie wasn't inclined to give him his three wishes.

"As you can see, Dr. Dinkelmann, who is head of the history department, will be observing our discussion today as well." Leslie smiled at her daunted students. "Here is your chance to impress Team Fuschia and nail that graduate school referral."

A ripple of laughter rolled through the hall, though Dinkelmann did not smile. He seemed particularly concerned with opening his notebook and taking the cap off his pen.

"As you know—or I hope you know—we will be discussing the emergence of the notion of the individual in medieval society today. This will be a free-ranging discussion, so please put up your hand when you have something to contribute. I'll try to ensure that you all have your chance to share what you've learned. I'd like you each to stand when you speak, as that will help your voice carry. This lecture hall has been designed, after all, to carry my voice to you, not the other way around." Leslie smiled and gestured to a familiar student. "Mr. Carmichael, would you like to start us off, maybe with a nice broad working thesis?"

He stood, a lanky kid who was both pompous and self-conscious. "Yes, Dr. Coxwell. I'd like to suggest that the emergence of the notion of the individual was both the culmination of medieval society, resulting in the highest achievements of the era, and its doom, as the notion of the supreme importance of the individual necessitated the end of the Middle Ages and the beginning of the Renaissance."

It was pretty good for something off the cuff. "Excellent. My only quibble is that the word 'necessitated' implies an inevitability, Mr. Carmichael. I'm not sure that anything in history is inevitable, but other than that one small item, it's an excellent working theory. Tell me more about what you mean or why you arrived at this thesis."

"Well, I focused on architecture, and the changes in the design of private residences over the course of the Middle Ages . . ."

To Leslie's delight, the discussion took on a life of its own. Mr. Carmichael talked about changes in architecture from a few large communal rooms to numerous smaller private rooms. A notable transition was to private sleeping arrangements.

Another student contributed some comments on walls, the increasing popularity of walled gardens for private contemplation, and the internal division of rooms in all buildings.

They talked about the pursuit of solitude and its fruits. They talked about the growing importance of identification of the individual creator with the work of art: of paintings being signed, of poets ensuring that their name was associated with their works, of even monks who copied chronicles making note of their own names in the margins when once they would have worked anonymously.

Someone brought up the notion of a personal relationship with the divine, of worshippers meeting God as an individual instead of en mass during Mass, of gnosis and Cathars and people reading the Bible for themselves, and how the Reformation was a natural outgrowth of that. That led them down the road of women's role in religious life, of visionaries like Julian of Norwich and Teresa of Ávila, who communed with God and shared their experiences. They talked about Joan of Arc, and her discussions with angels, as well as her abilities as an individual in rallying the troops and changing the military fortune of what would become France.

Another student had examined the notion of the solitary quest in poems and literature, particularly in the Arthurian cycle and the adventures of the Knights of the Round Table, who sought personal spiritual growth in order to glimpse or potentially possess the Grail. Previous to the popularity of these stories, a knight traveling alone was believed to be a threat or an outlaw fleeing his past, this student declared and Leslie concurred, but these stories defined the solitary traveler as a hero instead.

They talked about livestock being moved out of peasant huts

and into their own barns or outbuildings. That led to the inevitable discussion about sex and its presentation in popular medieval fiction, how it changed from being a deed done while surrounded by others—in a peasant hut or in a shared bed in a feudal castle—to an encounter requiring seclusion and privacy.

Leslie pointed out how *Le Ménagier de Paris*—a kind of domestic instruction manual written by a merchant for his young wife, and a familiar, beloved source for medieval social historians— insisted that arguments between man and wife belonged in the privacy of their own bed, and should not be conducted before servants or guests. Lines, she noted, were being drawn between public and private deeds, which was a facet of the same movement from community to individual.

Another student who focused on comparative literature noted about the emergence of first-person storytelling in literature, and the many various recountings of personal quests and dreams. Jean de Joinville's personal memoir, the first vernacular autobiography in French, was presented as another obvious example of this trend toward focus on the individual.

Ideas were flying across the lecture hall, the students were animated, and Leslie was having the time of her life. She was thrilled at the wide variety of topics they explored and how all of the information complemented the working thesis. She redirected and provided citations and made note of items that they had missed or that she felt should be granted greater emphasis.

Suddenly Fatima, one of her graduate students, looked up from the back of the hall and tapped her watch.

Leslie glanced at the wall clock and was shocked at the time.

"Ladies and gentlemen, we have two minutes to sum up," Leslie said, incredulous at how quickly the time had passed. She laughed and put her hands on her hips. "But that's impossible. We've had a fabulous exchange of information here today and have seen many facets of medieval society in transition. First of all, I'd like you each to write a short summary, either using Mr. Carmichael's thesis or one of your own, focusing on your particular area of research. Keep it brief, no more than three pages and a bibliography please, just so I'll have a firmer idea of what everyone explored. Although this won't be assigned a grade on its own, you can rest assured that one of the optional essay questions on the final exam will build upon this assignment. It will be good preparation for you. I promise."

She took a deep breath and smiled at her students, who were clearly waiting for the other shoe to drop. "In conclusion I have to say that this class far exceeded my highest expectations. I want you all to give yourselves a round of applause for a job well done. This was exemplary."

Leslie began to clap. She stood at the front of the room and applauded her students, their work and energy and enthusiasm, none of which she'd really glimpsed before. She was delighted as the students joined in. Their faces were alight and she knew they had learned something, maybe more than they had learned thus far in her course. They were engaged.

This was what teaching should be.

This was what she had signed up for.

Leslie had no chance to gloat, though. She looked up to where Dinkelmann had been sitting just in time to catch his scowl. He turned and marched out of the lecture hall, his shoulders hunched in disapproval.

She was going to guess that he wasn't persuaded of the power of what had happened here today.

In fact she wasn't going to wait for him to summon her. She packed up her notes, thanked her graduate students for their help, then left the hall, making a beeline for Dinkelmann's office.

Might as well beard this lion in his den.

* * *

"That went well, didn't it?" Leslie asked, sparing only a rap for Dinkelmann's door before she entered his office. He looked up from his desk and sputtered a greeting. Leslie continued with confidence. "I have to say that I was enormously impressed with how much preparation the students did and how much enthusiasm they showed for what can be a very elusive subject." She took the seat opposite him, crossed her legs and smiled triumphantly. "That was education! Those kids were totally engaged with the material, and it was sophisticated material."

Dinkelmann took a deep breath. "You needn't be so self-congratulatory about that fiasco."

"What fiasco? I was encouraging their academic passion."

"You can't teach like that all the time. You can't just let the class descend into chaos! What kind of exam question can you fabricate from that?"

"Oh, that's not difficult. One of the essay answer choices can be to write about their research for that class."

"But what are you teaching them, other than the fact that you are able to abdicate your responsibility?"

"I beg your pardon?" Leslie got out of her chair. "They each went into the library to research a specific facet of a major social change. There was no bibliography, no cheat sheet, no way they could ask each other, no breadcrumbs through the medieval studies section. They had to do research all by themselves, which meant they had to formulate a research plan and undoubtedly learned a great deal about the indices available as library resources, and then in class, they had to formulate and defend a thesis related to that research."

"You should have taught a lecture," Dinkelmann insisted grimly. "That's your job, Dr. Coxwell."

"My job, Dr. Dinkelmann, is to teach history and to teach academic skills to those who will go on to graduate work. Both of those objectives were met in that lecture hall today."

"You went too far. You obviously are distraught and are trying to pretend there is success in a failure on your part. I will not excuse this kind of behavior . . ."

"I am not distraught, though I am considering the merits of becoming so at this point in time."

Dinkelmann pushed to his feet. "I told you to take a week off. Do you see now the wisdom of my advice?"

"I have a family funeral to attend tomorrow, so I will not be in. I have canceled my lectures and appointments, but I will be back on Thursday." She straightened and looked Dinkelmann steadily in the eye. "I have a job to do here, Dr. Dinkelmann. There is academic excellence to be encouraged and the future of scholarship to be assured."

"You are going about this the wrong way."

"We have a deal, Dr. Dinkelmann, and I'm going to see it through. Have you had the grade point averages of my students calculated for comparison at the end of the term?"

"The dean will not support this kind of whimsy."

Leslie laughed. "I didn't know it was whimsy to try to improve students' marks. What is this institution coming to? Why will they need professors and department heads, Dr. Dinkelmann, after they decide to just give every registered student an A? Why bother teaching courses? They could just save the payroll cost and not have any professors at all." She leaned closer and tapped her fingertip on his desk. "You may think that you're compromising, that maybe it's just a little compromise, but as an historian, you should be able to discern the evolution of a trend. This is the beginning of the end and I will not capitulate. I will fight the good fight to my last breath."

She held his gaze for a long moment, then pivoted. "I will see you Thursday, Dr. Dinkelmann."

He cleared his throat. "I assume your graduate school referral letters are done?"

Leslie turned on the threshold of his office and smiled sweetly. "They're not due until Thursday. I had quite a number of requests this year and as I'm sure you can appreciate, personal events of this past week have interfered in my ability to complete them. They'll be done on time, though, you can be assured of that."

With one last achingly sweet smile, Leslie left Dr. Dinkelmann with something to think about.

She went back to her office, booted up her computer, logged on and replied to a message in her inbox.

Dear Graham,

    Please call me at home, at your convenience.

Leslie Coxwell

She included her home telephone number and hit *send* before she had a chance to reconsider.

*   *   *

Beverly Coxwell was certain that the demon child—as she had come to call Annette—would make her crazy. She'd left the funeral home, paused at the house to drop off the dogs, then gone shopping because she'd been certain the child would have nothing to wear to a funeral.

The quest for a suitable dark suit, one that was ladylike but not too old, one that was flattering but not too cute, one that also would fit a girl the size of Annette, had not been an easy one. It had, in fact, left Beverly in dire need of a shot of nice amontillado sherry.

Instead she had persisted against all odds, found a suit, haggled over the price and returned to the house triumphant (if sherry-free).

Where Annette had curled her nose. "I'm not wearing that!"

"You're not wearing *that*," Beverly retorted, gesturing to the black T-shirt and jeans with impatience. She didn't understand the logo on the T-shirt and didn't much care: Wearing clothing with writing on it was vulgar. "You must wear something appropriate and your mother won't have time to shop for you by the time she gets home."

"I'll wear something I have." Annette sulked in the corner of the kitchen. "What happened to all of those chocolate-chip cookies?"

Beverly could relate to the need for an indulgence all too well. "They're gone," she said dismissively, remembering that her sherry had been similarly discarded. "And there won't be any more of them in this house anytime soon." She drew herself up to her full height when Annette looked as if she might balk. "All right. What do you have to wear?"

Annette fidgeted. "Something."

"No. You show me exactly what."

Annette turned to face her, squaring her shoulders and standing up straight for once. "You're only worried about appearances, about what everyone else thinks . . ." she began, clearly gearing up for a teenage tirade.

But Beverly had survived four teenagers, more or less, and wasn't that easily ruffled. "You're right. I want people to think that my family had respect for my husband, and that means that you will dress appropriately or you will not go."

Annette's face lit and Beverly realized her mistake a bit late. "Bonus!"

"No bonus." Beverly smiled a slow cold smile, one that made Annette shiver just as children before her had shivered. "Because if you do not extend the courtesy of attending your grandfather's funeral, I will find a way to make you regret it. You can count on that."

Annette reached for Champagne's collar. "You won't take the dogs away."

"They have a trust fund," Beverly said, only realizing the import of that now. "It might be my obligation to house them in the style to which they've become accustomed, which would be, of course, in a condo downtown that is reasonably inaccessible without a car." She shrugged, though she was touched by Annette's horror at this prospect. "Which might mean that I had to get rid of the Jag, maybe for a Corolla or something more practical."

"I thought you were going to teach me to drive in the Jag!" Annette wailed.

Beverly arched a brow, letting the child do the math all by herself.

"You're not supposed to play dirty like this," Annette muttered. "Adults are supposed to take the high road and set an example."

"I decided a long time ago that I couldn't be an example, so I might as well be a horrible warning instead," Beverly said, quoting a quip she'd once heard somewhere.

Annette almost laughed. "You don't mean that."

"I'm serious about the funeral. You need to go and you need to look like the pretty young woman that you are." She held out the suit on its hanger, the plastic bag from the store bunched around the hook of the hanger. "You could at least try it on. You might be surprised. It is of excellent quality, because I don't believe in wasting my money on garbage."

The fact that it had been expensive kindled the girl's interest, which Beverly thought a good sign. "Do I have to get a paper route or something lame to pay you back for it?"

"No. It's a gift, even if it's one you don't want. Look at it this way: I'd rather not be buying you a suit to wear to your grandfather's funeral."

Annette looked surprised. "But then you mean you wish he wasn't dead."

Beverly held her granddaughter's gaze. "That's right."

"But he wasn't . . . I mean, he wasn't nice."

"Are you always nice?" Beverly shook her head, not waiting for an answer. "I'm not, but I hope that doesn't mean that there's a long line of people wishing me dead. If so, I don't intend to oblige them anytime soon."

Annette took the hanger with some reluctance and didn't move further. Beverly crossed the kitchen, shed her coat, and looked in the fridge. Great. There was cranberry juice. Hip hip hurray.

It would have to do.

She poured herself a glass, aware that Annette was watching her. She turned slowly and looked the girl up and down, ignoring her stricken expression. "You could have had the worst over with by now. It's not an enormous concession that I'm asking of you."

Annette passed the hanger from one hand to the other, looked away, then impaled Beverly with a glance. "Are you really sad that he's dead?"

"Yes." She smiled slightly at Annette's shock. "I knew him for a long time, and though we weren't always nice to each other, it was comforting in a way just to know that he was there."

She might have stopped there but the child was watching her so intently that she felt obliged to continue.

"I believed, even after we separated, that if I really needed anything, that Robert would have helped me. I'm not sure whether that was true, but it doesn't matter. The idea that there was someone I could rely upon was one that reassured me. And now he's not here anymore, which means there's no one to call. My parents and siblings are all dead already, and I think it's a bit tacky to keep counting on your kids to help you out." Beverly laughed a little, without humor. "Especially when you need as much help as I tend to."

"Maybe you shouldn't live alone."

"I have the girls now."

"I mean, without other people. Because then there'd always be someone around."

"I can't imagine that anyone would put up with me."

"We're doing it."

"Yes, I suppose you are. But then I've asked your mother for more than enough and probably should move soon." She frowned at the dogs, thinking of that trust fund and what it could buy. "I suppose the girls' money would enable me to move out and not rely on anyone."

"But you need someone you can call. You just said that."

"I guess I'll have to get over that."

"You could call me," Annette said, with heat and Beverly glanced up in surprise. "I mean, you've never asked me for anything except for a chance, and I said okay to that, so maybe I'd say okay to other things." She shrugged and flushed, uncomfortable with Beverly's silence. "I mean, it can't hurt to ask, right?"

Beverly put down the glass, touched beyond expectation. "No," she said quietly. "It never hurts to ask. The worst thing anyone can do is to say no, after all."

"I don't think I would," Annette said, then shrugged. Her tone changed, revealing that the moment between them had passed. "Unless you, like, asked me something totally gross, then I'd have to say no, you know?"

"That's only reasonable," Beverly agreed. She gestured to the suit. "Does trying that on qualify as totally gross?"

Annette smiled, looking so soft and pretty that Beverly's heart nearly stopped. "No. Not really. I'll go try it now." She ran for the stairs, which meant that the girls became convinced that they were missing something. They galloped after her, Champagne barking as they vaulted up the stairs. Annette giggled, then her door slammed, though Beverly could hear the tap of toenails on the hardwood floor overhead.

She sincerely hoped they were the dogs' toenails.

The child was trying so hard to eat properly, but Beverly knew that a radical change is the hardest one to stick to. That was why she'd been hunting cookies. It was far wiser, in Beverly's experience, to take a middle course over a radical change.

She thought a reward was in order.

Her own kids had always adored pizza and could have eaten it three times a day, instead of the three times a year or less that she'd permitted them to have it. She'd treat Leslie and Annette to pizza tonight: Undoubtedly Leslie would be relieved to not need to cook again. Beverly glanced through the yellow pages, dismissing the national chains without undue consideration, her fingertip landing firmly on the number for a local pizza place with a nice Italian name.

Macetti's. Perfect.

Beverly had no sooner hung up the phone from placing her order than it rang again. Mercifully, Leslie was just coming in the front door because the call was for her.

And it was a man.

"Leslie! There's a Graham Mulvaney on the phone for you."

Leslie's pleasure was clear as she hastened down the hall, dropping coat and bags en route. "Wonderful!" she said, looking younger and more vibrant than Beverly could ever remember her looking.

It wasn't just the pink.

Surely Leslie couldn't be in love with another man already?

The thought depressed Beverly more than she might have expected. The girls had leaped back down the stairs at the sound of the front door opening and were lobbying to go out into the backyard. It was no doubt a result of the excitement of everyone coming home, but this time Beverly went out into the snowy yard with them.

Although she was aching to hear what Leslie said, the tone of Leslie's voice told Beverly more than enough.

Why had Matt felt obliged to leave? It wasn't her business and Beverly knew it but for a heartfelt moment, she wished she'd had the chance to change his mind.

Although, really, she didn't think she would have had a chance to do so. The only person who might change Matt's mind was talking quite cheerfully to another man.

Damn James and those AA people.

*   *   *

Annette was thinking that the suit wasn't as bad as she'd feared. She heard her mom come home, let the girls out of the bedroom to thunder down the stairs, but stayed in her room to consider her reflection.

She liked the black. It was a deep rich black, and the fabric had a texture that made the black look even darker. It felt good beneath her fingertips, pretty deluxe.

She liked the skirt, too. It had a kind of flirty little hem with a flounce on the bottom that bounced a bit when she walked. It had stretchy stuff in the waist and didn't have one of those waistbands that made her feel like she was being cut in half, like an assistant in a magician's show. The skirt made her feel like a girl, and feeling like a girl wasn't all bad.

The jacket was short, stopping at her waist, and had a zipper up the front. It was kind of funky but restrained, too. Maybe she could even wear it with jeans. There was a package of panty hose in the bottom of the bag, black ones like adults wore and Annette felt a thrill of excitement that she'd been admitted to that class.

She had a pair of black shoes that weren't hugely exciting but she put them on anyway. They looked better than they did with her other skirt, which was long and straight and denim. She would have liked to have had a pair of slingbacks with long pointed toes, but it was probably too late to lobby for that.

Annette pivoted in front of the mirror and reluctantly conceded that the witch knew how to shop. The suit fit pretty well, and looked a lot better on her than it had on the hanger. She admired herself for a good chunk of time, imagining that the bra she had picked would feel good under this, picturing her legs looking sleek in those black stockings. She checked the panty hose package and was intimidated by the promise that the stockings within were ultrasheer and had cost twelve dollars.

Maybe she'd wait for help on those.

Could she press her luck for lipstick? Maybe not for a funeral.

The T-shirt, though, wasn't coming together with the suit. She needed a blouse, but a rummage through her jammed closet revealed that she had nothing even remotely cool enough for this suit. She zipped up the jacket and thought it would look as if she didn't have anything on underneath if in fact she didn't.

Then she remembered the scarf.

She had just pulled out the fabulous gold and orange box when the doorbell rang.

Incredibly no one answered it, because it rang again, ringing longer and louder than it had before.

At the third insistent ring, Annette wondered whether anyone else was still home. She chucked the silk across the bed, where it spilled like a splendid patch of sunlight. The doorbell rang again. She kicked off her shoes and ran down the stairs, flinging open the front door just as the bell started to ring again.

"What?" she demanded.

Anything else she might have said became a choking sound, because Scott Sexton himself—the amazing hunk Scott Sexton!—was standing on their porch with a pizza box.

"I thought there was nobody home," he said, flushing a little. "Sorry."

"Well, I don't know where everybody is."

"Well, somebody ordered a pizza."

Annette glanced over her shoulder, mostly to keep herself from staring at Scott, and saw her mother chatting on the phone in the kitchen, oblivious to what was happening at the door.

As if. This was probably a setup.

"So, how much is it?" Annette asked, feeling that the suit gave her a measure of dignity that she might not have had otherwise.

"It's paid already, on a credit card. I just have to drop it off." Scott passed Annette the hot pizza box, but didn't turn immediately to leave. "Don't you go to my school?"

"Doesn't everybody around here go to that school?" Annette asked, not wanting to show how thrilled she was that he had some clue who she was. Instead she sounded like a jerk, which she only realized too late.

Scott flushed. "Well, yeah, pretty much." He shoved one hand in his pocket, the insulated pizza bag hanging from the other. "I don't even know your name."

"It's Annette." She straightened. "And you are?"

"Scott. Scott Sexton."

"Oh," Annette said, as if she didn't know that already. "Hi." She would have turned away if he'd left, but he didn't go anywhere, just stood and looked at her.

"Are you going out or something?" he asked, gesturing to her suit.

"No. Well, sort of. I have to go to my grandfather's funeral tomorrow. My grandmother bought this for me to wear and I'm supposed to check that it fits."

"Looks nice."

"Oh, thanks." Annette tried her best to be cool but she felt herself blushing all the same. She couldn't look straight at him, but he didn't leave. The pizza was warm, exuding the scent of pepperoni and cheese, but Annette wasn't anxious to get inside and have a piece.

Weird.

"Sorry about your grandfather."

"Thanks." Annette shrugged. "I didn't know him very well."

"But it's still sad, 'cause everyone else is sad. Your grandma must be sad, for example. Mine was when my grandfather died."

"Yeah." Annette met his gaze and deliberately chose a different word to refer to the witch. "My grandma is sad." She didn't choke on the word and lightning didn't strike her dead.

Maybe Beverly was going to be her grandma, after all.

"You watch that?" Scott asked.

For a minute Annette didn't realize what he meant and then she saw that he was gesturing at her T-shirt. "Yeah, but I like the original series better." She took a deep breath, knowing that she was taking a big chance by stating her preference. "I mean, Starbuck is a man."

Scott grinned. "Absolutely!"

Annette felt her mouth fall open. They agreed on something, and not just anything, but something totally critical.

"And he was so cool," Scott continued. "Turning his character into a woman was like, just not right. And lame. I mean, not like I think girls can't do anything they want, but it just changed everything."

"Yeah, exactly."

"I'd like to see those old ones again, but they almost never come up on TV."

"I have them on DVD," Annette said, without meaning to do so.

"No way! That is so cool." Scott looked at her with new admiration, then sobered. "I mean, that's great that you can watch them and maybe compare the two. I know I've forgotten a lot about what made the original series so neat."

"You could buy the DVD." Annette nearly smacked herself for making such a dumb suggestion when she could have made a much better one.

Scott shook his head. "No, I'm trying to save for a car. You know how much they cost? No DVDs for me anytime soon."

Annette took a deep breath and fought to sound casual. She wasn't sure it worked. "Maybe you could come watch the ones I have sometime."

Scott didn't seem to care whether she was casual or not, and he certainly didn't trouble to hide his enthusiasm. "Yeah, maybe. That'd be cool, Annette." He held her gaze for a long delicious moment, while Annette savored the fact that he'd actually said her name.

Her heart was leaping all over the place and her mouth was dry and her palms were damp—though maybe that was the grease from the pizza seeping through the box. Either way, she couldn't just stand here all night and gape at him.

Could she?

"Pizza's getting cold," she said, with an apologetic shrug.

"Oh no!" Scott jumped in sudden recollection. "I've got three pizzas in the truck to deliver!" He looked at his watch, visibly panicked, and ran for the Macetti's truck idling at the curb. "I gotta go! I'll see you around, Annette."

"Yeah," Annette said, smiling to herself as she turned back into the house. "Yeah, I guess maybe you will."

Scott Sexton had recognized her.

Scott Sexton knew her name.

Scott Sexton wanted to watch her DVD of *Battlestar Galactica*.

Which meant that Scott Sexton probably watched all of the *Star Trek* series, too. Maybe he didn't have those on DVD, either.

Annette almost hugged the pizza in her delight, but remembered her new suit in the nick of time.

*   *   *

Leslie hung up the phone, excited beyond belief. Annette bounced into the kitchen in a gorgeous black suit, which made Leslie gape at the transformation in her daughter. It was more than the beauty of the suit: Annette was radiant.

And she was carrying a Macetti's pizza box. The math added up quite neatly then and Leslie chose not to pry into the delicate matters of the teenage heart.

"See what Grandma bought me?" Annette asked, and twirled for her mother.

Grandma even.

"It's beautiful, but you'd better change before dinner."

Beverly came in from the backyard with two snowy dogs who headed straight for the pizza box on the counter. They both sniffed so emphatically that Leslie thought the box would move, drawn by the power of their inhalation.

"Poodles do not eat pizza," Beverly said sternly, sending them to their corner with a single gesture. They collapsed there, chins on paws, eyes wide open and gazes fixed on the pizza box. Beverly set the table with brusque gestures, her impatience so clear that Leslie felt obliged to ask.

"Have a bad day?"

"No. I had an excellent day, thank you very much." Beverly put the plates down on the table with force, then turned to confront Leslie. "All right. It's not my business and I admit it, but I still want to know. Who is Graham Mulvaney and what exactly is going on between you? My son may have one foot out the door but he's not gone yet."

Leslie sat down in her astonishment. "You think I'm having an affair? Already?"

"What am I supposed to think? You come running down the

hall to take his call, looking like a young girl hearing from her lover . . ."

"He's a headhunter, Beverly. He's trying to entice me to interview for a job at another university."

Beverly sat down slowly, her expression watchful. "I thought you had tenure."

"I do."

"I thought you had always wanted to teach at your alma mater."

"I did, for a long time anyway." Leslie sighed. "But they keep changing the rules, moving the focus to giving the students what they want instead of encouraging them to work for it."

Beverly harumphed. "And this other place is different?"

"Apparently. They're establishing a new department in medieval studies, to which faculty from many departments will be cross-appointed. It will allow a kind of interaction of specialties that is really exciting. And they want to shift the balance, so that their senior faculty focus on research, not so much on teaching. They insist that faculty take a sabbatical every third year, just to pursue their research." Leslie shook her head, unable to imagine such an opportunity. "I haven't been able to do much research for the past couple of years, because of the burden of class size and the raw number of students I'm teaching and advising."

"You could, if you were a less conscientious teacher."

Leslie glanced up in surprise.

"You're a good teacher, Leslie. You're committed to it. I've seen it and Matt has told me about your dedication. I knew that you spent most weekends marking and composing lectures, but I never realized how much it was costing you."

"Well, how you teach is not something easily rewired." Leslie shrugged. "But I miss the research. I miss the thrill of discovery. And it's very tempting to consider the merit of having so much expertise integrated, just for the sake of discussion and direction."

"So what are you going to do?"

"I don't know. I said I'd let him know Thursday whether I wanted to interview or not."

"It sounds as if you have some reservations."

"Well, I have to think about the mortgage and the future, costs like Annette's education. I want her to be able to go to college and not have to work while she's doing so. I've been there and done that and it takes a lot of the experience away."

Leslie held up a hand when Beverly might have protested. "The compensation is commensurate and Graham said there's a good chance that the successful candidate will be tenured immediately, so it's not that."

"What is it, then?"

"I'd be leaving my safety net, leaving everything familiar. I thought I would teach where I am for my whole career. I never considered that I would have a home office, or that I would travel to do my research and present papers." She paused and frowned a little. "And it's a bit scary to be part of a new initiative, because there's nothing to guarantee that they won't decide in several years that it was a bad idea and that the program needs to be dismantled."

Annette reappeared and took her seat at the table. Beverly served out pizza and Leslie poured drinks and once they were all seated again, Beverly gave Leslie a glance. "So because there are no guarantees, you're afraid to take a chance."

"It's not that simple."

"Isn't it? You're not happy. Someone is offering you exactly what you want but you're afraid to take it because it doesn't come with a lifetime guarantee." Beverly shook her head. "The thing is, though, Leslie, that nothing does."

Leslie considered her mother-in-law, a woman who had probably expected an amiable marriage, a life without alcohol dependency, an easy retirement in her family home in Rosemount, and no dogs ever. Annette was watching the pair of them, her eyes wide even as she chewed pizza.

"Excuse me for a moment." Leslie got up from the table and referred to the number she had scribbled on the notepad beside the phone. "Hello, Graham? I've been thinking about this, and discussing it with my family, and I'd like to interview if you can arrange it. Early next week would be perfect, thanks." She glanced back to the table and smiled as Beverly nodded approval. "Nothing ventured, nothing gained, right?"

Chapter Sixteen

It was raining Wednesday morning.

It had turned warmer and the rain shrouded the world in gray, melting the snow to slush and turning everything to shadow. They drove separately to Rosemount because Beverly wanted some time alone. The girls sat at the living room window, sadly watching everyone leave, but Leslie promised Annette that she could take them for a romp when they got home.

Assuming the rain stopped.

It was a long drive to Rosemount, longer in the rain because there were a few accidents along the way. Leslie and Annette arrived in time to hear the bell tolling in the old church. Men from the funeral home, dressed in somber black, directed Leslie where to park for the procession, then escorted the pair of them to the church steps under large black umbrellas. Annette was visibly awed and Leslie realized that her daughter had never been to a funeral before.

And this one would be something.

The Episcopalian church in Rosemount was a magnificent piece of gothic revival architecture, with a high-pointed spire and a cavernous interior. Candles burned in quantities at the glittering altar of the church and the coffin reposed there. Robert's framed picture, the one that had been in the paper, stood on the closed coffin.

Organ music filled the sanctuary and a small group of mourn-
ers were gathered at the very front of the church. There were some
flowers arranged around the coffin, though Leslie supposed that
the scale of the church alone would make any display look modest.

Beverly stood by the door, chic, trim, and elegant. She greeted
those who attended but Leslie was surprised to find her mother-in-
law—who was always composed—looking shaken. Further evidence of this was James's presence beside his mother, his fingertips
on her elbow. Leslie thought it probably wasn't her imagination that
Beverly seemed to lean slightly toward, if not on, her eldest son.

Matt stood on her other side, his gaze fixed steadily on Leslie.

He was shaved and trimmed, his dark suit immaculately pressed.
He wore a white shirt and a dark tie, one that she didn't recognize.
Her sense that he was a stranger was emphasized by the remains of
a shiner around one eye and the shadows lurking in his gaze.

Leslie's heart stopped, plummeted, then began to palpitate. She
stood back, uncertain, while Annette hugged her father.

"Look," Annette said to Beverly. She opened her jacket to reveal an orange Hermès scarf tied like a halter top. "What do you
think?"

"Annette!" Leslie whispered, outraged that her daughter would
wear orange to a funeral. She could see the child's nipples! (And
she hadn't even thought about Annette having nipples before this
moment.) "That's not appropriate . . ."

But Beverly fingered the silk and smiled slightly. "No, you're
wrong, Leslie. It's absolutely perfect." She met Annette's gaze, then
the two hugged in a decidedly unexpected manner. "I don't know
where the joy went, but I think I can find it again," Beverly seemed
to say into Annette's hair, though that made no sense to Leslie.

"I'll stay with Grandma," Annette said, in a whisper, nudging
her father aside. "You go with Mom." She put her hand into Beverly's and visibly gave the older woman's hand a squeeze.

"Go," Beverly murmured when Matt might have hesitated. Her
gaze met Leslie's then flicked away.

Leslie gave Beverly a hug herself, something she had never done in all the years of their relationship. But then she'd never known Beverly to show so much raw emotion either.

The embrace apparently wasn't unwelcome.

Then Matt offered Leslie his elbow in silence.

She thought she might faint when she felt the strength of his arm beneath her fingertips. She could smell his cologne and the familiar heat of his skin and that old black magic was working as it never had before.

They both acted as if it was perfectly normal for him to escort her down the aisle of a church. In fact she was reminded of the day they had been married, in this very church.

Maybe that was why her knees were weak.

Maybe she was never going to get over this man. Leslie had a heartbeat to realize that, to fear its portent, before Matt lifted his right hand to interlace his fingers with hers. "I'm glad you're here," he said quietly, reminding her of what he had seen.

Leslie looked toward the coffin at the front of the church and wondered how difficult this was going to be for him. "I wasn't sure you would be."

"I had a session with a counselor yesterday afternoon who insisted that it was imperative." He took a ragged breath. "And she must know something about what she's doing because I almost slept last night, even though James and Maralys have a lumpy couch."

So he had gone to his brother, instead of coming home. That didn't seem to be a very good sign.

But then she was the one who had told him not to make assumptions about coming home.

They reached the front of the church and had a flurry of muted exchanges with family. Philippa and Nick were there with their toddler, and Leslie would have bet good money that Philippa was pregnant again. It was more than the way she stood; it was the way Nick stayed close. The display of their affection made tears rise in Leslie's eyes.

Maralys was dressed with dramatic flair, of course, even with a baby on her hip and two boisterous teenage boys in her company. Jimmy, James's older son, made a murmured joke to his brother and got a sharp word from his stepmother Maralys, a word that had him standing straight and silent in no time.

"I want to know what you said to him," Leslie murmured to Maralys when they greeted each other.

"It will cost you big," Maralys said, with a wink.

To Leslie's surprise, Matt stayed by her side, his fingers laced with hers. She decided that he had need of her strength for this ordeal, and she knew that she couldn't deny him whatever he wanted of her.

For now.

She held fast to his hand and let their shoulders brush, wondering all the while whether he would break her heart before the day was through.

* * *

The service wasn't as bad as Matt had feared it might be. He was glad that his mother had insisted on trying to keep it private, for the family, although a few old friends had attended as well. He was glad, too, that the coffin was closed, though in hindsight he wondered how he could have ever imagined that it would be otherwise.

It was James who the minister invited to give the eulogy for Robert, and Matt's older brother took his place at the pulpit with a slight frown. James had prepared something, but only referred to it a couple of times. He showed his usual courtroom flair and an enviable comfort with public speaking.

"We are here today to mourn the untimely passing of Robert Coxwell," James said, and the church was so quiet that everyone there might have been holding their breaths. James grimaced and shuffled his notes. "But I don't doubt that I'm the only one here with mixed feelings about my father's death. He was a demanding man, one with little patience for compromise. His moral code allowed no room for negotiation, something that my brothers and sister and I all discovered for ourselves."

Phil nodded and looked at the floor. Matt saw Nick capture her hand and hold it fast.

"For Robert, there was right and there was wrong and there was no in-between. He was not the kind of parent who would applaud any one of us having done our best, independent of the result. If you were right, if you gave your best, you would win. Victory was the only achievement worth celebrating. It was that simple for him."

James removed his glasses and considered the group assembled. "I would imagine that every one of us could tell a story about ending up on the wrong side of my father's accounting. As you all know, I have one of those stories, too. But that's not the only thing we should take away from having known him.

"My father believed in things that should be precious to us. He believed in nobility and honor. He believed in serving one's country and upholding the law. He believed in supporting his family and tithing to his church and offering support to the community around him. He believed in setting an example, and he did that. It's our responsibility to look at both sides of his legacy, to consider it in total.

"It's not so bad to teach your kids right from wrong; it's not so bad for kids to learn that you have to work hard for whatever you want; it's not so bad to be told that failure means an opportunity to try again, to try harder, to refine your game.

"The fact is that Robert taught us all to demand a lot from ourselves, to expect a lot from ourselves and from those around us. He taught me to make the right choice, even if it was a hard choice. He taught me not to flinch from what had to be done, whatever it might be or whatever it might cost me. He taught me that doing what's right is what's important, is what constitutes the measure of a man. He taught me that a moral man is a noble man."

Matt felt himself nodding as he agreed. Trust James to find the good in all of this.

"My father had a conviction in his decisions that I only wish I could emulate. He served three tours of duty in Vietnam when many people didn't even serve one. He did it initially because he believed it was his responsibility to his country to do his military service, but he stayed. I believe that he stayed because he believed that he could make a difference, maybe not to the war overall but to the men and women who also served there. There's nobility and honor in that choice, a nobility and honor that can inspire each of us to make choices for the greater good."

James cleared his throat and spared a glance to the coffin. "My father taught me also that his chosen path, the straight and narrow one, is a hard one to follow. Today we stand witness to the fact that perhaps Robert's high standards make a path that is impossible to navigate alone. I had no idea that he was so distraught as to do this, and I doubt that any of us did. He did not believe that a man should be so weak as to show his emotions, but we can all see what that cost him."

James straightened. "My father, Robert Coxwell, believed that everything that happens in life provides a lesson. So I think it's appropriate to consider the moral of this story, of his story, as he's not able to do so for us."

Matt saw James's eyes glitter with unshed tears, but there was no change in his brother's voice. "I suggest to you all that the moral of Robert's story is to live your life fearlessly, to adhere to your own moral code even if it's hard to do, with the caveat that if you falter, you should not be afraid to reach out for help. It is noble and honorable to be stoic and strong, but that doesn't mean it's weak to recognize and acknowledge your limitations."

James paused for a heartbeat and Matt sensed that this was becoming more difficult for him. "There is strength in numbers: My father told me that a thousand times, but in a critical moment, he just forgot." James's voice faltered ever so slightly. "So I ask you to remember that today, to find a lesson in tragedy, because I believe that Robert would have approved of our so doing. He would have been glad to know that we found a moral in his story, even if it was one he couldn't have seen himself."

James returned to Maralys and she held his hand tightly, even reaching to kiss his cheek. James lowered his head and Matt wondered what it had cost his brother to take the high road. Only James knew—and maybe Maralys did, too—just what Robert had said in their bitter dispute. Matt felt a surge of admiration for his brother, so different from him and yet similar on some level.

The minister returned to the pulpit to conclude the service and pronounce the blessings.

But it was James's words that made the strongest impression. His had been one of the most honest eulogies that Matt had ever heard and brought tears to every eye. Matt was glad to be beside Leslie, glad to have caught her sidelong glance. They had history together and he sincerely hoped they had a future.

But there were walls between them, words that one or the other of them had said. It wasn't that different from before he had left, even though so many things had changed, and it was harder to find the place to start in person than on the phone. Leslie seemed both brighter and more subdued, and he didn't know what to make of the change in her. He wanted to know what she thought of him, of his book, of the future, of everything, but she seemed closed to him in a way. Even the ease between her and Annette was both obvious to the casual eye and unexpectedly new.

Everything had changed in his absence, maybe because of his absence, and he didn't know where to begin.

He didn't know how to ask, how to explain, how to establish a link with his wife again.

Though he desperately wanted to do so. Matt wasn't sure what he had expected to happen when they met again, but it wasn't this. Was she already prepared to be rid of him?

A funeral maybe wasn't the best site for a reunion, as it led to the obvious conclusion that the relationship was dead, too.

That was when Matt remembered that Leslie had avoided this ritual with her own father. Was this funeral particularly painful to her? Was she thinking about her own past? She held fast to his hand and kept her gaze lowered so he couldn't tell whether she was crying.

But she was breathing quickly.

The minister led them all in the final prayers and last hymn. The music swelled and James stepped forward, leading the way for the pallbearers. Matt gave Leslie's hand a last squeeze and went to take his place opposite James. He was surprised to find his own bitterness losing its sting, maybe because of James's words, maybe because time dulled the wound, maybe because he was wishing that he had had more time to get to know his father.

Nick took the place behind James and four more cousins took their places. They were seven, and a bit uneven for a procession, but his mom had insisted on leaving one pallbearer's place empty.

Matt hadn't asked why, even though it was the space behind him. He figured it was some kind of tradition or family symbol.

He hefted his share now and at James's direction, the pallbearers lifted the coffin to their shoulders in even stages.

Matt's first surprise was that the coffin wasn't as heavy as he'd expected it to be. They might actually make it all the way to the hearse without missing a step.

His second surprise was that his mother was crying, something he had never seen her do.

His third surprise was that the door of the church opened at the end of the aisle. It was supposed to open when they got closer but they hadn't even left the altar yet. And it was supposed to open evenly, both doors swinging open in unison.

But a single door was thrown open and left to fall closed by itself. It did so with a resounding thump as the man who had opened it strode quickly down the aisle of the church.

It was Zach.

He ducked behind Matt, taking the place that had clearly been left for him, and Matt felt him take a share of the weight.

"Just in time," Zach muttered.

"Don't do us any favors," Nick muttered, and Matt found their animosity reassuring in a way.

He saw James's gesture, the one he had been watching for, and straightened beneath his burden. They began the processional march out of the church to "Amazing Grace." The doors at the end of the aisle swung open in unison as Matt had initially expected, the men in black from the funeral home doing their job of facilitating the ceremony.

The rain had stopped, though it was still overcast.

But the steps of the church weren't empty as they had been when Matt had arrived. The steps were lined with Marines in dress uniform and beyond them were other veterans in their dress uniforms, lining the course the hearse would take around the church's drive.

The pallbearers faltered as one at the unexpected sight, then carried on, matching James's pace. Matt recognized many of these men, knew that they had served in the military and that some of them were still in service. Some were his contemporaries but many were older.

They were his father's contemporaries. Matt had a glimpse of his father's history that he knew very little about and saw in the faces of these men an admiration that he had never expected.

As soon as the coffin cleared the church doors, the first man snapped to attention and saluted. The remaining men and women echoed his gesture with crisp precision, the salute rippling down the line.

The veterans of Rosemount had formed a spontaneous honor guard for Robert Coxwell, and at the sight of it, Matt realized that James had been right. Their father had touched many people, had insisted upon honor and morality, and was admired.

There was good mingled in the bad, black and white jumbled together instead of sorted out neatly as Robert would have preferred. Maybe the legacy from Robert was an ability to recognize right and wrong, which put the gray zones into perspective.

The coffin slid into the hearse and the pallbearers stepped back in unison. Matt looked up the steps as Leslie came out of the church and he felt that sense of rightness, that surety of purpose that Robert had encouraged in him.

He knew what he had to do to make things right.

He went straight to Leslie and claimed her hand again, not caring what anyone thought. "I think we need to talk, after the reception," he said to her. "Will you come for a drive with me?"

"But what about Annette?"

"She can come with me," Beverly said, with resolve. "Go now."

Leslie looked between the two of them, and Matt feared for a moment that she would decline. Then she smiled at him, a sad smile that didn't make him believe his chances of success were very good. "Yes, it's past time that we had a long talk."

*　*　*

The demon child had an innate fashion sense. Who would have guessed? Beverly had been surprised by the Hermès halter but also impressed.

The girl had potential, after all.

In fact, Beverly felt that life had more potential than it had before. Robert's funeral had been difficult, but she left the reception feeling lighter on her feet. The past had been laid to rest and the future beckoned.

Whatever it was, Beverly was ready.

After the service and reception, she drove back to Belmont with Annette to change and to fetch the girls. "The best thing about panty hose is taking them off," she informed her granddaughter, who actually smiled.

They went to a park together, one that Annette suggested, and the girls approved mightily of this endeavor. It was still overcast, the sky sulking like a teenager, though it wasn't raining. The snow had become messy slush in the field, but it was fenced so Beverly let the girls run. They always listened, so she wasn't too afraid. There was no one else around, just one man on the far side of the field, walking alone.

Annette ran with the girls, and it was obvious that all of them needed to let off some steam. Annette began to make snowballs, much to the girls' delight, and Beverly walked along the perimeter of the park where it was drier.

She tried to make sense of the buoyancy within her and failed. She was sober and though she knew she would want a drink again, she didn't want one now. She felt free of that desire, for the moment at least, and watched her granddaughter with an optimism that had become alien to her.

She caught up to the solitary man by accident and was surprised to recognize him. It was Ross Matheson, the vet, and he looked just as startled to see her as she was to see him.

"I thought you lived downtown," he said by way of greeting.

"I moved in with my son and daughter-in-law for the moment," Beverly said, hoping it was true.

"Ah, well, I won't disturb you," Ross said, with a polite smile. He seemed subdued today and less intent upon charming her. He was still charming, his manners impeccable, and Beverly wondered what had happened to sadden him.

"Is something wrong?"

He shrugged and she knew he lied. "No, it's just a good day for a walk, that's all."

"You need a dog."

He smiled. "Maybe I do." He glanced toward the girls playing with Annette and his smile broadened ever so slightly. "Your granddaughter?"

"Yes. She and the girls have really taken to each other."

"Probably good for all of them. I'll leave you to your snowball games."

Beverly looked at him hard. "I thought you might ask me out for dinner again."

"I thought you had declined. Quite emphatically."

"I thought you weren't the kind of man to take no for an answer so easily as that."

His smile turned rueful. "Maybe that's my problem."

"And what is that supposed to mean?"

He sighed, looked around, then met her gaze steadily. "My wife didn't want to get married, but I persuaded her. Maybe she just surrendered. Maybe she knew all along that it wasn't the right thing for her to do." He shrugged again. "And now she's gone and I really only have myself to blame for the whole mess."

"Hardly!" Beverly snorted. "She could have had the sense to say no, if marriage wasn't what she wanted."

"But I talked her into it . . ."

"Dr. Matheson, you are not as persuasive as you imagine yourself to be."

He chuckled. "And that's supposed to reassure me?"

"No, of course not. Reassurance comes from other things. A game of snowball with a dog, maybe, or a smile from a granddaughter."

"Or dinner with an enchanting lady?"

"Maybe." Beverly found herself smiling in turn. "Of course the possibility of that depends upon what kind of sherry you prefer."

"Not my charm?"

"We both already know that it's considerable."

"I thought you'd given up drinking, that you were getting help."

"I have and I am, but that doesn't change the fact that I've used taste in sherry as a measure of character for most of my life and am not about to change now."

"So what kind did you prefer?"

"I'll never tell. That's like asking a woman her age."

"I'll guess then. Not a cream sherry."

Beverly snorted. "That's for amateurs."

"Maybe an oloroso, round and rich and amber."

Beverly shook her head. "I'm sweet enough already."

Ross laughed slightly. "I don't imagine you so dry that a pale straw would be a good match."

"You know a lot about sherry," Beverly accused lightly. "And you're right, of course. What about you?"

He shoved his hands into his pockets and gave the matter the consideration that Beverly thought it deserved. "An amontillado is pretty much my favorite," he said finally. "Not too sweet, not too rich, not too frivolous or presumptuous." He looked up, met her gaze and his own eyes were twinkling. "It strikes a nice balance."

Beverly smiled at him. She found herself sure of something, sure that it was time to take a step forward. It fluttered in her chest, like a bright orange silk scarf loose in the wind.

"Take care, then," Ross said when she didn't speak and started to turn away.

Beverly wasn't quite ready to let him go. She cleared her throat, unsure in unfamiliar territory. He paused but didn't turn. "So are your office hours all booked tomorrow?"

He glanced back. "I can always fit someone in. Why?"

Beverly found herself blushing but she held his gaze. "I'm not sure that I know everything I need to know about having dogs. I wondered if you'd have a few moments to run through the basics with me."

Beverly found her heart taking a little optimistic skip when Ross Matheson smiled at her, really smiled at her. "You come in whenever you're ready," he said softly. "I'll be there."

Maybe joy wasn't so elusive, after all.

*　*　*

To Leslie's shock, Matt drove to Lowell.

"I haven't been here in years," she said, even as she unwillingly sought familiar landmarks.

"Not since we decided to get married," Matt confirmed.

There was another portent Leslie could have done without. Bring on the plague of locusts and the hail of comets: It had to be better than standing by to watch her marriage dissolve.

Once she wouldn't have asked, once she would have just waited to see what he intended to do. But she wasn't the same person she had been a week before.

Or maybe she wasn't prepared to play the same games. "Why are we going to Lowell now?"

"Because there's something you never did here, something that maybe you need to do."

"Like?"

Matt frowned as he took the exit from the highway. It was starting to rain again and the ramp looked slick. "I didn't want to go to the funeral today. That therapist told me I needed to go to find closure, and that if I didn't go, I'd never again have such a good chance to put the past behind me where it belonged. So I went, and it wasn't so bad."

He turned at the end of the ramp, going in the opposite direction of the house where Leslie had grown up.

"Not the cemetery!" she said, with alarm.

"Yes, the cemetery. You never went to his funeral, so this is as good as it gets."

"But there might not be a stone. We could spend all day wandering around in the rain . . ."

"No, there is a stone and I know exactly where it is."

Leslie turned to look at her husband, startled by what an enigma he could be. "How?"

"You and your father still weren't speaking at the end. Your mother asked me to help her have the stone installed." He shrugged. "So I did. You know she didn't drive, so I used to take her there a couple of times a year."

"I never knew," Leslie said, with wonder.

"You weren't supposed to. She insisted upon it." He cast her a rueful smile. "I used to pick her up at the T so you wouldn't guess the truth."

"Am I that scary?"

Matt laughed a little. "No, but I think your mom thought that both you and your dad were pretty strong willed."

Leslie thought about legacies unexpected, then sat up straight in recollection. "There used to be a greenhouse and nursery up here. Could you stop?"

"Of course I can."

It was right where Leslie remembered it. They had to run through the rain to the door, and Matt shook his head over the state of his suit. The lady was very helpful and they left with a Christmas Rose that she insisted would not only continue to bloom in the snow but would survive the winter quite nicely.

The car filled with the smell of wet wool as they drove onward and Leslie wrinkled her nose. "The dry cleaner is going to love us."

"Oh well, it's only money."

That seemed to be about as good an opening as she'd get. Leslie braced her hand on the seat and twisted to watch Matt's expression. "I'm probably going to quit my job."

Matt blinked, then he smiled. "That's probably a good thing. You've been pretty frustrated. Any idea what you're going to do?"

Leslie stared at him in awe. "You really believe that things just work out, don't you?"

"Well, yes. I mean you have to believe that if you're going to take a chance on anything. Why would anyone get married, if we couldn't believe that it was going to work out? Why would anyone have children or buy a house or buy a car or take a vacation, if we couldn't have that optimism that it could work out, or that it *would* work out."

Leslie watched the rain hit the windshield, her fingers caressing the waxy blossom of the Christmas Rose in her lap. "Your book is good, you know."

The car swerved a little. "No, I didn't know." Matt stopped at a traffic light and turned to face her. "You're not putting me on, are you?"

Leslie shook her head and smiled. She crossed her heart with her fingertips, touched them to her lips and saw the tension leave his shoulders.

"You're sure?"

"I'm positive." Leslie shook her head. "Matt, you have such a gift. It's such a powerful story and so well told, and the characters are so real that they could just step off the page. I halfway thought you'd had a secret life without my knowing about it. It seemed so true. I couldn't tell where the fiction ended and the truth began."

"I have no secret lives," he said, with quiet fervor as he parked in the cemetery. He turned off the ignition and the rain beat on the roof. "You know everything about me, Leslie."

"New Orleans?"

He sighed. "I thought I knew what I wanted, but the truth is that I didn't have the nerve to ask you for what I wanted." He met her gaze, a little wonder of his own in his eyes. "But you gave it to me anyway. You told me your truth and you asked me for mine. I'm sorry. I should have known better than to have assumed that you would insist on my sacrificing my dreams for the sake of yours."

"You couldn't have known," Leslie said, but before she could say more, she found the heat of his fingertips against her lips.

"I should have believed," he whispered, close enough that she could see not just the myriad hues in his eyes but the sincerity there. "I should have asked. And I should never have hurt you. I'm sorry."

Leslie lifted his fingers from her mouth, closed her hand over them. "I'm sorry, too. We stopped talking. We both stopped asking and stopped listening." She looked down at his hand within hers, took a breath and asked what she really wanted to know. "Did you sleep with her?"

Matt's fingers moved, he touched her chin and tilted her face so that she was looking straight into his eyes. "No. I thought Sharan was what I wanted. I thought she was my future. But by the time I got there, I knew that Sharan was my past. I'd not only left my future behind, but quite possibly jeopardized it."

"In your book—" Leslie said, hearing that her voice was uneven. "In your book, at the end, you say that there are times when something has to be taken completely apart—"

"—into its component pieces, in order to rebuild it better than it was before," Matt finished. "Yes, I did write that and I believe it."

Leslie dared to look at him again. "Is this one of those times?"

"I hope so." He swallowed, his gaze filled with all the candor and integrity that had stolen Leslie's heart in the first place. "I want it to be, if you'll give an unemployed lawyer one more chance."

"You're not an unemployed lawyer," Leslie chided softly. "You're a writer in search of a publisher."

She saw how the words pleased him and then, just because she had so seldom initiated anything sexual between them before, she kissed him.

She immediately tasted the change in the balance between them, felt not only that old black magic but a new appreciation for each other. They were embarking on a new journey together, one that maybe they had undertaken once but which had had an obscured path in recent years.

One more chance was all they needed to get it right. Leslie knew it and so, she saw, did Matt.

"We'd better go see your father before we start steaming the windows," Matt said, when their kiss broke. "I don't even want to know what will happen then."

"Maybe he'll haunt us."

"No, he's done that already." Matt peered out the window, perhaps unaware of the truth he had uttered. "Come on, it's letting up. Let's go."

Chapter Seventeen

Two weeks after Robert's funeral, the Coxwells gathered at James and Maralys's house for dinner. Leslie had been astonished by the invitation, given that they'd never socialized much before, but Matt had insisted they accept.

"It's different since he's gone," he said simply. "It's easier."

Once Leslie would have argued, once she would have demanded more of an explanation: Now she trusted Matt's instincts. He was different since his return and yet still the same. The determination with which he revised his book, the demands he made of himself, his sheer intensity reminded her of why she had fallen in love with him in the first place.

She could feel the new balance in him and it made her smile even more when she came home at night. They had shared some hot kisses and she knew that he was waiting for her to invite him back to bed.

Tonight was the night. Leslie knew it.

She'd worn that black camisole, just for him.

Matt was at ease in James's house, perhaps because he had stayed there those few nights. Maybe the camaraderie was because Zach had declined the invitation. Theirs was a noisy kitchen, especially with so many in attendance.

"Can we be excused?" Jimmy asked as soon as forks hit the dessert plates.

"You just want a rematch," Annette said, smug in her earlier triumph.

"Well, duh," her older cousin said. "Can we?"

"May we?" James corrected in a tone that told Leslie that he knew he wouldn't win the grammatical battle.

She could relate to that.

"Whatever," Jimmy muttered, then flashed his father a smile. "Can we? Please?"

"Go. It'll be quieter without you," James said, with a flick of his hand. There was a clatter as three teenagers leapt from the table in unison.

"Me first," Johnny, the number two son, insisted.

"Forget it," his older brother said. "It's my turn."

"Then we'll play each other."

"Hello!" Annette interjected. "I am the champion."

"Wasn't that a song?" Matt asked, and the adults smiled.

"Think what we have to look forward to," Nick said to Philippa who put her hand over her rounded belly.

"We'll have enough of them to have them take care of each other," she said.

Nick chuckled. "Is that how it works?"

James leaned closer to him and dropped his voice. "Never. It never works that way. Just so you know."

"Thanks a lot. It's not going to change much now, though. This one's on her way."

A chorus of congratulations echoed around the table, and Philippa had her cheek kissed by her mother. "A girl?" Beverly asked.

"That's what the ultrasound technician said. So Michael will have a baby sister."

The toddler in question squirmed and once Nick let him down from his seat at the table, he set off in pursuit of his older, more interesting cousins. The sound of laser fire carried from the living room, as well as good-natured bickering.

"You didn't put your dishes in the sink!" Leslie called after the kids would have just bolted from the room. They came back sheepishly and did her bidding, moving quickly so they didn't delay their game much.

Then they disappeared. Champagne and Caviar ran after them, Champagne barking that she was being left behind. Caviar paused to sniff something on Michael's overalls, then to lick it off. The toddler seized a handful of the dog's coat and steadied his balance. He grinned triumphantly at his mother, then continued to the living room.

"Always the tough guy," Matt teased Leslie, but he was smiling.

"Well, you'd have to be," Maralys said, taking sides with Leslie. Her little one, Zoé, began to fuss, so she plucked her out of the high chair and bounced her on her lap. Zoé seized a tablespoon and seemed to find it fascinating. "I can't imagine what it's like to teach college kids."

"You just remember what a challenge you were," James said, and Maralys laughed.

"Pretty much. I didn't make anybody's life easy."

"Imagine that," James said, looking too innocent to be believed. The pair exchanged a hot glance across the table and Leslie met Matt's gaze in surprise.

He smiled a slow smile that heated her to her toes, then leaned forward. "Go ahead, Leslie, tell them your news. Being the tough guy has its spoils."

"Well, I guess. I've accepted a new position." She named the college and told them a bit about the program, unsurprised that they were surprised she'd leave her alma mater. "I needed a new challenge and this is it. Plus I want to focus on my own research more than I've been able to in recent years. I'll finish this term, then spend the summer settling in there."

"But the best part is how you were recruited," Matt prompted.

Leslie laughed. "Oh, the headhunter was a kid I failed twice. He told me that I was the only person who'd ever demanded more of him than he could easily do. He ultimately graduated summa cum laude."

"Score one for the good guys," James said, and the group applauded her.

"There's a bottle of sparkling wine in the fridge," Maralys said. "Let's drink a toast to Philippa and Nick and their new baby, and to Leslie in her new job."

And to Matt's book. Leslie met Matt's gaze, knowing that it was still their secret because he wanted it that way. She smiled at him, hoping he could see her pride, and liked the gleam that lit his eyes.

"I shouldn't have any alcohol," Philippa protested.

"Have a sip for luck and give the rest to me," Nick offered.

"A martyr to the cause," Matt teased, and the men laughed together. It turned out that each of them only got a sip once the bottle was split seven ways, but it was the principle of the thing. Leslie felt buoyant—and it wasn't from the bubbles. It was the way Matt watched her over the rim of his glass, silently toasting her from across the table.

"They'll give you a nice office, I hope," Beverly said, and Leslie laughed.

"I don't much care. Actually I expect to telecommute more and do some work at home. It will be nice to see Annette, at least in passing, more than I have."

"But where will you work?" Beverly demanded.

It seemed rude to point out that if Beverly moved her stuff out, then there would be room in the living room—sort of—to set up a desk. Leslie had herself been concerned about the space issue and thought she had found a compromise solution.

"Well I might just set up a desk in the basement . . ." she began but got no further.

"Basements are for potatoes," Beverly interrupted her crisply. "I have a better idea."

Everyone looked at her, probably expecting her to announce that she'd taken an apartment somewhere.

"Gray Gables." Beverly considered each of them, her smile as victorious as little Michael's had been. Leslie gasped but Matt appeared to be considering the idea. He frowned and leaned forward in the same moment as James.

"It's my family home," Beverly said. "And my moving back there makes perfect sense. The girls need space to run. I don't want to sell the house, it has too many memories, but I don't want to live alone, either."

"We're close by, at Lucia's house," Philippa said, referring to Nick's grandmother. The couple had been living with Lucia in Rosemount since their wedding.

Beverly shook her head. "No, I think I need someone in the house. And Leslie needs an office and Matt needs an office and the house has room to spare."

"But any of us could use more space," Leslie argued, even as her heart began to pound at the possibility.

James shook his head firmly. "It's an hour and half drive from Boston, and only if there's no traffic."

"When you go to work, it'll be bumper to bumper," Maralys said. "It would take you three hours each way." She nodded at Leslie. "We're better off right here, where we can see more of him."

"They're not likely to move the courthouse to suit me," James said, with a grin.

"But . . ." Leslie protested.

"We have Lucia's place," Nick said, "and believe me, no one alive needs the responsibility of two old houses."

Philippa laughed. "It's not that bad!"

"But it's a lot of work. One house is plenty for me."

"What about Zach?" Leslie asked.

"He'll never live out there," James said. "He couldn't wait to be gone."

"But it's not fair to everyone else," Leslie said.

"It's my house," Beverly insisted. "I want to live there. When I die, it will be divided between the four of you anyway."

Matt grabbed a sheet of paper and started to scribble. "So, let's figure out whether Leslie and I can afford to buy the rest of you out. What do you think the house is worth?"

James named a figure that made Leslie blink. "That's too low," she argued. "It's a beautiful house."

"But it's in Rosemount. It's too far to commute."

"Location, location, location," Maralys agreed.

"We could check with a Realtor, but I think that's a reasonable working number," Nick said, bending to look at Matt's calculations.

A moment later he shoved the paper across the table to Leslie. He'd subtracted a quarter of the total, done a side calculation of their house's value, subtracting how much they still owed. When that was taken from the sum, there was still a hefty balance left.

Leslie did a little mental calculation, then swallowed and shook her head. "I don't think we can manage this."

"Of course you can," Beverly said sharply. She took the pencil and scribbled a number at the bottom. "There's the monthly rent the girls will pay. They need room, and to be accommodated in the style to which they've become accustomed."

"The girls can pay that much rent?" James and Nick demanded simultaneously.

"They have a trust fund and I see no reason not to use it," Beverly said haughtily. "After all, I couldn't rent a nice apartment in Boston for that much per month."

No one could argue with that.

"So, it's decided?" James asked. "Since Zach is Father's executor, I'll have him check that the power of attorney didn't extend to the property . . ."

Zach was Robert's executor? Leslie blinked but didn't comment. No one else seemed surprised so they must have known.

"Gray Gables was explicitly excluded from that agreement," Beverly said. "I wasn't that drunk."

"Which reminds me," James said, sparing a glance to the clock on the wall. "It's that time again."

Beverly sighed with forbearance and rose to her feet. She drained the last of her mouthful of sparkling wine and gave her eldest son a glare. "Tell them about this mouthful and I'll ensure that you regret it."

He laughed, unafraid. "You'll have to do penance for it and go to another meeting Friday."

"Not me," Beverly said, as she swept out of the kitchen. "I have a dinner date Friday night."

If she intended to give everyone left in the room something to think about, she certainly succeeded.

"Details!" Maralys hissed, as James followed his mother. "Get us the scoop!"

"We want to know who it is!" Philippa agreed.

"You're a nosy bunch," James teased, then winked. Maralys chucked a napkin at him and he laughed. "I'll see what I can do." He showed little resemblance to the courtroom shark Leslie had always believed him to be. She looked around the table, wondering how much else she didn't know about these people who had been part of her life for almost twenty years.

And she resolved to find out.

She found Matt's gaze upon her again and smiled at him. "Maybe we should get going, too, as it's a school night. I'll just give Maralys a hand with the dishes first."

"We all will," Matt said, and rose from the table.

* * *

The dishes were done quickly, so many hands making light work, then Matt and Leslie and Annette were in the Subaru, heading home. Matt was keenly aware of his wife's presence and he couldn't help but think of that night a few weeks before, when the atmosphere in the car had been almost toxic.

Tonight it was filled with promise. Magical.

Of course there were two dogs in the back seat as well, which made the car seem particularly crowded.

"Jimmy is such a pig," Annette ranted in the back seat. "I can't believe how he thinks he's so hot. No one in my school would even give him the time of day . . ."

Leslie put her hand on Matt's thigh and his heart stopped. He was still getting used to her taking the initiative: It shocked him and excited him both. He turned a corner, then closed his hand over hers. In his peripheral vision, he saw her smile.

"I was thinking," she said softly, so softly that Annette's rank flowed uninterrupted. "I was thinking that your toes must be black and blue."

Matt couldn't make sense of that, so he waited.

"From tripping over the furniture in the living room," she said quietly. "I don't know how you find the couch every night."

Matt grinned. "I don't. I just fall and sleep wherever I land."

Leslie laughed, causing Annette to fall silent.

"What are you two whispering about now?"

"Nothing that concerns you," Matt said.

Annette flung herself against the back seat. "SEX. You're talking about sex. I seriously don't want to know anything about you two having sex. Parents shouldn't be allowed to do that. It's like so *gross*."

Matt nearly stalled the car in his shock, which would have been a trick given that it was an automatic. "Excuse me?" he said finally, and Leslie laughed as if she'd never stop.

"Be gentle with your father, Annette," she said, when she caught her breath. "Dads never want to know that their daughters have even heard of sex."

"You can say that again," Matt grumbled.

"Besides, he doesn't even know about Scott Sexton . . ."

"I told you that in confidence!" Annette cried. "I should never have trusted you. I should never have told you." She settled into a rant while Matt focused on driving.

He heard Leslie laughing softly, then she leaned closer. "At least you weren't part of the expedition to buy her a vibrator," she whispered.

The car swerved. Matt couldn't help it. "This is seriously more than I want to know." He shook a finger at Annette in the rearview mirror, knowing he was foolish to be surprised. "You're not allowed to grow up. You hear me?"

She tossed her hair. "As if." She sat back and sighed theatrically, then grinned at him. "Don't worry, Dad. I'm not stupid."

"I know. You're smart enough to be careful and to ask questions when you need to."

"Well, yeah, but I do have some reference materials."

Matt slanted a glance at his wife, primary source of reference materials and found her smiling a Cheshire smile. She undid the top button of her blouse and slid her finger down her chest, parting her clothes. She watched him, still smiling, her gaze heated. Matt saw the creamy slice of her skin, then the lacey edge of a bra.

It was black. That was all he needed to know.

It was the invitation he'd been waiting for, and he didn't intend to decline with regrets. He squeezed her hand, still trapped within his, and Leslie squeezed his back.

It was indisputable that he drove home a bit faster than he'd initially planned.

*   *   *

Runt dunt dada dadala dunt da.

Leslie finds herself on the end of the tightrope. Her father is there, but remarkably silent. The crowd murmurs as the barker's cry fades. All proceeds as it has a dozen times, until her father tries to hand her a box.

"No, thank you," Leslie says, to his obvious astonishment. "I'll have a pink parasol instead."

And suddenly there is a pink parasol, leaning against the wall of the big top, just a few paces away. It's frilly and feminine and pre-

cisely the way she has always imagined she'd want a pink parasol to be. It is precisely the parasol that she always expects her father to hand to her in this dream, the one she expects when she gets a box instead.

Has it been there all along?

Or did it manifest only after she dared to voice her desire? What came first: the parasol or the request? Leslie doesn't know and the dream doesn't allow her much time to consider the philo-sophical ramifications of the parasol's existence. Her father, with a familiar grunt of disapproval, gets the parasol and hands it to her.

"Careful what you ask for, lass," he says, with a bright glance. "Lest you get it when you're least expecting it."

And Leslie sees with painful clarity that her father was afraid to ask for anything for himself. She can't teach him this lesson or give him this gift: It is her parasol and her journey across the wire and she can only provide an example.

She smiles and gives him a kiss farewell, the one she never gave him in real life, then turns and steps out onto the wire. She is jubi-lant, triumphant, her parasol held high, her steps proud and confi-dent.

She walks like a woman who knows what she wants and isn't afraid to ask for it. She sees a little girl in the front row, far far be-low, and on impulse, casts her parasol down to the little girl. She waits until the little girl catches it, until the little girl's face lights with joy and the crowd cheers.

Then Leslie leaps off the tightrope and flies with the greatest of ease.

Without a trapeze.

When the crowd disappears and the floor of the tent drops down down down, Leslie swoops low, toward the eternal fires burning far below. To her astonishment, the letters they form don't make the word FAILURE.

She sees the message emblazoned against the darkness, the last *message she would have expected to see. She reads it again, then laughs aloud and soars high once more.*

GO FOR IT *is what the letters urge.*

* * *

Leslie awakened smiling in the cool darkness of the morning. The house was quiet, as was the street outside, but someone somewhere was whimpering.

It was a poodle dream.

Leslie nestled deep into the covers, content in so many ways that she'd lost track. It was early, too early to be awake, but she was filled with such optimism from her dream that she knew she wouldn't sleep again. She snuggled closer to Matt's warmth and recalled every detail that she could before the dream completely faded.

Her strongest memory was of how wonderful it had felt to fly. How simple it was. How elegant and effortless and joyous. She yearned already to do it again.

She also felt a confidence that was new to her, another gift from the dream. Leslie now had a curious conviction that her job would work out just fine, that she had been offered the job because she had wanted it.

No, because she had wanted it and she had dared to ask for it.

It was hard not to love the idea of living in Gray Gables, a house the like of which Leslie had only dreamed about in the past. She liked the idea of Beverly not living alone, too. Annette loved the idea of living with the girls for perpetuity. The house was everything Leslie had ever wanted, and was coming to them in a way that she never could have anticipated.

A little bonus prize from the universe for believing.

Matt had said that he would make his office in another room than his father's study, but it was clear that he had good feelings about returning to his childhood home.

And Annette would learn to drive in the Jag.

It was a perfect solution. Mrs. Beaton would have new neighbors to worry about, but Leslie decided she could live with that.

Matt's book would sell, Leslie believed, or if it didn't, his next one would. She knew with quiet certainty on that drowsy Saturday morning that he would be fine, that he would recover from the shock of that gruesome discovery, because he had reached out to all of them for help. He was strong and resilient and he would force honesty from himself.

And he had a support network to please the most demanding therapist. There was Leslie and Annette and Beverly and the girls, but even more than that, Matt's siblings seemed more intent on being close than they ever had been.

They even had fun together.

She watched Matt sleep and felt blessed as she hadn't in years. She was profoundly grateful for a second chance to make her marriage come right. Leslie knew as she watched the sky lighten that she would never have her recurring dream again. In a way, that was sad.

But, in another way, it wasn't sad at all.

Claire Cross makes her home in Canada with her husband, far too many books, and a variety of undisciplined houseplants. She is an avid knitter and often sorts out plot tangles while knitting funky socks. Claire travels as much as possible, rides her bicycle everywhere, and cooks with enthusiasm—as long as someone else washes the dishes. Claire also writes historical romances uner the name Claire Delacroix. Visit her websites at www.clairecross.com or www.delacroix.net.